continued . . .

FOR ALL ETERNITY

The passionate story of Maeve Tremayne—a beautiful vampire who haunts the battlefields of Gettysburg like an angel of death ... and who dares to lose her soul to a mortal soldier.

"The reigning queen of supernatural romance ... Ms. Miller has brilliantly written a haunting love story."
                                        —*Affaire de Coeur*

"Highly recommended."   —*Booklist*

"Absolutely fascinating ... intriguing ... the mesmerizing Valerian steals the show once again."
                                        —*Romantic Times*

"Linda Lael Miller's fabulous time-travelling vampires are back ... the exciting plot and fast pacing will keep readers enthralled to the very last page and eager for the next installment."   —*The Talisman*

"This page-turner will keep you on the edge of your seat ... a fast-paced, mysterious tale woven by a master storyteller."   —*The Time Machine*

"Ms. Miller takes the reader into the world of the damned [and] carries the reader on a river of emotions that are hot and sensuous."   —*Heartland Critiques*

TIME WITHOUT END

*Once every century, Valerian's lost love, the
enchanting Brenna, returns in human form.
But this time, as the new millennium draws near,
Valerian vows never to lose her again . . .*

"Her best work to date. A keeper to treasure, remember, and savor."
                                    —*Affaire de Coeur*

"Heart-wrenching scenes . . . engrossing historical characters and period atmosphere."   —*Publishers Weekly*

"Mesmerizing . . . Ms. Miller comes up trumps in this intricate tale featuring the sexy, arrogant vampire destined to become an all-time favorite with romance readers of every persuasion. Long live Valerian!"
                                    —*Romantic Times*

"Ms. Miller takes us from past to present with ease, giving the reader a look at how it all started and leaves us hoping for more . . . Valerian and Daisy are powered with such intensity that the sparks between them leap at the reader."
                                    —*Rendezvous*

LINDA LAEL MILLER

Tonight AND *Always*

BERKLEY BOOKS, NEW YORK

TONIGHT AND ALWAYS

A Berkley Book / published by arrangement with
the author

PRINTING HISTORY
Berkley edition / November 1996

The Putnam Berkley World Wide Web site address is
http://www.berkley.com/berkley

ISBN: 0-425-15541-2

BERKLEY®
Berkley Books are published by The Berkley Publishing Group,
200 Madison Avenue, New York, New York 10016.
BERKLEY and the "B" design
are trademarks belonging to Berkley Publishing Corporation.

PRINTED IN THE UNITED STATES OF AMERICA

10 9 8 7 6 5 4 3 2 1

FOR JUDITH STERN PALAIS,

THE CONSUMMATE PRO AND A LOYAL FRIEND,

WITH LOVE, APPRECIATION, AND

GREAT ADMIRATION.

THANK YOU.

For love is a smoke raised with the fume of sighs;
Being purged, a fire sparkling in lovers' eyes;
Being vex'd, a sea nourish'd with lovers' tears:
What is it else? a madness most discreet,
A choking gall and a preserving sweet.

Romeo and Juliet

PROLOGUE

LONDON
WINTER, 1872

The new governess leaned down from what seemed to the child a great height, smiling her brash American smile. The woman was pretty enough, with her auburn hair and shining green eyes, and smart, too, or Mummy wouldn't have engaged her in the first place. Still, a stranger was a stranger.

"Kristina Tremayne Holbrook, is it?" Miss Phillips inquired in a nonobjectionable tone of voice. "Such a big name for so small a girl."

Kristina came out of the voluminous folds of her nanny's skirts to correct an apparent misconception on the part of the newcomer. "I am not so very little," she said. "I'm five—six next April—and I can already read and count to a hundred. You may be on your way now—we won't be needing you because I shall learn all I need to know from Mama and Papa and Valerian."

Mrs. Eldridge, the plump nurse with whom Kristina spent the majority of her time, laid a fond and encouraging hand atop her charge's head. "Hush now, child," she scolded benignly. Then, to the governess she confided, "You mustn't mind our Kristina. She's too bright by half, she is, and sometimes it makes her a mite saucy, but she's good through and through." She paused to emit a heartfelt sigh. "Now, come right in and settle yourself next to the drawing room fire, Miss Phillips, and welcome to you. It's a blustery day out, isn't it, and I daresay a nice cup of tea would go well with you just now."

"Thank you, Mrs. Eldridge," Miss Phillips said, removing her dowdy bonnet and cloak, both of which were dappled with snow, and handing them off to Delia, the handsome downstairs maid, whose duty it was to greet and announce guests and look after their belongings while they were being entertained. Delia collected Miss Phillips's battered carpet satchel—it was dripping on the Persian rug—and bore that away as well.

Kristina lagged behind as Mrs. Eldridge and Miss Phillips hurried into the drawing room, arms linked, whispering to each other. She lingered just inside the double doors, half hidden behind the marble pedestal that supported a bust of Socrates, while Miss Phillips was made comfortable beside the coal fire.

When Mrs. Eldridge went out to arrange for tea to be served, Miss Phillips put her small feet in their scuffed black boots on the chrome rail edging the hearth, and sighed contentedly.

"I do like to toast my toes on a winter's day," she said cheerfully. "Don't you, Kristina?"

Kristina had believed herself invisible, dwarfed as she was by Socrates and his pillar, and was both disgruntled and pleased that her new teacher had taken notice of her. Mama and Papa were loving and attentive, but they were never about during the daylight hours, and both of them were very busy—Papa worked in his laboratory belowstairs, and Mama was the queen of something, though Kristina didn't know exactly what.

"Yes," she said tentatively, drawn to the young woman with bright hair and shabby clothes and a gentle voice.

"Won't you join me by the fire? I feel a little lonely, sitting here all by myself."

Kristina understood loneliness well, though she was but five. It was a mysterious ache in one small corner of her heart, and always with her, even when Mama or Papa or Valerian or Mrs. Eldridge was nearby. Most of the time she felt as though she were lost from someone she did not yet know, and must find that person to be truly happy. Given her age and size, and the fact that she was not allowed to go farther than the wall at the rear of the garden by herself, the objective seemed very daunting indeed.

She stepped nearer to the hearth, leaning on the arm of Papa's wing-back chair. Miss Phillips sat smiling in the matching seat, which was Mama's. The approach was concession enough, for the moment—Kristina did not speak.

Miss Phillips smoothed her skirts, which were clean but frayed at the hem and mended in at least two places. "I do not think you are really so shy as you pretend to be," she said. "Are you afraid of me, Kristina?"

"No," Kristina said in a sturdy voice. "Not now. I was for a few moments, though."

"Why?"

"Because I don't know you," Kristina responded reasonably. "I've been told never to speak to strangers."

"Good advice," Miss Phillips agreed. "We shall be fast friends, you and I, as well as student and tutor. I think you like to learn, and there is much I can teach you. I would like to begin our association by taking you to St. Regent's Lecture Hall tomorrow afternoon. The topic is the mythology of ancient Greece."

Kristina felt her eyes widen. She rarely left the house, except with Mrs. Eldridge for carriage rides through the park in good weather, and she loved the sights and sounds and smells and people—so *many* people—that made up the great city of London.

"I don't know anything at all about Greece," she confessed solemnly. "Or mistology, either."

"All the more reason to attend a lecture," replied Miss Phillips, tucking away a smile.

That night, after Mrs. Eldridge and Miss Phillips and Kristina had taken their supper by the nursery fire, the nanny and the governess went off to their own quarters, and Mama came to help Kristina get ready for bed.

It was her favorite time of the day, for Mama was beautiful, and full of stories, and she could do all sorts of marvelous tricks, like making dolls dance with each other, or causing real snow to drift down from the ceiling. She never entered or left the room in the customary fashion, either, but simply appeared and disappeared. Kristina wondered, when she took the time to ponder such questions, why Mrs. Eldridge and the maids didn't move from place to place the way Mama did, instead of bothering with stairs and doors and other such ordinary things.

"I'm going to hear a lecture on ancient Greece tomorrow with Miss Phillips!" Kristina blurted, so excited that she bounced on her feather bed and wheeled her arms.

Mama laughed as she wrestled Kristina's warm flannel nightgown over her small head, which was dark like her own. "Well, now," she said. "I shall want to hear all about that adventure." She paused to smooth Kristina's silken hair. "Do you like Miss Phillips, darling?"

"Oh, yes. She's wonderful." Kristina's happiness faded a little as she considered a possibility that had not occurred to her before. "Will Mrs. Eldridge be going away, now that I'm big enough to have a governess?"

Mama kissed her forehead, her blue eyes shining with love, and embraced her daughter tightly. "No, sweetheart—she'll stay. Since Papa and I can't be with you in the daytime, it's important that Mrs. Eldridge be here."

Kristina was relieved, for the nanny had been her constant companion for as long as she could remember, and it would be terrible indeed if she ever went away. "Why is that, Mama?" she ventured to ask. "Why are you and Papa never at home before dark?"

Mama hesitated, then answered in a soft and somewhat wistful voice, "I'll explain that soon, when you're just a little older. In the meantime, you must be patient."

After a grave nod, Kristina sat down on the bed and pulled the warm covers up to her chest. "All right," she said. "But I want to know the *instant* I'm old enough."

Her mother laughed again, and Kristina was struck anew by her loveliness; she was a magical creature, with her pale, flawless skin, her flowing ebony hair, her exquisitely fitted white gown. "I promise to tell you all the family secrets as soon as I think you're ready to hear them," she said.

Kristina snuggled deeper into the bedclothes, already fighting sleep but determined to make the time with Mama last. "Make the puppets tell a story," she whispered. "Please?"

Mama drew a chair up beside Kristina's bed, sat down, and gestured grandly toward the ornate toy puppet theater, a gift from Kristina's Uncle Valerian, which stood on the window seat. Instantly the tiny stage was flooded with light, and the small, colorful figures rattled to loose-jointed life and began to perform.

Kristina was asleep before the end of the first act.

The lecture was fascinating, full of gods and goddesses, minotaurs and mazes. Kristina perched on the edge of her chair throughout, and even though she did not understand much of what was said, she left the public hall with a storm of bright, strange images raging in her mind.

She and Miss Phillips rode home together in the carriage, with a heavy quilt over their laps and warm bricks tucked beneath their feet, chattering excitedly about all they'd heard.

It was that night after supper, and after Papa had come to the nursery to read a chapter from a novel by Mr. Mark Twain in his deep and somehow reassuring voice, that Kristina first realized that she was different from other children.

She'd been sleeping, and dreaming of Athens, the city that had figured so prominently in the lecture, when the warmth of her bed was suddenly gone, replaced by a chill that seemed to wrap itself around her very bones. She opened her eyes and found herself standing in the middle of a vast marble pavilion, an eerie place, splashed with cold silver moonlight and utterly silent.

This, Kristina knew, was no dream. The cool stone beneath her bare feet was solid and real, and so were the chipped columns and fractured statues looming all around her. This was certainly not London, and she did not know how to get home.

She cried out in fear.

Instantly Mama appeared and knelt to draw a trembling Kristina into her arms. "It's all right, darling," she whispered. "Don't be afraid."

Kristina clung tightly to her mother. "How did I get here?" she pleaded. "What is this place?"

Mama cupped Kristina's face in her cool, soft fingers and looked into her eyes. "This is Greece, my love. You were dreaming about it, weren't you? And your thoughts brought you here."

"My thoughts?"

Mama smiled and gave Kristina a tight hug before rising to her full height again and taking her daughter's hand. "Yes. Come, let's go home—think hard about your room and your toys, sweetheart, and we'll be there in a trice."

It happened just as Mama said; in a twinkling the two

of them were safe in the nursery, and Greece was far away, where it belonged.

"The time to speak of magic and mysteries came sooner than I expected," Mama began, sitting down by the dying fire and lifting Kristina onto her lap. They rocked together, Kristina's head resting against her mother's shoulder. "A long time ago there were two small children, your uncle Aidan and me. One day our mother took us to see a gypsy, and we had our fortunes told. . . ."

CHAPTER 1

SEATTLE, WASHINGTON
PRESENT DAY

Kristina found the packet of letters tucked inside a small cedar box, in a far corner of her attic, while searching for a ceramic jack-o'lantern to set out on the front porch in honor of Halloween. In an instant the witches' holiday was forgotten; the mere sight of those heavy vellum envelopes, with their faded, curling stamps, struck her a bittersweet blow to the heart. She had not thought of her beloved governess, Miss Eudocia Phillips, in at least fifty years.

Now, in that cramped and dusty chamber where bits and fragments of the past were stored, memories nearly overwhelmed Kristina. She sat down on the arched lid of an old steamer trunk, heedless of potential damage to her white silk slacks, and was only mildly surprised to find the ribbon-bound stack of letters clasped with fevered gentleness in her hands. She did not recall reaching for it.

For a long time she simply sat there, holding the letters, remembering. There was no real need to read the words, some penned in her own handwriting, some in Miss Phillips's ornate Victorian script. Just touching the paper evoked those vibrant, colorful, and often painful days with breathtaking clarity, bringing tears to Kristina's eyes and stealing her breath.

Presently Kristina looked up, blinked several times, and saw her reflection in the murky surface of the large antique mirror she'd purchased in Hong Kong. She looked just as she had for upwards of a hundred years, except that she'd worn her dark hair long before the nineteen-twenties, like everyone else. Her skin was still unwrinkled, and her figure remained slender and supple.

Pretty good, she thought, with a slight and rueful smile, *for a woman of my maturity.*

Kristina shifted her attention from her image to the ornately ugly contours of the mirror itself, pressing the back of one hand to her face. She'd gone traveling after her husband Michael's death in the 1890s, roaming the world like a restless wind, never staying in one place for long. One bleak and rainy afternoon she'd found the piece in a seedy back-street shop and bought it.

To this day Kristina had no idea why she'd wanted the monstrosity. She'd done a number of strange things after Michael was killed—and many of her experiences and emotions were recorded, in great detail, in the letters she held. Miss Phillips's private nurse, engaged by Kristina, had returned her letters after the old woman succumbed to pneumonia in 1934.

A distracted thought flitted through Kristina's mind: She ought to clean the mirror and have it moved to her exclusive and suitably snobbish little antiques and fine art shop on Western Avenue. One woman's junk invariably proved to be another's treasure, as the success of Kristina's business proved.

The correspondence resting in her fingers reclaimed her attention, and with uncommonly awkward fingers she opened the first envelope. The fragile paper was turning to dust, and Kristina held it carefully. Reverently.

The faintest scent of lemon verbena, the fragrance she'd favored then, rose delicately from the vellum, arousing other remembrances, effectively carrying Kristina back to a time that no longer existed for her . . .

> Cheltingham Castle
> Somerset
> June 14, 1897

My very dear Phillie,

By now, I know you will have heard of Michael's death, but I find I must recount all of it, as I could to no one else, in order to lay down some of the burden. A mortal's death is a mere trifle to my parents, though they have respected my pain and grief and done what they could to lend me comfort, but their kindness does not reach deep enough to soothe the bruises upon my spirit. As for Valerian, who is, as you are well aware, my confidante and friend—well, suffice it to say I believe he secretly thinks me better off without Michael. He always believed my husband was weak, and thus utterly unworthy of my affections. He would, of course, have had that same opinion of virtually anyone, for such is his devotion to me.

Valerian could never understand, as you always have, beloved Phillie, that one need not be especially worthy to be cherished by another. So often love simply occurs, all on its own, like an earthquake or a case of the grippe, and to seek rhyme or reason in such an event is to seek in vain. That, of course, is how it was with Michael and me.

But I must start at the beginning, if I am to tell the tale properly. . . .

My memories spin so beautifully in my mind just now, Phillie, bright-hued and vivid, brimming with sorrow and joy and all the emotions in between. Life is, as you always asserted, rife with paradoxes.

I was already twenty-two the day I met Michael Brad-

ford, an old maid by anyone's standards. You had long since gone to live with your sister, far away in Boston, and I had completed my formal education in Switzerland and London. I visited you sometimes, though I was careful not to draw your notice, out of fear that I might frighten you. I had not yet learned to trust my magic in those days, and there are times when I doubt it still.

But I digress.

I was alone at Refuge, my parents' cottage near Cheltingham Castle, except for the servants, and it had been raining all that morning. The house, spacious as it was, seemed close and dark, and I was fitful, with the beginnings of a headache throbbing in my temples. Just after lunch the blessed sun came out at last, and I asked a groom to saddle my pony, Pan, thinking a ride would clear my muddled brain.

Pan, you may recall, was a wretched beast, spawned no doubt in some corner of hell where the devil himself will not venture, and we hadn't traveled a mile before he'd pitched me headlong into the ditch alongside the road. I was not injured, but my favorite riding habit, a lovely gray velvet with a divided skirt to match, was torn and muddied beyond repair.

I was livid and barely resisted the impulse to turn that odious creature into a tree stump teaming with termites as he raced back toward the stables at Refuge, where the stable hands would no doubt reward him for his villainy with grain and perhaps even a lump of sugar. It was the way of grooms, I supposed, standing there covered in wet dirt, my hair straggling and my hat still floating in the ditch, to care more for horses than for people.

I could have willed myself home, or exchanged my spoiled garments for fresh ones in a twinkling, of course, but even then I liked to do things in the ordinary human way, wherever possible. You taught me that, Phillie, that

I was more mortal than monster, and may heaven bless you for it. (And for so many other kindnesses that I can't begin to count them.)

Michael came round a bend in the track, mounted on a spectacular dapple gray gelding, just moments after I'd shouted a particularly ungracious malediction to the retreating Pan. I had known Michael to be a pest and a bully when we were children—he was the second son of the Duke of Cheltingham, and his resentment of his elder brother Gilbert's splendid prospects had fostered a corresponding nastiness in his nature—but there could be no denying now that he had changed.

Or so I thought, at the time, in my naiveté. Even though I was unquestionably a woman grown by then, I had led a very sheltered life, as you are certainly aware, and there was so much I did not know.

Michael had grown into a spectacular man, with golden hair and eyes of the palest green—just the color of the tree-shaded pond behind our house. He sat his horse well, for he, like most young men of his social class, had spent virtually every free moment in the saddle from earliest childhood, and was an expert rider. I knew from the servants' gossip that he won every race he entered, that he drank and gambled with a vengeance, and had been put out of several schools for unseemly behavior.

He had many shortcomings, my Michael—there is no denying that. Being apprised of these imperfections, I should have fled the scene with all haste and spared myself much suffering, but in that curious way of females, I was instantly and powerfully attracted to him instead. I am otherwise quite intelligent, as Valerian has since and often pointed out, always with a telling emphasis on the word otherwise.

Michael reined in his horse just short of trampling me

and smiled indulgently at my dishabille. "Are you hurt?" *he inquired with what I deemed an unnecessary note of delight in his voice. I did not think, from his tone and manner, that it would dampen his spirits in the slightest if I said I'd fractured every bone in my skeleton, and I was stung to flushing fury. A few weeks spent as a toad, I reflected uncharitably, might have a salutary effect upon his character.*

"No," *I said, giving him one of my most quelling looks.* "I'm fine, though it's no credit to you that I wasn't stomped to a bloody pulp in the mud! How dare you ride in so reckless a fashion?"

Michael laughed, and his steed danced beneath him, but he managed the beast with no more conscious effort than he would have ascribed to breathing or causing his heart to beat. "You were in no danger from me, Miss Holbrook. I am, after all, an accomplished rider." *He leaned down, the rich leather of his saddle creaking as he moved, to offer me his hand.* "Come along, then, and I'll see you safely home."

"I can take myself home," *I insisted, still blushing. My heart pounded like the hooves of a great horse passing over hard ground, and I thought I'd be violently ill, right there in the road. For all of it, I knew a rash and heated pleasure at the prospect of pressing my person against his.*

I gave him my hand, after wiping it hastily on my skirts—I can hear your voice now, Phillie dear, saying, Life is paradox, Kristina—*and I confess I used just a smidgeon of magic to mount the horse behind Michael, thus allowing him to fancy that he'd raised me up by means of manly strength alone. Little is required, I have discovered, to surfeit the masculine ego, but once again I stray from my subject.*

We rode back to Refuge, and my arms were round

Michael's lean waist, and that innocent contact stirred the most wondrously wicked feelings within me, desires that I had only read about and imagined until then. And alas, Phillie, knowing better all the while, I began to fall in love. . . .

"Not one of your more salient moments," a male voice intruded, wrenching Kristina out of her reverie and back to the dusty attic.

She looked up to see Valerian towering between her and the mirror, then glanced toward the fanlight set high in the outside wall. Sure enough, full darkness had come, without her noticing. Where had the time gone?

The vampire was majestic, as always, clad in his magician's cape and impeccably tailored tuxedo and carrying a walking stick that doubled as a wand when he was onstage. His Las Vegas act was sold out for a full year in advance, and he obviously planned to perform that night. A mortal would have been justifiably concerned, being in Seattle with curtain time only minutes away, but for Valerian the commute was no more difficult than a blink of his sapphire eyes.

"Falling in love with Michael, I mean," he clarified when Kristina failed to respond to his original remark. "I can't think what happened to your judgment."

"How fortunate," Kristina said dryly, "that I did not require your approval then any more than I do now."

The vampire smiled, his shaggy chestnut hair gleaming in the moonlight. "It is a relief to find you as insolent and willful as ever. I should not know how to react if you were the least bit sensible."

Carefully Kristina folded the letter she had been holding and slipped it back into its envelope. She did not set the packet aside, but instead held it close against her middle, as if she feared her formidable friend would snatch it from her. "I have gotten by these many years," she commented, "despite my ineptitude."

"I did not say you were inept," Valerian pointed out, twirling the wand idly between his long fingers, like a baton. "Never that. You know full well, Kristina, that I could not adore you more if you were my own child."

She stood and felt an odd and unaccustomed ache in her knees. Was she beginning to age at last, like a normal woman? She dared not hope it was so; she hadn't changed significantly, after all, since she was thirty.

Except to become lonelier.

"What brings you here?" she asked, making her way toward the stairs.

Behind her Valerian muttered and grumbled. He, like her mother—and even her more practical father, to some extent—could not comprehend why she so seldom used her powers to move from place to place. To want mortality was an enigma to them, she knew, though her uncle Aidan would certainly have been sympathetic.

"I sensed that you were in a melancholy mood," he replied, "and I came to see what could be done about it. You're very lonely, aren't you, Kristina?"

She felt her shoulders slump a little, despite her effort to be strong. Valerian had recently found his soul mate, a mortal by the delightful name of Daisy Chandler, and the experience had turned him into something of a romantic. "What good would it do to deny it?" she asked, gaining the second floor landing and taking the rear stairway that led to the kitchen. "You know me better than I know myself. Tell me, O Guardian Vampire—what is your sage advice?"

Valerian loomed near the table, looking pensive, imperious, and vaguely annoyed, while Kristina took a pot from the cupboard and filled it with water for pasta. "Find yourself a nice mortal and settle down," he said at length.

Kristina laughed, but she was painfully conscious of her heart, which felt cracked and brittle, and as fragile as translucent porcelain. "Don't look now, but I *am* a nice mortal, and I have long since settled down. Look around you." She gestured with a distracted wave of one hand. "I have a house filled with antiques and exquisite art. I have a successful business."

"You are not a mortal," Valerian insisted quietly, disregarding everything else she'd said.

Kristina felt fresh tears sting her eyes. "Then what am I, will you tell me that? Not a vampire, not a woman. Neither witch nor angel, fish nor fowl—"

The magician's magician crossed the room in his faster-than-light fashion and enfolded her in his arms, and she wept disconsolately onto the white linen ruffles of his shirt. "You are unique, Kristina," he told her tenderly. "There is no other like you."

"But I want to be a woman!" Kristina wailed, tilting her head back to look up into the aristocratic face. "I want to love and be loved, to marry and have a baby and gain too much weight and get stretch marks. I want to grow old with someone special and die when it's my turn and be mourned by my children and grandchildren and great-grandchildren!"

"I know," Valerian replied, and this time his voice was sorrowful. He was almost certainly thinking of Kristina's uncle, Aidan Tremayne, whom he had loved with devotion and singular passion. Aidan, made a vampire against his will in the eighteenth century, had wanted nothing so much as to be a flesh-and-blood man again. His transformation had separated him forever from those who had known him as a fiend, for he had no memory of his original existence.

Kristina collected herself quickly, sniffling and turning from Valerian's fatherly embrace. He could do nothing to change her situation, and it was not only wrong but unkind to burden him with her grief.

"I'm sorry," she said.

Valerian was silent for a long moment. Then he made the pretense of a sigh—being an immortal, he had no breath—and said, "You're bound to meet someone—or something. Just be more careful this time, if you don't mind. I will not tolerate another wenching wastrel like Michael Bradford."

Kristina welcomed the anger that surged through her, knew Valerian had deliberately inspired it in an effort to give her a way out of her gloomy mood, if only for a little while. "*You* won't be asked to tolerate anybody," she said, dumping a handful of tortellini into the water boiling on the stove and slamming the lid onto the pot with a heartening, cymbal-like crash. "My love life, pitiful as it may be, is none of your damned business!"

The vampire shook an imperious finger under her nose, but she saw fond amusement in his eyes. "You only wish it were so," he warned sternly. "And see that you don't take up with that warlock Dathan, either!"

"Go to hell!" Kristina yelled, vastly cheered.

"I've been there!" Valerian retorted at equal volume, his nose within an inch of hers. "It's overrated and they *don't* take American Express. Good-bye!"

With that, he vanished.

As always, it was an impressive exit, smoky and sudden.

Kristina smiled, shook her head, and turned back to her tortellini. Just this one night, she decided, she would indulge herself and have pesto with her pasta instead of marinara.

It was beyond a doubt the most ferociously hideous piece of furniture he'd ever seen, Max Kilcarragh reflected, circling the antique mirror once more. It would do nicely.

He reached for the price tag, turned it over, and winced.

A woman came into the main part of the shop from a back room, and Max caught his breath when he saw her image in the highly polished looking glass. She was truly lovely, with her short ebony hair and intelligent silver eyes, and he couldn't help thinking that her reflection had transformed the awful mirror into a thing of beauty.

He smiled as she approached. Attractive she definitely was, but she wasn't his type. He liked wholesome, athletic women, and this one exuded sophistication and class. She looked, he decided, sort of art deco, as though she'd just slinked out of an Erte print.

"May I help you?" she asked. Her voice reminded him of the tiny silver chimes Sandy had hung in a corner of the girls' bedroom, just weeks before she died. Musical, delicate, somehow magical.

Max cleared his throat. *Get a grip,* he told himself. *Even if she was your type, which she isn't, a woman like this wouldn't be attracted to a high school football coach.*

"I think I may be beyond help," he confided. "Anyone who would even consider buying this mirror definitely qualifies as a serious case."

She raised one dark eyebrow, and he watched the hint of a smile tug at one corner of her heart-shaped mouth. "Oh? *I* bought it, a long time ago, and I hardly consider myself a lost cause."

Max raked his brown hair with one hand, oddly nervous. It was just plain ridiculous, he thought impatiently, to be so damned edgy. After all, he'd never see this woman again after today.

"It's a vengeance present," he said.

"I beg your pardon?"

Max grinned, feeling awkward and even bigger than his six-foot, four-inch frame. "The mirror, I mean. I'm thinking of giving it to my sister Gweneth for her birthday. To pay her back for the moth-eaten moose head she gave me at Christmas.''

Now she didn't suppress the smile, and Max felt as though he'd just run, at full speed and head down, into a goalpost. ''I see. On gift-giving occasions each of you tries to present the other with a truly ugly object.''

Suddenly the tradition seemed slightly sophomoric, though the antiques dealer had not implied that in any way. ''Yes,'' Max said wretchedly, wishing he'd gone somewhere else to shop, like that store down the street, with the rubber snakes and the souvenirs and the mummy on display. A nice, tacky ashtray in the shape of Washington State would have been just the ticket, or maybe one of those floating plastic eyeballs.

She laughed, and the sound made something ache, deep down in Max's gut. ''That's wonderful,'' she said. ''Tell you what. It just so happens that I share your opinion of this particular piece, though it's quite old and—mercifully, I think—rare. I'm willing to let you have it on a very slim profit margin.''

''How slim?'' Max inquired. He wanted to ask her name, if she was married or otherwise involved, if she liked Chinese food and old movies and Christmas. But he didn't. If there was one thing Max prided himself on, besides his daughters, it was self-control.

She named a price, and he agreed to it, producing a credit card.

While she was writing up the purchase and arranging for delivery, Max idly took a business card from a small brass holder on the counter and scanned it. *Kristina's*, the raised script read. *Antiques and Fine Art for the Discerning. Kristina Holbrook, Prop.* This was followed by the shop's address and a phone number, and Max tucked the information into the pocket of his brown sports jacket.

''Max Kilcarragh,'' Ms. Holbrook read aloud from his

Visa card. "That's a very unusual last name. I don't believe I've ever heard it before."

Was she trying to prolong the conversation?

He couldn't be that lucky.

"It's Irish," he volunteered, and immediately felt stupid. Anybody with a brain in his head would know *that*, for God's sake. He just hoped he wasn't blushing, like some pimply second-stringer with a bad case.

She smiled. "Yes," she said, handing back his card along with a receipt. "I'll have the mirror delivered to your sister's house this afternoon, if that's suitable. Heaven help the poor woman."

The wisecrack put Max at ease again, but he felt giddy, as if he'd just downed a six-pack of Corona in a few gulps. He grinned like a fool and leaned against the counter, his big linebacker's hands leaving smudges on the gleaming glass.

"Was there something else?" Kristina Holbrook asked.

Max cleared his throat again and realized he was sweating. "No," he said hoarsely and turned to leave the shop.

"Thank you," Ms. Holbrook called after him, soft laughter playing like a chorus of distant harps in her voice. "Come back soon."

Come back soon. The words were innocent, ordinary— merchants said them to departing customers every hour of every day. Especially the ones who were dense enough to pay good money for a mirror so ugly that even Sleeping Beauty's stepmother wouldn't have believed a word it said.

Max went to the door and pulled it open, feeling the late-October chill rush up from the busy sidewalk to turn his perspiration to ice. The little brass bell overhead tinkled merrily to indicate that the big, bad jock was leaving at last, but Max just stood there.

Kristina was at his side before he'd finished telling himself he was an idiot.

"Are you all right?" she asked. She really cared, really wanted to know, he could see that. And he was so touched by that one small sign of tenderness that the backs of his eyes began to burn.

"Yes," he replied, closing the door. "No. I don't really know."

Kristina touched his arm, and he fancied that he could feel her warm fingertips even through the fabric and lining of his jacket and shirt. "Maybe you'd better sit down for a few minutes. Or I could call someone—your wife, perhaps?"

The word *wife* wounded Max like an arrow fired from a crossbow at close range. It had been two years, and he'd worked through his grief. When, he wondered, would he stop stepping into emotional booby traps?

"Sandy is dead," he said, as though he were telling Kristina that it was about to rain.

"I'm sorry," she replied.

"So am I," he answered, and then he opened the door again, stepped over the threshold, and strode off down the sidewalk.

He hadn't gone a block when he found himself turning around and retracing his steps to the door of Kristina's shop. He hesitated for a moment, then stepped inside.

"I'm back," he announced.

"Good," Kristina said, with a smile that tugged at Max's insides. "I rather expected you."

He looked around, out of his element and yet wishing to be nowhere but exactly where he was. "Do you have a husband?" he asked bluntly, for it was not his nature to beat around the proverbial bush. "Or a boyfriend?"

"Neither," Kristina responded, gesturing toward an elegant old wing-back chair upholstered in dark crimson velvet. "Sit down. I'll make tea—or would you prefer coffee?"

Max had that bull-in-a-china-shop feeling again; he was a big man, broad in the shoulders and muscular, and he was afraid he'd smash the spindly legs of the chair. "I'll stand, if you don't mind," he said.

Way to go, Max, he mocked himself silently. *You've got all the style of a high school freshman trying to make time with a cheerleader.*

"If you're worried about breaking the chair," Kristina said from the doorway that led into the rear of the store, "don't be. They don't make 'em like that anymore, as the saying goes. That thing would support a Sumo wrestler."

Max figured he'd only imagined that she'd read his mind, and sank gingerly into the seat of an antique that probably cost more than he made in a month. He was pleasantly surprised when it withstood his weight without so much as a creak.

"I'll take coffee," he said belatedly in answer to her question. "Please."

She smiled and left him alone with the paintings and chairs and breakfronts and figurines.

He felt clumsy, off balance, as if there should have been prom tickets in his pocket and a corsage wilting in his hands. It was crazy; even Sandy hadn't affected him like this, and he'd loved her as much as any man had ever loved a woman. Even now, two long years after her death, he would have surrendered his own life gladly if that would bring her back.

Kristina returned, carrying a tray with two steaming cups on it, and sat down on a footstool with a fancy needlepoint cover. She handed Max his coffee and sipped from a mug of her own, surveying him with those remarkable silvery eyes of hers.

He tasted the brew and was startled to find that just the right amount of sugar had been added, along with a little milk. "How did you know how I take my coffee?" he asked.

She took her time answering, still watching him with that expression of gentle speculation. "I'm a good guesser," she finally replied, and he had an odd and completely unfounded suspicion that she knew all his secrets. Right down to the fact that he wore his wedding band on a chain around his neck, tucked under his shirt.

"You're very kind." Max drank more coffee and was almost his old self again.

Kristina's wide eyes twinkled. "It's the least I could do, now that you've taken that dreadful mirror off my hands. Your sister can return it if she really hates it."

Max beamed. "She will," he said. "Hate it, I mean. But she won't bring it back because that's against the rules. The only legitimate way to unload a vengeance gift is to find somebody who really wants it and give it to them."

"A tall order, in this case," Kristina observed.

"I got rid of the moose head," Max boasted with a shrug and spontaneous grin.

Kristina leaned forward slightly, and Max basked shamelessly in her warmth and her innate femininity, breathing in the faintly spicy scent of her hair and skin. "Who would want something like that?" she demanded, eyes narrowed, hair glistening like onyx in the muted light of the shop.

Max couldn't remember for the life of him.

CHAPTER 2

Kristina was working out on the stair climber in her family room the next morning when Daisy Chandler arrived, wearing blue jeans, worn-out running shoes, a pink-and-white-striped shirt, and an oversize letterman's jacket with the name Walt stitched onto one sleeve. Her beautiful copper-gold hair was pulled into a ponytail, which cascaded through the hole in the back of her blue baseball cap in a wild profusion of curls.

"You're demented," she told Kristina, who was still diligently climbing, and sweating in the bargain. "You couldn't get fat if you tried. Why exercise?"

Kristina was asking herself that same question just about then, but she kept going. "You know why. I want to be normal."

Daisy flung her arms out in a gesture of exclamation. Looking at her in those crazy clothes, it seemed ironic that she was the center of a certain very sophisticated vampire's life. "What's normal?" she railed with good-natured irritation. "I haven't met anybody yet who really qualifies."

Kristina was in no mood to discuss her penchant for doing everything she could in the ordinary human way. She'd been thinking about Max Kilcarragh ever since their encounter at the shop the day before, and the temptation to use her singular powers to explore every nook and corner of his life and psyche had been nearly overwhelming.

"I have," she replied in a somewhat bleak tone. Mr. Kilcarragh was *wonderfully* normal, sound and stable and genuine, yet strong, too, and utterly masculine.

Drying her hairline with the white towel draped around her neck, Kristina continued the workout and changed the subject. Daisy was her best friend, but she wasn't ready to talk to anyone about Max because there was too much— and nothing at all—to say. "I trust Mrs. Prine let you in," she said. "Or did you pick the locks?"

Daisy, who had been a police detective, now ran a thriving private investigation service. She beamed, shrugged out of the second-hand athletic jacket, and tossed it onto the couch. Her cap sailed after it. "I'm still working on basic breaking and entering. In this case, your housekeeper is the culprit." She crossed to the refrigerator in the small kitchenette and helped herself to a bottle of sparkling water. She frowned. "I must have rung the doorbell ten times. Does Prine always go around with earphones stuck to her head?"

"Yes." The timer on Kristina's stair climber started to beep, and she shut it off and stepped gratefully down from the machine. Mrs. Prine's name didn't suit her; she was not a plump and proper matron, as one might expect. She appeared to be in her late forties, had a body like Jane Fonda's, wore well-scuffed cowboy boots and big belt buckles with an assortment of old jeans and tank tops, and had a tattoo on her upper right arm that read *Garth Forever*. She bleached her hair and probably hadn't said more than half a dozen sentences to Kristina in the five years she'd worked for her.

Daisy watched Kristina towel her leotard-clad body and shook her head once in apparent disbelief. "Aren't you going to ask if there's a point to my visit?" the gumshoe inquired, plunking down on the overstuffed sofa with her bottle of water.

Kristina shrugged. "You're my closest friend. Friends drop in on each other." She sighed and hung the towel over the handrest on the stair climber. "But since it seems important to you, I'll ask. What are you doing here, Daisy?"

"Tonight is Halloween," Daisy said, "and I've decided I want to have a party for some of the kids in our neighborhood."

Daisy's neighborhood was one of Seattle's poshest; she and Valerian shared a marvelous, spooky old mansion with seven gables and at least that many secret rooms. The property was surrounded by a high brick wall, and there were gardens and fountains everywhere. Instead of being intimidated by the place, however, children came from blocks around to peer through the high wrought-iron gates, waiting for Daisy or Valerian to appear. They fed the white wolf, Barabbas, tidbits from their brightly colored lunch boxes and tucked letters written in crayon into the ornate mailbox out front.

What delicious irony, Kristina thought. The vampire and his ladylove throwing a Halloween party for a horde of miniature mortals. "It's a terrific idea," she said in all sincerity. "I suppose Valerian plans to set a coffin in the center of the parlor and lie in state?"

Daisy made a rueful face. "I suggested it, and he nearly bit my head off, if you'll forgive the expression. Once I'd really thought the thing through, I had to admit that a coffin with a real vampire in it would probably be a touch too scary."

"A touch," Kristina agreed with a slight twitch of the lips. "I have to shower and hie myself to the shop. Could we fast forward to the part of this that has something to do with me?"

Daisy reached for her baseball cap and jacket. "I'd like you to be there, that's all," she said happily.

"And do what?"

Daisy bit her lower lip. "Stir a cauldron. And it would help if you wore something long and black—"

"No doubt I could borrow an outfit from Morticia Addams," Kristina teased. "But where would I get a big pot of foul and bubbling brew?"

"I thought you could conjure one up," Daisy said, pulling on her jacket.

"You know how I feel about doing things like that."

"Come on, Kristina—you don't have to be stuffy just because you're old."

"Thanks."

"Will you do it?"

"I must be crazy," Kristina said with a nod of acquiescence. Daisy was a hard person to refuse.

"Great!" Daisy cried, adding the cap to her jaunty ensemble. Then she gave her friend a quick hug. "Come at four-thirty if you can. It'll be dark by then."

Kristina promised to be on time, suitably garbed and in possession of a large cast iron pot emitting green steam. When Daisy had gone, she asked herself why she didn't spend Halloween in seclusion, as did most of the vampires, warlocks, and other supernatural creatures she knew.

As she stepped under a shower of hot water minutes later, Kristina answered her own question. She participated in mortal holidays for the same reason she exercised, traveled by car, cooked her own meals, and bought her clothes in stores. When she did those things, she could pretend to be fully human.

The old Tarrington estate was a great place for a Halloween party, Max thought as he led his small daughters, in their masks and costumes, through the open gates and up the long brick driveway to the front door. Eliette, seven years old and dressed as Princess Jasmine, chattered happily about any number of things, while Sabrina, better known as Bree, age four and garbed as a clown, was unusually quiet.

"Everything okay, Shortstop?" Max asked, crouching to tweak Bree's red foam nose when they'd reached the front steps.

Bree glanced nervously in one direction and then the other. "They have a big dog," she confided. "*I think it's a wolf.*"

"That's only Barabbas," said Eliette, who feared neither man nor beast. Her reckless acceptance of everyone and everything worried Max; for obvious reasons, he wished she were not quite so brave.

"Listen," Max said, holding Bree's gaze with his own. "If you're scared, I'll take you home. You can help Aunt Elaine pass out treats while your sister the party animal and I bob for apples and swig cider."

The tiny clown shifted from one floppy orange foot to the other and cast a yearning glance toward the elegant brick porch, which was lined with the flickering smiles of at least a dozen jack-o'lanterns. "What about Bob's apples?"

Max suppressed a grin. "That's *bobbing* for apples, honey—"

"It's a game, stupid," Eliette grumbled, impatient to get in on the action. The house emitted an intriguing combination of moans, shrieks, and maniacal laughter—none of which seemed to frighten Eliette in the least.

"Bad choice of words," Max told his older daughter. "Your sister isn't stupid."

"Sorry," Eliette said with limited conviction.

"I guess I want go in," Bree announced. "But if we see that dog—"

Eliette had forged ahead and was already stomping up the steps. "I already told you Barabbas wouldn't hurt you," she reiterated.

Bree slipped her tiny hand into Max's and looked up at him with Sandy's solemn brown eyes. "You'll save me if the wolf comes, won't you, Daddy? You won't let him gobble me up?"

Max swallowed, and though he tried to sound casual, his voice came out hoarse. "Count on it, Babe," he said. "You're safe with me."

He was thinking, while Eliette rang the doorbell with verve, that Barabbas was a damned strange name to give a mutt.

One of the twelve-foot double doors swung open with a theatrical creak, and just like that she was there—Kristina Holbrook, the woman he'd been thinking about almost nonstop since yesterday.

Even with green paint on her hands and face she was elegant, and her gray eyes sparked with surprise, then humor, as she recognized Max.

"Come iiiiiin," she said in a very witchy voice. Eliette went past her like a shot, eager to join her friends, but Bree stood still at Max's side, staring up at Kristina in awe.

"You can do magic," the child said without a trace of fear.

"Yes," Kristina replied simply. Max had a brief, odd flash that she wasn't kidding. "Won't you come in?"

Bree released her sweaty hold on Max's thumb and padded past Kristina into the shadowy hall.

The lovely witch smiled and gestured for Max to step inside as well. "Hello, again. Did your sister hate the mirror as much as you hoped?"

Max grinned, getting over the shock of seeing her again so easily, and so soon. He wondered, as he had for the past twenty-four hours, what she'd say if he asked her out for dinner. "More," he replied. "Gweneth has sworn vengeance."

Kristina laughed. "I'd watch it if I were you," she told him. "It's Halloween, after all. She might find a way to cast a spell over you."

Max took a chance. "Somebody already did that," he told her quietly. "You're looking at an enchanted man."

She might have blushed—he couldn't tell, because of the dim light and her green makeup—but she did lower her eyes for a moment. "Do you like it?" she asked in a voice so soft he barely heard it. "Being under a spell, that is?"

"Yes," Max answered. "Which isn't to say I'm not scared."

Before Kristina could say anything in reply, the doorbell rang again, and she went back to being a witch and greeting guests. Max stood and watched her for a few seconds, then found an assemblage of adults in a nearby room, where a mob of noisy, delighted kids was watching a magician perform.

After helping himself to an hors d'oeuvre and a cup of mulled wine, Max chatted amiably with a few neighbors and then went to the doorway of the parlor to watch the magician. All the while his mind was full of Kristina—her scent, her voice, her supple, shapely body.

Their host and hostess hadn't spared any expense, he thought, watching the conjurer. This was no hobbyist or clever college kid moonlighting; the guy was a definite pro. His tuxedo was custom made and probably cost about as much as a midsize car. Over it he wore a black silk cape, lined in glistening red, and his skin had a pearlescent quality Max had never seen before. His hair was brown and somewhat shaggy, lending him an oddly old-fashioned look, as if he actually belonged to another time and was just visiting the present.

While Max watched, the wizard gestured toward a tall

vase of carved jade, which was probably priceless, with a graceful, white-gloved hand. A sparkling light surrounded the piece, which stood alone in the middle of the floor, glowing more and more brightly until it dazzled the eyes. The children—Max had long since located Eliette and Bree—were spellbound and utterly silent. A feat in itself, he thought with amusement.

The curious, electrical mist dissipated as Max watched, and a small monkey wearing a red velvet fez and a matching vest perched where the vase had been.

The kids shrieked and clapped with joy, believing. Accepting it all at face value.

Max frowned, stumped. No trapdoor, no table, no box on wheels. How the hell had he done that?

"It's a night for magic," commented a feminine voice, and he saw Kristina standing beside him.

"Who is that?" Max demanded in a whisper as the fog of light returned and the vase reappeared. There was, of course, no sign of the monkey.

"His name is Valerian," Kristina said, watching the magician with pride and affection shimmering in her eyes.

"He's damn good," Max allowed, but he felt grumpy all of a sudden. Especially when all the kids, including his own, turned as one to shush him.

Kristina took his arm and pulled him away, into the hall. Her cauldron was there, doubling and bubbling, toiling and troubling. "I didn't realize you lived in this neighborhood," she said.

Max felt a surge of crazy, drunken joy. God, it was pathetic when a thirty-five-year-old man could be this grateful just because an attractive woman made small talk with him. He needed to get out more.

"Our house isn't quite this fancy," he replied. "It's just an ordinary colonial with green shutters and a fanlight over the door."

"Your wife must have loved it," she said dreamily. Then she put a hand to her shapely chest, plainly embarrassed, and gave a sigh. "I'm sorry. I don't know why I said that."

Max wanted to put her at ease, and more. He wanted to ford rivers and scale peaks for her, to slay dragons and build cities of gold that she could rule over.

Get a grip, he told himself. "It's okay," he said aloud. "Sandy never saw the house—we lived in a condo on Queen Anne Hill when she was killed. After—afterward, well, Eliette and I seemed to stumble over a memory every time we turned around, and we weren't making much progress with the grief, so I bought this place—" He stopped, flustered, wishing he could refill his cup. He hadn't said that much about the move to his parents, his closest friends, or even Gweneth. "I guess I told you more than you wanted to know."

She touched his arm with gentle albeit green fingers and smiled. "No," she said softly. There was a brief, tender pause, then she went on. "Eliette is a beautiful name—I don't think I've ever heard it before."

"My wife's father was with the diplomatic corps, and the family spent a lot of time in France. Sandy spoke the language fluently and loved everything about the place— the people, the food, the music, the art. We were going to take a trip to Paris the next summer—"

Damn it, he'd done it again.

"It's all right," Kristina insisted. "What about your other daughter—the little one?"

Max smiled. "That's Sabrina—we call her Bree," he said. "She thinks you can do magic."

"Maybe I can," Kristina replied with a smile and the slightest of shrugs. "Unlike most adults, children know enchantment when they see it. The lucky ones have yet to be blinded by disbelief—they still trust themselves."

Max cleared his throat, went to take a sip of his wine,

remembered that the cup was empty, and blurted out, "I like you." He was wondering if there was such a thing as classes for the dating-impaired. "I mean—"

She laughed that wonderful, chiming laugh. "I like you, too, Max," she said, and waited, her eyes dancing, her makeup beginning to run. Beneath the green grease-paint, her skin was very fair and cameo-perfect.

"I thought maybe we could go out to dinner somewhere. Tomorrow night, I mean." He held his breath.

"I'd enjoy that," she said. "I keep the shop open until seven on Friday nights. Would you like to pick me up there, or should I meet you at the restaurant?"

Max was wildly pleased and wanted to run outside and dance on the lawn like a kid celebrating the first snowfall. Fortunately he managed to subdue those urges. "I'm an old-fashioned guy," he answered. "I'll pick you up at the shop."

"I knew that."

"That I'd pick you up at the shop?"

"No," she said with a twinkle. "That you were an old-fashioned guy."

It sounded like a compliment, so Max took it as such.

Kristina waved stained fingers as Max left the party some-time later, carrying a sleepy Bree in the curve of one strong arm. His free hand rested lightly, affectionately, on Eliette's small head. He nodded to Kristina, and she felt a sweet pull, deep down, that was both physical and emotional.

Daisy, aka Marie Antoinette, stood next to her, holding her head in the curve of one elbow. Her green eyes peered at Kristina from inside the French queen's latex bosom, above which rose a stump of a neck.

"Good looking guy," said Marie's cleavage.

Kristina sighed. She didn't know why she was letting herself dream about dating Max Kilcarragh, let alone mar-

rying him and having children by him. He was mortal, and
she was God-only-knew-what. Things could never work out
between them.

"Yeah," she said sadly. "He's good-looking all right.
Even better, he's decent, and funny, and kind."

Daisy shifted the plastic head from one arm to the other
and shifted uncomfortably. Evidently Marie's dainty satin
slippers were beginning to pinch. "Shall I run a check on
him for you? You know, find out if he's got any bad
habits—more than one wife—stuff like that?"

"Don't you dare," Kristina said, prodding at the bloody
stump of Her Highness's neck with one finger and frowning. "Max and I are having dinner together, not getting
married. If he's got any bad habits—and I doubt it—I don't
want to know about them."

Daisy pulled off the top part of her costume, to Kristina's
relief, so that her own unsevered head was revealed, and
tossed the debris onto the hall table. "Don't you read pop
psychology or watch talk shows?" she demanded. Her cop-
per hair was wildly disarrayed, and the look in her green
eyes said she was serious. "You can't go around *ignoring*
bad habits in a man. That's denial!"

The house was empty except for the two of them and
Barabbas, who was upstairs somewhere, sleeping under a
bed. Valerian had already done his vanishing act; he would
want to feed before materializing in his dressing room at
the Venetian Hotel, in Las Vegas, to prepare for that night's
performance. So Kristina spoke freely. "Don't talk to me
about denial, my friend," she said cheerfully, taking her
coat and purse from the hall closet. "The love of your life
is a real, live, card-carrying, neck-munching *vampire*, remember? Talk about bad habits!"

Daisy shoved fingers stained with novelty-store blood
through her hair and grinned. It had been hot inside that
costume, apparently, for her face glistened with perspira-

tion. "I never said I wasn't kinky," she said, and they both laughed.

"Good night," Kristina said moments later, pulling on her coat and rummaging through her drawstring bag for her car keys. "And thanks for a sensational party."

"Thank you," Daisy countered. "You made a really great witch. But, uh—" she glanced back at the cauldron. "What am I supposed to do with the brew? Is it toxic, or can I pore it down the storm drain?"

"Not to worry." Kristina looked at the pot and snapped her fingers, and it obediently disappeared.

Daisy smiled. "You've got a future with the Environmental Protection Agency," she said, following Kristina out onto the porch, where the jack-o'lanterns still projected gleaming grins into the darkness. "Could you just make the stuff in the landfills disappear, for a start?"

Kristina waggled a finger at her friend, walking backward while she spoke. "You know the rules, Dase. No interfering with the course of history."

Daisy leaned against one of the pillars supporting the porch roof. "At least your attitude is better than Valerian's—when I ask him questions like that, he says something like, 'You mortals made your bed, you can lie in it.' Who makes these rules, anyway?"

Standing beside her car, a white Mercedes 450SL, Kristina shrugged and pushed a key into the lock on the driver's side. "I haven't the faintest idea," she called back. "All I can tell you is, I was born knowing I'd better obey them. Good night again, Daisy. I'll see you soon."

"Let me know how the date goes," Daisy replied with a nod and a wave.

When Kristina looked into her rearview mirror, as she drove down the driveway, she saw the white wolf join Daisy on the porch, its coat gleaming in the moonlight. One by one, the faces of the jack-o'lanterns winked out.

* * *

The girls had both washed their faces, brushed their teeth, said their prayers, and gone to sleep. No doubt they were already dreaming magic dreams, Max thought as he closed the door of the room they shared, and turned to go back down the hall to the head of the stairs.

Elaine, Sandy's sister, was standing by the front door, wearing her coat. She was wrapping a muffler around her neck when Max reached the bottom step.

"Thanks," he said. "For holding down the fort while we were visiting the neighbors tonight, I mean. Did you get a lot of trick-or-treaters?"

Elaine resembled her late sister, but only physically. She was shy and uncertain, while Sandy had been a dynamo, full of opinions and ideas and eager to express them. "Not so many," she said, pulling the muffler up over her head like a shawl. "I guess most of the kids were at the party."

Max nodded. He always felt vaguely guilty around Elaine, as though there was something he was supposed to do or say or notice—something that eluded him completely. "I'll walk you to your car," he said.

Elaine smiled, and for a moment she was almost pretty. "It's in the driveway. Just watch me from the porch, if you would—"

Max opened the door and took her elbow lightly in one hand. He saw Elaine to the late-model Toyota parked behind his red Blazer, despite her earlier suggestion, and waited until she'd locked the doors, started the engine, and driven away. The neighborhood was a peaceful one, but crime was on the rise in Seattle like everywhere else.

Turning to go back inside, Max saw the sleek, silvery-white form of a dog streak across the lawn next door. In mere moments the animal leaped the fence, trotted over, and sat on its haunches on Max's front walk.

Standing still, more fascinated than afraid, Max saw that

this was no dog, after all, but a wolf. The creature's eyes were an uncanny blue, and they glinted with an unnerving intelligence.

"If you aren't the infamous Barabbas," Max said, slipping his hands into the pockets of his brown corduroy slacks, "you're certainly a candidate for the all-around best costume."

A shrill whistle pierced the night, and Barabbas perked up his ears in response.

"Damn it, Barabbas," a female voice called, "do you want to end up in the pound?"

Barabbas made a whimpering sound and then uttered a dutiful yelp, and an attractive woman in jeans and a plaid flannel jacket appeared on the sidewalk in front of Max's house. He recognized her immediately as his neighbor, the party-giver, and he was happy to see her. Relieved, too.

The wolf trotted over, took the fence in another graceful bound, and proceeded to lick one of the woman's hands.

"I'm Daisy Chandler," she said, holding out the other hand over the fence. "I saw you at the party tonight, but we didn't get a chance to talk."

Max walked to the gate and shook her hand. "Max Kilcarragh," he said. "It was a terrific setup—especially the witch." He was embarrassed all of a sudden, fearing he'd revealed too much about his attraction to Kristina. "The magician wasn't bad, either."

She laughed. "I guess that's a matter of viewpoint," she said. "Sorry about Barabbas, here. I hope he didn't scare you."

Max saw the humor of the situation, now that White Fang was on the other side of the fence and completely enthralled by his mistress. "It was the first time I ever had an aerobic experience without moving anything on the outside of my body," he said. Mindful of recent chilling headlines concerning wolves kept as pets, and of Bree's fear of the animal, Max turned serious. "Maybe it isn't—well, maybe it's dangerous, keeping a wild animal in a residential area."

"Oh, Barabbas isn't wild," Ms. Chandler said with supreme confidence. "He wouldn't hurt anybody unless they deserved it."

Eliette had said a similar thing earlier, Max recalled. He wondered what made his daughter—and Ms. Chandler—so sure the wolf was tame. "All the same, I wonder—"

"Trust me, it's okay," Ms. Chandler broke in, speaking as cheerfully as before, and Max found that he wanted very much to believe her. Some instinct, born long, long ago in the mind of some distant ancestor and passed down to him through uncountable generations, told him that this woman was a friend. "Barabbas loves children."

Max felt his mouth slant into a grin. "That's what I'm afraid of," he said. But in truth he really wasn't worried about the wolf any longer. Maybe some passing witch had cast a spell over him. "My daughters enjoyed the party, and so did I. Thanks for inviting us."

"Thanks for coming," she said. "It was a nice turnout, wasn't it? I would have been disappointed if nobody had showed up." She flashed him another smile. "Well, Barabbas and I had better be getting back now. See you around, Mr. Kilcarragh."

"Max," he corrected, starting toward the house. No need to fear for Ms. Chandler's safe passage home, with a wolf to escort her.

"Daisy," she answered and went her way, with the Hound of the Baskervilles trotting along behind her like a puppy.

Max went back inside and wandered into the living room, which had been cluttered when he left for the party earlier in the evening. Now, thanks to Elaine, the place was as tidy as an old maid's parlor—except for the pumpkin.

The jack-o'lantern, which he had carved a week before, with close supervision by Eliette and Bree, sat forlornly in the middle of the coffee table, caving in on itself and smelling like what it was—a scorched squash.

Max took it in both hands, carried it into the kitchen, and dropped it into the trash. "Sorry," he told the discarded vegetable as he washed his hands at the sink, "but that's life. Ask last year's Christmas tree."

"Who are you talking to, Daddy?"

Max turned to see Bree standing in the doorway, clutching her "blankie." "Myself," he said, scooping the child into his arms and giving her a quick hug. "What are you doing up, anyway? It's late."

"I was thinking about the witch lady," Bree answered, rubbing one eye with the back of a dimpled hand. "The pretty one we saw at the white wolf's house. Do you think she's green all over?"

Max started up the rear stairway, still carrying Bree. "No," he replied, hiding a smile. "She isn't green anywhere, Poppet. She's a regular woman, not a witch. Her name is Kristina, and she's very, very nice."

Bree laid her head on Max's shoulder and sighed sleepily. "Maybe she isn't green, and maybe she's nice, too. Maybe she's even regular, but she *is* a witch."

Max kissed his daughter's downy temple. "No, honey. She was only pretending. For Halloween."

Bree yawned big and gave his cheek a sympathetic pat. "Grown-ups," she said with another sigh. With that, she promptly fell asleep again.

CHAPTER 3

After blitzing her costume back into the nothingness from whence it came, and scrubbing off the green greasepaint in the shower, Kristina brewed herself a cup of herbal tea. Bundled in the comfortable cocoon of her favorite robe, a pink terry-cloth number with deep pockets and a zipper in front, she sat in her darkened living room, watching the moon through the huge leaded-glass windows opposite her chair.

"Here's to you," she said, raising her teacup in a friendly salute to all things lunar. The massive translucent disk almost seemed to be hovering just beyond the glass, hoping for an invitation to tea.

Kristina settled back in her chair and closed her eyes, haunted by images of Max and his beautiful children. Her yearning to be mortal was, in those moments, so poignant, so deeply rooted in the center of her being, that it threatened to splinter her very soul.

If indeed she *had* a soul, Kristina thought as one tear slipped down her cheek.

"Depressed, my darling?"

Kristina jumped and opened her eyes wide to see Dathan, the golden-haired warlock, standing next to the fireplace.

Of late, he had taken to wearing capes and tuxedos, à la Valerian, though the two politely despised each other.

"Don't call me 'darling,' " Kristina snapped, nearly upsetting her tea as angry adrenaline surged through her system. "And I won't have you just *appearing* in my house, either. It's bad enough when my mother and Valerian do it."

Dathan's smile was charmingly rueful and quite heartrending—if one didn't know him for the scheming wastrel he was. Despite his guileless brown eyes and choir-boy looks, his capacity for devilment rivaled Valerian's own. "Sorry," he said. "I was passing by and—"

"Flying across the moon, you mean," Kristina scoffed. She remained in her chair and held her teacup in both hands to keep from spilling the contents on her bathrobe.

He pressed one palm to his chest and splayed his fine, tapered fingers. "You wound me," he said. "I'm here out of concern for you, Kristina."

"Right."

"And it is Halloween, after all. Surely I can be forgiven for popping in on a friend." He crossed to a table inlaid with marble, a piece Kristina had acquired at Sotheby's in 1921, and helped himself to a handful of brightly colored candies.

"You are not a friend," Kristina pointed out coolly. "I hope the candy corn will suit. We're fresh out of dead rats and flies' wings."

"A second blow," Dathan cried around a mouthful of treats, clutching his chest again. "More crippling even than the first!" He swallowed with a tragic gulp. "I've come here expressly to save you from making a dreadful error, and how do you repay me? With insults!"

Kristina sighed. "Please do not add bad acting to your other crimes," she said. "Just tell me what you want and get out."

He executed a sweeping bow, eyes twinkling, and began to pace the length of the room in long, aristocratic strides, showing off his cape to excellent advantage and putting away more candy corn with every step. "You may know that I seek a vampire bride," he said. "Imagine the possibilities, the powers that might result, if a warlock and a blood-drinker were to mate!"

Kristina rubbed her temple. "Well, you're barking up the wrong tombstone this time," she said wearily. "Despite my illustrious heritage, I'm definitely not a vampire. And even if I were—"

"Stop," Dathan warned, halting, with a majestic, rustling swirl of silk in the center of the room. "You've made your disinterest in my romantic attentions plain enough already. I wasn't suggesting that we get together, I merely hoped that you might have a friend—"

"Ah," Kristina said, her headache intensifying. "You want me to fix you up. I thought you and Roxanne Havermail were an item. How's the family, by the way?"

Color surged into Dathan's face. "Kindly do not mention that creature, or her horrible children, again!"

Kristina smiled, recalling Benecia and Canaan Havermail, Roxanne's five-hundred-year-old babies, who were vampires in their own right and all the more savage for their doll-like, little-girl beauty. "Valerian will be disappointed that his matchmaking didn't work out," she said. "And since Avery Havermail ran off with that fledgling a few years ago, Roxanne and the girls have been—lost."

Dathan seethed in silence for a few moments, then, with admirable resolve, regained control of his temper and spoke in a moderate, even cordial, tone. "Kristina," he began again, in slow, measured tones. "Do you know any unattached vampires?"

She couldn't help it—she laughed. His phrasing had been unfortunate but highly visual. "No," she said when she'd recovered. "Except for my mother—who is madly in love with my father and will be for all eternity—and the Havermails, I am not acquainted with any female nightwalkers." Her tea had turned cold, but she took a sip anyway. "Now, before you go, please explain that comment you made earlier, about saving me from making a terrible mistake."

The warlock looked so defeated and so forlorn that Kristina almost felt sorry for him. Almost, but not quite. She'd been around long enough to know a first-class flimflam artist when she saw one. "You shouldn't become involved with the mortal," he said. "Max Kilcarragh, I mean."

Kristina stiffened. Valerian, her parents, the Havermails—all of them could defend themselves against the warlock if the need arose—but Max was different, of course. He had no magical powers and would thus be no match for the likes of Dathan. "What do you know about Max?"

The magnificent warlock toyed with one of the emerald cufflinks glittering at his wrists. "Enough," he replied gruffly, "and stop worrying. I'm no threat to him or to his children. It's just that he can't give you his heart, my dear—it's buried with his dead wife. He adored her, you see."

Kristina's eyes stung, and she blinked a couple of times in an effort to hold back tears. "Stay away from Max Kilcarragh," she said evenly and quietly. "If you dare to bother him in any way—"

Dathan held up both hands, immaculately gloved, in a bid for peace. "I give you my word, Kristina. I mean him no harm."

"Valerian has told me about the word of warlocks."

The splendid, graceful creature sighed. "Your friend the vampire is hardly objective where we are concerned, is he? Be fair, Kristina—what have I ever done to deserve your rancor, except admire you and make a fool of myself over you?''

Kristina was not good at holding grudges, especially against beings, human or otherwise, who had never hurt her in any way. She let Dathan's plaintive question pass unanswered, however, and countered, ''How would you know anything about the state of Max Kilcarragh's heart?''

He shrugged. ''I saw you with him earlier, and flipped through a few mental files, that's all. Poor Max. He'd give up his own life, even after two years, if it would bring his Sandy back.''

Kristina ached inside, because she understood Max's pain, had felt something similar herself, once upon a time. Far from putting her off, Max's devotion to his lost wife increased his appeal. Along with all his other fine characteristics, he was loyal.

''Yes,'' she said softly, ''I'm sure he would do that. That's part of what makes him Max. Now, if you don't mind—''

Dathan uttered another sigh, gave his cape a dashing swirl, and vanished.

Kristina carried her teacup into the kitchen and set it on the drainboard. Then she climbed the rear stairway and moved along the hall toward her bedroom. On the way she passed one of her favorite pieces of furniture, a small lacquered chest purchased long ago in Florence, and ran her fingers lightly over its smooth surface.

The thick packet of letters from the attic waited on the nightstand in Kristina's bedroom, in the cedar box, and she did not need to open them, or even touch the dried, crumbling paper, to bring their contents flooding into her mind, word for word. . . .

. . . and you can probably imagine, Phillie dear, how my beloved parents reacted to the news that I was in love

with Michael Bradford. Why, they hardly took it better than Valerian did—he was in a terrible rage for weeks, and when that finally passed, he remained inconsolable for some time.

But I'm getting ahead of myself again. I'm afraid I've never quite broken that habit, despite all my efforts to slow down and take matters one by one.

It began to rain again, that afternoon when Michael brought me home to Refuge after my tumble from Pan's back, and we were quite drenched by the time we reached the stables. Naturally I offered the hospitality of our cozy drawing room, where there would be a warm fire burning, with hot tea and biscuits close at hand, and Michael accepted graciously.

I still recall the mingled and not unpleasant scents of damp wool, brandy, horseflesh, and some manly cologne as my childhood enemy stood before the hearth, smiling down at me while he waited for his clothes and hair to dry.

"You've grown up to be a very lovely woman, Kristina," he said.

My heart rate quickened at his words and so, however imperceptibly, did my breathing. I wondered how lovely I could be, sitting there on Papa's leather hassock with my garments torn and wet and covered in mud, and my tresses straggling untidily from their pins. Only then did it occur to me that I might have gone to my room to wash and change and do something with my hair before sitting down to tea with a gentleman.

I fear the social graces were not emphasized in our home after your time with us came to an end. Mama would have thought it demeaning for a woman to prink and preen for a man, and Papa was only interested in Mama, then as now, and in his endless scientific exper-

iments. Manners and conventions seem silly to him, I'm sure.

But Michael had paid me a compliment, and I was charmed and quite smitten even then. I had to set my tea aside, for fear of spillage, and my face felt much too warm, considering the distance between myself and the fire.

"Thank you," I said, as you taught me, keeping my eyes down.

"You're here all alone, in this vast house?"

I made myself look at Michael and replied, "Not really. The servants are here, and it's not a large place, really. Not like Cheltingham."

"That haunted ruin," Michael scoffed, dismissing several centuries of very distinctive history with the wave of a hand. "It's a cold dungeon of a place, filled with drafts and dust motes and wailing specters, and I abhor it."

The word haunted *did not intrigue me, as it might have done another girl, for I knew a thing or two about such phenomena, of course, and in fact found them so commonplace as to be boring. "But Cheltingham is your home," I protested. "Your family lives there, after all."*

Too late I recalled Michael's antipathy toward his elder brother, Gilbert, the future Duke of Cheltingham. He turned away quickly, ostensibly fascinated by a small figurine on the mantelpiece, but not before I saw the look of wretched misery flickering like dark flames in his eyes. "So they do," he said, trying to sound disinterested and failing utterly.

I rose from my hassock and went to lay a bold hand on his arm, whispering his name, wanting to offer him some small comfort, some reassurance.

He turned suddenly and took me into his arms and held me close, out of some secret desperation rather than passion. I felt him tremble against me as he struggled to contain his emotions, and although I am ashamed to admit it, I wanted him to go on holding me like that forever.

Alas, Michael remembered himself and released me within a few moments, and I stood tottering on the hearth, speechless and flushed, while he stepped away, shoving a hand through his rain-dampened hair. "I'm sorry, Kristina," he said. "I had no right to take such a liberty."

I did not speak; I could not have done so for anything, for my foolish heart was wedged into my throat, and my eyes were filled with the tears of a besotted virgin. Which, of course, is exactly what I was.

He apologized again and promptly took his leave, and I was left behind to adore him in hopeless solitude, as I would be many times in the future. But I knew nothing of heartache then, nothing of suffering.

I was so very innocent.

The following day, Phillie, he was back—Michael, I mean—to bring me a blue hair ribbon and invite me to go riding with him. I accepted happily and sent a maid to the stables to speak to one of the grooms. I would not ride Pan again, I had decided. The fractious beast could just stay in his stall until he'd learned to behave himself, as far as I was concerned. If he toppled over from old age first, so be it.

A fine palomino mare was brought around for my inspection—Mama had probably acquired it for one of her adventures—and I was more than pleased. Here was a mount that would not embarrass me.

I allowed Michael to assist me onto the saddle—being in the company of a gentleman, I did not sit astride as I normally would have done but perched demurely on the animal's back, hoping I looked pretty.

I was such a fool in those days, but I don't mind it so much now—looking back on that time, I mean. I was absurdly happy, you see, and the dazzling sunshine of that day will surely warm my heart whenever I remember how it was.

Michael came to call often in the weeks and months that followed, and on those occasions when he was occupied with other things, I missed him so badly that I could not eat or sleep. I might have gone to him, by means of my powers, but even then I was determined not to take unfair advantage of those around me.

Since then, as you might imagine when you've heard the whole account, I have often wished I had not been so noble.

Michael proposed marriage exactly eight weeks after our first rainy encounter on the road between Refuge and Cheltingham, and I accepted eagerly.

I did not need to go searching for Mama and Papa to tell them my news; they appeared that very night in the drawing room, where I was sipping tea and sketching wedding gowns for the dressmaker in the village.

"Kristina Holbrook!" Mama said, so sternly that I started in my chair. I had not noticed my parents' arrival until she spoke, for they had long since foresworn the flamboyant entrances and exits Valerian generally employed.

"What is this nonsense about your marrying Cheltingham's younger son?" Papa demanded.

I held out my hand to show the promise ring—a sizable sapphire brought from some far-off country many years before, for Michael's great-grandmother to wear— and smiled. I was pleased to see my mother and father, and not even faintly intimidated by their obvious displeasure. "His name is Michael," I said, well aware that a certain stubborn light had come into my eyes. "And I love him very much."

"This will not do!" my father informed me. "The boy

is a waste of skin—Cheltingham's been threatening to make a remittance man of him for years!''

''I shall be his salvation,'' I said.

I recall that my beautiful mother rolled her indigo-blue eyes at this pronouncement. ''All he needs is the love of a good woman,'' she muttered in clear disdain.

''Well, it's true!'' I cried, leaping to my feet.

Papa folded his arms. ''Kristina, I forbid you to see this young man again. Do you understand? I forbid it.''

''Don't be a fool, Calder,'' Mama said, nudging him lightly with one elbow. ''Kristina is an adult. You cannot forbid her to do anything.'' She drew close to me and laid cool, calming white hands on my cheeks. ''You are infatuated with the lad, darling,'' she reasoned. ''But that will pass in time, I promise. In the meanwhile, you mustn't do anything rash.''

I was to think of my mother's wise counsel often in the years to come, but at the time I thought she only wanted to spoil my fun and keep me a spinster forever.

''I'm tired of being alone,'' I said with some bitterness, pulling away and establishing a little distance between myself and the splendid vampires who had raised me with love. ''Good heavens, I'm already older than most girls are when they marry.''

''We're not saying you shouldn't take a mate, my dear,'' Mama said cautiously. Papa was glowering at me in silence, his hands in the pockets of his trousers, his sleeves rolled up for laboratory work, as always. ''It's simply that Michael is—''

''A mortal?'' I demanded rudely. ''May I remind you, Mama, that Papa was human, too, when I was conceived?''

''Kristina,'' my father warned in a quiet voice I had long since learned to obey. ''Have a care what you say.

No one, not even you, is permitted to address your mother without respect.''

I swallowed hard, closer to tears now than tantrums. "I'm sorry. It's just that I do love Michael and I want my own life. I've waited long enough."

We had the same conversation many times in the following weeks, but I was immovable. Finally, in despair, my parents gave up the cause of dissuading me from marrying Michael Bradford and told me sadly that they loved me, that I had only to summon them if I needed anything.

They did not attend the wedding, nor did Valerian, whom I had adopted as an uncle when I was very small. I wept secret tears, before and after the ceremony, because my cherished family refused to share my joy.

I confess, Phillie, that I went so far as to hire a man and woman from a neighboring village to pose as my parents, lest I be shamed before my bridegroom's kin. Yes, I know it was a cheap and even reprehensible deception, but what else should I have done, old friend? Should I have told the aging duke and duchess, the heir apparent, and my own proud young husband, before their friends and relations, that my mother and father never went abroad during the daylight hours because they were vampires?

Of course I could not. And I must close this letter now, dear, before it becomes too fat for its envelope. I shall write more soon, and I warn you, Phillie, I mean to leave nothing out. You must brace yourself for some ugly truths.

Love Always, Kristina

Max paused outside the door of Kristina's shop at exactly seven o'clock the next evening, loosened his tie, which felt like a noose, and asked himself what had made him think he had anything in common with this woman. He was an exceptional father, a good football coach, a loyal American, and an all around regular guy, but Kristina Holbrook was way out of his league. He wasn't even sure what to say to her.

He forced himself to cross the threshold, and the tinkling of the small brass bell heralding his entrance vibrated in his head like the toll of an enormous gong.

Kristina was standing behind the counter, wrapping an exquisite rosewood music box for an upscale woman with a stylish haircut. The silly thought flashed in Max's mind that Bree would be glad to hear that Kristina was no longer green.

"Hi, Max," she called with a friendly wave. "I'll be with you in a moment."

"No hurry," he said, and turned away to browse while Kristina and the customer finished their business.

He was pondering a grotesque bronze monkey when Kristina joined him a few minutes later.

"This might be perfect for Gweneth," he mused. "Christmas is coming, after all."

To Max's surprise, Kristina snatched up the monstrosity and carried it into the back room. She was pale when she returned, and there was a stubborn set to her jaw.

"That thing is not for sale," she said.

"Why not?" Max asked, puzzled. He didn't know Kristina well—there hadn't been time for that—but he *had* figured out that she wasn't given to mood swings.

"Because it's evil, that's why," Kristina replied, and immediately looked as though she regretted explaining.

"Evil?"

"Never mind, Max," she said, her silver eyes softening with some old sorrow as she linked her arm with his. "It's late, and I'm hungry and very anxious to lock up and leave."

He smiled down at her, noting the lingering sadness he saw in her delicate features and wondering what he could do, or say, to drive it away. "I tend to be too curious for my own good sometimes," he said. "Come on, let's go get something to eat."

He took her to his favorite restaurant, just off Pioneer Square, where a jazz band played on weekends and the food was Creole and Cajun. It was a loud jumble of waiters and customers, always jammed to the baseboards. The wooden floors were uneven, and the pipes in the rest rooms were exposed and you had to pass the supply closet to find them.

As they followed the hostess through the throng, Max felt a wild stab of doubt. What had he been thinking, bringing a woman like Kristina to a place like this? She was probably used to quiet, elegant restaurants with sweeping views and parchment menus with no prices.

He glanced down at her face, and his heart hurtled upward on a swell of relief because her smile was brilliant. She *liked* the noise, the crowds, the rickety tables, and the vinyl-backed chairs.

Glory be.

Max put a hand to the small of Kristina's back, and his touch was light but undeniably protective. Perhaps even a little possessive.

He wished to God he knew how to act.

Kristina was still smiling when they were seated at their table. Although there were plenty of well-dressed people in the restaurant, along with the jeans-and-T-shirt crowd, she stood out in her slim dress of glimmering gray velvet. Her hair was like polished onyx, catching the light, and Max wanted to slip his fingers through it, find out if it felt as silky-soft as it looked.

"This is great!" she shouted across the Formica tabletop, opening the menu.

"I'm glad you like it!" Max yelled back, smiling, but

he was thinking about the music, which was so loud that he felt his liver quivering. Why hadn't he noticed that before, when he came here with the kids, or Gweneth, or his buddies from school and the gym? He reached for his own menu and pretended to examine it carefully, even though he always had the Seafood Etouffe.

Kristina ordered first and chose the special, Craw-Dad pie. It was impossible to talk with all the noise, and Max wondered if he hadn't subconsciously chosen the place for just that reason. He hadn't been this fascinated by a woman since he and Sandy had met and fallen in love when they were in college, and he was scared because the depths of what he felt were uncharted ones. Because he didn't want to say something stupid that would make her dislike him.

They ate, and Kristina smiled and moved her head in time with the music, and Max thought, *Even if this is all there is, it's enough. Just let it last forever.*

It didn't, of course. They finished their meal, Max paid the bill, and they left the restaurant, making their way through a crowd of new customers swelling in from the sidewalk.

"Nice night," Max said.

Kristina pulled her camel-hair coat closer and laughed. "I was about to say it was unseasonably cold, even for the first of November."

Max debated with himself. Should he slip an arm around her, or was it too soon to touch her at all? "Well," he said from the horns of his dilemma, determined to strike a positive note, "at least the stars are out."

"You're an optimist, Max Kilcarragh," Kristina told him as he took her hand and pulled her across the street, between honking cabs, smoking clunkers with dragging mufflers, and BMWs polished to a blinding shine.

They reached the opposite sidewalk safely, but Max didn't let go of Kristina's hand. There were a lot of panhandlers on the street, he reasoned, and even though most of the poor devils were harmless, you couldn't be too careful. Not these days.

It was ironic, his thinking thoughts like that when Kristina had just accused him of being an optimist. "What's wrong with looking on the bright side?" he asked as they approached the parking lot where he'd parked the Blazer earlier.

Her expression was serious in the neon glow of Pioneer Square and the streetlights. "It can be so dazzling that it blinds you, that's what," she said.

Frowning, Max opened the passenger door, helped Kristina in, and walked around to the other side. He was behind the wheel, with the engine started, when he spoke again. "Where did that come from?" he asked.

She settled back against the seat with a sigh so deep and so weary that Max wanted to put his arms around her. Even more than he had before, that is. "I found some old letters in the attic the other day," she said. "I guess they've brought back a few feelings I thought I'd already dealt with."

"The past can sneak up on a person, all right," Max agreed, switching on the lights and pulling out into the brisk Friday-night traffic. "Sometimes it's tough to stay in the present."

"Yes," Kristina said, turning her head and looking at him with those spectacular gray eyes of hers. They reminded Max of the sparklers he always bought for the kids on the Fourth of July. "You're a nice guy, Max Kilcarragh."

"Thanks," he answered with a touch of regret in his voice. "Just once, though, I'd like some woman to say I was—"

"What?" she prompted, grinning, as they drove up one of Seattle's many one-way streets.

"Dangerous," Max admitted with a grin of his own.

"I'd like for mothers to say to their daughters, 'Watch out for that one. He's trouble.' "

Kristina's laughter pealed through the car like the chiming of a celebratory bell. "No, you wouldn't," she said when she'd calmed herself a little. "You're sweet and you're strong and you're good, and trouble, my friend, is definitely *not* your middle name."

Max was mildly insulted. "You make me sound like a real wimp, to use today's vernacular."

She touched his arm, and Max felt the proverbial electric shock snake through his veins and explode in his biceps. "Never," she said quietly. "Don't you understand, Max? You're the complete opposite of a wimp. You're a genuine, grown-up, secure-in-his-masculinity *man.*"

He was grateful that it was dark inside the Blazer, because he blushed. He hadn't reacted quite like that since the beginning of adolescence, when his hormones, dormant one moment, had been running amok the next.

"Max?" She wasn't going to give him time to think of something clever to say, which was just as well, because it might have taken the rest of his life.

He cleared his throat. "Yeah?"

Kristina's fingers brushed the side of his face, so lightly, so briefly, that he was afraid he'd only dreamed it. "I'm not what you think I am."

Max turned his head, smiling with his eyes as well as his mouth. "You used to be a man," he teased. "You were born on another planet." He snapped his fingers, as if struck by a sudden revelation. "I've got it. Bree was right—you're a witch."

Kristina's silver eyes shimmered, and when she answered, her voice was hardly more than a whisper. "Close," she said. "You almost guessed it, Max."

CHAPTER 4

Kristina turned in the passenger seat of Max's car and regarded him solemnly, so he'd know she hadn't been joking when she'd said his guess that she was a witch was close to the truth. Their brief evening together was about to end, she thought with dismal resignation, and once he'd heard what she had to say, there wouldn't be another date.

The thought stirred an unbearable sadness in Kristina. How had she come to want so much from this man, so soon?

Max glanced at her, navigating the traffic with a skill born of long practice. He was a good driver, yet another trait Kristina admired in him, for she herself had never really gotten the knack of motoring. Probably because of her nineteenth-century beginnings, she still yearned for horse-drawn carriages and spirited riding ponies.

"What is it?" he prompted in a gentle voice.

Kristina sighed. "I'm different," she said.

Max kept driving, but he was plainly listening, waiting for her to go on. There was something very nurturing in his attentiveness, something Kristina had craved all her adult life, without being aware of it until that moment.

She folded her arms, gnawed briefly on her lower lip.

"A moving vehicle is hardly the place to discuss something like this," she observed, thinking aloud more than addressing Max in any specific way. "Could we go to my place for coffee?"

"I'd like that," Max answered simply, apparently ascribing no other meaning to the invitation, as many men might have done. Another point in his favor: He didn't think buying dinner entitled him to spend the rest of the night in Kristina's bed.

She murmured directions, and they soon pulled into the driveway of her house. Without thinking, she turned on both the interior and exterior lights with the flip of a mental switch. Despite her unique heritage, or perhaps because of it, Kristina did not care for dark places.

A bright glow spilled around them, pouring through virtually every window. Max, in the midst of helping Kristina out of the Blazer, merely grinned. "These electronic motion-detectors are great, aren't they?"

Kristina nodded in reply. Her resolve to tell all was already waning. The deep, unutterable loneliness that had plagued her since her disastrous marriage to Michael would surely return, once Max had taken his inevitable leave, and she dreaded that empty ache the way mortals dreaded death.

She did not normally lock her front door; vampires and other immortals could not be kept out by such simple means, and she was more than a match for human criminals. Kristina gave a moment of thought to a certain doorstop on display at the shop, an ugly brass monkey that had once been a living, breathing man—a thief and a would-be rapist. He'd broken into her store one night when she was working late, going over the books, and threatened her with a knife. She'd dealt with him accordingly.

One of these days, of course, she would have to change him back and hand him over to the authorities. For the time being, though, he could remain a brass monkey, quietly contemplating the error of his ways.

Kristina pretended to use a key, for Max's benefit, and stepped into the house. "This way," she said, and set out for the kitchen.

Max followed. "This is a beautiful place," he remarked as they passed through the large living room, with its elegantly faded Persian rugs and French antique furniture.

"Thank you," Kristina replied, proud of her possessions, which she had gathered from all over the world, in nearly a century of travel. "That writing desk in the corner next to the fireplace belonged to Marie Antoinette." Naturally she did not add that Valerian, whom Max knew only as a neighbor and a magician, had been personally acquainted with the queen and indeed been a member of her court until, inevitably, he'd managed to offend her.

Max gave a low whistle of appreciation, pausing to examine the workmanship of the piece, and then they proceeded into the kitchen, where lights blazed and the large refrigerator, with its stainless-steel door, hummed.

"Have a seat," Kristina said, gesturing toward the tall stools lining the breakfast bar, which overlooked the family room. It was there that she exercised, read, and occasionally watched television. "What will you have—coffee or tea?"

He perched on one of the stools, looking a little awkward there because of his size, though he was not an ungainly man.

"Coffee sounds good," he said quietly, watching her. He was surely waiting for her to confide in him, as she had promised to do earlier, but he didn't press. There was something so restful about him, so easy. With Max, Kristina thought, there would be no games, no subterfuge, no guessing. He was exactly who he appeared to be.

She sighed inwardly, envying him a little. If she were ever so open about herself, her life would become a circus in short order. "Regular or decaf?" she asked in order to fill the silence, comfortable though it was, opening cupboard doors and taking down cups with brisk clatters and clinks.

"Regular," he answered with a smile in his voice. "Nothing keeps me awake."

A vivid image came to Kristina's mind, unbidden and fierce; she saw herself and Max making love, and sudden heat suffused her, beginning in the very core of her being, in regions at once physical and spiritual, and surging to the surface to throb beneath her skin. She was very glad that her back was turned to Max, that he couldn't see her high color or trembling hands. "You're lucky," she said, hoping she sounded even remotely normal.

"Kristina." Max spoke calmly but firmly, causing her to turn toward him before she'd thought about it. "What is your terrible secret?"

She hesitated, imagining herself saying, "Well, both my parents are vampires, you see. I'm a hundred and thirty years old, and I have magical powers. Except for those things, I'm perfectly normal."

Her considerable courage failed her in that instant, and she said the first thing that came to mind. "I was married once."

Hardly a shocking confession in this day and age, she reflected, wishing she'd thought of something more dramatic.

Max shrugged, his hands still resting comfortably on the countertop, fingers loosely intertwined. "So was I," he said.

The four-cup coffeemaker began to chortle and hiss. "I know," Kristina answered, thinking of his beautiful children, the little girls she'd seen at Daisy and Valerian's Halloween party. "Please—tell me about her."

"I thought we were going to talk about you." It was an

unvarnished statement, with no underlying meaning and no hint of secrecy or irritation.

"We will," Kristina said. She felt shame, because she wasn't sure she could manage complete honesty with this man. Not if it meant driving him away.

"Her name was Sandy," Max said, and a certain sorrow came into his brown eyes, as though he were looking inward, seeing some tragic scene. And no doubt he was. "She was killed two years ago, just before Christmas, in a car accident."

Kristina felt his pain in a shattering rush, making it her own, and steadied herself by moving close to the breakfast bar and grasping the counter's edge in both hands. "You loved her," she said. It wasn't a question, or an accusation, or a protest. Just a plain fact.

"Yes," Max answered. "We were very happy together. I met Sandy in college, and we were together from then on."

The coffee had finished brewing, but Kristina did not move to fill the cups. "I'm sorry," she said and then blushed again. "Not that you were happy, of course—I only meant—"

Max smiled and reached over to brush calloused fingertips across the backs of her knuckles. "Relax, Kristina," he said. "I know what you meant."

She looked down at his hand, now resting lightly upon hers, and marveled that such an innocent contact could rouse so many violent sensations. Nerve endings crackled in every part of Kristina's body, as if she'd grasped a lightning bolt, and her heart felt like a smooth stone, skittering over ice.

"It's just that—well—I don't want to say the wrong thing," she admitted. That much, at least, was true. Kristina could not remember a time when making a good impression had been so important to her.

"I don't think you could," he replied. "You have to be the most elegant, well-spoken woman I have ever met." With that, Max got off the stool, came around the end of the breakfast bar, and took Kristina's arm. Once he'd seated her at the table in the family room, he went back to the kitchen, poured coffee into the two cups Kristina had gotten out earlier, and then rejoined her.

These small ordinary courtesies pleased her to a ridiculous degree, and so did the compliment. In all her long life Kristina had never known a man quite like Max Kilcarragh. She thanked him for bringing the coffee, lowering her eyes, feeling shy and awkward and anything but well spoken.

"I'd like to see you again, Kristina," Max said when a long but untroubled silence had unfurled between them.

Kristina met his eyes, swallowed hard. *Tell him*, commanded some sensible inner voice, but she couldn't bring herself to comply. "I'm a pretty good cook," she said. "Would you like to come to dinner tomorrow night with the girls?"

He grinned. "Just tell me what time to be here," he said.

"Seven-thirty?" Kristina replied, even as she called herself a reckless fool. It was bad enough to risk her own heart, but there was much more at stake than that. Through her, Max and his children would be exposed to creatures they couldn't begin to imagine—vampires and warlocks for certain, and possibly other monsters, too. She did not have the right to unleash such forces, she knew that, and yet she seemed unable to stop herself.

"Seven-thirty," Max confirmed. Then, glancing at his watch, he sighed and rose from his chair. "I'd better go. It's a school night, and I don't want to keep the babysitter out late."

Kristina stood up, too, and walked with him to the front door. There he kissed her gently on the forehead, said good night, and went out. She watched until he'd gotten into the

Blazer and backed out of the driveway, her heart brimming with contradictions—guilt, longing, sorrow, and hope.

Once Max was gone, Kristina climbed the stairs to her bedroom and took the packet containing her old letters to Phillie, her governess, from the top drawer of her writing desk. Then, after mentally shutting off all the lights in the house, except for the lamp beside her chintz-covered chaise lounge, she sat down and began to read . . .

My dearest Phillie,

I am certain that my last letter must have caused you considerable worry, and I do regret any anxiety you may have felt while waiting for me to continue my tale.

Michael and I were married in the family chapel at Cheltingham, under a shower of colors from the splendid medieval windows of stained glass that grace the wall behind the altar. My fraudulent "parents," engaged by Valerian (because I pleaded and wept until he gave in), sat on the bride's side of the church, along with the servants from Refuge and a few mortal friends I'd managed to make along the way. They were well behaved and fashionably dressed, this hired mother and father, but given the circles Valerian travels in, I shudder even now to think who, or what, they might have been.

But that is beside the point. Our vows were exchanged, and there was music and great merriment on the south lawn of Cheltingham, my new home, where pavilions of silk had been erected for the occasion. Never, since the days of the dissolute Romans, has there ever been so much food and wine arrayed in one place. There was dancing and laughter, and I felt welcome and wanted, despite the fact that most of the wedding guests had been invited by Michael's family. I actually believed that I belonged, at long last.

After the sun went down, I began to look for Mama

and Papa and Valerian, though I knew none of them would appear. They did not approve of the marriage, and besides, they were notably different from everyone else and would have attracted unwanted attention.

Still, I was wretchedly disappointed.

Michael's brother, Gilbert, Lord Cheltingham, had arranged for fireworks. When the last of the day's light had truly gone, and only the stars and the red and blue and yellow Chinese lanterns suspended from wires crisscrossing the lawn offered any illumination at all, Gilbert gave the order for the fuses to be lit.

Oh, Phillie, it was splendid! The sky was black and cloudless, and suddenly there were great bursts of brilliantly colored light blooming overhead, like massive celestial flowers. I was awestruck, my arm linked with Michael's as we, like everyone else, gazed up at that incredible spectacle.

Michael was a bit drunk by then, for he and his friends had been offering toasts to marital bliss ever since the ceremony ended, but I didn't think much of it until later. I had only one concern, as I have told you, and that was the marked absence of my own, true family.

The fireworks ended, and Michael staggered off somewhere, leaving me quite alone. Before I knew what to make of that—it was our wedding night, after all, and I had been looking forward to being deflowered, though I admit I was fearful, too—an argument erupted between my bridegroom and one of his guests.

I could not have guessed then how serious the repercussions of what seemed like a simple disagreement would turn out to be. Gilbert broke up the shouting match before it could become a brawl, and gave his younger brother a subtle push in my direction.

I suppose it is indelicate to speak of what happened next, but I must if I am to tell the story in an accurate fashion. Michael put his arm around my waist and guided me toward the darkened house, with only a candle, plucked from one of the Chinese lanterns, to guide our steps.

I was shivering with excitement and the peculiar sort of dread all innocent brides must feel, and by the time we had entered the castle and gained Michael's room on the second floor, my husband had sobered considerably.

In light of future events, I suppose it would make more sense if the evening had brought disillusion, even pain, but it did not. I loved Michael thoroughly, and I believe he felt the same toward me, insofar as he was capable of tender sentiments. He was uncommonly gentle as he removed my wedding gown and all the many troublesome garments beneath, each in its turn and its own good time. He caressed me, and whispered pretty words, and though there was some hurt when, at last, he took me as a husband takes a wife, pleasure soon followed. Am I wanton, Phillie? I enjoyed the things Michael did to me in his bed that night—I thrashed upon the mattress. I moaned when he promised that strange, sweet satisfaction I craved without understanding, cried out when at long last he gave it.

I understood, after that introduction to marriage, the tremendous passion my parents felt for each other, a caring that transcended time and space, existing in a dimension of its own creation. I actually believed, in my naïveté, that Michael and I shared such a love.

When I awakened, my bridegroom was gone, though it was not yet dawn. I had sublimated my powers in my desire to be human, but that morning my intuition would not be ignored. I threw back the covers, full of a sick and sudden terror, and pulled on my silk wrapper. I might have gone to him then, disregarding all the care

I had taken to hide my magic, but for the sound of a single shot echoing through the air.

I froze, there in the bedroom I was to share with my husband, while the whole terrible scene unfolded before my eyes, as clearly as if I'd been on that fog-shrouded hillside to witness the tragedy. . . .

"And still the rascal wasn't dead," said an imperious male voice, startling Kristina out of the lost world of the letter. "More's the pity."

Kristina folded the fragile vellum pages carefully and put them aside on the lamp table. Her father, Calder Holbrook, stood at the foot of the chaise, looking both spectacular and miserable in his formal evening clothes. He fiddled with one of his diamond cufflinks—a gift from her mother, of course, since he would never have purchased or conjured such a frippery for himself—and glowered down at his daughter.

"Mother often appears unannounced," Kristina said, with a wry, affectionate smile, while he took off his top hat and laid aside his heavy silk cape. "Valerian, too. But this isn't like you, Papa. Is something wrong?"

He was beside her in much less than an instant, bending to kiss the top of her head in greeting. "I simply wanted to look in on you, that's all," he said, drawing up another chair to sit down. Calder glanced uneasily at the letter Kristina had been immersed in when he arrived. "I didn't mean to intrude, but your thoughts were so plain that you might as well have been reading those words into a bullhorn."

Kristina smiled. She did not want to discuss the letter. "How is Mama? Or should I ask *where* is Mama?"

Calder sighed, looking exasperated. "There is a ball tonight, to honor Dimity. I have promised to meet your mother there, though I dislike the prospect heartily."

She laughed. "If it weren't for Mama," she pointed out,

"you would never leave that laboratory of yours, except to feed. Tell me, Papa—have you found what you've been looking for all these years?"

At the mention of his singular quest—to find a means of curing vampirism, while retaining the best of that creature's powers—Calder Holbrook beamed, and Kristina was struck by how handsome he was, with his dark hair and patrician features. He had been a doctor in mortal life, and a good one, serving in the American Civil War. He'd become a vampire, according to her mother, because he wanted to explore a blood-drinker's singular gifts and use them, if possible, for the good of his beloved humans. Kristina knew that had only been part of the reason; Calder adored Maeve and could not have borne being parted from her.

"I am making progress," he said.

Kristina thought of Max and his children, and the babies she wanted so much but would probably never have. "If you come across a way to make me normal, let me know, will you?"

Calder's smile faded to an expression of intense concern. "'Normal'?" he echoed. "You of all people, Kristina, should know that no such blissful state exists." He regarded her even more closely. "You've met someone. A mortal."

There was no sense in denying it. Vampires were perceptive creatures, and they read the secrets of those with lesser powers easily. "Yes," Kristina admitted, bracing herself for the same sort of censure she'd gotten when she fell in love with Michael, over a century before. "His name is Max Kilcarragh," she said almost defiantly, "and he's a high school football coach."

To her surprise, Calder looked excited, even happy. "That's wonderful!" he enthused. "Just wait until I tell your mother."

"Tell her mother what?" demanded Maeve Tremayne Holbrook, appearing out of nowhere in typical fashion. She too was dressed for Dimity's ball, in a white gown shimmering with thousands of tiny diamonds. Her black hair, showing not a strand of gray, flowed down her back in a gleaming fall of curls, and she stood imperially erect, as always, with her hands resting on her hips.

"Kristina has fallen in love," Calder announced before his daughter could move, let alone offer a greeting. He was already on his feet, in that quicker-than-a-wink way vampires had, gazing with fond triumph upon his wife.

The Queen of all Vampires turned slightly, to regard her daughter with thoughtful, ink-blue eyes. In a trice she'd read the complete story from Kristina's mind, just as Calder had moments before.

Kristina loved both her parents beyond measure, but she resented the lack of privacy their tremendous powers afforded her. Rising at last from the chaise, she faced her mother, her stance as regal, in its way, as Maeve's own. "I hope neither of you will take it upon yourselves to interfere," she said.

As if she had any recourse should these two magnificently beautiful monsters decide to turn her entire life inside out and upside down! Her magic, though formidable by mortal standards, was nothing in comparison to theirs. They could travel back in time, for one thing, which meant they could change the present significantly, and that was only the beginning of their abilities.

Maeve drew herself up, looking more queenlike than ever. "If we didn't step in when you married that wretch Michael," she pointed out, "what makes you think we would involve ourselves in this new romance?"

"It isn't a romance," Kristina said wearily.

Calder cleared his throat to get his wife's attention and offered his arm in that elegant, old-fashioned way so rare in modern times. "We are late for the ball, are we not?" he inquired.

The tension was broken, for both Maeve and Kristina knew he had no wish to attend the event, and they laughed.

Maeve linked her arm with Calder's. "So we are," she said, smiling up at him in plain adoration. A moment later her gaze shifted to Kristina. "We are not through discussing this situation," she warned. Then, in the merest shadow of a moment, the two vampires vanished.

Kristina felt more alone than ever. She was neither vampire nor mortal, and in certain ways both worlds were closed to her because of that.

She glanced back at the letter she had been reading before her father's arrival, but she suddenly felt too downhearted to go back to it. She'd been kidding herself, inviting Max and his daughters to dinner, letting her heart go wandering where it would, dreaming dreams that could never come true.

What had she been thinking of? Her attraction to Max Kilcarragh meant trouble at best and, at worst, absolute calamity for all of them.

Tomorrow, Kristina promised herself, she would telephone Max, make up some excuse, call the whole thing off before any harm had been done.

The trouble was, she suspected that it was already too late.

"Daddy?"

Max was standing in front of the living room fireplace, staring at a framed photograph of Sandy, the children, and himself, and he turned at the sound of his youngest daughter's voice.

Bree was in the doorway, clad in pink footed pajamas, her dark hair a-tumble, clasping her beloved teddy bear in one arm.

"What is it, sweetheart?" he asked. "Bad dream?"

Bree shook her head. "How long till Christmas?" she asked.

Max shoved a hand through his hair, feeling mildly exasperated. Halloween was barely over, and Thanksgiving was almost a month off, but the commercials on TV were already pushing toys at every opportunity. "It's quite a while," he answered, crossing the room to lift the child into his arms, teddy bear and all. "Why?"

"I have to get in touch with Santa Claus," Bree said with the special urgency of a four-year-old. "Do you think we could send him a fax?"

Max grinned, already mounting the stairs, Bree solid in his arms. "When I was a kid," he said, "we just wrote the old boy a letter."

"A fax is quicker," Bree reasoned. "Besides, this is an emergency."

He wondered where she'd picked up a fancy word like *emergency,* but only for a moment. Bree was smart, like her sister, and she spent most of her time with adults. "Okay," he said. "You tell me what you want to say, and I'll get a message to the North Pole first thing in the morning. There's a fax machine in the office at school."

They had reached the upstairs hallway. Bree yawned in spite of herself, then rested her head on Max's shoulder. "Ask Santa to please bring back Mommy," she said. She yawned again, more broadly. "Do you know his number?"

Max could barely speak. He'd been ambushed by his emotions again; his throat was thick with tears he dared not shed, and his eyes burned. Where had Bree gotten the idea of asking for something like that? She'd been barely two when the accident happened and couldn't possibly remember Sandy the way Eliette did. "Sure," he said gruffly. "I know his number. But there's a problem here, Button."

Bree raised her head and looked at him with Sandy's eyes. "What?"

Max swallowed hard and blinked. "Nobody can bring Mommy back, honey. Not even Santa."

"Oh," Bree said.

"Shhh," he whispered, carrying the child into the room she shared with Eliette, putting her gently back into bed, tucking the covers under her chin and kissing her forehead. "You don't want to wake your sister, do you?"

Bree shook her head. "What do you want Santa to bring you, Daddy?" she asked, barely breathing the words.

Max thought of Kristina Holbrook. Try as he might, he couldn't imagine her living in this spacious but essentially ordinary house, sharing his life, helping to raise two little girls. Nor could he picture her accompanying him to high school football games and social gatherings for the faculty members.

"I've got everything I want," he answered. "Now go back to sleep."

Obediently Bree closed her eyes and snuggled down into her pillow with a soft sigh. Max checked Eliette, who was sleeping soundly, and then slipped out of the room, closing the door softly behind him.

In the hallway he stood still, collecting himself. He'd told Bree he had everything he wanted—two fantastic kids called him Daddy, his health was good, his extended family really cared, and he worked at a job he loved—but he had to admit, at least to himself, that he'd stretched the truth a little. For a year after the accident he'd concentrated on just getting through the days and nights without cracking up from grief. Then, at his friends' insistence, he'd started to date again.

God, that had been terrible at first. He'd felt awkward and somehow guilty, as though he were cheating on Sandy. Dating had become tolerable, though, little by little, and then he'd actually begun to enjoy it. He hadn't expected to care deeply about any woman, ever again, however. He'd thought he'd lost the capacity for the kind of passionate, romantic love he and Sandy had shared.

Now, after one evening with Kristina, he wondered.

He made his way down the hall to his own room. They'd moved to this house after Sandy's funeral, when the memories at the condo had become too much for him and for Eliette, and no one had ever slept in his new bed except him. He was grateful now that there were no memories lurking there, because that night it wasn't Sandy he was thinking about, it was Kristina.

Max hauled his sweater off over his head and tossed it onto a chair. He'd been faithful to Sandy, from the day he met her, and even though he'd dated several women in the last year, he'd never gone to bed with any of them. Now he wanted someone else, and the fact was difficult to face and even harder to square with his personal code.

He took off the rest of his clothes and stepped into his bathroom, reaching for the shower spigot. After just a moment's hesitation, Max turned on the cold water, full blast, and stepped under the spray.

The next morning, despite a restless night, rife with disturbing dreams, things looked brighter to Kristina. She was simply cooking a meal for Max, not marrying him and promising to raise his children, and she'd made too much of the whole matter. Surely there was no danger from the supernatural world, either—the vast majority of mortals lived their whole lives without encountering anything but other human beings.

Coolly, while she got ready to go to the shop, Kristina considered the menu for that evening's meal.

Pasta, she decided, donning a loose dress of rose-colored silk, purchased on a buying trip to the Orient. After studying her reflection in the vanity mirror, she added a long strand of pearls and touched her lips with soft pink lipstick.

A person had to keep things in perspective, that was all, she thought. Max was an attractive man, and there was no denying that she was drawn to him, but they really didn't have much in common, and after a few dates they would probably lose interest in each other.

Half an hour later Kristina entered the shop. The weather was cold, but the day was unusually bright for Seattle in November, and as she was opening the cash register, a stray beam of sunshine struck the brass doorstop.

Kristina frowned. Valerian had warned her that such flamboyant spells were unpredictable; he'd said that the ugly monkey might turn back into a criminal at an inconvenient moment. Suppose that happened, he'd asked, and her magic failed, as magic sometimes will, just when she needed it most?

She took a moment to ponder again the foibles of the justice system, which would probably set the man free to hurt other, more defenseless people, and promptly put the whole matter out of her mind.

Business was brisk that morning, with Christmas just appearing on the far horizon. By noon Kristina had sold a set of sterling silver combs, a lacquered bureau made in China in the eighteenth century, and a painting of two young girls in frilly gowns, weaving flower crowns in a Victorian garden.

She was just beginning to think about lunch when Daisy came in, wearing her customary jeans, letterman's jacket, T-shirt, sneakers, and baseball cap. It amused Kristina that, for all his sophistication and incredible power, Valerian loved this particular woman. Every time she thought about it, in fact, she gave thanks for his good judgment.

"I hope that contains food," Kristina said, indicating the large, greasy bag Daisy carried with a nod of her head.

Daisy smiled. "Fish and chips," she said. "With extra tartar sauce."

"Let me at it," Kristina answered. She put the *Closed* sign in the window, locked the door, and led the way to the back room, where a gracious old table stood, surrounded by crates and boxes.

"I resent the fact that you can eat stuff like this without worrying about the fat content," Daisy said a few minutes later, holding up a french fry as Exhibit A. "Some of us can actually gain weight from what we eat!"

Kristina didn't laugh, as she might have done another time. Her thoughts had taken a serious turn again, because food had reminded her that Max and his daughters were coming to her house for dinner that night. "You and Valerian seem to be making your relationship work," she mused, swirling a piece of deep-fried fish in the tartar sauce. "Even though he's immortal and you're human."

Daisy widened her eyes at Kristina in mock surprise. "Now, there's a quick change of subject," she said. Then she sighed in a way that revealed deep contentment and caused a flash of envy in Kristina. Her smile was dreamy and faintly wicked. "Yeah," she went on after a moment of mysterious reflection. "It works, all right."

"How?" Kristina pressed. "You're so different from each other."

"An understatement if I've ever heard one. You know the story, Kris," Daisy replied gently. "It was fate. Valerian and I have been together before, in other lifetimes and all that mystical stuff." She paused and grinned devilishly. "Of course, it helps that the sex is only terrific."

Kristina blushed. "I don't even want to know about that, so don't tell me."

Daisy laughed. "Okay, I won't."

"It doesn't bother you that he—that he's a vampire?"

"I think of it as a mixed marriage," Daisy said, eyes twinkling. "As for the thing about his having to stay out of the sun, well, I just tell people my husband works the graveyard shift.''

Kristina thought about Max again—actually, she'd been thinking about him all along, on some level—and tried to imagine making a life with him. It seemed impossible, given the fact that he was a down-to-earth sort of guy who probably didn't believe that vampires and other such creatures existed, outside of movies and books. Meeting up with one, an inevitability if he spent much time with her, would probably have him rushing out to consult the nearest mental health professional.

And he certainly wouldn't want his children to encounter such monsters.

Suddenly tears sprang to Kristina's eyes, and she covered her face with both hands and sobbed.

''What's the matter?'' Daisy asked quickly, full of concern. ''Kris, what is it?''

Kristina struggled to compose herself, but the effort was a failure. ''The most awful thing has happened,'' she wailed. ''I've met a wonderful man, and I think I'm falling in love with him!''

Daisy raised her eyebrows in mock horror. ''That *is* terrible,'' she teased. Then she went to the water cooler, filled a paper cup, and brought it back to the table for Kristina. ''Drink up, kiddo,'' she said. ''There's no 'I think' about it. You're crazy about the guy, whoever he is. And all I can say is, it's about time.''

CHAPTER 5

Max surveyed his varsity football squad with pride as they finished their daily laps and trotted off the field toward the locker rooms. None of them would ever play college ball, let alone get a crack at the pros, but they were good kids who knew how to set goals, think on their feet, and work as a team. To Max, implanting those qualities in his students was the most important part of his job. Winning was a secondary consideration, as far as he was concerned, but because the boys were so focused and so dedicated, they took their share of games.

Max himself had been preoccupied for much of that day—once he'd gotten Eliette and Bree off to school and play group respectively, he'd found his thoughts continually turning to Kristina Holbrook. Although he loved his children more than his own life, he found himself wishing they weren't invited to that night's dinner.

It wasn't that he was ashamed of his daughters or afraid they would misbehave. It was pure selfishness on his part; he wanted Kristina to himself, wanted to concentrate on getting to know her, with no distractions.

Inside the locker room, Max ignored the noise, towel-snapping, and good-natured bickering—it was standard adolescent stuff—and walked through to his office. A pink message slip lay on his desk amid the general clutter of diagrams of potential plays, evaluation forms, magazines and mail.

Max picked it up, feeling a small tremor of fear as he did so. Since the accident, and Sandy's instantaneous death, he had been well aware of the fragility of human life. On some level he was always braced for disaster, and knew it could come from any direction. Even a simple telephone message could sometimes shake him up.

"Dr. Kwo called," one of the clerks in the high school's reception office had written in a neat, loopy hand. "Don't forget your appointment."

Max realized that he *had* forgotten, probably because he'd been thinking about Kristina all day. He glanced at his watch and considered foregoing the visit to his chiropractor because he still had to pick the girls up and get them ready to go out again. Then he thought of the pain he might suffer in his neck and shoulders—residual effects of the wreck, after which he had spent more than a month in the hospital—and rummaged for the telephone.

Fortunately his mother, who was in her third year of law school at the University of Washington, happened to be at home. She agreed to collect Bree and Eliette, take them to Max's place, and wait with them until he arrived.

He thanked her with genuine sincerity—if it hadn't been for his mother and Gweneth and Elaine, Sandy's sister, the transition to single parent would have been even more difficult and wrenching than it was.

When he arrived at his chiropractor's professional building, Stan Kwo was ready for him. They were old friends, having gone to college together, and Max had been visiting Stan's office ever since the accident. Kwo's treatments, which he called adjustments, had enabled Max to recover without an undue dependence on drugs. He had begun with three adjustments per week and was now down to a couple of sessions a month.

"You seem to be doing well," Stan observed, watching Max through the lenses of his wire-rimmed glasses. "The last few years have been rough, but maybe now you are coming out on the other side of your grief?"

Max sighed, remembering the way Bree's inquiry about faxing Santa Claus had broadsided him the night before. "Sometimes I think so," he agreed. "Other times?" He shrugged. "Who knows? Maybe you never get over it completely."

"Maybe not," Stan allowed. "But I see something new in you, old buddy. There's a light in the back of your eyes that hasn't been there since before Sandy died."

Because of Kristina, Max thought, but he wasn't ready to talk about her yet, even with a close friend. Things were still delicate, and he sensed in Kristina a reluctance to let down her guard that was equal to, or even greater than, his own trepidation. "One day at a time, allowing for a step back every once in a while, things get better," he said.

Stan slapped him on the shoulder. "See you again in two weeks. I'll have Doreen call with a reminder. And how about a game of racquetball one of these evenings?"

Max grinned. "Sounds good," he said and took his leave.

Traffic was thick, since it was the height of the rush hour, but Max was in no hurry. He'd called the house on his cell phone as soon as he climbed into the Blazer, and the kids were home, having milk and fruit with their grandmother, Alison Kilcarragh, future attorney.

When Max pulled into the driveway, Bree burst out of the house to hurl herself toward him, her little face bright with joy. He swept her up in his arms and swung her around once, before planting a smacking kiss on her forehead. "Hi, Monkey," he said. "How's my girl?"

Bree wrapped her arms around Max's neck and held on tightly. "I'm being *really* good," she said. "Because Santa Claus is coming to this very house!"

Max hoped they weren't going to have a discussion like the one the night before; he wasn't sure he could handle explaining again that Santa couldn't bring Sandy back. "I'd say it's a safe bet that he'll show up," he answered. "But Christmas is still a ways off. Why don't we think about Thanksgiving first? Aren't you painting turkeys or pilgrims at play group?"

They had reached the gaping front door, where Eliette stood, reticent and serious. Max suspected his elder daughter was already wise to the Santa gambit and hoped she wouldn't spill the beans to her little sister. Kids had to give up believing in magic all too soon, he reflected, saddened by the thought. Maybe he'd go to the video store, a week or two after Thanksgiving, and rent a copy of *Miracle on 34th Street.* . . .

"Can we go out for pizza tonight?" Eliette asked as they went inside.

Max ruffled her mop of curly brown hair. "Sorry, sweetnik," he replied. "We're invited to have dinner with a friend of mine."

Eliette wrinkled her freckled nose. "Who?"

Max's mom appeared in the doorway that led to the dining room, chin-length silver hair sleekly cut, clad in a beige wool skirt, a long maroon sweater, and high boots. Her arms were folded and her brown eyes were twinkling.

"Yeah," she said with an inquisitive smile. "Who?"

"Her name is Kristina Holbrook," Max replied, setting Bree down and getting out of his jacket. He met Eliette's piercing gaze. "You met her the other night at the Halloween party. She was dressed as a witch."

"The green lady!" Bree crowed, obviously delighted.

Eliette said nothing, but merely looked thoughtful. She

was a very bright kid, and damnably perceptive at times. Max suspected there was a wicked-stepmother scenario going on in that little head.

"I take it she's only green when she's dressed as a witch?" Alison inquired of her son, putting an arm around Eliette and holding the child close against her side for a moment. Perception ran in the family, at least on the female side.

Max gave his mother a look in reply and rubbed the back of his neck with one hand. Again he wished he'd hired a sitter, or arranged for the girls to spend the evening with Gweneth or Elaine. Alison had class that night, had probably brought her textbooks along, so that she could go straight to school.

"I don't want to go," Eliette announced. "To dinner, I mean."

Here was a convenient out, but Max's instincts told him not to take it. In his experience, things that seemed easy in the beginning often turned into major snags later on. He stifled Bree's rising protest by laying a gentle hand on top of her head and addressed the eldest of his daughters.

"Why not?"

"Because my stomach hurts."

Max glanced at Alison, but her expression said, *You're on your own with this one*.

"Is that really true," he began, "or are you just trying to get out of going to dinner at Ms. Holbrook's place?"

Eliette lowered her gaze for a moment. She was an honest child, and Max could usually get to the bottom of whatever happened to be bugging her by simply asking a few direct questions. He sat down on the lower part of the curved stairway and made room beside him for Eliette. Alison took Bree by the hand and led her back toward the kitchen.

"It's really true," Eliette said in a very small voice.

Max put an arm around his daughter. "Are you just nervous, or do you figure you're coming down with something?"

Eliette scooted a little closer to her father and looked up at him with wide, worried eyes. "I don't know," she confessed.

Max gave her a gentle squeeze. "Fair enough," he said. "Ms. Holbrook is a very nice person, you know. There's no need to be afraid of her."

"She's not Mommy," Eliette pointed out.

Another stab of mingled pain and guilt struck Max's heart and splintered into shards. "No," he said gruffly. "Mommy's gone, and there's never going to be anybody just like her."

"Are you going to marry Ms. Holbrook?"

Max frowned. Kristina certainly wasn't the first woman he'd dated, and yet Eliette had never asked that particular question before. "I don't know," he replied presently. "Why?"

"Marcy Hilcrest's dad got married last summer. Now Marcy doesn't get to visit him as much as before, because he's always busy. She says he doesn't love her anymore— that he only cares about his new wife."

"Ah," Max said, understanding at last. "You must be worried that I wouldn't love you and your sister as much if I got married."

Eliette swallowed hard, then nodded.

"That isn't going to happen, sweetheart. Whether I get married or not."

The child smiled tentatively. "Marcy's dad is a jerk," she said.

"Yeah," Max agreed. "I think you're probably right about that. But don't quote me, okay? That would only make Marcy feel worse."

Eliette leaned close and whispered. "I won't tell."

Max kissed her forehead. "I'll give you a dollar," he whispered back, "if you can persuade your sister to take a bath and put on a dress."

Delighted to be a part of the conspiracy, Eliette nodded again and bounced to her feet. "Bree!" she shouted, hurrying into the kitchen.

Both his daughters were upstairs when Alison got into her coat, with Max's help, then gathered her purse, notebook, and books.

"You are a good father, Max Kilcarragh," she declared, pausing beside the kitchen door.

Max thrust a hand through his hair and sighed. "Thanks."

"Gweneth showed me the mirror you gave her," Alison said, grinning as she reached for the doorknob. "It truly is ugly. I think you should know your sister has sworn revenge."

He chuckled. "Has she found anybody to palm the thing off on yet?"

Alison shook her head. "That little rule about the other person having to want the item is getting in her way," she answered. "Have a good evening, Max."

He went to her and kissed her forehead. "Thanks, Mom. For everything."

She patted his cheek. "I think it would be wonderful if you fell in love with the mysterious Green Lady," she said. With that, she left, carrying her books. Max watched through the kitchen window until he saw her get into her silver Volvo and back out of the driveway.

For perhaps the thousandth time that day, Kristina's image took shape in Max's mind. He could hardly wait to see her again.

The last customer of the day entered the shop at 4:45, just fifteen minutes before closing time. Kristina, anxious to get to the Pike Place Market for fresh pasta, vegetables, and a bouquet of fresh flowers, wished she'd put the *Closed* sign in the window of the front door at 4:30, as she'd been tempted to do.

The woman was well dressed, perhaps forty years old, with graying blond hair and dark, inquisitive eyes. Kristina did not need her magic to guess that the visitor was related to Max; despite the difference in hair color and her diminutive size, the resemblance was marked.

"May I help you?" Kristina asked. Family relationships and resemblances had always fascinated her. As the only child of supernatural parents, she had been lonely for much of her life, even though Maeve and Calder had given her all the love and guidance anyone could want.

"My name is Gweneth Peterson," the woman said, holding out a gloved hand. Her cloth coat was beautifully made, and her general appearance implied an upscale profession, such as medicine, academics, or law. "I'm Max Kilcarragh's sister. I believe he bought that terrible mirror from you?"

Kristina couldn't help smiling a little, though she suspected Ms. Peterson was about to ask for an exchange, if not a refund. "Yes," she said. "He told me you would hate it."

Gweneth laughed. "And of course he was right."

"Perhaps you'd like to choose something else," Kristina offered, gesturing toward her large and varied stock of antiques.

Gweneth sighed, but her eyes were still sparkling. "Alas, that's against the rules. I came here seeking something equally hideous—a present for my dear brother, naturally. What do you have?"

Kristina was amused; Max had this coming, after inflicting that monstrosity of a mirror on his own sister. "Believe it or not, Ms. Peterson, I don't specialize in horrendous merchandise. But if you look around—''

''Please—call me Gwen,'' she said.

''And I'm Kristina.''

Gwen scanned the shop, her attractive features narrowed into a speculative frown. Then, as luck would have it, she zeroed in on the brass-monkey doorstop, the one item in the place that Kristina wouldn't have sold.

''Perfect!'' Gwen cried, bending over to hoist the thing from the floor and set it carefully on a table to examine. ''It *is* dreadful, isn't it?'' she marveled. ''What possesses people to make such atrocious things?''

Kristina remembered the vicious young man who had broken into her shop, intending to rob, rape, and perhaps even kill her. ''You might be surprised,'' she replied, hovering. Valerian was something of an alarmist, and he enjoyed pondering the unthinkable, but if he was right in maintaining this thing could come back to life unexpectedly . . .

''I'm afraid the doorstop isn't for sale. I've—I've promised it to another client.''

The next time Kristina saw Valerian, she would ask him to dispose of the brass monkey, no questions asked.

Gwen looked disappointed, but took the refusal sportingly. ''Do you mean to say there are other people in this world who play the same game Max and I do? Surely no one would actually *want* to own it.''

''There's no accounting for taste,'' Kristina answered, carrying the heavy piece into the back room. Was it her imagination, or did the thing feel slightly warm to the touch? When she returned to the shop, Gwen was still there, pondering a vase with the roller coaster at Coney Island painted on one side. After a moment Max's sister shook her head and turned back to Kristina.

"I can see surpassing that mirror Max bought is going to take some real effort," she said.

Kristina smiled. "I think you're up to the challenge," she said. "Max told me about the moose head you gave him in the last round. How did this contest get started, anyway?"

"It was Max's bright idea," Gwen replied, tugging at her gloves and lifting the collar of her coat against the twilight chill outside. Her smile was genuine, full of happy, hilarious memories. "When he was eleven and I was turning fifteen, he gave me a neon beer sign he'd bought at a flea market as a birthday present. I was about to throw it away—or better yet, break the thing over his head—but Mom and Dad wouldn't let me. They said a gift was a gift, and I had to find someone who wanted it. I did, though it wasn't easy. And after that I prowled the thrift shops and souvenir stores, a woman with a mission. I retaliated at Christmas with a bronze statue of a hula dancer with a clock in her belly. Our little competition became a family tradition."

Once again Kristina felt a whisper of envy, far back in the darkest reaches of her heart. Then she brought herself up short, ashamed. Her own childhood might have been unconventional, to say the least, but she'd been deeply loved, and she'd had everything she needed and most of what she wanted.

She almost confided that she was having dinner with Max and his daughters that night, but in the end she held her tongue. It was fragile, this thing with Max, and she didn't want to jinx it with too many words, too many expectations.

Gwen took a card from her handbag and laid it on the polished counter. "Here's my number," she said. "Please call immediately if you get something in that I might be interested in." She glanced wistfully toward the storeroom.

"Or if that misguided soul who bought the monkey doesn't come back for it."

Kristina barely suppressed a shudder as she reached for the card. "That particular client is pretty reliable," she lied. "But I will keep an eye out for something that would suit."

Gwen, according to the card, was a CPA with a highly respected Seattle firm. She smiled and raised one hand in farewell before leaving the shop.

Kristina glanced at the clock on the shelf behind the cash register—five-fifteen. She still needed to stop at the market, and there was a good chance she would be caught in traffic on her way home. She drew a deep breath and released it slowly, in order to calm herself. It was silly to be so stressed out over a simple dinner.

Hastily she reversed the *Open* sign to say *Closed*, then locked the door. She put the day's cash and checks in her purse, snatched her coat from the peg in the storeroom and almost tripped over the brass monkey as she passed it. Yes, indeed, it was time to get rid of the reprehensible thing once and for all.

She'd speak to Valerian soon.

"You're not wearing your green makeup," the smaller of Max's daughters remarked, the moment Kristina opened the front door to her guests. The child sounded somewhat disappointed.

Kristina exchanged a grin with Max and stepped back to admit the Kilcarragh family to the warmth of her living room. It was chilly out that night, though the sky was clear, with a few determined stars winking through smog and city lights. Once the door was closed, she stooped to offer her hand, careful to speak as she would to an adult.

"I'm afraid I've run out of green makeup," she confided, as though sharing a secret, noticing that the elder sister was just as interested as the younger one, though not so willing to trust. "I used it all up on Halloween."

"For what it's worth, I think you look terrific, even without the greasepaint," Max offered quietly as Kristina straightened again, tugging self-consciously at the hem of her white angora sweater. Her tailored wool slacks matched perfectly and her only jewelry was a polished sterling medallion on a long chain.

"Thanks," she said and blushed. It was such a small compliment, and yet she felt as moved as if Max had knelt at her feet, like a knight pledging fealty to his queen. "Is everybody hungry?"

The girls nodded shyly, and Max helped them out of their coats. Kristina summoned their names from her memory—the little one was Bree, short for Sabrina, and the eldest was Eliette.

Kristina had set the glass-topped table next to the breakfast bar, instead of the formal one in the dining room. She wanted Max and his children to be comfortable, rather than impressed.

Bree and Eliette were well behaved during the meal, though it was soon apparent that tortellini in pesto sauce was not their favorite dish. Max didn't urge them to eat, but it was all Kristina could do to keep from offering them sugared cereal, pizza, or hamburgers. Whatever it was that kids liked—she hadn't had enough experience with them to know.

Max seemed to sense her concern; at one point, while they were talking about a recent development in local politics, he touched her arm lightly and said, "Relax, Kristina. They won't starve."

The remark took the pressure off; Kristina let out a mental breath and stopped worrying. Max was right; his daughters were well nourished and would no doubt survive one scanty meal.

"May we be excused, please?" Eliette asked, her expression sweet as she took in both Kristina and her father in a single glance.

Max deferred to Kristina with a slight inclination of his head.

"Of course," Kristina said.

"Sit quietly," Max told his daughters with another nod, this time toward the family room sofa. "An in-depth report on any goofing off will be faxed to Santa the minute I get to work tomorrow morning."

Eliette smiled coyly at this threat, but Bree looked impressed.

Kristina and Max finished their meal in peace, chatting cordially, and then cleared the table together. Once Kristina had convinced Max that the dishes could wait until morning, she approached the two little girls, perched side by side on the couch. Eliette was paging through a travel magazine, while Bree peered over her shoulder, her tiny brow furrowed with concentration.

"I have something I'd like to show you," Kristina said.

Both children looked up with interest.

"Is it magic?" Bree asked, brightening.

"Don't be silly," Eliette scolded.

Kristina felt, rather than heard, Max's inward sigh. He didn't say anything, though, but simply waited.

"I think we'll save the magic for another time," Kristina replied. "Follow me, and I'll show you the things I played with when I was your age."

Both Bree and Eliette complied eagerly, and Max trailed behind them. When Kristina glanced back at him once, as they all mounted the rear stairway leading to the second floor, their gazes met and held, and Kristina felt a powerful jolt of emotion.

Upstairs, she opened the door of the attic-like room where she kept the priceless memorabilia of her childhood.

There were dozens of dolls, most with painted china heads and elaborate dresses, along with miniature furniture of the finest craftsmanship. One end of the room was dominated by the magnificent dollhouse Valerian had given her for her seventh birthday—it was a close replica of the Palace of Versailles, complete with a Hall of Mirrors and the Queen's sumptuous boudoir. The creation was seven feet wide and over five feet tall, and it dwarfed the intricately made puppet theater resting on the floor beside it.

Bree and Eliette were plainly enchanted, but Kristina felt immediate chagrin. Maybe it was macabre for a grown woman to have a room full of toys, however precious they might be. Suddenly her treasures seemed more like artifacts in a museum or an ancient tomb than the innocent belongings that had brought her so much joy as a little girl.

"Wow," Max said.

"Can we touch something?" Bree cried, almost breathless with excitement.

"Please, Ms. Holbrook?" Eliette added in a soft, awed voice.

"Everything is very sturdy," Kristina said, "specifically made to hold and touch." She sounded a little shaky, to herself at least—she had referred to these things as her own, mentioned playing with them when she was small. How was she going to explain the rather obvious fact that they were priceless antiques?

Max bent to look inside the gigantic dollhouse, with its paintings and marble fireplaces and velvet-draped windows. Bree lifted a porcelain baby doll from its hand-carved cradle and held it as gently as if it were a newborn, while Eliette crouched to examine the puppet theater, her eyes wide and luminous with wonder.

"Where did you get this?" Eliette asked, touching the tiny stage curtain, made of heavy blue velvet and trimmed in shimmering gold fringe.

"It was a gift from my mother. I had the measles and couldn't leave my nur—my room, so she put on puppet shows for me." Kristina didn't add, of course, that Maeve had made the puppets move and speak and dance without touching them.

"Our mommy died," Bree confided, holding the baby doll, in its exquisitely embroidered christening gown and matching bonnet, close against her little chest. "I don't remember her face."

Kristina's throat tightened, and her eyes stung. "I'm—I'm sorry," she managed to say.

Max, standing just behind her, laid a gentle hand on her shoulder.

"All you have to do to see Mommy's face is look at her picture, silly," Eliette taunted, still concentrating on her examination of the puppet theater, but the words were spoken with affection, not rancor.

"Is your mommy still alive?" Bree asked, standing very close to Kristina now, and gazing up into her face. She continued to cradle the doll.

If the situation hadn't been so touching, Kristina might have smiled at the singular irony of that question. *Alive* was probably not the precise word to describe the reigning Queen of the Vampires, but it was close enough, she supposed.

"Yes," she said simply.

"This stuff is really old," Eliette commented. There was nothing critical in her tone; she was merely making an observation. A very astute one, for such a small child. "You couldn't get these things at Toys R Us."

Both Kristina and Max laughed at that, and Kristina's tension eased significantly.

"Some people like old things better than new ones," Max told his daughter a moment later. "And I think it's time you ya-hoos were home in bed." Both girls joined him in comical chorus to finish the statement with, "Tomorrow is a school day, after all."

Kristina laughed again, wondering why she was so dangerously close to tears. It had been a wonderful evening, even if it was ending too quickly. For this little while, she'd felt part of a normal mortal family, and the sensation was sweet and warm.

"I've raised a couple of smart alecks," Max confided out of the corner of his mouth, to the enormous delight of his daughters.

Kristina led the way back downstairs, blinking hard and sniffling once or twice, so Max wouldn't guess what a sentimental fool she was. "I'm sorry to see you leave so soon," she said in the entryway, while Max helped Bree into her coat. Eliette would have scorned assistance with such a task, Kristina thought—she was trying very hard to be a big girl.

"We had a great time," Max said, straightening, towering over Kristina now and looking straight down into her eyes. "I'd like to see you again—without the entourage."

"He means us," Eliette said.

Max rolled his eyes, and Kristina found herself laughing yet again. She couldn't remember the last time she'd felt such a range of emotions in such a short interval.

Bree tugged at her dad's leather jacket. "I want Santa to bring me a doll like that one upstairs," she crowed. "*Exactly* like it!"

"Oh, great," Max murmured, but his eyes hadn't strayed from Kristina's face. There was something so strong in his expression, and yet so tender. What manner of man was this, managing two small girls with such love and skill? Kristina had been married to a mortal, and had dated any number of others, over a very long period of time, but Max Kilcarragh was different from them all. Evidently he was so confident of his masculinity that he didn't need to assert it at every turn.

Charming, Kristina reflected, more intrigued than ever.

Max caught her by surprise when he bent his head and brushed her lips lightly with his own. The girls, already out the door and headed for Max's Blazer, which was parked at the curb, were engaged in a lively conversation of their own.

"Thank you," he said in a low voice. "May I call you?"

Kristina wondered if there were stars in her eyes. "If you don't," she said, "I'll call you."

He grinned and turned away to follow Bree and Eliette, who were arguing by that time over who got to sit in the front seat.

"The answer is: nobody but me," Max told them in a game-show host's exuberant tone of voice.

Kristina watched, smiling, until he'd settled both children in the backseat and made sure their seat belts were fastened. Then, after a wave to her, Max got into the Blazer and drove away.

Suddenly the big house echoed around her, full of nothing. At that moment, as she closed the door, Kristina would have given all her possessions and the fortune she'd accrued over the decades for a family of her own.

She allowed herself to dream as she winked off the lights.

Oh, to be getting children off to bed, reading them a story, making sure they'd brushed their teeth and washed their faces and said their prayers. And once they were asleep, to talk quietly with a man like Max, to share the events of the day with him, to be held in his arms . . .

"Stop it," Kristina whispered brokenly, standing there in the darkness, alone, just as she would always be alone.

There was no place for her in the flesh-and-blood world of mortals, nor in the realm of supernatural beings, for she was neither one nor the other. Forgetting that fact would not only be rash, but also dangerous.

CHAPTER 6

The nightmare was upon Max, like some monster lying in wait, the moment he drifted off to sleep. He knew he was not awake, and yet the dream was excruciatingly vivid, in color and dimension and sound. He struggled to escape its hold, to rise to the surface of consciousness, but he was trapped, entangled, like a diver flailing in seaweed. . . .

He was riding in the passenger seat of the late-model van he and Sandy had just bought, to accommodate their growing family. It was a Saturday in mid-December, around seven o'clock in the evening. They'd spent the day shopping at one of the area's major malls, and the rear of the vehicle was jammed with Christmas presents, mostly toys and clothes for Bree and Eliette, who were with Sandy's parents for the weekend.

Max and Sandy were tired, triumphant, and very, very happy. They were fortunate people; they knew that and were grateful. They had each other, their children, their career plans and personal goals, their home. And in six months Sandy was going to have another baby.

Max was hoping for a boy.

They'd had dinner at their favorite Mexican restaurant after braving the crowded stores, and Max, feeling unusu-

ally festive, had consumed two sizable margueritas along
with a plate of enchiladas. After the meal, they'd discussed
stopping off to see a movie, but in the end they'd decided
to spend a romantic evening at home instead.

Although Max did not feel drunk, he and Sandy had
agreed that it would be best if she drove home, and she had
gotten behind the wheel. He recalled that she'd adjusted the
seat and the mirrors before carefully fastening her seat belt.

That was Sandy—responsible, conscientious, competent.
The best of wives, the most devoted of mothers, somebody
who took being a good citizen very seriously. Although
she'd taken a few years off from her own career as an
elementary school teacher, she made a point of keeping up
with every new development in the field of education.
When the time came to go back to work, she would be
ready. Max had not only loved Sandy, he'd admired her,
too.

Again he tried to wake up, to break out of the dream.
Again he was unsuccessful. Sandy was about to die, and
there was nothing he could do to prevent it. No way to
warn her, or even to say good-bye.

He was caught inside his smiling, dreaming self. He tried
to memorize the look of her—slender, tall, with laughing
eyes and curly light brown hair—the clean, fresh-air scent
of her, the sweet sound of her voice.

They left the restaurant parking lot, cruised along city
streets, pulled onto the freeway. Traffic was fairly heavy
and moving at a moderate pace as a consequence.

She winked at him and checked the rearview before sig-
naling and changing lanes. There was no rain, no thick fog,
no ice on the pavement.

It should have been perfectly safe.

Should have been.

Waking and sleeping, Max wanted to weep at the seren-
ity he saw in Sandy's face in those final moments of her

life, of their life together. She looked so happy, so trusting. She had no reason to think the future was about to be canceled.

The semi-truck, loaded with Christmas trees, roared up beside them, appearing suddenly, then pulled out to pass. In the next instant there was a terrible metallic screech, the only warning they had, followed by a fleeting interval, surely only seconds long, of what seemed like suspended animation. That pulsing void was shattered by a thunderous crash, a bone-jarring impact, a spinning sensation so violent that Max did not have the breath to cry out.

And then, darkness. Pain, fierce and heavy.

Voices—horrified, reassuring. Disembodied.

Sandy.

The grief and terror gave Max the impetus he needed; he lunged upward out of the nightmare, breathing hard, his flesh chilled beneath a cold sweat. Groping for the switch, he turned on the bedside lamp and lay gasping in its thin light for several moments, waiting for the shock to subside. Finally, when he was no longer trembling, when he had freed himself from the last tentacles of the dream, he got up, reached for his robe, and pulled it on.

He hadn't had that particular nightmare in months, but its return wasn't exactly a surprise he thought, as he descended the rear stairs leading to the kitchen. Max didn't need a shrink to explain the situation—he was deeply attracted to Kristina Holbrook, and he had some conflicts about it.

He flipped on the light over the sink, poured himself a glass of milk, and leaned against the counter. He still felt the chill of the dream, and there was a lingering ache in the pit of his stomach. His strongest instinct was to push the memories out of his mind, but he made himself walk through them instead.

Max had awakened in the Intensive Care Unit of a Seattle

hospital some four days after the crash. His parents had been there when he opened his eyes, his mother on one side of his bed, his father on the other. And the sorrow he'd seen in their faces had been far worse than the relentless pain in his body.

He'd known before either of them spoke that Sandy was gone. His dad had wept unashamedly as he related the grim facts of the accident. Sandy had died instantly.

Max had spent what seemed like an eternity in the hospital, staring up at the ceiling, enduring, undergoing constant physical therapy. He'd missed Sandy's funeral, and Christmas, and when he was finally able to go home, he needed crutches to walk. It would have been easier to go under, body and soul, in those dark days and even darker nights, if it hadn't been for his daughters. Eliette, only five but formidably bright, had been bewildered and hollow-eyed. Bree was just a baby then, barely two, and she'd cried for Sandy at night, and searched every room and closet of the condo by day, as though hoping this was only a game. She clearly expected her mother to pop out of some hiding place and say "Boo!", the way she'd done when they played.

Max had done his share of weeping, though always in private, so that the children wouldn't see or hear. And it had often seemed to him that Sandy *couldn't* be dead—that she would breeze in one morning or afternoon or evening, saying it had all been a mistake, making everything all right just by being back.

He finished the milk and set the glass in the sink, but he wasn't really seeing the spacious kitchen around him. Instead he saw himself going through Sandy's things with help from Elaine and Gweneth and his mother, giving some of her possessions away, keeping others for the girls to have when they were older. He'd finally sold the condo, when he knew in his heart, as well as in his reasoning mind, that

Sandy was never coming home. It was simply too painful to stay.

Even now, as he remembered, Max's throat tightened, and his eyes burned. If he had problems squaring whatever he felt for Kristina with all he and Sandy had shared, it was his own fault. Had his wife lived, Max was sure they would have grown old together, for their commitment to each other had been the kind that lasts. But Sandy was gone, and he knew that she would want him to find someone else.

"You're not cut out to be alone, Max," he recalled her saying, one winter night when they were newlyweds, snuggled before the cheap fireplace in their first apartment, neither one guessing how brief their time together would be. "You need somebody to love and protect."

Max flipped off the light. There was no question that he'd loved Sandy, but in the end, when it really counted, he hadn't been able to protect her or their unborn child. He climbed the stairs slowly. If he'd been driving the night of the accident, instead of Sandy, maybe she would have survived. He would have gladly died in her place.

Pausing on the threshold of his empty bedroom, Max sighed and shoved a hand through his hair. He'd been over the tragedy a million times, second-guessing fate, tormenting himself with the inevitable regrets—if only he hadn't had drinks with dinner he would have been the one driving. If only they'd lingered in the restaurant for even another five minutes, or gone to the movies instead of heading straight home.

If only, if only, if only.

As Max climbed back into bed and stretched to turn off the lamp, however, he found himself thinking about Kristina again, and wondered if he was ready for all the things she made him feel.

* * *

After Max and the children had gone, the house seemed emptier than ever. Kristina, though fond of her elegant home, suddenly felt a need to leave it, at least for a little while.

She focused her thoughts on her parents' London residence, the stately mansion where she had passed much of her childhood, and arrived there in the blink of an eye. It was around five A.M. in England, and dawn was not far off.

Her mother might still be hunting, Kristina knew, but her father would have fed early, in order to spend as much time as possible in his lab.

Having assembled herself in the kitchen, still empty at that early hour, Kristina reverted to human habits, went to the cellar door and descended the steep stone steps. There was grillwork on the windows, which were just above ground level, and the area was in no way spooky, as a more fanciful soul might expect. No cobwebs, no coffins, no candelabras or ghostly shrouded furniture.

"Papa?" Kristina rapped at the door of Calder's lab as she called to him. Only her mother and possibly Valerian would have dared to enter unannounced.

The heavy panel swung open on well-oiled hinges, and Dr. Holbrook stood in the opening, wearing a lab coat, his dark hair rumpled. He was plainly surprised to see her, which in turn surprised Kristina, for vampires are perceptive creatures, rarely caught off guard.

"Hello, sweetheart," Calder said, a glorious smile dawning in his handsome face as he took her hand and drew her into his inner sanctum. He kissed her forehead. "What are you doing here?"

"I couldn't sleep," she said.

Calder glanced at his watch, hastily drawn form his vest pocket, and frowned. In truth, he did not need such a mechanism to discern the time for, as a blood-drinker, he was always intuitively aware of approaching daylight. Dr. Holbrook still practiced many small, mortal rituals, though whether out of habit or preference Kristina didn't know. "What I wouldn't give for the luxury of insomnia," he said, and his serious expression was replaced in an instant by a wry grin. "I could accomplish so much."

Kristina raised herself on tiptoe to kiss her father's cheek. He had not aged, since becoming a vampire in his mid-thirties, and thus did not look much older than his daughter. "You work so hard," she chided gently. "Why can't you be self-indulgent, like Valerian? Or adventurous, like Mother?"

Calder chuckled and shook his head. There was no love lost between her father and the vampire she thought of as an uncle, although he had been the one to transform Calder to an immortal more than a century before. "Heaven forbid," he said, "that I should be anything like Valerian, beguiling monster that he is. As for adventure—I get all I need just living with Maeve Tremayne."

Kristina saw that Calder was growing wearier by the moment as morning drew near; he spoke slowly and seemed unusually distracted. She smiled. "You need to rest now," she said, "so I won't keep you from your bed. It's all right, isn't it, if I spend some time here?"

He squeezed her shoulders lightly. "Of course it is—this is your home." Discreetly he guided her toward the door of the lab. "Perhaps you'll still be here at sunset, and we can talk further."

Eased out of her father's private domain, Kristina waggled her fingers in temporary farewell. "Sleep tight, Papa," she said and took herself back up the stairs to the kitchen.

Mrs. Fullywub, the housekeeper, was there, standing in front of the open door of the refrigerator. She was clad in a yellow chenille robe, and her gray hair was tied up in the old-fashioned way, with many little strips of cloth.

"Mercy, child," she protested, laying one hand to her heart, "you scared me!"

Kristina was fond of the woman; though mortal, Mrs. F. had been with the family for many years, and she knew what was what in that unconventional household. "I would have thought you'd be used to people appearing and disappearing by now," she observed. The refrigerator was still open, and she reached past the housekeeper for a bottle of mineral water. "I use the word *people* loosely, of course."

Mrs. F. took packages of sliced cheese and cold cuts from the shelves and carried them to the counter, where she began making a sandwich. "It's very good to see you again, Miss Holbrook," the old woman said warmly. "I hope I didn't make you feel unwelcome or anything like that."

Sipping her water, Kristina pulled back one of the stools at the breakfast bar and sat. "I could never feel unwelcome here," she replied. "And I'm sorry for startling you."

Mrs. F. rolled her wise, merry eyes. "I'm getting too old for this job," she confessed, still busy with her snack. "A body never knows who—or what—she'll meet in the passage."

Kristina chuckled. "Valerian, perhaps?"

"Oh, him," Mrs. F. muttered, discounting one of the most powerful vampires in existence with a motion of one hand. "He's gentle as a lamb, that one, if you know how to manage him." She paused and shivered. "It's creatures like those dreadful Havermail children—Benecia and Canaan, I believe they're called—that I dread."

Kristina's amusement faded; she felt a flicker of alarm. Benecia and Canaan were hardly children, as each had lived more than five centuries as a vampire. "They've been here?" she asked in surprise.

"Oh, yes," Mrs. F. answered. "Are you hungry, dear?

I must be sleep-fogged—it only occurs to me now that you might like something to eat as well.''

"No, thank you," Kristina said automatically. Her mind was still on the Havermails—two ghouls all the more hideous for their appearance. They looked like little girls, exquisitely beautiful ones at that, because they had been transformed as children. "When were Benecia and Canaan in this house?"

Mrs. F. trundled across the kitchen and took a seat at the table, a few feet from where Kristina sat, her sandwich on a china plate before her. "Just the other night, dear," she answered after pausing to make mental calculations. "Don't you worry, though—they came in response to a summons from your mother. I doubt they'd dare to show their awful little faces under this roof unless Maeve invited them, though I admit it gave me a turn to stumble across them the way I did.''

Kristina was not reassured. Benecia and Canaan might be afraid of Maeve, the acknowledged queen of all blood-drinkers, but they probably wouldn't fear a half-mortal like herself. Suppose their deadly attention was drawn to Max and Bree and Eliette through Kristina? Just the thought of that made her raise one hand to her mouth in a mute expression of horror.

"Oh, dear," Mrs. F. fretted, pushing away her food. "You mustn't be frightened, Kristina—horrid as they are, those creatures wouldn't have the gall to trouble you. They know your mother would finish them if they did, and she'd have to get to the little demons before Valerian found them, at that.''

Kristina swallowed hard, her eyes burning with hot, sudden tears. "If only it were that simple," she murmured. She wanted desperately to speak to Maeve, but by now the sun had risen, and her mother would be sleeping, probably side by side with Calder in the special vault beneath the house. "It's not myself I fear for, Mrs. F. There are—there are mortals I've come to care about. And by that caring, I've made them vulnerable."

Mrs. F. rose and went to stand beside Kristina, patting her hand once with cool, aged fingers. "Here, now. Human beings are *born* vulnerable. Yes, your love may endanger these special mortals of yours, but you are also in a unique position to protect them. You must not forget your own powers."

"I've sublimated my magic," Kristina confessed, still near tears. "All this time I've wanted so much to be fully human—I've pretended—"

"Then you must become strong again. You must be what you are, Kristina, and stop resisting your own nature."

Kristina nodded. "Yes," she said after a long, reflective silence. "You're right, Mrs. F. It's time I explored my powers, found out what I can and cannot do."

"Your mother will help," the housekeeper agreed gently. "And I have no doubt that Valerian could advise you in the matter, too."

Valerian. It was eight hours earlier in the western United States. He would still be awake, if he had not gone abroad to hunt.

Yes, Valerian was definitely the vampire of the hour. Kristina stood, stepped back from Mrs. F. and the breakfast bar, smiled, and gave the old woman a nod of farewell.

Her thoughts took her not to Seattle, as she had expected, or even to Las Vegas, where Valerian still mystified the masses with his magic act four times per week, at the Venetian Hotel. Instead she found herself on a moonlit street, in a tropical clime. The paving stones were broken and uneven, the houses squalid and close together. The stench of raw sewage mingled with that of ripe garbage, and Kristina wrinkled her nose.

There was no sign of the vampire, no sign of anyone,

though she sensed the slumbering residents of the hovels crowding both sides of the narrow street. She heard rats rummaging in the mountains of refuse crammed into every alleyway, piled outside every door. Somewhere, a couple made sleepy love; from another direction came the faint mewling of a hungry baby.

What is this place? Kristina asked herself, standing still on the street, waiting, listening to her intuition.

"This is Rio," a familiar voice answered from just behind her. "Great Zeus, Kristina—you *are* rusty."

She turned to see Valerian an arm's length away, looking spectacular and arrogant, as usual. Perhaps for the drama of it—he was impervious, of course, to the smothering heat—he wore one of his many tailored tuxedos and a voluminous cape lined with cobalt blue satin.

"This is a really depressing place to hunt, if that was what you were doing," she said, in a futile effort to deflect his attention from her neglected skills.

"*All* the places where I hunt are depressing," Valerian retorted, looming over her now, his patrician nose nearly touching hers. "Did you think I would go to Disneyland?"

Kristina felt uncomfortable, though she had traveled to virtually every part of the world, sometimes with the aid of a train or airplane, sometimes without. "I don't like it here."

"The answer to that is so obvious I can't bring myself to utter it."

She sighed, then a new thought occurred to her, and she studied the imperious vampire with narrowed eyes. "So help me, Valerian, if you're hunting something besides your dinner—"

He drew himself up, so that he seemed even taller than his already intimidating height, folded his arms and glared. "Have a care, Snippet," he said, seething. "To insult me in that manner—or any other—is most imprudent."

"Before Daisy came into your life, you were a notorious rake," Kristina reminded him.

"The key words in that statement," Valerian replied evenly, his tone no less lethal for its softness, "were *before Daisy*. I am here, if you must know, because there is a child—"

Kristina's eyes widened in surprise. "*You've* sired a child?"

Valerian bristled, then smoothed his countenance by means of his will, like a majestic bird settling ruffled feathers into sleek array. "Please," he snapped, thereby dispensing with the possibility, as though his word were universal law.

"Well, you can't just snatch one off the streets," Kristina retorted, growing impatient. "Kids are people, you know, and they have rights."

Valerian arched one eyebrow, which made him look, if possible, even more imposing. Then, a moment later he relented, and Kristina saw sorrow in his magnificent face. He might have been sculpted by Michelangelo, a statue brought to life at the whim of a favored angel, so perfect were his features, his build, his graceful manner. "Thank you for that sermon," he said, but then he took Kristina's hand and drew her along the street, through an alleyway, up a set of crumbling stone steps to a wretched, attic-like room.

The heat was sweltering, the air close and fetid.

On the floor sat a little boy, probably three or four years of age, though it was hard to tell. His clothes were mere rags, he was filthy, and he raised great, luminous brown eyes to the vampire.

"His mother is a prostitute," Valerian said to Kristina, without taking his eyes from the child. "Tonight, in a cantina not far from here, she sold him, her own son, to a procurer who specializes in pretty boys. They'll be coming to fetch him at any moment.''

Kristina felt sick. Her own problems were forgotten, at least temporarily. ''What are you going to do?''

Valerian did not reply. Instead he dropped to one knee and addressed the boy in rapid, facile Portuguese. The child raised his arms to the vampire, obviously wanting to be held. He spoke to Valerian in the same language, and although Kristina did not speak it, she got the general drift.

Valerian meant to take the boy away, perhaps even home to Daisy in Seattle, to be raised as their son.

As Kristina watched, the magnificent vampire drew the little boy into his arms and rose to his feet.

''His name is Esteban,'' he said to Kristina as the lad nestled against Valerian's broad shoulder and buried his face in his neck. With a shudder of relief, Esteban gave himself up to sleep.

She was moved by the sight of the monster cradling the frightened child. ''Valerian,'' she whispered, ''he's *mortal*. This is very dangerous—''

''Are you implying that I would do him harm—this— this baby?''

''Of course not,'' Kristina replied, annoyed. The situation had reminded her, however, of her own concern for Max and his daughters, and the singular dangers she might have brought into their lives. ''But you have enemies. He could be hurt.''

''Would any fate be worse than what awaits him this night, at the hands of his mother?'' Valerian affected a sigh, having no breath to fuel a real one. ''He will be my son,'' the vampire added patiently. ''The fiend who dares to touch him will suffer a reprisal that would make hell itself seem trivial by comparison.''

Kristina had no answer, for she knew that Esteban's world was a place where children such as he could be shot in the streets like vermin. Despite the perils he might face, even with Valerian to protect him, he would undoubtedly be better off in Seattle.

A woman's laughter sounded from the street outside, shrill and somehow ugly. Instinctively Kristina took a step closer to Valerian and touched the child's matted ebony hair with a tender, protective hand.

Valerian gave Kristina a meaningful glance, covered the sleeping child with his cape, and vanished. She had no choice but to follow on the vampire's coattails.

They popped into the mansion in Seattle simultaneously, and Esteban was still sleeping, undisturbed, when Valerian laid him gently on the plush sofa in the large front room Kristina thought of as a parlor. There was a fire crackling in the grate of the beautiful chiseled marble fireplace, and Barabbas lay on the hearth, his muzzle resting on his paws, his eerie eyes watchful.

There was no sign of Daisy, but it was a vast house, and both Valerian and Kristina knew she was around somewhere.

Kristina felt awkward, but she held her ground. It was important that she speak with Valerian.

"What is it?" the vampire asked without looking at her, covering Esteban's small, thin body with a cashmere afghan as he spoke. "I know you didn't seek me out for nothing."

"I wanted to speak to you because I'm—I'm afraid."

That statement drew Valerian's gaze straight to Kristina's face. "Afraid? Of what?"

"Of Benecia and Canaan Havermail, to name just two of a great many ogres."

He raised an eyebrow in that familiar expression of irritation. "If those soulless chits have threatened you, I shall put stakes through their miserable, atrophied hearts!"

Barabbas rose from his warm resting place on the hearth to pad over to the couch and sniff the little boy's grubby face. Kristina shook her head. "I'm not afraid for myself," she said. "It's Max and his children. Without meaning to, I've made them vulnerable."

"Without meaning to?" Valerian echoed, somewhat skeptically. "Come now, Kristina—you may have let your powers go to an alarming degree, but you are not stupid. You must have known, from the moment you met this man, that he was only a mortal, and thus prey to all manner of fiends, human and otherwise."

Kristina could not refute Valerian's claim. She had been selfish, wanting Max and the girls to be part of her life, however briefly, but she had not admitted them unwittingly. "All right!" she snapped, panicked. "I knew! I was lonely—Max is so gentle and kind and intelligent and—"

"Shhh," Valerian said, taking her shoulders in his hands, as her father had done earlier in London. "You needn't justify what you feel, my sweet."

"But what about the dangers? It will be my fault if—"

"It is your task to protect those you love, Kristina. And you have the means to do so—you were born with a great deal of your mother's magic."

Before Kristina could argue that she was no match for ancient vampires like the Havermails, Daisy entered the room, clad in a blue and white flannel nightshirt and fuzzy slippers. Her gaze went straight to Esteban, as though drawn there by a magnet, and Kristina marveled that she had not seen how much her friend wanted a child until now.

"Who is this?" Daisy asked in the softest of voices, kneeling by the couch and smoothing the boy's hair back from his forehead with feather-light fingers. He stirred and made a fearful, whimpering sound, but did not awaken.

Valerian was watching Daisy with a tenderness so poignant that it wrenched Kristina's heart. She knew she could not stay another moment; to do so would be an inexcusable intrusion.

She did not feel like blinking herself back to London, however. She'd done enough traveling for one day, and wanted only to return to her own house.

She used no magic to do so, but simply let herself out and walked the short distance. Once there, she gathered all the letters she'd written to her aged governess over the years, settled herself in the big, cozy chair in the family room, and began to read.

Max entered the shop at four-twenty the following afternoon, carrying a bouquet of snow-white peonies in one hand.

"For you," he said, laying the perfect flowers in front of Kristina. The glass counter was a barrier between them. He spoke shyly, though there was something in his brown eyes—an invitation, or perhaps a promise—that roused desires in her that she'd thought she'd forgotten how to feel.

Kristina could not resist the peonies. She gathered them up, held them to her nose for a moment, enjoying their scent. "Thank you," she said, and went to fetch a small crystal vase to put them in.

Max followed her into the back room, watched as she filled the vase with water at the sink, then arranged the flowers. They were breathtakingly beautiful, in their simplicity and purity, and Kristina felt another surge of emotion as she admired them.

"I thought all the peonies were gone for the season," she said. The comment was the least of what was in her heart, but all she could manage at the moment.

"My sister has a greenhouse," Max answered, standing in the doorway with his hands braced on either side of the frame. As big as he was, he did not look intimidating, only solid and strong. "I stole them from her."

"Great," Kristina replied with a smile, carrying the vase

in both hands as she approached, meaning to go back to the main part of the shop.

Max did not step aside, as she had expected him to do. Instead he took the flowers from her and set them on a shelf next to the door. "Kristina, there's something I need to say," he told her. "The problem is, I'm not sure you want to hear it."

Kristina's heart missed one beat, then careened into the next. She couldn't speak, so she nodded, looking up into Max's eyes.

"I care about you, Kristina," he said quietly, returning her gaze unflinchingly. "I don't know if what I feel is love, or if it will ever turn into that, but it's there, and I can't ignore it, even though I've tried." He paused, as if gathering his courage, and then went on. "I'm a high school football coach and I like what I do, but I'm never going to make a lot of money. I have two kids, one of whom still misses her mother very much. I guess what I need to know is, do I have a chance with you?"

Here was her chance to do the noble thing, to end a potentially disastrous romance with Max Kilcarragh before it got started. Kristina took a step closer, when she knew she should retreat, and put her arms around Max's neck.

"Oh, yes," she answered. "You've got a chance. In fact, I'd say you're a sure thing."

He smiled and bent his head to kiss her, tentatively at first, then in earnest. And all that had slept within Kristina awakened, full of yearning.

CHAPTER 7

To Kristina, Max's kiss seemed like a miniature eternity, during which she was born as a new creature, to live, to die, and then to begin the magical cycle all over again. She was breathless when the intimate contact ended at last, and clutched Max's upper arms with both hands to steady herself. Her heart was thundering, as if to escape her chest and take wing, and there was a vibrant quickening in all her nerve endings and pulse points, accompanied by a warm, tightening sensation deep between her pelvic bones.

She had never felt so much before, even in her wildest, most abandoned moments with Michael, and did not know what to make of this new capacity, this new depth of response. If a simple kiss could stir her so profoundly, what would happen when—if—she and Max made love? The thought was both worrisome and alluring, for while Kristina yearned for the sort of soul fusion she knew Daisy and Valerian shared, she was also afraid of baring not just her body, but her very being, to another person.

Max sighed, his brown eyes dancing with mischief and undisguised pleasure. ''Wow,'' he said, and wrapped his arms loosely around her waist, keeping her close but not crushing her.

Kristina let her forehead rest against his rock-hard shoulder. He was wearing a corduroy sports jacket, and the fabric smelled pleasantly of cologne, misty rain, and man. She was moved, almost overwhelmed, by the realization that Max had found the kiss special, too.

He rested the fingertips of one large but incredibly gentle hand at her nape, sending a tremor through her entire system. "Kristina," he murmured. That was all, just her name, and yet she was stricken with joy, as though some part of herself, long missing, had been restored.

She struggled not to weep from happiness and wonder, and with effort looked up at Max, her eyes shimmering. "Oh, Max," she said softly, "it is dangerous to care for me—I'm not what you think—"

Max cupped her chin firmly in one hand, ran a calloused thumb over her mouth in a way that sent sharp quivers of sensation into every part of her body. He spoke tenderly, but his eyes were dark with passion—Kristina knew that, like her, he wanted very much to make love, then and there.

"What are you, Kristina Holbrook, if not a beautiful, intelligent, fascinating woman?"

She did not want to tell him, could not bear the prospect of his horror, his rejection, but she had already let things go too far. "You'll think I'm mad when I tell you," she said fearfully. She had known Max for such a short time, but already he had a place in her life, and when he left, she would be devastated.

The shop bell tinkled before Max could reply; he looked exasperated and amused at the same time.

"I'll—I'll take care of this customer and then close up," Kristina promised. "We have to talk."

Max didn't reply verbally, but the sparkle in his eyes indicated that he had more than conversation in mind. Clearly he did not expect Kristina's impending confession to be anything too dire.

Still feeling aftershocks from the kiss and at the same time dreading the task that lay ahead, Kristina left Max in the back room and proceeded into the main part of the shop.

She stopped in her tracks when she found the warlock, Dathan, standing next to the counter. He looked quite ordinary, despite his suave good looks, like a lawyer or an accountant or perhaps a professor. He wore a beautifully tailored camel-hair coat over a dark suit, and carried an umbrella and a briefcase. His guileless eyes twinkled as he met Kristina's startled gaze; he knew he had taken her unaware, and he was enjoying that small triumph.

Kristina stifled an impulse to turn him into a piece of bric-a-brac—he would surely resist, and his magic, unlike her own, was state-of-the-art.

"May I help you?" she asked, for Max's benefit rather than Dathan's or her own. With her thoughts, she warned the warlock not to make a scene, unless he wanted yet another eternal enemy. "We were just about to close, but if you have something particular in mind—"

Dathan's gaze slipped past Kristina, went unerringly to the door of the back room. He smiled impishly and had probably known Max was with her even before his badly timed arrival.

"My card," he said, extending one expensively gloved hand. "I was hoping to find a silver snuffbox, like one I'd seen in London. It was inlaid with ground malachite and the interior of conch shells, in the fashion of Italian marble."

Kristina accepted the bit of heavy card stock, frowning. Reading it, she realized that, of course, Dathan had conjured it for the occasion. *I must speak to you in private,* it read. *I will visit you this evening.*

Kristina shook her head. "I'm sorry," she said in the most ordinary tone she could manage. "I don't have anything like that in stock." She had several similar items, but that was beside the point. "I'll get in touch with you if I ever have reason."

She hoped the message was clear. *Don't call me. I'll call you.*

Dathan merely smiled and inclined his head slightly, indicating the card Kristina still held. The print had been changed. *This is serious, Kristina. I will arrive at midnight.*

Kristina let out a long breath in frustration. If Dathan wanted to pop in on her at the witching hour, there wasn't a great deal she could do to prevent him. Here was yet another obstacle between herself and any reasonable life she might have shared with Max or any other mortal man—gregarious warlocks who couldn't take a hint.

"You arrived just at closing time," she said sweetly, ushering Dathan toward the door.

His eyes twinkled merrily. "What a pity," he replied, and went out.

Kristina promptly locked the door behind him—a useless gesture if ever there was one—and glanced once again at the card. *Be there,* it said.

She crumpled the bit of paper and tossed it into the trash, where it dissolved with a chiming sound, like the thinnest crystal.

Show-off, Kristina thought, and made another vow to practice her magic.

Max was sipping herbal tea from a mug as he came out of the storeroom. Just looking at him reawakened all the physical hungers Kristina had felt before when they kissed. Obviously their relationship—if indeed it *was* a relationship—had undergone some subtle but very important change.

The knowledge filled her with a strange mingling of joy and guilt. There was no question that she loved Max Kilcarragh, but it was a selfish love, promising fulfillment and even rapture for Kristina, and terrible danger for Max and his daughters.

She had no choice but to give him up, she knew, and she was swamped with sorrow at the thought. Once he knew the truth, he would no longer want her—in fact, he might well recoil in disgust and horror.

Kristina gazed up at Max with tears of grief welling in her eyes. She could not help thinking of her uncle Aidan, her mother's twin, who had been made a vampire against his will, and so hated what he was that he had undergone a truly torturous process in the hope of becoming human again. He had succeeded, though barely, and made a life for himself with the mortal woman he loved, but he was forever separated from Maeve, from Valerian, from Kristina herself. All memory of his existence as a vampire had been eradicated from his mind for all time.

She thought she understood now, longing for complete union with Max, why Aidan Tremayne had been willing, even eager, to make such a sacrifice.

She took his hand, led him to a corner of the shop and the lovely Victorian settee that was part of a nineteenth-century parlor display. It was a private place; they could not be seen from the shop windows.

When Kristina would have withdrawn her hand from Max's, out of a nervous need to smooth her lightweight woolen skirt, he did not let her go. His patient expression nearly broke her heart.

She drew a deep breath, let it out slowly, and began. "You remember the first time we went out—I started to tell you how I was different—"

Max merely nodded. The shop telephone rang, but neither of them paid any attention; they were, for that brief interval at least, in a world of their own.

Kristina forced herself to go on, dreading the inevitable reaction with her whole soul. Michael, she recalled, had laughed at her when she finally confessed her secret, and accused her of taking too much laudanum.

"I have never been as attracted to another man as I am to you," she said.

"That's good news," Max interjected quietly.

Kristina shook her head. "No. No, it isn't," she replied. "I'm not human, Max—not exactly."

Now he looked worried. It would be a short leap from there to outright abhorrence—or mockery—or, worst of all, pity. His grasp on her hand tightened ever so slightly, and he waited in silence for her to go on.

"It's all too incredible for any sensible person to believe—I know that—but it's very important that I tell you because—because being closely associated with me could be deadly." She paused and closed her eyes for a moment while she gathered her courage. When she looked at Max she saw only compassion in his rugged face, and incredible tenderness. "My father was mortal when I was conceived, but now, like my mother, he's—he's—" Max squeezed her hand again, lending encouragement. "He's a vampire."

Max stared at her; his expression revealed amazement, but no other emotion. No revulsion, no judgment—yet. "A vampire?"

"I know how it sounds," she said miserably, feeling as though she would shatter, fall apart into a thousand irretrievable pieces. "Ridiculous, impossible, even ludicrous. But nevertheless, Max, it's true. I'm a sort of half-breed—I have powers, but I'm not a—I'm not like my parents—"

He let out a long sigh and shoved a hand through his hair. "You're right, Kristina. It's hard to comprehend. I mean, *vampires*?"

"Yes." She waited a beat, struggling to hold on to her composure. "I know that most people don't even believe in such creatures, and in most cases the vampires prefer that. But they are real, Max—as real, maybe more so, than you or I.''

Max didn't bolt and run, or jump to his feet and form a protective cross with his index fingers, but he was plainly confounded all the same. He had surely decided that Kristina was deluded, and therefore to be avoided from then on. He was right on one count, anyway.

"My God," he said.

"You don't believe me," Kristina replied with resignation. "You must think I'm insane. Sometimes, Max, I truly wish I were."

Slowly, Max Kilcarragh shook his head. "No," he insisted calmly, still making no effort to flee or even to release Kristina's hand. "No, you're no more insane than I am. Still—"

She was going to have to prove that she was telling the truth; it was, after all, the least she could do under the circumstances. Focusing her attention on a small Dresden figurine, standing on an intricately crocheted doily in the center of the coffee table before them, she raised it several inches off the green marble surface, let it hover in midair for a few moments, then carefully lowered it.

Max frowned and raised his eyes toward the ceiling, clearly looking for a string of fishing line or some other form of trickery. Kristina knew, without invading the privacy of his mind, that he was thinking of Valerian's magic act at the party on Halloween night, no doubt concluding that hers was a family of necromancers.

"Impressive," he said.

"But obviously not enough to convince you," Kristina said with another sigh.

He laced his fingers through hers. "I'm a skeptic," he conceded mildly.

"Brace yourself," she murmured. Then, by mental

means alone, she raised Max himself some six inches off the settee.

To say he was surprised would be a supreme understatement, but, to his credit, Max did not flail or cry out as another man might have done. He had to know Kristina would never hurt him—not intentionally, at least.

Gently she lowered him back to the cushioned seat of the small sofa.

He was pale and understandably somewhat ruffled. "I know this is a mundane question, but I have to ask it. How in hell did you do that?"

"By what you would call magic," Kristina answered with great reluctance.

"And what would *you* call it?"

Kristina shrugged slightly. "Actually, such things are natural functions of the human brain. It's just that most mortals haven't evolved the ability to utilize all their faculties."

Max's dark brows came together in a thoughtful frown. "Are you saying that we all have the potential to do things like that?"

She nodded. "Some mortals naturally use more of their mental capacities than others, of course—and can do things that would appear magical to the average person. The Russians, in fact, were making significant strides in opening new frontiers of the mind until their political structure finally collapsed under its own weight."

Max narrowed his eyes. "This is truly fantastic."

"You do believe me, then?" A brief, shining hope lighted Kristina's spirit before logic snuffed it out. "By your association with me, Max," she forced herself to say, "you and your children would be in peril from other supernatural beings. I would of course do everything I possibly could to protect you, but—"

He laid an index finger to her mouth to quiet her. "It

isn't your job to protect me, Kristina, or my daughters. I have no idea what I'm dealing with here, but I do know from personal experience that life can be very fragile, and that all human beings are in constant jeopardy. But evil isn't the only force in the world—there is good as well.''

Kristina didn't know what to say, so she just sat back against the settee and looked at Max, waiting for him to go on.

''Obviously my first priority is to make sure Eliette and Bree are as safe as possible. We're going to have to take this situation one step at a time and move slowly. But I care about you, Kristina, and I'm not willing to just walk away—it's too late for that.''

Kristina's eyes were beginning to smart, but she didn't cry. ''Where do we go from here?'' she asked, letting her head rest against his shoulder.

He chuckled ruefully. ''I guess I don't need to tell you where I'd *like* to go from here,'' he replied, ''but I don't want to scare you off.''

She laughed at the amazing irony of that statement, but her heart felt tremulous and very, very fragile, like a bubble of newly blown glass, still shivering and insubstantial. ''There is so much I need to explain,'' she said. ''To begin with, there's my age. Then my marriage. And my family.''

''I think my brain circuits are overloaded,'' he said with a grin. ''Let's have some dinner in some quiet place and talk about ordinary things, just for a little while. I'm still getting over my first experience with personal levitation.''

She watched him, marveling, wondering at her good fortune in encountering such a man.

''I hope you weren't frightened,'' she said.

''More like baffled,'' Max admitted. ''That was a really weird feeling.'' He stood and offered his hand to Kristina, helping her up.

They had an early supper in a small, secluded restaurant

down the street from Kristina's shop—Bree and Eliette were spending the evening with their aunt Gweneth—and after coffee they drove in separate cars back to Kristina's house.

After starting a cheery fire in the family room fireplace and offering Max a seat at the table, she went upstairs for the stack of letters she'd written to her governess, Miss Phillips, over a span of some fifty years. Reading them would explain more to Max about who—and what—Kristina was than anything she might say.

Noting the date on the initial page of the first letter, and probably the worn, fragile state of the paper, Max looked at Kristina and grinned. "There's a slight age difference between us," he remarked.

"Almost a century," Kristina confirmed. She wasn't smiling.

"This is incredible," Max muttered, and turned his attention back to the letters before him. He read through her meeting with Michael, her marriage, the account of her wedding night, all without flinching. Kristina, for her part, was painfully aware of one particular passage.

. . . He was uncommonly gentle as he removed my wedding gown and all the many troublesome garments beneath, each in its turn and its own good time. He caressed me and whispered pretty words, and though there was some hurt when, at last, he took me as a husband takes a wife, pleasure soon followed. Am I wanton, Phillie? I enjoyed the things Michael did to me in his bed that night—I thrashed upon the mattress. I moaned when he promised that strange, sweet satisfaction I craved without understanding, cried out when at long last he gave it.

Finally Max reached the incident of the shooting, and Kristina, seated across the table from him, saw those neatly penned words as clearly as if she were reading over Max's shoulder. . . .

. . . with the blast of a pistol still thundering in my head, I dressed hastily in a simple chemise, slippers, and a loose gown—I could not trouble myself with corsets and the like—and raced out into the passageway and down the main staircase.

The great house was abuzz with consternation, for it seemed that all within those thick, august walls had heard the report of gunfire, though it was still so early that the sun had not yet risen. At that hour even the servants would not have arisen, but for that dreadful, singularly ominous noise.

I encountered Gilbert in the entry hall—Lord and Lady Cheltingham, my mother- and father-in-law, were nowhere to be seen. Gilbert wore rough huntsman's clothes, and his brown hair had not been tied back but instead fell loose around his face. I glimpsed pity in his eyes when he spared me a glance, and despair.

"There has been a duel," I said, grasping one of his arms as though I thought he could somehow undo the morning's tragedy. I knew that was impossible, of course, and I had seen the incident by means of my magic, even before leaving the bedchamber. "Michael is hurt—"

For a moment Gilbert's strong jaw tightened, but his mind was veiled from me, and I could not discern his thoughts. "You must stay here, Kristina," he told me. "It is unseasonably cold this morning and raining. Besides, there may be more trouble."

With that, he turned and hurried out, joined by several rumpled male wedding guests summoned from their beds by the clarion of calamity.

I obeyed my brother-in-law's edict, not because I was

daunted by his authority, but because I knew I could be of no real help on that dismal knoll behind the parish church, where two men lay bleeding on the dew-dampened grass. One was dead, having taken a bullet through the heart; the other, my Michael, had been shot in the right knee.

I hurried back upstairs, breathless in my urgency, went straight to the main linen cupboard, and began pulling out Lady Cheltingham's finely stitched sheets with their borders of Irish and Italian lace. When I had torn a sufficient supply of bandages, I carried these back into our bedroom and sent a mewling maid to fetch hot water, a large basin, and a selection of whiskey from the cabinet in Gilbert's study belowstairs.

While she was gone, I stripped the linens from our marriage bed and replaced them. Then I ran back down-stairs again and waited fitfully by the stables, heedless of the drizzling rain, for the men to return.

Michael was astride his own horse when they arrived, drenched with blood and rain, plainly only half-conscious. After reining in the great stallion, my husband promptly collapsed and would have landed in the mud of the stableyard if Gilbert and another man hadn't been there to catch him. A litter was brought from one of the sheds, and Michael was placed upon it, out of his head now and raving.

Concern for my badly injured husband was, of course, my paramount emotion, but I did not fail to notice the other man, draped over the back of a horse led by one of the other guests. I recognized him with a pang of sorrow—he was the eighteen-year-old cousin, come all the way from London to celebrate the marriage, with whom Michael had argued so vociferously on the lawn. His sister, even younger at fifteen, ran sobbing through the rain in bare feet and a wrapper, her hair unbound, trailing and sodden, her pretty face twisted into a mask of unfathomable anguish. She flung herself at the lad's narrow, lifeless back and clung to him, wailing.

Gently one of the men drew her away, lifted her into his arms, and carried her back toward the house.

I returned my attention to Michael, prostrate on his litter, but I knew I would never forget what I had just seen. I believe my feelings toward my husband began to change in that very moment, Phillie, for I had seen the confrontation between the two men, remember; I was well aware that Michael had been the instigator of these sorrows.

They carried Michael to our room, where Gilbert and I stripped away his coat and boots, his muddy shirt, and bloodstained breeches. My new husband was groaning, and though he could not have left our bed more than an hour before, and the sun was just then topping the eastern horizon, he reeked of ardent spirits.

"Damn you," Gilbert said to his brother, soaking one of the cloths I'd torn earlier in the basin the maid had brought, as requested. He sat on the edge of the plump feather mattress and began gingerly to clean the terrible wound to Michael's knee. "You've killed poor young Justin, and for what cause? In the process, it appears that you've made a cripple of yourself!"

I could not feel anger toward Gilbert, righteous or otherwise. "Has the doctor been sent for?" I asked stupidly—for of course the village physician would have been summoned immediately—and moved to the opposite side of the bed, where I knelt and held Michael's pale, long-fingered hand in both my own. I desperately wished for my father in those moments, for there was no finer surgeon in all of creation, but daylight had come, and I knew that Papa would have gone underground to sleep, as all but the oldest vampires do. . . .

Max stopped reading to rub his eyes with the thumb and forefinger of his right hand. Kristina had made a fresh pot of coffee, and she carried two cups to the family room table, once again sitting down across from him. There must have been a thousand questions he wanted to ask; Kristina watched his expressive eyes as he sifted through his thoughts, sorting, trying to assign reasonable priorities.

"What kind of man was your husband?" he asked at last. It would have been unnecessary to ask if she had loved Michael, for it was obvious that she had—just as Max himself had cherished his lost wife, Sandy.

"He was rich and handsome and very spoiled." Privately Kristina compared the two men—Max was attractive, but in a rugged, straightforward and intensely masculine way. Michael had been the boyish type, charming and superficial and selfish.

"I'm surprised you were interested in him," Max said without rancor before taking a sip of his coffee.

Kristina smiled; remorse might come later, but for now she was happy because Max had heard her terrible secret, and he was still around. "I was younger then," she said.

Max laughed. "I'll say," he replied, squinting at her. "But you're very well preserved." Some of his amusement faded. "Will you ever age, Kristina? I mean—and this is hypothetical, of course—if you and I were married, would you get old, as I will?"

"I don't know," Kristina replied, and suddenly she felt like crying again. She sipped some coffee to steady herself. "Vampires, theoretically, that is, are immortal. I don't—er—hunt, or sleep during the day, and I can't travel through time the way my parents and Valerian do—"

Max held up one hand. "One second, please. Valerian is a vampire? That guy who was doing magic tricks for the kids on Halloween night?"

Kristina drew a deep breath and let it out slowly. "Yes,"

she answered. She thought of Esteban, the urchin Valerian had rescued from the mean streets of Rio only the night before. She would never forget the sight of the illustrious vampire cradling that scared, wretched little boy against his shoulder. "But you needn't worry—he would never harm a child."

"I had already figured that out," Max said. "You're obviously fond of him, and that is as good a character reference as I need. But knowing what Valerian is explains how he pulled off all those fantastic tricks at the party the other night."

"You're in on a world-class secret now," Kristina said, feeling a bit less weary, a bit less ancient. She leaned across the table a little way. "But you must swear not to tell, for your own sake—no one will believe you, and your sanity will be suspect—and because magicians fly in from all over the world to watch Valerian's act in Las Vegas and try to figure out how he manages such fantastic feats. It's all part of his mystique."

Max frowned, looking down at the letters scattered before him in peculiar neatness. "This is all so personal—are you sure you want to share it?"

Except for her feelings for Max, Kristina could not recall the last time she had been so certain of anything. "It's important for you to understand," she said.

He began to read again, taking up where he had left off.

. . . and while I knew a great many pretty tricks, levitation, altering the form of things, making objects and people disappear and then appear again, I was ignorant of the healing arts.

Michael started to come round, once the doctor had arrived and set himself to sorting out that shattered knee. Gilbert, for all his fury with his younger brother, looked as though he would have changed places with him in a moment and borne the pain himself. I know I would gladly have done that, but I wonder if it was generosity that prompted me. Watching *a loved one suffer is perhaps the greater agony, making the desire to usurp that pain an act of cowardice, rather than nobility. It was no comfort that Michael had brought this anguish upon himself, that he might even have deserved to bear it, after taking another man's life.*

I do not know.

The surgery was dreadful to witness, and yet I could not leave Michael's side. I absorbed each scream, each moan and curse, in my spirit, every one like a violent shock, and when it was over, and he collapsed again, however mercifully, into a near comatose state, I also swooned.

Gilbert, poor, beleaguered, stricken Gilbert, carried me to another room, where I was to be looked after by a maid. I was exhausted by Michael's ordeal, and went immediately to sleep.

But I must leave the tale here for a little while, dear Phillie, for I fear I have run on too long, and my story, while dramatic, is also grim. I do not wish to tire you overmuch, so I shall wait a week or so before I write another letter.

Thank you, beloved friend, for your understanding heart and gentle comments. You cannot know what comfort your wise letters have brought me.

Love always,
Kristina

Max folded the aged vellum pages carefully, almost reverently, and tucked them back into the appropriate envelope. Instead of reaching for another, he looked at Kristina, seeming to see into the farthest corner of her bruised heart, and she knew he saw her loneliness, her pain, her doubts. He pushed back his chair a little way.

"Come here," he said gently. "You look like somebody who needs to be held."

Kristina didn't require a second invitation. She was around the table and seated on Max's lap, with her arms encircling his neck and her head resting on his shoulder, almost before her next heartbeat.

Max held her tightly. He smelled good, and felt good, too—hard and strong and yet incredibly tender. Although Kristina wanted him powerfully, she appreciated that he did nothing in those moments except to keep her within the warm circle of his embrace.

"You're too good to be true, Max Kilcarragh," she said against his neck.

He chuckled. "I wish I could keep you thinking that for the rest of your life," he replied, his breath a soft caress at her temple as he spoke, one that set her tingling and roused the legion of needs that had been slumbering within her. "Unfortunately it won't be long before you find out the truth. I have a temper. I'm opinionated, especially when it comes to politics. And somewhere deep inside, I have to admit, I wish women still wanted to stay home, cook, and raise kids. How's that for a shocking confession?"

Kristina sat back far enough to look into Max's face, albeit reluctantly. No man had ever held her so lovingly without expecting, even demanding, something in return, and she loved the intimacy of it. "In comparison to my being one hundred and thirty years old and having vampires for parents, you mean?"

Max sighed heavily, but his eyes were still warm, still smiling. "I don't think I've absorbed that yet," he confessed.

"When you do," Kristina predicted, suddenly sorrowful again, "you'll never want to see me again. You'll tell me to stay away from you and your beautiful children.''

He brushed her mouth with his. "It's more likely, lovely Kristina, that you will become bored with me one day.''

The sound of clapping and the chiming of the mantel clock in the parlor were simultaneous. It was midnight— where had the evening gone?—and Dathan stood in the kitchen doorway, still applauding.

"An accurate prediction, I'm sure,'' the warlock said, ignoring Kristina's murderous glare. "What, I pray you, is duller than a mortal?''

CHAPTER 8

Max, always so unflappable, in Kristina's experience at least, tensed at the sight of the warlock and moved without hesitation to confront him. Kristina put out an arm to prevent that. There were any number of ways an immortal could defend himself against a human being, no matter how brave that feckless mortal might be, and most of them were unthinkable. Especially in connection with Max.

Dathan was at his most charming—but with an edge. "Oh, dear," he said with a sly glint in his eyes and a soft exhalation of breath. "Here we have that most foolhardy of all creatures—a *brave* mortal. Perhaps I was too hasty, Mr. Kilcarragh, in declaring you to be dull. Though you would be oh-so-much better off as a dullard than a martyr, it's true."

"Enough," Kristina said firmly, her gaze never leaving Dathan's face. She still had the back of one hand pressed against Max's chest, as though that would stop him if he decided to pounce.

"Who the hell is this guy?" Max demanded.

Dathan chuckled. "Who indeed?"

Kristina sighed. "Max Kilcarragh," she said, "meet Dathan—warlock among warlocks."

Max seemed to feel a grudging fascination, rather than fear. He narrowed his eyes, studying the splendid beast who stood before him; Dathan's manner was almost as imperious as that of Valerian. "Is that your religious persuasion," Max asked, "or were you born that way?"

Dathan's deceptively soft brown eyes gleamed with delighted amusement. "Religion has nothing to do with it," he replied at some length. "And, yes, I suppose I was born a warlock, but I couldn't say when that momentous event occurred. I've quite forgotten."

"Vampires are made," Kristina explained, looking back at Max over one shoulder. A deep sorrow possessed her; the understanding he had displayed earlier would be short-lived, once he really comprehended the full spectrum of fiends he might encounter, just by association with Kristina. "Created by other vampires, I mean. Warlocks"—she tossed a malevolent glance toward Dathan"—probably *hatch*, like reptiles."

"I'm getting a headache," Max said. He looked as though every muscle in his body was poised for a fight. "Just tell me, Kristina—is this guy welcome here?"

"*Welcome* is hardly the word I would use," Kristina answered, and Dathan pretended to be wounded by her remark. "He's quite harmless, however. Where I'm concerned, at least."

Max looked skeptical, assessing Dathan again with undisguised dislike and suspicion in his eyes. "Are you sure?"

Kristina spoke lightly, her tone, as well as her words, calculated to irritate the arrogant warlock. "Dathan wouldn't dare do me mischief," she said. "If he did, he would have my mother to contend with, not to mention Valerian."

Dathan flushed. "I am not afraid of that—that *stage magician*!" he snapped. He and Valerian were sworn adversaries, actively antagonistic toward each other.

Kristina noticed that he had not raised the same protest in regard to Maeve. As queen of the nightwalkers, she was among the most powerful beings in this dimension and several others. Dathan, while an accomplished necromancer, was no match for the legendary vampire, and he was smart enough to know it.

She linked her arm with Max's. "It would be better if you left," she said. "I'm in no danger, and the sooner I hear Dathan out, the sooner he will leave me alone."

The warlock adjusted his diamond cufflinks, somewhat huffily, but offered no comment.

"You're sure?" Max asked, looking deeply into Kristina's eyes.

She nodded and stood on tiptoe to kiss him lightly on the mouth. "We'll talk tomorrow," she said.

"Count on it," Max replied. Then, with the utmost reluctance, he collected his coat from the back of one of the chairs at the table in the family room, gave Dathan a long, unfriendly once-over, and left.

"The nerve," Dathan complained when Max was gone.

"Go near him," Kristina answered evenly, "ruffle one hair on his head, bother him in any way, and I promise you, Dathan, I will find a way to destroy you if it takes my share of eternity. Do not take my warning lightly, thinking my magic small, either, for I have not begun to explore the extent of my powers."

"A stirring speech," Dathan said, removing his cloak with a graceful gesture. "Though, alas, all for naught. You have nothing to fear from me, Kristina—I shall not trouble your mortal."

"Then what do you want?"

"You touched upon the purpose of my visit yourself, just a moment ago. Your magic is rusty, and woe betide you, my dear, if you find yourself in need of it, without your mother, myself, or a certain ill-tempered vampire within rescuing distance. I have appointed myself your tutor.''

The idea was not without merit, though Kristina would have dearly loved to hurl the suggestion right back in his face. The nearly unpalatable truth was that she desperately needed to polish her skills. ''What's in this for you?'' she asked warily. ''And don't say you're willing to offer your time out of simple generosity. You're not the charitable type, and we both know it.''

Dathan released a long sigh. Unlike Valerian's sighs, which were always feigned, for vampires do not breathe, Dathan's was quite genuine. Warlocks, unlike their blood-drinking counterparts, had beating hearts and functioning lungs, among other humanlike appurtenances.

''I wish to find a mate,'' he said.

Kristina recalled that Dathan had once made some unholy bargain with Valerian, to that end. The warlock did not wish a union with another witch, or even a mortal; he sought a vampire. Part of the antipathy between the two was based in the indisputable fact that Valerian had tricked Dathan.

She felt herself softening a little toward the warlock, for she certainly understood what it was to be lonely, to yearn for love. ''I don't know how you think I can help,'' she said, after mulling Dathan's announcement over for a few more moments. ''It may have escaped your notice, but I don't exactly have a wide circle of friends—or even acquaintances—in the world of nightwalkers. And I'd prefer to keep it that way.''

''You are your mother's daughter,'' Dathan insisted with a quiet earnestness Kristina did not think was a pretense. ''As such, there are doors open to you that would be closed to me.''

Kristina turned away, went to the table where she and Max had been reading the letters she had written so long before about her marriage to Michael Bradford, and began gathering them together. She felt a need to be busy.

"Why don't you take a witch for a mate?"

"Witches are notoriously independent," Dathan answered in a vaguely defensive tone. "They tend to regard intimate relationships as bothersome."

Kristina barely suppressed an urge to roll her eyes. She was not without sympathy—toward the viewpoint of the female of the species, that is. If Dathan was a representation of the average warlock, they could be obnoxious creatures.

But then, so could vampires. And men.

"What can you teach me?" she asked.

"Virtually everything, with the probable exception of time travel. That is quite tricky—requiring either a great age or a conversion from mortal to blood-drinker, as in the case of your parents, for example."

Kristina raised one eyebrow slightly and indulged in a crooked smile. "I'm a hundred and thirty," she said. "Isn't that a great age?"

"Not in this crowd," Dathan replied, folding his arms. His cloak lay over the back of the family room couch in a familiar way, as though he'd tossed it there a thousand times. Which, of course, he hadn't. "Put an end to my suspense, Kristina. Do we have an agreement or not?"

"With reservations," she answered, standing still now, the gathered letters in her hands, watching him. "I run an antiques shop, not a preternatural dating service. I'll do my best to help you out, but I can't promise miracles."

Dathan snatched up his cloak in a practiced motion of one hand. "I hardly think it should be that difficult," he said. "I am not, after all, ugly or otherwise objectionable."

"You are definitely not ugly," Kristina agreed, sensing that, at least temporarily, she had the upper hand. "Whether or not you could be described as objectionable is certainly open to debate. But if finding a mate were not difficult, you would have done it yourself by now, wouldn't you?''

The warlock donned the cape in a theatrical swirling motion reminiscent of Valerian, although Kristina judiciously refrained from pointing out the similarity. "As you know," he said coolly, "vampires and warlocks do not commonly interact."

"Perhaps because the blood of warlocks is poisonous to nightwalkers, and so many have been tricked into partaking," Kristina commented. "Why are you set on attaining this? Vampires are among your oldest and most ardent enemies."

"It does not have to be so," Dathan replied with faint umbrage rather than acquiescence. "Between us we could create a new race of beings." There was a hint of the crusader in the warlock's bearing, putting Kristina in mind of her father, who spent practically every spare moment in his laboratory, searching for a way to enhance the positive side of vampirism while eliminating the negative aspects.

"I'm not sure I want to participate," Kristina said.

"Consider my proposition well," Dathan advised. "I will return for your answer tomorrow."

Kristina inclined her head in silent agreement, and Dathan vanished within the instant.

She went slowly up the stairs, carrying the letters, tucking all but one away in the drawer of the night table beside her bed. She wanted very much to consult with her mother, but it was eight hours later in London, which meant that Maeve had taken refuge in her lair.

Leaving the letter that took up where the account of the duel, Michael's terrible injuries, and poor Justin's death, had left off, Kristina went into her bathroom to indulge in a long, soothing shower.

The flow of warm water calmed her, helped her to think more clearly. She faced a paradox in considering Dathan's bargain; on the one hand, she would be better able to protect Max and his children, not to mention herself, if she took instruction from the warlock. On the other hand, that same crucial training would inevitably lead her deeper into the very world she found so threatening and so abhorrent.

She might have asked her mother for help, of course, or even Valerian, but Kristina had lived thirteen decades, not thirteen years. She had loved and lost, she had traveled the world, she had built a highly respected and lucrative business. Always, always, Kristina had steered her own ship, albeit with more success at some times than others. Now she found that she did not relish the prospect of asking either vampire to lead her through the elementary steps of magic like a preadolescent stumbling through a lesson in ballroom dance.

As she stepped out of the shower, toweled her body and her hair dry, Kristina allowed herself the indulgence of thinking about Max again. He could not have guessed what it meant to her, his readiness to believe in her, to share her memories by reading the letters. While he had certainly been shocked by her revelations—who wouldn't be?—he had also gone to remarkable lengths to understand. Even more important, he hadn't shown disgust, or any sort of judgment.

Nothing had really rattled Max, she reflected, until Dathan had materialized. At that point, Max had been ready to protect her, a noble if highly imprudent act.

While the memory definitely troubled her—the range of horrible things Dathan might have done in response was almost unlimited—Kristina couldn't help feeling a little pleased by Max's gallantry. She did not recall another instance, in all her adult life, when she'd been the object of such reckless chivalry.

She pulled on her white terry-cloth robe and ran a comb through her cap of sleek, dark hair, which was already drying nicely. She was smiling as she went through her bedroom and into the hallway, intending to brew a cup of herbal tea.

Her amusement faded as she passed the room where she had taken Max and Bree and Eliette, to show them the toys from her childhood. She heard two chilling, little-girl voices through the door.

Kristina froze in the hall, almost too startled to think, let alone act. Then, summoning all her paltry powers, she reached for the knob.

The lock clicked before her hand closed on the brass handle and the heavy wooden panel swung silently open. An eerie wash of moonlight lit the otherwise darkened room, but Kristina could see only too clearly.

She stood on the threshold, torn between fury and terror, unable, for the moment, even to speak.

Benecia Havermail, demon-child, all blond, blue-eyed perfection, with her ringlets and ruffled dress, was perched on the cushioned window seat, holding the very baby doll Bree had so favored during her visit. She smiled, showing tiny, perfect white teeth. Teeth capable of tearing the throat out of a rhinoceros.

"Hello, Kristina," she chimed.

Canaan, the younger of the two monsters, was dark-haired and smaller than her sister, though just as exquisitely beautiful. And just as deadly. She was seated cross-legged on the floor, in front of the toy theater, while the puppets whirled in a ludicrous, drunken dance. This, like Benecia's attentions to the baby doll, was a subtle but effective parody of the Kilcarragh children's visit, for Eliette had been fascinated by the little stage, with its colorful, inanimate players.

"What are you doing here?" Kristina managed to croak. She knew it was unwise to show fear—and fear wasn't precisely what she felt—but hiding her emotions from these two ancient blood-drinkers was more than she could manage at the moment. "How dare you?"

Benecia smiled sweetly, but did not stir herself from the window seat. She might have been a mannequin, a model of Alice in Wonderland come to life, Kristina thought with an involuntary shiver. So flawless were her features. "You mustn't be rude," Benecia scolded in that musical voice. She glanced toward the array of priceless porcelain dolls Kristina had collected, displayed in a cabinet on one wall, behind glass doors.

Silently the doors opened. The dolls climbed daintily down from their shelves, murmuring among themselves.

"Stop it!" Kristina gasped.

The treasured dolls joined hands and made a circle, going round and round in a stiff-jointed caricature of some schoolyard game. Their voices were a singsong, chantlike sound that made the hairs on Kristina's nape stand upright.

"Stop!" she said again. "Now!"

Canaan only laughed, but Benecia gave a somewhat petulant sigh, and, at some mental command from her, the dolls returned to their cases, closing the doors behind them, striking their familiar poses. Their small voices, however, seemed to echo in the room for a long time.

"We didn't mean to frighten you," Benecia said.

"The hell you didn't," Kristina shot back. "I want you out of my house—now. And don't ever come back!"

"What will you do—complain to Valerian? Or to your mother? Or perhaps to your father, the mad scientist?"

Kristina ignored the jibe at Calder Holbrook's fascination with mysterious experiments, but she was incensed by the idea that she needed Valerian or Maeve to protect her. Even though that was, in essence, the truth of the matter. "Valerian is just looking for an excuse to drive a stake through your rotten little hearts, and as for my mother—"

Canaan got to her feet. "Valerian won't have time for

you now that he has Daisy, and that filthy, awful little street urchin he's brought home from Brazil," she said. "And Maeve happens to be quite busy, if you haven't noticed. There is another political problem, you see, between vampires and angels, and Her Majesty"—she gave these last two words a note of mockery—"spends every waking moment trying to resolve it."

Kristina felt a stab of guilt, as well as trepidation. Relations between the realms of darkness and light were always dubious, of course, but a conflagration, if serious enough, might well bring on the cataclysm mortals referred to as Armageddon. Kristina had not even suspected that her mother was facing another such crisis. "Why did you come here?" she asked. If she could not keep the panic out of her psyche, perhaps she could at least sound normal. "What do you want?"

As usual, Benecia, being the eldest, was the spokesperson for the dreadful duo. "We have heard that the warlock, Dathan, desires a vampire wife."

Kristina's stomach rolled. Surely even such fiends, such ghouls as these two, would not, *could* not, suggest . . .

"I should like to offer myself," Benecia said.

Kristina barely kept her dinner down. "You have the body of a child," she pointed out in what she hoped was an even, reasonable tone.

"I am nearly as old as Valerian," argued the ancient woman imprisoned forever in the size and form of a little girl.

"No," Kristina said, retreating a step.

"Do you know what it is like, Kristina?" Benecia demanded bitterly, advancing with a delicate tread. "Can you even guess what it means to be trapped for all of time? If I had been left alone, I would have grown to womanhood, married, lived, and died, and then been born again, through a procession of lives. Instead I must spend eternity just as I am!''

Kristina stopped retreating; this was her house, damn it. But before she could say anything, Canaan entered the conversation, addressing her sister. It was well known among immortals and their consorts that the two, though invariably together, were not always in accord.

"Do stop being so dramatic about it, Benecia," Canaan said without a trace of tenderness or sympathy. "It's not as though you were made a vampire against your will, like poor Aidan Tremayne. You begged Papa until he changed you, and you knew full well what you were doing!"

Kristina stood her ground, frantically trying to figure out a way to use the sisters' antipathy toward each other in order to defend herself. "I have no desire to listen to an account of the Havermail family history," she said with bravado. "You will both leave this house immediately and stay away."

Benecia and Canaan looked at each other and laughed. The sound was like crystal chimes, dancing in a soft breeze, and it raised a cold sweat on Kristina's skin.

"If you don't do as I say," Benecia said sweetly, patiently, as though explaining something elemental to a slavering idiot, "Canaan and I shall simply have to strike up a friendship with—what were their names again?—oh, yes. Bree and Eliette. I'm sure we could convince them we were angels—mortals are such gullible creatures, and we've made good use of that trick in the past."

Kristina was outraged. She was also more convinced than ever that she needed to bring her magic skills up to speed ASAP. "Dathan is a warlock," she said when she could trust herself to speak without shrieking in uncontrollable fury, "but he is not a deviate. If I suggested such a vile thing to him, he would be as revolted as I am."

Benecia had evidently fed copiously earlier in the evening, for a blush rose beneath her nearly transparent ivory skin. "I have told you. I am not a child, I am an adult!"

"Then go find someone else whose development was arrested in a similar fashion," Kristina replied. She did not know where she got the audacity, for here was a creature who could burn her to cinders with a mere glance. And that would be one of her more merciful punishments.

"We could transform a small boy," Canaan said thoughtfully.

"Fool," Benecia spat. "I have the mind of a woman. I desire a mature mate, not a child! Besides, the making of vampires is forbidden, by Maeve's order."

Kristina was silent, hoping the argument would escalate, carrying the Havermail sisters away—*far* away—on a swell of indignation or at least sibling rivalry.

"I thought you weren't afraid of Maeve," Canaan taunted.

So far, so good, Kristina thought.

"You know, Canaan, sometimes I wish I'd been an only child."

Unfortunately the phrase *only child* turned their attention back to Kristina. They assessed her with glittering, gemlike eyes.

"I am not going to forget this, Kristina Holbrook," Benecia said. "You have made an enemy by insulting me."

Kristina refrained from saying that she had been an enemy for a very long time. She simply gestured toward the door, tendering a silent invitation to leave.

Benecia and Canaan disappeared in a blink.

Kristina, for her part, gave up all hope of getting a good night's sleep. She dressed in dark jeans and a matching cashmere turtleneck, then added a long, buttonless cardigan in the same ebony color. After only a moment's hesitation, she willed herself to Max's house.

Invisibility, being a fairly simple trick compared to some

others, was still part of Kristina's repertoire. The dark clothes were a safeguard, in case she had overestimated her talents.

Her reasons for paying this late-night, uninvited visit were altruistic—she meant to watch over little Eliette and Bree until dawn, when the Havermails would be forced into their lairs by the light of the sun—but she still felt like a trespasser, a sort of inverse Peeping Tom.

Perhaps it was not an accident, on an unconscious level at least, that Kristina first projected herself into Max's room. He lay sprawled across the large bed, sound asleep, his naked athletic body only partially covered by a sheet. She admired him for a long time, hoping his dreams were sweet but suspecting otherwise by his restlessness, and then sought and found the room his daughters shared.

It was a spacious chamber, nearly as large as Max's own quarters, furnished with two canopied beds in the pseudo-French Provençal style so popular with little girls, matching dressers, a desk, and a miniature vanity. On Bree's side of the room was a toy chest, overflowing with vinyl dolls in various states of undress, a scattering of clothes, a coloring book, still open, with crayons in the seam like logs in a flume.

Eliette's territory, on the other hand, was almost painfully neat. The desk and vanity were tidy, and even in sleep the little girl looked as though she were bracing herself, expecting tragedy. Kristina knew that this child had felt the loss of her mother more deeply than anyone suspected, including her very caring father.

Kristina's heart ached; she almost made herself solid again, so strong was her desire to smooth Eliette's little brow with her fingertips, to kiss her and tell her that everything was all right, that she was safe now.

But that promise could not be made, in honesty, to any mortal on earth, no matter how beloved, for inherent in the glorious miracle of life, of course, was the certainty of death.

Kristina moved to stand beside Bree's bed and saw with an inner smile that the younger child was utterly relaxed in sleep, still trusting and vulnerable. She had only deep-seated, almost instinctual memories of her lost mother and did not yet suspect that love could be treacherous.

In those moments a new sort of love was born in the very center of Kristina's being, one she had never known before. The fathomless devotion a mother feels for her children.

It was silly. Even preposterous. But there it was. She cared so much for these little girls that she would have laid down her own life for them.

It was no great leap, from that conclusion, to the realization that she loved Max, as well. Truly and completely, in an adult fashion that bore no resemblance at all to the reckless, superficial and somewhat fatuous fondness she had felt toward Michael.

Kristina settled in to keep her vigil, reflecting upon these revelations while she waited for the dawn.

Perhaps an hour had passed when Bree awakened, groped her sleepy way into the bathroom, and crawled back into bed. She sat up for a few moments, a tousled moppet gilded in silvery moonlight, as though she sensed someone's presence. Then, with an expansive yawn, she collapsed onto the pillows and tumbled back into the sort of consuming slumber Kristina suspected only vampires and small children can attain.

The remainder of the night passed quickly for Kristina. After a last stolen look at Max, who was sleeping peacefully now, she willed herself back to her own house, her own bedroom.

The letter she had intended to read the night before lay on her bed, where she had left it before her shower the night before. Still wearing the dark clothes she'd put on after the encounter with Benecia and Canaan Havermail, she hurried down the hall.

Stepping over the threshold, Kristina scanned the room. The dolls were in their cabinets, staring and silent, and there was no sign that the tiny vampires had ever fouled the place with their presence.

"Behave yourselves," Kristina told the dolls before closing the door and returning to her room to dress for work.

Dathan was waiting inside the shop when she arrived, making himself at home on a Chippendale chair and reading the current issue of *USA Today*. He smiled benevolently, like an indulgent husband whose docile wife has just brought his breakfast on a tray.

"Well?" he said, laying aside the newspaper and rising. He was wearing battered jeans and a tweedy brown sweater, but he bowed as elegantly as if he were clad in a coat and tails.

Kristina was more than irritated at his presumption—he could at least have waited until she'd arrived at the shop herself instead of entering like a common thief—but she put her annoyance aside. Last night's visit from the Havermails had convinced her that she needed someone's help, and at the moment Dathan was the best available candidate.

"We have a bargain," she said, extending one hand to seal the agreement.

Dathan looked mildly surprised. "Acquiescence? So easily and so soon? Great Zeus, Kristina, I confess I'm almost disappointed!"

He deserved a jab, she decided. "You've already had one offer of marriage," she said, "though I doubt you'll find it suitable."

"Was it a vampire?"

"*It* is certainly the appropriate word and, yes, Benecia Havermail is indeed a vampire."

Dathan all but spat his response. "Why, that's revolting—the creature is a child!"

"She only looks like one," Kristina replied. "Apparently she's decided she made a bad bargain in becoming a vampire and passing up her chance to go through the normal sequence of lifetimes. In addition, she seems to be smitten with you."

Dathan's expression was a study in revulsion. "Needless to say, my dear, that particular monster will not do."

Kristina went to the back of the shop to hang up her coat, set her purse on a shelf, and put a mug of water into the microwave for tea. She had not taken the time for breakfast and felt the beginnings of hunger in the pit of her stomach. "I completely agree that Benecia is not suitable. I hasten to remind you, however, that all vampires are monsters, in one way or another."

"As are all witches and warlocks," Dathan said, though he glossed over the concession pretty quickly. He gave Kristina a pointed look as she took the mug out of the microwave and swirled a teabag around in the hot water before discarding it in the trash bin. "Lesson one, Ms. Holbrook," he said. "Why do you brew tea in the mortal way, like a common scullery maid, when you could simply conjure it up in the first place?"

Kristina considered her long-cherished preference for doing things in human fashion. "I wanted to live as normal a life as I could," she said.

"Normal for you, Kristina? Or normal for the mortal you wish you were? 'This above all,' as the Bard so wisely said, 'to thine own self be true.' "

"Point taken," Kristina replied, deflated. "I've been playing make believe for a long time. The problem is, I'm not sure *what* I am—clearly I'm not human, but I'm no vampire, either."

"You are Kristina Holbrook," Dathan said, touching the

tip of her nose with an index finger in the same fond way that her father and Valerian had often done, while reassuring her. "You are utterly unique, and you should celebrate that, *glory in it*, rather than fretting and trying to pretend you're someone else."

Kristina knew he was right, but just knowing didn't mean she could change right away. After all, she'd been posing as a mortal woman ever since that long-ago day when she'd taken a spill from her horse on an English country road and just as surely fallen for Michael Bradford. A habit of more than a century's standing would take time and effort to break.

"Okay," she said. "What do I do first? How do I start?"

Dathan studied her speculatively. "I assume you know the basics—appearing and disappearing, changing the outward appearance of simple objects and all that?"

Kristina flushed with indignation. "I'm not an idiot," she said.

"Now, now," Dathan scolded, waggling a finger under her nose. "The mark of a good student is humility. To achieve mastery, one must assume the attitude of a beginner."

Indignation gave way to a singular lack of enthusiasm. "Terrific," Kristina muttered.

CHAPTER 9

For the first time in his life, as he drove the short distance between Kristina's house and his own, Max Kilcarragh questioned his sanity. He cared—more than cared—for a woman who professed to be one hundred and thirty years old, with vampires for parents. He had seen a genuine warlock pop into the room like a character on *Bewitched*.

Seeing was believing, they said. He didn't know which was crazier—that he'd seen, or that he believed. Even more insane was the fact that he wasn't running as fast as he could in the other direction.

He was at risk. More important, so were his children.

Yet there was something inside him, a part of himself he'd never explored, that urged him to stand his ground.

Stand his ground? How could one mortal, however athletic, hold his own against creatures with magical powers? Maybe it was already too late to protect his daughters, himself, and Kristina.

Now *there* was a grandiose idea—that he, a high school football coach just five years short of turning forty—would have so much as a prayer against the likes of that warlock, Dathan, or any of the other monsters Kristina had so haltingly described.

He was nearly home, but suddenly there it was—the neighborhood church he had avoided assiduously since the accident. Although he'd sent Bree and Eliette to Sunday School every week, knowing Sandy would have wanted them to stay in touch with their personal heritage, he hadn't set foot in the place himself. Hadn't been inclined to worship a God who would take somebody like Sandy out of the world, though he guessed he still believed. Grudgingly.

Maybe, he thought, pulling over to the curb and staring up at the darkened structure, it wasn't a case of not having a prayer after all. Maybe, in fact, that was *all* he had.

He gripped the steering wheel in both hands and lowered his head, motivated mostly by discouragement, rather than reverence. His supplication was silent. *Show me how to handle this. I don't care what happens to me, but I'm asking You to look out for Kristina and Eliette and Bree. Please.*

That was the extent of Max's entreaty; he hoped it would be enough. When Sandy was killed, he hadn't had time to ask for help; everything had happened too fast.

He shifted the Blazer back into gear and went home.

Elaine was there to babysit, and her face brightened as Max entered the house. He greeted her with a nod and bounded up the stairs without taking off his coat or asking how the kids were. He had to see his daughters for himself; a report from his sister-in-law wouldn't suffice.

They were safe.

Bree was tangled in her blankets, though the expression on her little face was one of sweet repose. Eliette seemed to be on guard, even in her sleep, but that was normal for her. Max's heart ached because he couldn't take away the pain, make up for the loss that had wounded her so terribly.

She awakened, this elder daughter of his, who remembered the death of her mother all too clearly, and looked at him with large brown eyes. "Hi, Daddy," she whispered, conscious, as always, of Bree. Eliette was too serious, too responsible, but he didn't know how to help her.

"Hi," he said in a gruff, gentle whisper.

"I'm glad you're home."

"Me, too. Everything go okay tonight?"

Eliette nodded soberly. Max wondered if she was thinking what he was—trying to reason out how things could be okay in a world in which your mom could be snatched away forever, without a moment's notice. "You were with Kristina," she said.

It was only a statement, not an accusation. Not a protest.

Max felt a twinge of guilt all the same. What new kind of suffering might he have brought into Eliette's life, and Bree's, by involving himself with Kristina Holbrook?

"Yeah," he said.

"Bree says she's going to be our mommy now. Miss Holbrook, I mean."

Max tucked Eliette in, in an approximation of the way Sandy had done it. "Just a second here," he said softly. "Mommies come one to a customer, and yours is gone to heaven. Miss Holbrook—if I did marry her, and trust me, things haven't gotten that far—would be your stepmother."

Eliette's nose crinkled. "Like in *Cinderella*?"

The word stepmother had been a poor choice, Max thought. While he knew in the center of his soul that Kristina wasn't wicked, she was no Mary Poppins, either. "No," he said quickly. "Kristina isn't mean."

"Would she get to boss me around?"

Max suppressed a smile, in spite of the fact that the evening's events had left him feeling as though he'd been pushed five miles by a snowplow and then run over. "If you mean could she tell you to do your homework, quit picking on your sister, or clean up your room, yes. Now, go to sleep. We'll talk about this in the morning." He kissed Eliette's forehead and left the room.

Elaine was lingering downstairs, sipping herbal tea. She always lingered, it seemed, but then Max wouldn't have wanted her to walk to her car alone. She was a good friend to him, an attentive and loving aunt to the children, and she had been Sandy's sister. But she got on his nerves sometimes.

She looked at him with big, soulful eyes, and Max was confronted, yet again, with a fact he usually managed to deny. Elaine wanted more from him than he was willing to give. She wanted to step into Sandy's shoes, raise the girls, share his bed every night.

"Bree and Eliette were good, like always," she said.

Max shoved a hand through his hair, much rumpled because it had been a night for that sort of gesture, and manufactured a smile. "I really appreciate your coming over here on such short notice to take care of them," he said. "But it occurs to me that I've been taking advantage of you by asking. I'm sorry, Elaine—I haven't been very thoughtful."

She drew nearer, and Max unconsciously stepped back.

Her smile was tremulous. Her hair was like Sandy's, her face and body were similar. It would be so easy to pretend . . .

And so unfair. So cruel.

Besides, it was Kristina who occupied his mind and heart these days, for better or worse. He didn't even want to think about the worse part.

"Max," Elaine said quietly as if she were holding out a handful of seeds to a bird on the verge of taking wing, "the girls need a mother."

While Max privately agreed, the remark rankled. In an ideal world, every child would have two loving, nurturing parents, but this one was another kind of place entirely. He'd done his best in spite of that, making sure Eliette and Bree knew that he would be there for them, no matter what.

If there was a single thing he was sure of, in a universe full of surprises, it was that he was a good father.

"I don't think we should pursue this, Elaine," he said with a sigh. "I'm really tired and . . ." *And tonight I found out that vampires and warlocks, to name just two of a variety of fiends, are real. Not only that—I learned that I'm in love with a woman who is a hundred and thirty years old.*

Elaine did not advance, but neither did she retreat. Max was developing a pounding headache, and he was still wearing his coat. The room felt hot and close, though he knew the temperature was set at sixty-eight degrees, as always.

"I've been patient," she said.

Max felt a chill. Patient? Her sister had died violently, tragically, instantaneously. He said nothing, but started toward the door, hoping to lead Elaine in that direction. Her coat, a simple one of gray tweed, hung on the hall tree. "It's late," he said, offering the garment, holding it out so that she could slip her arms into the sleeves.

She smiled somewhat sadly and got into the coat. Max wished he loved her; it would have made everything so much simpler. Elaine looked like Sandy. She cherished the girls, and they were fond of her. And there were, to his knowledge anyway, no vampires in her family tree, no warlocks amidst her small circle of lackluster friends.

"I've watched you," she said with her back still turned to him, her hands busy with the buttons of her coat. "First you grieved, like all of us, of course. Then you started dating . . ."

Max closed his eyes for a moment. *Damn. She was going to push it.*

"Elaine—" he began awkwardly, reluctantly.

She turned and placed a finger to his lips. Her eyes were brimming with tears, and her chin trembled. "Just listen," she said. "I've always loved you—even when you and Sandy were first dating. I kept hoping. But then you married her."

He had an image of Elaine as a shy, knock-kneed kid in a bridesmaid's dress. Sandy had tossed her bouquet to her younger sister. Elaine had had too much champagne at the reception, he recalled. She'd sobbed and made something of a scene when he and Sandy left for their honeymoon.

He'd felt sorry for the kid, ascribing her behavior to excitement and the champagne she and some of the cousins had been sneaking all afternoon, but Sandy had touched his arm and shook her head. A signal that she didn't want to discuss the matter.

"Don't," he said now, in the entryway of his home. "Please. Don't."

She ignored his plea. "I can make you happy, Max."

He let out a long, raspy sigh and put a hand to the small of her back, ushering her to the door, turning the knob. "Come on," he said as if she hadn't spoken. "I'll see you to your car."

"Max."

He didn't push her over the threshold, but he did guide her a little, increasing the pressure just slightly. "No, Elaine," he said firmly. Wearily. "I won't talk about this with you. Not tonight, not ever."

"Couldn't you just pretend I was Sandy?" They were in the middle of the front yard. Only a few more feet to her car.

"My God," Max answered, opening the car door for her, waiting for her to slip inside. "I'm going to forget you even suggested that. You don't mean what you're saying, Elaine." He felt compelled to offer a reason, an explanation, for her behavior. "It's the grief that's making you say these things. You haven't worked through losing Sandy."

She got behind the wheel, but Max couldn't close the

car door because she hadn't swung her legs inside. "You think I didn't love her, don't you? Well, I did. I do. And I miss her as much as you do."

Max shivered, but he didn't think it was the cold November wind that was biting at him, even through his coat. "I know you loved her," he said patiently, carefully. "We all did."

"It's what Sandy wants, you know," she told him. "For us to be together. A family. She told me so."

Max didn't speak. He wouldn't have known what to say.

"In dreams," Elaine explained, all the way inside the car now, at long last. Switching on the ignition. "Sandy comes to me in dreams. Talks to me. Tells me things."

Max still didn't answer. He was a pragmatic man who did not believe the dead spoke to the living, waking or sleeping, but that night he'd learned, in an unforgettable way, that there were indeed other realms, other realities besides the one he knew.

"I'll ask her to visit you. Sandy, I mean. Maybe that will convince you." Having uttered those incredible words, Elaine closed the door, clicked the electric lock button, and backed out of Max's driveway.

He was scared, and not just because of what had been revealed to him at Kristina's house earlier that evening. Nor did he believe that his late wife would show up in his dreams, at Elaine's behest or for any other reason. He knew because he'd tried often enough to summon Sandy, during the early, dark days, when the loneliness had been almost too much to bear. No, what worried Max was the state of his sister-in-law's mind.

He stood in the driveway long after Elaine's car had disappeared around the corner.

"Slow," Dathan said critically, "but a little better than your last try."

Kristina glared at him. She'd willed herself to China and back—the whole process couldn't have taken more than a minute—but she felt as if she'd made the journey on foot. "I'm half mortal, you know," she said.

"No excuse," Dathan replied. They were standing in the center of her living room, where they had materialized moments before; Dathan first, of course, then a disgruntled and somewhat breathless Kristina. There was a subtle change in his expression as he studied her. "You know," he said, "maybe I don't need a vampire for a mate after all. You might do very well."

Kristina felt herself flush with indignation and something not unlike revulsion, although the warlock was a beguiling creature if she'd ever seen one. "Forget it," she said. "My family is weird enough without stirring you into the mix."

Dathan's tender brown eyes flashed with annoyance, and he spread one long-fingered hand over his chest in a gesture of injured pride. "You lack grace," he said. "Verbally, as well as in regard to your magic."

Kristina was exhausted. She wanted to crawl into bed and lie there for a hundred years, like Sleeping Beauty. When she woke up, Max and his sweet, innocent children would have lived out their lives and gone on to some brighter, safer realm where she would no longer be a danger to them.

"I'm not going to apologize, if that's what you're waiting for," she told Dathan.

"Don't you see that it's your very insistence on pretending to be mortal that has gotten you into this mess?" the warlock demanded. "And yet you persist. You're in love with, of all things, a *high school football coach*. A jock, Kristina. That's what humans call men like him, isn't it? Jocks?"

She felt incredibly defensive. "There is nothing wrong

with being athletic,'' she said. ''Besides, Max is smart. And sensitive.''

Dathan rolled his eyes. ''You may already be beyond hope,'' he said, folding his arms. He looked magnificent, standing there in the center of Kristina's beautifully appointed living room, but she felt nothing except irritation.

''Maybe I am,'' she said. It was only too true. If anything happened to Max and the girls because of their association with her, she would not be able to bear it. It was the one prospect with the impetus to drive Kristina to destroy herself.

''No,'' Dathan insisted. ''I won't let it happen.''

She wondered if he'd been reading her mind, hoped not. There were a great many things she didn't know about warlocks and their singular powers. Or those of vampires, for that matter. ''Won't let what happen?'' she asked suspiciously. She kept some very private things in her mind and didn't want Dathan or anyone else rifling through them.

''You're not going to give up on your magic, Kristina,'' Dathan decreed. He tilted his handsome head to one side, considering. His exquisite features were taut with concentration. ''Come with me,'' he went on after a long and, for Kristina, uncomfortable silence. ''Be my bride. You will learn to love me in time, and forget your little mortal.''

Little was hardly the word Kristina would have used to describe Max; he was well over six feet tall and probably weighed better than two hundred pounds. And that didn't take the size of his spirit into account; she had known from their first encounter that Max had the soul of a gentle warrior. Even if he'd been small physically, his character would have made him a giant.

''If I thought going with you would keep Max and his daughters safe, I would probably do it,'' Kristina said. She hadn't considered her words ahead of time; they simply came tumbling out of her mouth. Straight from her heart.

"But it's too late now. The damage has been done."

"Exactly whom do you fear so much?" Dathan asked. He was standing behind a Queen Anne chair now, his elegant hands grasping the back. "Surely it can't be Valerian. He dotes on you."

"It's the Havermails," Kristina said, and shuddered superstitiously, lest mentioning the little demons' names might summon them from whatever hellish pursuit they'd chosen for the night. As soon as Dathan was gone, in fact, she would go to Max's house and keep watch again.

"Avery? Roxanne?" Dathan raised one eyebrow, and his fine, angelic mouth twisted slightly in a delicate expression of contempt. "Those cowardly creatures? Neither of them would dare cross Valerian, let alone your mother."

Kristina shook her head. "Benecia and Canaan."

"The devil's children," Dathan said. The contempt in his face changed to revulsion, and there was nothing delicate about it. "Surely they, too, would be afraid—"

Kristina recalled the recklessness of Benecia's taunts the night before when she'd found them in the room where she kept her childhood toys, her collection of dolls. "Something is different. I don't know about Canaan, but Benecia is—well—it's almost as if she wants to be destroyed." Before Dathan could offer to oblige, Kristina held up one hand to stay his words. "Which isn't to say she won't fight to defend herself, Dathan. She is five hundred years old, remember, and her powers are beyond reckoning."

"Maybe for you. Compared to me, she is but a babe."

"But she is powerful."

"She must sleep in the daytime, like most other vampires. Warlocks suffer no such disadvantage. I have only to find her lair and drive a stake through her heart to put an end to her."

"Not good enough," Kristina answered. "Canaan would avenge her, and even if you managed to destroy her as well,

other vampires would seek retribution, if for no other reason than that a warlock had given them cause.''

''They would defy your mother's command, that there
must be peace between vampires and warlocks, lest Nemesis and his angels be sent to destroy us all?''

''Eternity is a long time,'' Kristina answered. ''I believe
some vampires—perhaps many of them—are weary like
Benecia. Maybe destruction, even damnation, would be a
welcome release after century upon century of being just
what they are. Humans pass through a variety of lives, you
know, shedding each body like a skin when they are
through with it. They go on, change, make progress. I've
never spoken of it with my mother, Papa, or Valerian, but
I suspect that sometimes a blood-drinker hates being
trapped in one identity for all of time. Perhaps they've denied themselves the very thing they sought in the first place,
in becoming vampires—life.''

''They live forever,'' Dathan reminded her in a quiet
voice.

''No,'' Kristina replied. ''They *exist* forever, or until
they are destroyed. There is a big difference.''

''I will concede that, if for no other cause than courtesy.
What does it have to do with the hideous Benecia Havermail and her equally charming sister?''

''They have nothing to lose,'' Kristina said. The realization weighed so heavily on her spirit that it threatened to
crush her. ''They may be desperate enough, lonely enough,
bored enough, to risk hellfire on the chance that they could
encounter oblivion instead. Valerian says the afterlife is
what each one of us expects it to be, and he has reason to
know.''

In a blink Dathan was standing before Kristina, his hands
resting lightly on her shoulders. ''Let me show you wonders beyond your greatest fantasies, Kristina.''

She smiled, though the last thing she felt was amusement. "Let you take me away from all this? No, Dathan. I don't care for you and, anyway, as I told you before, it's too late."

"Then I shall find Benecia's lair, and that of her sister, and before the first crow of the cock—"

"No," Kristina said quickly. "You mustn't interfere, Dathan. Not in that way. No conscious, reasoning creature kills with impunity."

"More philosophy?"

"Call it a hunch," Kristina replied. "Now, will you please leave? I need some time to myself."

Dathan snapped his fingers; the cloak he'd worn earlier, when he arrived, appeared in his grasp. He donned it with the customary flourish, his soft eyes fiery as he regarded Kristina. "Don't forget our bargain," he warned. "I will train you in magic, and you will find me a suitable mate. In the meantime, I intend to woo you by any means I can devise."

She suppressed an urge to slap her self-appointed mentor across the face. Kristina might have let her powers slip, but she was no fool. "That last part wasn't in the deal," she pointed out. "I don't love you. I don't want you. In fact, I wouldn't have anything to do with you if I didn't need your help. How's that for philosophical?"

Dathan smiled, though both her words and her manner had been poisonous. One warlock's venom was another's ambrosia, she supposed.

"You have your mother's magnificent spirit," he said. "That only makes you more desirable, as far as I'm concerned." He executed a suave little bow, more a motion of his head than his body. "Farewell, lovely Kristina. For now, at least."

With that, he was gone, leaving no trace of smoke or sulphur in his wake.

Kristina hesitated only a few moments before willing

herself to the Kilcarragh house. The children were sleeping soundly, but Max was in his living room, sitting in the dark, without even the television screen to provide light.

He sat in a recliner, a drink in one hand, looking rumpled but plainly not intoxicated. Kristina's heart ached as she stood a few feet away, hopefully invisible, watching him. Little wonder that he was upset, she reflected. He'd just been introduced to a world where things that went bump in the night were real, not just imagined. He'd lost that precious mortal innocence because of her.

As if Max sensed her presence, he set the glass aside and peered into the gloom.

Kristina retreated a little way; he knew she had powers, but she didn't want him to think she was going to pop in on him for no reason, like some supernatural stalker. Maybe he could see her; maybe what was developing between them made that possible.

"Kristina?"

She did the mental equivalent of biting her lip and said nothing.

"Damn," Max muttered, rising from the chair with a sudden motion that almost startled Kristina right out of her spell and into full visibility. "You're not that lucky, Kilcarragh."

Had Kristina been solid, she knew tears would have filled her eyes.

He started toward the stairway, moving confidently in the familiar darkness.

Kristina waited until he was asleep before following him up the stairs and slipping into his room. She was tired from her session with Dathan, and her invisibility was shaky at best. At any moment, she might be seen, and explaining would be difficult.

She stood at the foot of Max's bed for a long while, watching him sleep, searching her mind and heart for a way to keep him and his children safe. But no one was really beyond harm except the dead; Kristina knew that and so, surely, did Max.

Reluctantly Kristina finally turned away, forgetting her spell, opening the door, stepping into the hallway.

Bree was standing there, just outside the bathroom door, wide awake and staring in Kristina's direction.

"You really *can* do magic," the child said in a tone of awe rather than fear.

"Or you could be dreaming," Kristina suggested, somewhat lamely, and in a very soft voice. She hadn't planned on being caught, and now that she had been, she didn't know what to say. It would be cruel and foolish to tell an innocent little girl that monsters, whether hiding in the closet or otherwise, were not necessarily imaginary. That sometimes children needed guarding.

"I'm not dreaming," Bree said firmly. She took a few steps toward Kristina, dragging her blanket behind her, holding a worn teddy bear under one arm. "I can sort of see through you. Are you a ghost, like my mommy?"

"No," Kristina answered. "I'm not a ghost, and neither is your mommy."

"How do you know? About Mommy, I mean?"

Kristina shrugged. She didn't know how she knew that Sandy Kilcarragh had gone on to better things, but she was as sure of that as she was of anything else. "I guess by magic," she said. "Now, don't you think you'd better go back to bed?"

Bree wasn't ready to cooperate, though she yawned broadly. "You're getting pretty solid." She reached out, touched Kristina's hand to test the theory. "Yep. How come you're here? Walking around in our house in the middle of the night?"

"I just wanted to make sure you were all right," Kristina

said. It was as close to the truth as she dared to venture, at the moment.

Bree pulled, so that Kristina bent down to her level. "I'm okay," she confided in a stage whisper, "but Eliette is really sad. And Daddy needs somebody grown up to talk to and stuff like that."

"I understand," Kristina whispered. "Why is Eliette sad?"

"She thinks about Mommy a lot," Bree explained. "It makes her lonesome."

Kristina shared the sleeping Eliette's sorrow, felt it keenly in that moment. Her own upbringing had been anything but normal, but Maeve had been a devoted mother, for all her temperament and dramatic flair. Kristina could barely imagine what it would have been like to grow up without her. "It's good to remember people we love," she said gently. "Even if it hurts sometimes."

Bree frowned, her small, pixie-like face solemn. She clutched both blanket and bear just a little closer. "Is it bad that I can't see Mommy's face in my brain, even when I close my eyes?"

Kristina kissed the little girl's cheek. "No, darling, it isn't bad. And deep in your heart, you do remember. I promise."

Bree smiled brilliantly. "I do?"

Kristina nodded, no longer trusting herself to speak. She watched in silence as the little girl toddled back into the room she shared with her sister, there to sleep and, Kristina hoped, to dream sweet dreams.

Not bothering to cloak herself in invisibility again, not even sure she could manage the spell if she tried, Kristina waited a while, then followed, sitting in the wooden rocking chair in the corner of the room, keeping her vigil and waiting.

The night passed without incident, and Kristina went

home a few minutes before sunrise, marveling at the weariness she felt. Was she finally beginning to age, after all these years? It seemed too much to hope for.

Only after Kristina had filled the glass carafe with water and started the coffee machine in her kitchen did she turn and see the note resting prominently on the counter. It was written on expensive, handmade parchment, and the elegant, flowing letters could only have been shaped by one hand.

Her mother's.

Come to London at once, Maeve had written. *I must see you.*

Kristina frowned. Sunset was still a few hours away in England, so she didn't have to hurry. It wasn't the summons that troubled her, either, but the fact that Maeve had not simply come to her at Max's house. Why had her mother left a note, instead of seeking Kristina out, or wrenching her home again, by means of her formidable magic?

In the end, it didn't matter why. Maeve had commanded her, as a daughter and as a subject, to make an appearance at "court." There was never any question of disobeying.

Kristina showered, applied careful makeup, and put on a suit of dove-gray silk. Then, after taking a few minutes to psyche herself up for the task, she blinked herself to London and the lovely old house where so many secrets lived.

It was not yet sunset when Kristina arrived. Having materialized in the outer hallway—she was grateful it hadn't been the coal bin, considering the strain she'd been under lately—she made her way to the library, which was situated at the back of the first floor. The room was spacious, overlooking the garden, and a polished suit of armor, empty as far as Kristina knew, guarded the double doors.

She stepped inside the vast chamber and went straight to her mother's collection of volumes on the subjects of alchemy and general magic. The tomes were very old, some still in manuscript form and in danger of turning to dust at a touch, and the language was strange. Kristina was puzzling out a spell to forestall evil spirits when a voice startled her out of her contemplation.

"You are here," Maeve remarked, sounding at once imperious and relieved. "I daresay I feared you would not obey."

Kristina laid the book gently aside and smiled at her mother. Maeve was a splendid creature, with flowing dark hair, flawless ivory skin, and eyes of a singular indigo shade. She wore a gossamer white gown, as was typical of her, for she loved spectacle and glamour. Which was not to say that she didn't have a somewhat raunchy side, uncontested queen of the vampires though she was.

"Of course I am here," Kristina answered. "When have I disobeyed you?"

"When you married that mortal—what was his name?— Michael Bradford."

"Mother, that was more than a century ago. I was young and foolish."

Maeve came near, bringing the scent of jasmine with her, and kissed her daughter's cheek. Her smile was warm, full of love and humor, but also tinged with worry. "I fear, from what I am told," she said, "that you are *still* foolish."

CHAPTER 10

Maeve's words trembled in the air.

I fear, from what I am told, that you are still foolish.

Kristina was not intimidated by her mother; she knew Maeve would never hurt her. Would indeed perish to protect her daughter, if such a sacrifice were to prove necessary. Still, she was unsettled by the troubled expression she saw in the queen's dark blue eyes, behind the welcome and the joy.

"Foolish?" Kristina echoed, in a tone of false innocence, stalling.

Maeve's brilliant eyes flashed with impatience and temper. Creatures of every sort quailed before that look, and not without reason, but Kristina held her ground. She was about to hear a lecture about her involvement with Max, and she fully intended to fight back.

"Yes, foolish," Maeve snapped. "You've been consorting with warlocks! Kristina, how could you?"

Kristina was taken aback. While she had certainly known that there was a polite rancor between her mother and Dathan, she was also aware that the two had once joined forces to destroy a particularly evil vampire called Lisette. "This is about *Dathan*?"

"Yes," Maeve said with a little less impatience this time. "How can you be so foolhardy as to trust that—that viper?"

Kristina sighed. She had the beginnings of a headache, though she didn't know whether the tension behind it stemmed from her transatlantic blink or the stress she'd suffered of late. Perhaps both. "I expected you to rail against Max," she said, turning, finding a chair and sinking wearily into it.

All her life she'd been able to go days, even weeks, without sleep, but she had never been sick. Still, something was wrong; she wasn't herself.

Maeve was beside her in an instant, seated gracefully on a hassock, holding Kristina's hand in both her own graceful, chilly ones. "He's done something to you," the great vampire fretted. "I swear, if he's poisoned you, I'll find him and make him long for the mercies of hell!"

"Dathan hasn't harmed me, Mother," Kristina said patiently, gently. "He's helping me with my magic, that's all. Frankly the strain is getting to me."

Maeve narrowed her eyes. "Why should a warlock wish to help the child of two vampires?" she demanded suspiciously.

"We have a bargain," Kristina answered. She conjured a cup of tea, hoping that would restore her a little, and while it appeared in her hands, as ordered, it proved slightly bitter and none too warm. She sipped it anyway. "My part is to find him a mate."

Maeve frowned at the teacup, which rattled against its saucer as Kristina set it aside. "Why doesn't he find a partner from his own species?"

"He says witches are too independent," Kristina explained. "He wants a vampire."

"Why?" Merely suspicious before, Maeve was now a

study in irritated disbelief. "Does the arrogant bore think *us* weak and pliable?"

"It's something about blending the powers of warlocks and blood-drinkers." Kristina had no intention of mentioning that Dathan had suggested *her* as a romantic possibility. Maeve would have come unwrapped if she did, and that was an event to be dreaded by monsters and mortals alike.

Disbelieving annoyance had finally turned to rage. "That *idiot*!" Maeve hissed, letting go of Kristina's hand, surging to her feet. "How can he think Nemesis would tolerate such an aberration for so much as a moment?"

Nemesis, Kristina knew, was a powerful angel. A warrior feared, and rightfully so, by the very demons of hell. For centuries, Nemesis had been straining at the celestial bit, wanting to destroy the supernatural world once and for all. Maeve, Valerian, and Dathan had barely prevented that from happening before Kristina was born. Clearly the danger was still very real.

Kristina made another attempt at conjuring tea and this time got it right. She supposed caffeine was a mistake, given the situation, but she needed something to raise her energy level. "I ran into Benecia Havermail the other night," she said cautiously. "She implied that you have your hands full with some new crisis. What's going on, Mother?"

As easily as that, the tables were turned. Kristina had become the inquisitor, instead of the one being questioned. Maeve began to pace smoothly and gracefully, as she did everything. But she was clearly agitated.

"There has been an—incident."

"What sort of incident?" Kristina pressed.

"Do you remember Dimity?"

The image of a beautiful vampire came to Kristina's mind. Dimity was fair of hair and flesh, and she'd played a string instrument of some sort, a small harp or dulcimer.

Her most distinguishing characteristic, however, was her friendship with Gideon, an angel under the command of Nemesis himself.

"Yes," Kristina said. "I remember." She'd always thought Dimity looked more like an angel than a fiend, but then that was an attribute of evil—it was so often gentle of countenance, beguiling to the eyes, deceiving the heart.

"They have vanished, the pair of them."

Kristina made no further attempt to drink her tea. The ramifications of her mother's words were earthshaking. If Gideon had been destroyed or wooed to the dark side, there would literally be hell to pay. Dimity, for her part, would be on her own as far as her fellow vampires were concerned, but angels were protected, each one accounted for and cherished by their Maker. As were mortals.

"Surely Nemesis would know where—"

Maeve interrupted her with a shake of the head. "That's the mystery of it. There's no sign, anywhere, of either of them."

Kristina let out a long breath. "What's your theory, Mother? And don't say you haven't one, because I know you too well to believe it."

The vampire queen ceased her pacing and gave her daughter a level look. "I've discussed the matter with your father, of course. And the only possibility we've been able to come up with is that they've gone into some other dimension, some alternate reality."

Kristina was nearly speechless. "A place even Nemesis doesn't know about?" The implications of that were staggering, because the warrior angel was privy to the greatest secrets of heaven itself. How could there possibly be a place, a realm, that was beyond his ken, out of his reach?

"You've been searching for them."

Maeve nodded. "To no avail, obviously. Nemesis has been turning the universe upside-down as well, and he is fit to be tied, as you can imagine. He thinks we're plotting against the Light, we vampires, planning to take over, extinguish the sun—'' She flung her hands wide in a gesture of bewilderment, an extremely rare emotion for her.

"Are those things possible?'' Kristina asked, awestruck as well as frightened. If they were, she had underestimated her mother's powers and Valerian's by an immeasurable margin.

"No,'' Maeve said, "but Nemesis can be utterly unreasonable when his temper is roused. The fact that his every effort to locate Gideon has failed only compounds his frustration, of course.''

"Dear heaven,'' Kristina murmured.

"I wish you wouldn't use that word,'' Maeve replied crisply. She gathered herself, as imperious as ever, and stood before Kristina, willing her daughter to rise. Kristina could no more have resisted than a jonquil bulb could defy the warm, incessant tug of spring sunlight. "We must still discuss the warlock.''

Kristina thought of Max and Bree and Eliette, how vulnerable they were. "I have reasons of my own for forging an alliance with Dathan,'' she said evenly. "Just as you once had. Besides, I doubt that a warlock and a vampire *could* conceive a child in any case.''

"Do you?'' Maeve asked, arching one ebony eyebrow in an expression that might have been disdain, had it been directed at anyone else except her daughter or her beloved mate. "You forget, then, that you yourself were born of a nightwalker and a mortal. That, too, was thought to be impossible.''

Kristina sighed. "I haven't forgotten,'' she said. "But my conception was a rare occurrence, wasn't it? There has been no other birth like it, before or since—isn't that true?''

"Yes,'' Maeve admitted, but only after a long and stubborn silence. "It's true.''

"Then we can safely assume that any union between Dathan and a vampire would be childless."

"We can safely assume nothing," Maeve said fiercely. "But you are right about one thing—I simply cannot concern myself with this affair, not at the moment. The other situation must take precedence over virtually everything else."

Kristina faced her mother and kissed her cool, alabaster white forehead. "I will be very careful," she promised. "Don't expend your energies worrying about me."

Maeve made a sound that might have been a sigh in a creature with breath. "Warlocks are the most treacherous of monsters," she said. "And they are the natural enemies of vampires."

"Yes," Kristina replied, "but it isn't only politics that makes strange bedfellows. I need Dathan's help, and apparently he needs mine. Never fear, though—I won't make the mistake of trusting him."

"That will have to be good enough, for the moment at least," Maeve conceded. "I *am* glad to hear that you are giving up this silly pretense of being human and finally exploring your powers. It's about time you came to your senses."

Kristina bit her lip and gestured toward the shelves behind her, where the manuscript she had been perusing still lay. "May I borrow some of those volumes? There are some interesting, if ancient, spells recorded there—difficult to decipher but worth the effort, I think."

"Of course," Maeve said. She made a gesture with one hand, and the books Kristina wanted to read vanished into thin air, to land neatly on her desk at home, no doubt. Express mail, vampire style. "I must go now, darling," the queen continued. "First to hunt, then to seek the ever-illusive Dimity. Your father is probably in the laboratory if you'd like to see him."

Kristina smiled and nodded. "Good luck in your search."

Maeve vanished in a draft of cool air and a whiff of jasmine.

Kristina hesitated only a few moments before heading belowstairs, to her father's favorite place. Still oddly weary, knowing she would need her energy for the return trip to Seattle, she took the stairs in good mortal fashion and knocked at the laboratory door.

Simultaneously a lock clicked, and Calder's voice called out, "Come in, Kristina."

She entered to find her father busy at one of his tables. He appeared to be performing an autopsy on something, and Kristina felt bile surge into the back of her throat. "What is that?" she asked, holding back.

Calder grinned at her over one shoulder. He was handsome, and more than one female vampire had dared to flirt with him over the years, but he cared only for Maeve. "Sorry, I should have warned you," he said. "This is— was—a vampire."

Kristina's revulsion was overruled by her natural curiosity, much of which had been inherited, no doubt, from Calder himself. She stepped closer, looking down at the creature on the table, saw a humanoid shape with fangs and sunken, staring eyes. There was none of the gore that would have accompanied such an examination of a mortal, however—the vampire, a female, was dried out and crumbling, like a wasp's nest long abandoned.

"Who-who was she?"

"No one you knew," Calder said, returning his attention to his work.

"How was she killed?"

"An infusion of warlock blood, I would guess. There have been a number of such cases lately, though Dathan and his underlings deny all knowledge of the matter."

Kristina shivered. ''Why the autopsy?''

''Part of an experiment,'' Calder said.

Of course. He was still trying to find the method and the magic that would ''cure'' blood-drinkers of their ghastly obsession, without robbing them of their singular powers.

She spoke quietly, gently, because she needed for him to look at her, needed his full attention. ''Papa, I want to be mortal—I want to have babies, get gray hair, and eventually die. Can you help me?''

Calder's splendid face contorted for a moment with pain and perhaps with understanding. He said nothing just then, but left the autopsy table to cross the room where he shed his lab coat and scrubbed his hands with disinfectant soap and a brush, like a surgeon.

Kristina followed him, stayed close by his side. ''Can you?'' she repeated.

''I don't know,'' Calder answered. She saw true suffering in his eyes as he looked at her. To do what she asked would be, in his view, to kill her.

''Don't you ever get weary, Papa?'' Kristina pressed. ''Don't you long sometimes for peace, for oblivion, for cool, dark nothingness?''

Calder was drying his hands on a starched, spotless towel. He tossed the cloth into a hamper beside the sink before replying. ''I am young, as vampires go,'' he said. ''There is still much I want to accomplish.''

''But someday—?''

He closed his eyes for a moment, this vampire who had once been a man, a surgeon on the bloody battlefields of the American Civil War. He had seen anguish, of both the flesh and the spirit, and despite his intense focus on his experiments, he was not insensible to the shared sorrows of men and monsters. ''Perhaps someday I will grow weary, yes. Kristina, why do you ask these questions? Is it because of that mortal you have become enamored of?''

"Mostly, yes," Kristina admitted. There was no use in lying to Calder, even if she'd felt the inclination. Because of the scientific bent of his mind, he was far more focused than Maeve, and attempts to dissemble were lost on him. "I love Max very much, Papa. You of all people"—they both smiled at the misnomer—"er—vampires—should understand."

"I do," Calder said with a nod. He frowned and narrowed his eyes, studying Kristina more intently than usual. "You do not look well. What is wrong?"

Kristina shrugged. "Love, I suppose," she said. "And I am so very tired."

Calder's frown deepened. "Sit down," he said, indicating a nearby stool. Behind him, the half-dissected vampire was clearly visible, lying still on its gleaming stainless-steel autopsy table. Calder took a syringe from its sterile packaging and skillfully drew blood from the vein in Kristina's right forearm.

"What's the diagnosis, Doctor?" Kristina asked with a wan smile.

He set the vial of blood carefully on a countertop and smiled back, but there was a shadow of consternation in his dark eyes. "Probably nothing," he replied, "but it will take some time to determine the exact nature of the problem."

Kristina felt a little shiver of uneasiness. Was it possible for her to be ill? She'd never had so much as a case of the sniffles, in almost a century and a half of life, though she did occasionally suffer headaches. Even those tended to be more psychic in origin, however, rather than physical. "You'll be in touch as soon as you know?"

He came to her and laid a comforting hand on her shoulder. "Of course, and in the meantime, I don't want you fretting. I took that blood sample as a precautionary measure, and for no other reason."

Kristina stood. "But there is another reason. You must study the specimen closely, Papa." She paused to draw a resolute breath. "Please. I want to know what I am, if there's a definition."

Calder squeezed Kristina's shoulder lightly before letting go. He did not speak again but simply nodded.

Kristina summoned all her strength and willed herself back to Seattle. Although she had aimed for her house, she materialized in the shop instead. Then, too tired to do anything more, she curled up on a settee in the back of the store and tumbled into a deep, all-encompassing sleep.

The shop remained closed that day. The telephone went unanswered, and so did the postman's knock at the door. Kristina was oblivious, almost comatose.

When she awakened, it was dark, and for a few moments she could not remember where she was. She felt groggy and disoriented, as though she'd been drugged, and the thin light coming in through the windows cast eerie shadows all around her.

Only then did Kristina recognize her surroundings.

She pushed splayed fingers through her hair. The Victorian settee was hard, stuffed with bristly horsehair that smelled faintly musty, anything but comfortable. She sat up slowly, shaken and filled with a strange sense of urgency, as though there was somewhere she was supposed to go. Something she needed desperately to do.

But she couldn't think, couldn't concentrate. What was wrong?

Kristina made herself stand and flip on a light. She still had enough magic for that, at least, but the effort sapped her strength all the same, made her feel dizzy.

Someone rapped at the shop door; Kristina made her way through the maze of old furniture and umbrella stands and statues to peer through the glass.

Jim Graham, a policeman who patrolled the area on foot,

greeted her with a concerned smile after she'd fumbled with the locks and opened the door to the chilly night breeze.

"Everything okay, Ms. Holbrook?"

"I'm just working late," Kristina said. She hadn't really shaped the excuse; it just fell from her tongue, ready-made.

"You look like you could use some rest." The cop was a nice middle-aged man, and Kristina liked him. She wished it was so simple, that all she needed was a day in bed or a short vacation.

"You're right." A smile fluttered near her lips, but she couldn't quite bring it in for a landing. "But you know how it is these days."

Jim nodded sagely. "You want me to walk you to your car? I could wait while you get your coat and lock up."

Kristina's car was parked in her garage at home, her coat still hanging in the hall closet. She didn't explain, of course. "That's really kind of you," she said, and meant it. "But I have a friend picking me up in a little while."

"Well, just make sure you keep the place locked up tight until he gets here," the officer said. "Can't be too careful, you know."

Kristina thought belatedly of the intruder who had broken into the store some months before. She'd turned him into a doorstop, handily enough, but she wondered now how trustworthy her magic had been, even then, and shuddered to think what might have happened if her skills had failed her. "That's for sure," she agreed as the policeman stepped away from the door. He waited, she noticed with appreciation, until all the locks were in place again.

The brass monkey was still on his shelf in the back room, where Kristina had left him. Dredging up all the strength she could summon, she reinforced the original spell, and promptly sank to the floor in a faint.

When Kristina opened her eyes, only moments later, she found herself at home, lying on her own bed. Dathan bent over her to lay a cool cloth on her forehead.

"What's the matter with me?" she asked in a small voice. She wanted Max, wanted to go to him, to make sure he and the girls were all right, but she couldn't seem to move, except in slow motion.

The warlock sat down beside the bed. He looked incongruous in the delicate, chintz-covered chair, given his size and his almost regal elegance. "It's only a guess," he said, "but I'd say that all these years of pretending have finally caught up with you. You've allowed your magic to be depleted and, thus, the very essence of your being."

"Am I going to die?"

Dathan smiled. "Probably not. You come from sturdy— not to mention stubborn—stock."

Kristina wasn't sure whether to be relieved or disappointed, and the dilemma made her slightly testy. "What are you doing here?"

"You're welcome," the warlock said pointedly.

"Thank you." Kristina gave the words a grudging note. "What happened?"

"You swooned. I dropped by on a lark, and did the— er—gentlemanly thing. Lifted you into my arms, brought you here, all that."

Kristina closed her eyes for a moment, trying to absorb what was happening to her, to make some sense of it. Dathan's theory, that she had expended vital powers in her efforts to live as a mortal, seemed the most likely. "I'm in big trouble," she said.

"That's true," Dathan agreed, but lightly.

"My mother warned me not to trust you."

He smiled as beatifically as an angel. "Maeve is a suspicious vampire."

"She is also a *smart* vampire. I need a spell, Dathan. Something to keep the Havermails away from Max and the children, at least until I can get myself together. Will you help me?''

"It is a good thing for you, my dear, that you are virtually irresistible." The warlock sighed in a long-suffering fashion. "Yes, I'll arrange to shield your precious mortals, for tonight at least, though I don't think Benecia and Canaan will trouble them."

"I can't take the chance." But Kristina knew there would have been nothing she could do if Dathan had refused to help. She simply had no strength left.

Max paced. He'd tried to call Kristina intermittently throughout the day. There was no answer at her shop or at her house.

She was a businesswoman, an adult with a life of her own, and he had no claim on her, no right to obsess about where she was or what she was doing. Yet something in his gut, some instinct he had never felt before, was telling him there was trouble.

He shoved a hand through his hair. It was late, and the girls were already in bed. He couldn't leave them alone and, after the exchange with Elaine the night before, he wasn't about to ask his sister-in-law to come over and babysit. The teenager he hired when Elaine wasn't available was probably sound asleep, and if he called his mother or Gwen in the middle of the night, they would be frightened, not to mention angry.

Max returned to the telephone on the desk in his study and punched the redial button; there was no need to go through the sequence of numbers that would make Kristina's home phone ring, because he'd been calling there since six o'clock.

This time she answered. Her voice sounded small, fragile.

"Hello?"

"It's Max." He closed his eyes, feeling both relieved and foolish.

"I guessed that," she said. There was a smile in her softly spoken words.

"By magic?"

The smile came through again, though Max knew in his heart of hearts that all was not right with Kristina. He was scared.

"No," she answered. "I was just hoping."

He wanted to hold her, to draw her into his arms and shelter her against whatever threatened her. He had never felt so protective before, even with Sandy—but then, he'd been naive in those golden days before his wife's death. He hadn't known how quickly and finally tragedy could strike. Hadn't dreamed.

"Are you all right?"

"Just tired," she said.

Max's gut clenched hard. He was torn between his children and the need to go to this woman who had finally caused him to put away Sandy's wedding band, which he had worn on a chain around his neck ever since his wife's death. He ached to see with his own eyes that she was safe and well.

"Do you need anything?"

He could almost see her shaking her head. He knew she was in bed, though he wasn't sure how, and he felt guilty because the image stirred him in a profoundly sexual way. So much for the altruistic wish to embrace Kristina and lend his manly strength. Max wanted more—a whole lot more—and he wasn't proud of the fact, given that she was so obviously vulnerable.

"No," Kristina replied. "I'm all right, Max, really. What about you? Are you okay? And the girls?"

"Don't worry about us," Max said firmly. "We're fine."

There was a short, pulsing silence, during which their hearts communicated.

I need you, Max told Kristina.

And I need you, was her reply.

"Can I see you tomorrow?" Max finally asked aloud. He was leaning against the desk now, the receiver clutched in his hand, still wanting to go to her right then. Not in an hour, not the next day, after football practice.

Now.

"I'd like that," she said. "I'll be at home, taking it easy. I've been meaning to read through the rest of those letters anyway."

Just the prospect of seeing Kristina again made Max ridiculously happy, even though he still wished he could go to her immediately. "Couldn't you just—well—blink yourself over here? You could stay in the spare room—"

"Not tonight, Max," she interrupted gently. "I need to sleep now."

A thick knot formed in his throat; he wanted to weep, could not imagine why. "Yeah, okay, me too," he said. "Good night."

Another pause. "Good night, Max." Kristina had not just spoken to him, she had caressed him. He replaced the receiver, crossed the room, and switched out the lights before heading toward the stairway.

If he'd looked out a window, he might have seen the strange, cloaked sentries standing guard in the night, but Max was thinking only of Kristina that night.

"Take this," Dathan said, holding out a spoonful of something.

Kristina, resting against her pillows and still fully dressed, eyed the offering suspiciously. "Like I told you, my mother warned me to be careful of warlocks and their tricks."

"Give me a little credit, will you?" Dathan demanded. "I didn't bring you here and tuck you into bed just to destroy you. I could have done that at any time if that was what I wanted."

"What is this stuff?" The spoon was closer; Kristina saw that it contained a brownish fluid, some herbal concoction, judging by the noxious smell. One she had never come across before and hoped never to encounter again.

"Call it witches' brew if you must," Dathan answered with a touch of impatience. "It will make you sleep, and thus restore some of your strength. Not a cure, but it's a start."

Kristina deliberated a moment longer, then opened her mouth and took the medicine. It tasted bitter, but she swallowed it. "I'm not going to grow horns, am I?" she asked, falling back against her pillows once more.

Dathan's expression said he wasn't about to dignify such a question with a reply.

"You'd better not take advantage of me while I'm sleeping, either."

He bent close and smiled wickedly. "I hadn't thought of that. What a delightful prospect—thank you for suggesting it, Kristina."

Already she was drifting, spinning, sinking. This, she thought, must be how it is for vampires when they lie down in their lairs, far out of the sun's reach.

Kristina did not dream and awakened many hours later, in the same position in which she'd fallen asleep, in the same clothes. There was no sign of Dathan, but Max was standing at the foot of her bed, wearing jeans and a bright blue sweatshirt, his face beard-stubbled and his hair rumpled.

"How long?" she asked. "Since we talked, I mean?"

"About twenty-four hours," Max replied.

She sat up, yawning. The room was brilliant with sun-light. "You're missing work."

"It's Saturday."

"The girls—"

"Forget about Bree and Eliette," Max said gently. "They're with my folks for the weekend. Kristina, what's going on with you? What knocked you out like this?"

She sighed. Dathan's potion, whatever it was, had cer-tainly done its work. She felt strong again, energetic, almost her old self. Almost.

"Maybe it was the supernatural equivalent of the flu," she said. "In any case, I feel fine now."

Max grinned. He looked tired, though, and she wondered how long he'd been watching over her. "If you don't mind, I'd like to borrow your shower," he said. "And a razor, if you have a spare. I forgot mine."

There was a certain intimacy in sharing space with Max, letting him use her shower, her things. She felt a sensual, stretching sensation deep inside, just looking at him. "Okay," she said. "Help yourself to whatever you need."

Another silence ensued, rife with possible interpretations. Then Max turned and went into the bathroom, carrying a gym bag he'd apparently brought from home.

Kristina heard the water go on, imagined Max stripping off his clothes, stepping naked and muscular under the spray. He was so blatantly, unapologetically male.

She wondered what he would say, what he would think, if she joined him.

In the end she didn't quite have the courage. She took a peach silk robe from her closet and went down the hall to the guest bathroom, where she took a long, hot shower of her own. The flow of water did nothing to soothe the ache inside her, the one only Max Kilcarragh could reach and assuage.

Kristina toweled her hair dry, ran a brush through it, and

then dried her body. The silk robe clung a little as she stepped out into the hall.

Max was there, clad in a pair of clean, worn jeans and nothing else. The encounter seemed accidental, but Kristina knew that it wasn't, that they'd both wanted to be together. That had been in the cards from the first moment of history.

Slowly, deliberately, Kristina untied the belt of her robe.

CHAPTER 11

Max did not move from where he stood, just outside Kristina's bedroom door, until she was near enough to touch, her robe untied, hanging loosely from her shoulders. He put his hands on either side of her face and, with a low sound, part growl and part groan, took her mouth with his.

The kiss was passionate from the first; there was no hesitation this time, only a hunger that had been denied too long. Max entered her with his tongue, conquered her, his silent command presaging all that was to come.

Kristina sagged against him, weakened by her own wanting, by a yearning she had never felt before. When at last he drew back and lifted her into his arms, there were tears of wonder in her eyes.

He kissed her lids, her cheeks, and carried her over the threshold of her bedroom.

"Are you sure you want this?" he asked, still holding her.

Kristina was in a daze. "Oh, yes," she said. "Yes."

Max set her on her feet, ever so gently, and smoothed the robe back off her shoulders, down over her arms. He tossed the garment aside and consumed her naked form with his eyes, arousing her to a fever pitch of desire just by admiring and cherishing her.

"You are so unbelievably, impossibly beautiful," he said.

Kristina leaned forward, brushed his hairy chest with her lips, teasing hard brown nipples with the tip of her tongue. Her fingers strayed to the zipper of his jeans; he halted the motion with both hands, though he did not put her away from him.

"There's a problem," he confessed. "I didn't plan—"

She smiled. Her magic might be rusty, but it was still magic. She held out one hand, in a rather cocky gesture, and a small packet appeared on her palm.

Max chuckled, took the condom, and laid it on the nightstand, within easy reach of the bed. "Impressive," he said.

"Thanks." Kristina slipped her arms around his neck and tilted her head back to look up into his eyes. She knew she was casting a spell, and that it had nothing to do with supernatural powers. In that moment, in that private place, she was not a freak, but a woman, pure and simple.

He unfastened his own jeans and shed them, along with his underwear, and then simply held Kristina against him for a long, heated interval. Just that simple intimacy nurtured her on the deepest level of her being; she could have stood there, cradled in Max's arms, for an indeterminate length of time. Even that small contact was better than anything she had ever felt with Michael.

Finally, however, Max raised his hands to cup Kristina's small, firm breasts. A searing shiver went through her at his touch, for the contact was at once possessive and inexpressibly tender. Hard-edged thumbs stroked her nipples, causing them to stiffen into little peaks.

Kristina emitted a long sigh and closed her eyes. Max bent his head and kissed her again, teasing now, tasting and tempting.

She was still standing, was amazed that her legs would support her. She moved her hands up and down the muscled length of Max's back, in a slow yet conversely frantic motion. She had waited so long, suppressed the yearnings of her body so often, that patience was nearly beyond her.

"Max . . ." she pleaded against his mouth.

"Shhh," he whispered, and continued to caress her, to adore her with his hands.

Kristina made a soft, whimpering sound; it was all she could manage because he had stolen her breath, stilled her heartbeat, frozen her in one fiery moment of time.

Max laid her down on the bed and stretched out beside her. She wanted him to take her, but he was conducting some primal ritual; she knew he would make her feel every nuance of their lovemaking, that her responses were, to him, a vital part of the encounter.

He kissed her again and again, until she was drunk with the need to have him inside her, but it still wasn't enough. While Kristina entangled desperate fingers in his hair, Max brushed her earlobes with his lips, nibbled at her neck, finally moved down over the quivering rise of her breasts.

She gasped with pleasure and arched her back in an ancient, instinctive gesture of surrender as he took one nipple into his mouth and drew at it greedily.

He went on suckling, meanwhile parting her legs with one hand. She ached to accommodate him; her hips rose and fell as he parted the moist curls at the junction of her thighs and teased her with a soft, plucking motion of his fingers.

Kristina sobbed, with joy, with triumph, with frustration. Her body arched, again and again, seeking, reverberating like the strings of a fine instrument drawn tight.

At last, Max relented. He reached for the condom on the bedside table while kissing Kristina's belly. Once he was ready, he cupped both hands under her buttocks and raised her to receive him.

His eyes searched hers one last time, and then he plunged into her, delving deep, as if to touch the very core of her.

Kristina thrashed beneath him, in a physical plea for him to move faster, to thrust himself even further inside. She wanted all of him, not just his powerful body, but his mind, even his soul. She did not wish to own Max, it wasn't that, but to be a part of him, to meld the very essence of her being with his.

Max set an even pace, driving Kristina insane with long, slow, methodical strokes.

Finally, as she flung herself up to meet yet another thrust, a cataclysmic orgasm exploded within her, thrusting her legs even wider apart, splintering the heavens, altering the path of uncounted planets orbiting innumerable stars. While Kristina flexed beneath Max, seized by spasm after spasm, he stiffened upon her, and cried out in hoarse ecstasy.

Kristina lay still, stunned, spent, but Max got up and disappeared into the bathroom. He was back in a few moments, stretching out beside her again, gathering her close against him. She was trembling, even then, in the aftermath of satisfaction.

Max kissed her temple. "What are we going to do now?" he asked.

She snuggled even closer, loving the feel of him, the substance and power and the scent of him. "After that, anything else would be anticlimactic."

He groaned at the play on words, but there was a smile in the sound.

Kristina laughed and buried her face in his neck.

"What?" Max prompted.

She lifted her head to look into his eyes. "You're the first man I've slept with in a hundred years," she said. "That's got to be some kind of distinction."

Max rolled over so that she was pinned beneath him, his brown eyes bright with mischief and the beginnings of fresh desire. "Was I worth waiting for?"

Kristina put her arms around his neck, kissed his chin and then his mouth. "Oh, yes, Mr. Kilcarragh." She felt him growing hard against her thigh, while her own body prepared itself to receive him again.

"Do you think you could work that little trick again? This time without the package and all the groping around?"

She nodded, and Max was instantly outfitted with a fresh condom.

"Pretty fancy," he said, grinning.

"Stop talking," Kristina replied, putting her arms around his neck. "And let's skip the foreplay."

Max wouldn't hear of it; he worked Kristina into another fit of longing, and by the time she was in the throes of her second climax, a pleasure even keener and more strenuous than the first, she was glistening with perspiration and completely incoherent.

Much later, when Max was dozing, Kristina got out of bed, took another shower, and put on jeans and a T-shirt. Her earlier exhaustion was gone; making love with Max had restored her, it seemed.

She was in the kitchen, humming and filling the teapot at the sink, when Valerian appeared at her elbow, unheralded as usual. Kristina was so startled that she nearly dropped the kettle.

"I wish you wouldn't do that," she snapped.

Valerian folded his arms and glowered at her. "Wish away," he replied.

Kristina sighed. There was no reasoning with him when he was in one of his moods, and she could only guess at what was bugging this most temperamental of vampires. Her controversial arrangement with Dathan or her blossoming affair with Max? Or perhaps Valerian was finding parenthood to be less than wonderful.

"Okay, I give up," she said. "What is it now?" She moved around him to set the teakettle on the stove and switch on the burner.

"If you wanted to polish your magic, you might have come to me. I do know a thing or two about the craft, as it happens!"

Kristina hid a smile. She'd injured Valerian's formidable pride, without meaning to, of course. "You've been busy," she said reasonably. "With Daisy and your magic act in Las Vegas and now Esteban. I didn't want to bother you."

"So you took up with a *warlock!*"

"You sound just like Mother," Kristina answered, no longer smiling. She was an adult by anyone's definition of the word, and she was getting tired of being scolded about the company she kept. "I didn't 'take up' with Dathan. We have a bargain, that's all."

"What sort of bargain?" Valerian's magnificent face was thunderous, and his cloak and tailored tuxedo made him resemble some great, beautiful bird of prey.

Kristina sighed, hoping Max wouldn't awaken and come downstairs. He'd already met a warlock; it was too soon to introduce him to a vampire. "You know damn well what sort of bargain," she retorted. "He's tutoring me in magic, and I'm—I'm going to help him find a bride."

Valerian loomed, in that singular way he had. Kristina drew herself up to her full if unspectacular height, trying not to seem intimidated.

"Great Zeus, is he still harping on that?" the vampire demanded. "I thought I'd cured him of the obsession by setting Roxanne Havermail on his trail."

"Dathan is as stubborn as you are. He won't rest until he has what he wants."

"You realize, of course, how dangerous he is—that he

is the leader of all warlocks everywhere? That his mate will share in that power?''

Kristina knew only too well that Valerian could read minds when he tried; she hoped he was too annoyed and distracted to focus on hers and learn that Dathan had proposed an unholy marriage. "He has been an ally in the past," she said to deflect the vampire's attention. "It seems to me that you welcomed his help at one time."

"That was an armed truce," Valerian snapped. "There was never any question that we would be enemies again, once the common threat had been eliminated."

The common threat, of course, had been the vampire Lisette, who had reigned over the nightwalkers before Maeve. "That's silly. If vampires and warlocks made peace once, they can do it again."

Surprisingly Valerian subsided a little, and Kristina had a sudden insight. It wasn't just her relationship with Dathan that was troubling him, but something deeper and much closer to home. *His* home.

"Things aren't going well with Esteban, are they?" she said softly, touching his arm. She had been so occupied with her own concerns that she had not had the time to visit Daisy or Valerian.

The vampire, so imposing, so fearsome, suddenly appeared vulnerable. "He sleeps on the floor like an animal," he said. "He hides food in his room and won't acknowledge anyone except Barabbas."

Kristina considered the environment from which the little boy had been rescued. "Things like this take time," she said.

Valerian was downright crestfallen. "I wanted to give Daisy a child," he whispered, staring off into some realm Kristina couldn't see. "She's so beautiful, so smart and so good. She deserves a normal life."

Kristina felt a wrench far down in her heart. Whatever

his faults, and they were many, Valerian adored Daisy. He had sought her out through lifetime after lifetime, only to lose her again and again. Clearly he feared that history would repeat itself. "Daisy loves you," she reminded him gently.

"Yes," he said, his tone dark with misery. "She loves a fiend, a monster, an inhuman ghoul who dares not sire a child for fear of creating something far worse than himself."

Kristina bit her lip. "I was conceived by a vampire and a mortal," she pointed out, "and I didn't turn out so badly, did I?"

Valerian touched her cheek, not as a lover would, but in the way of a devoted uncle or a godfather. His smile was beautiful, and full of sorrow, and Kristina began to fear for him. He had been known, in his long history, to succumb to terrible fits of melancholia, during which he could lie dormant for decades. One of the oldest vampires, Tobias, had gone underground long ago and never resurfaced.

"No," Valerian said. "You are a miracle, Kristina. But your splendid mother and honorable father are far better creatures than I have ever been."

Kristina willed Max not to come downstairs, but she sensed that he was stirring in his sleep, soon to awaken. Although he had seen Valerian at the Halloween party, meeting the legendary vampire up close and personal was something else again. An experience for which any human being would have to be carefully prepared.

She couldn't help thinking of her private theory that some vampires must grow weary of their existence, of watching mortal loved ones live and die. Though they were predators, blood-drinkers were fascinated by human beings and often became enamored of them, appointing themselves as their guardians or wooing them as lovers. Perhaps Valerian, who had been born as a mortal in the fourteenth century, secretly yearned to rest in peace.

"Do you ever wish you'd never become a vampire?" she asked. The kettle was whistling insistently on the stove, but they both ignored the noise.

"Yes," Valerian answered. "Each time I've found Daisy in a new incarnation and loved her, only to lose her again." For a moment a haunted expression clouded his fathomless sapphire eyes. "It is always with me, Kristina. The knowledge that she will grow old and die, and that I will live on, alone, and wait for her, search for her yet again—"

Kristina thought with sorrow of all the people she'd cared about throughout the years she'd lived—a very short time in comparison to Valerian—her beloved governess, Miss Phillips, for instance. Gilbert Bradford, her husband's brother, and certain mortal friends she'd made along the way. She'd seen all of them age and finally leave her behind. It would happen with Max, too, if they managed to make a life together, and the dread of that pierced her heart like a shard of ice.

"I would gladly surrender my immortality, if indeed that's what I have," she confessed, taking the kettle off the burner at last, pouring hot water over loose tea leaves she'd spooned into a crockery pot earlier. "To me, it's a curse."

Valerian closed his eyes for a moment, as though she'd struck him. "And yet you would suggest that I sire a child by Daisy," he said, meeting her gaze again.

"I would not presume to advise you one way or the other," Kristina answered, "except to say that I think you should forget your Las Vegas show for a while and concentrate on Daisy and Esteban. You yourself said that human life is fleeting—why spend so much time away from them? You certainly don't need the money or the notoriety."

"You're right," he conceded, though somewhat ungraciously. Valerian preferred to play the mentor and guide, not the pupil. In the next moment he assumed a stern expression. "Remember my warning. Warlocks are not to be trusted."

Upstairs, the shower was running. Max was out of bed; he would be downstairs within a matter of minutes.

Valerian arched an eyebrow. "The mortal?"

"Yes," Kristina said with a hint of defiance.

"Is it for him that you are willing to risk so much?"

Kristina knew Valerian was referring to her contract with Dathan. She nodded. "Do you dare to chastise me for that—you who have pursued one woman, one human being, down so many crooked corridors of history?"

"No," Valerian said softly, almost tenderly. "But I sympathize. It would almost be better, I think, if you took a warlock for a mate. At least then you'd be spared the terrible grief, the vulnerability."

"But that would mean giving up the joy as well," Kristina pointed out.

At last he smiled, and when Valerian did that, he was as much a work of art as Michelangelo's *David*. "Wise words," he said. He kissed her forehead and vanished.

There lingered a faint draft in the room, from the vampire's passing, when Max came down the rear stairs and into the kitchen, fully dressed, his hair still damp from the shower. In that moment of simplicity and silence, Kristina knew for certain not only that she loved Max Kilcarragh, but that he had been chosen as her beloved long, long ago, in a time before time, and a place neither of them remembered.

He approached, laying a hand to either side of her waist. He smelled pleasantly of soap, shampoo, and toothpaste as he bent to kiss her lightly on the mouth.

"Hungry?" Kristina asked.

Max drew her against him, gently but firmly enough that

she could not doubt his attraction to her. He slid a second, featherlight kiss from the bridge of her nose to the tip. "Yeah," he answered, eyes twinkling, "but I'll settle for food."

Kristina laughed softly and turned in the direction of the refrigerator. Max caught her hand and pulled her back. "Sit down," he said. "I'll cook."

She was amazed again; so much about this man surprised her. In her adult life, especially during her marriage to Michael Bradford, Kristina had never been taken care of by a man. She had essentially looked out for herself, with occasional interference from her mother or Valerian.

Kristina allowed Max to seat her at the breakfast bar. The tea had finished brewing by then, and he brought her a cup before opening the refrigerator door and taking out the ingredients for an omelette—onions, peppers, mushrooms, fat-free cheese, and a carton containing an egg substitute.

"Is it possible for you to develop high cholesterol?" he asked, frowning at the collection of healthy foods.

Kristina flushed a little, embarrassed at this small, harmless reminder of just how different she was from Max himself and virtually everyone else on earth. "I don't know," she said. "I guess it's all part of the act."

Max's expression was thoughtful as he explored the cupboards, finally producing a nonstick skillet. "The act being your need to be—how shall I put it—ordinary?"

She nodded. Her cheeks still felt warm, and she was just a touch defensive. "I've wanted that all my life," she said.

He set the skillet on the stove, turned on the appropriate burner, and began mixing and chopping with a deftness that indicated long practice. There was a twinkly smile in his brown eyes when, at last, he looked at Kristina. "You've been overlooking one very important fact," he told her. "You, Kristina Holbrook, could never be ordinary, in any sense of the word. Even if you were mortal, you would still be utterly unique.''

Kristina looked away for a moment, wanting to believe he meant what he said, but skeptical. He was trying to be kind, to spare her feelings. ''I know what I am, Max,'' she said a little impatiently.

But it wasn't true, of course. She wasn't a witch, woman, angel, or vampire. What did that leave? Were there creatures on other planets like her? In alternate universes and parallel dimensions?

He poured the omelette concoction into the pan and added pepper and salt from the shakers on the back of the stove. He didn't reply to her statement, which made her uneasy.

''What do you think I am?'' she asked, trying to hide the vulnerability she felt. When Michael, her husband, had learned of her powers, he had said she was unnatural, a bestial freak. Even after more than a century, the memory had the power to wound her.

''Beautiful,'' Max replied without hesitation, managing the omelette while at the same time meeting her gaze directly. ''Intelligent. Generous. Responsive. Shall I go on?''

Tears gathered along her lower lashes; she blinked them back quickly. Her reaction was contradictory—on the one hand, she was relieved, but Max hadn't really had time to absorb and assimilate the various realities of the situation. It was too soon, even for a man as bright as Max, to comprehend what it meant to be involved with her.

Again he nodded, smiling a little now, dashing at her eyes with the back of one hand. ''Yes,'' she said in a raspy whisper. ''Tell me more.''

''You have the elegance of a goddess and the mind of a philosopher. Making love to you was like being taken apart, cell by cell, and then put back together, but better than before. Stronger.''

Kristina sniffled and then gave a soft laugh. Her hand trembled a little as she reached out for her teacup. "You either have a poetic soul or one hell of a line," she said.

Max found plates, divided the omelette, and slid the halves expertly out of the pan. "And you have a trust problem," he answered without rancor. "I guess that's pretty common these days, with both sexes."

She didn't point out that she didn't really qualify for the analogy; there was no sense in harping on the fact that, for all practical intents and purposes, she was some kind of mutant. "How about you, Max? Do you have a trust problem?"

He set the plates on the breakfast bar, found forks, and joined her, taking the stool next to hers. "No," he said after a few moments of thoughtful silence, during which he surveyed his half of the omelette as though he thought it might offer some sort of input. "I was raised in one of the few functional families in America. Nobody drank, gambled, or hit anybody else. We all went to church every Sunday, yet neither Mom nor Dad could be described as fanatical in any way. I was still in college when I fell in love with Sandy, and she happened to be an emotionally healthy individual, too. The toughest thing that ever happened to me—to all of us, really—was her death."

Kristina took up her fork, more because Max had gone to the trouble to cook for her than because she was hungry. It was a terrible injustice that someone talented and beautiful, with a loving husband and two precious children, could be taken in her youth, while jaded vampires yearned for the solace of death and were denied it.

"I'd like to know more about your life with Michael," Max said in that straightforward way he had that so often caught Kristina off guard. "What happened after the duel?"

Kristina started to rise from the stool, her food forgotten.

She wanted, even needed, to share the remaining letters, and the story they contained, with an objective person. If indeed Max could be described as objective, after the way he'd made love to her.

"I'll get the letters," she said.

Max stopped her, taking her wrist in a gentle grasp. "Not now, love," he said. "After breakfast."

Kristina realized that she was hungry, and returned to the omelette. "You're a good cook," she said with some surprise after she'd taken a few bites.

Max grinned. "I'm a nineties kinda guy," he said. "I also do laundry, clean bathrooms, and scrub floors. Once I even mended a tutu fifteen minutes before Eliette was due to perform in a dance recital. Naturally I wouldn't want the guys on my team to find out about that last part."

She smiled at the image of this large, powerfully built man stitching a little girl's ballet costume. The thought stirred a poignant sweetness in the bottom of her heart. "You're a good man, Max Kilcarragh," she said.

He sighed. "Don't give me too much credit. I didn't say I *liked* sewing and cleaning. It was just that somebody had to do it."

Because Sandy was gone, she thought sadly. It was almost as if Max's late wife were there in the room with them, and only then did Kristina fully realize that even if she herself were a normal mortal woman, there would still be an obstacle to overcome. Max had loved Sandy with a rare intensity. Perhaps he did not have the emotional resources to care so deeply again.

"Was—was Sandy that sort of wife?" she asked in a cautious tone. It wasn't really any of her business, she knew, but she still wanted to know what Sandy Kilcarragh had been like. She, who had always had servants, traveled the world, and, in recent decades, concentrated almost completely on building a business that was international in scope. "The domestic type, I mean?"

Max didn't take offense to the inquiry, didn't seem to mind it at all. He took his plate and Kristina's, seeing that she was finished eating, to the sink. "We shared the housework in the beginning," he said, "but once Eliette was born, Sandy decided to take a few years off from her teaching career and stay home. She did more than her share after that, but I helped with the kids as much as I could."

Kristina got off the stool, ready to go upstairs for the other letters. Her throat felt tight, painfully so, for she would probably never be a mother. She and Michael had never conceived a child, and besides, like Valerian, she was afraid of producing a monster of some sort.

"I—I don't think I can have children," she said very softly. She had very good reason to believe as she did.

Max, who had been running water over the breakfast dishes, left the sink to cross the room and take her shoulders tenderly in his big hands. "That hurts you, doesn't it?" he asked. And then, without waiting for her answer, which was probably visible in her eyes, he drew her close and held her tightly for a moment.

Kristina was starved for tenderness; she did not trust her judgment or her perceptions, so great was her need. She was intoxicated by Max's caring, it affected her like opium. She allowed herself to cling to him, just for a few seconds, then pulled away and went upstairs.

She found the letters where she had left them, hesitating only briefly before going back down to the kitchen again. Max was in the family room, sipping from a mug of steaming coffee, probably brewed in the microwave, and gazing out the window, watching a ferry head out of Elliott Bay, lights blazing.

With a smile, Max put down his coffee, went over to the fireplace, and built a crackling fire. It was still dark; dawn was at least an hour away, and there was a certain trenchant intimacy in being together when much of the city was still sleeping. A silent resonance echoed between them, too—a lingering sense-memory of their lovemaking, as though their passion had imprinted itself forever, in the very cells of their flesh.

Kristina stood still, watching Max, allowing herself the fantasy that there could be a thousand other mornings like this one. A lifetime of days and nights.

Max rose to his feet, dusting his hands together, and turned to face Kristina. He ignored the packet of letters in her hand. "Did you ever have one of those moments that you wished could last forever?"

"I think I'm having one right now," Kristina replied.

Neither of them moved.

"It scares me," Max confessed.

"What?"

"Caring so damn much. Kristina, I don't know if I can let myself feel what I'm starting to feel. I don't know if I can risk it."

She understood, or thought she did. "You don't have to be afraid of—of warlocks and vampires. I'll find a way to protect you—"

Max shook his head, and she fell silent. "That isn't what I meant."

Kristina swallowed hard. "Oh."

"I think I'd lose my mind if I loved a woman the way I believe I could love you and then lost her. I've been down that road before, and if I hadn't had Bree and Eliette to live for, I'm not sure I would have made it."

Kristina didn't remind Max that she was already a hundred and thirty years old, that she would probably be the one to grieve, not him. That would have been self-pity, even martyrdom, and those were states of mind she tried hard to avoid, though it wasn't always easy.

She might have said that there were no guarantees, that everyone takes chances, that caring is worth the risks involved, but all those things were too easy, too glib. Max's concerns were valid, and so were her own.

There were so many questions, and so few clear answers.

CHAPTER *12*

My beloved Phillie, the next letter began. Max had settled comfortably on the overstuffed leather sofa to read, with Kristina beside him, her eyes following the lines she herself had penned so long before. For her the experience was almost equivalent to reliving those dreadful times, and yet she knew she had to do it, in order to put that most disturbing part of her past to rest . . .

I had intended to write sooner, my patient friend, but it is not so easy remembering those dark days, even now, when considerable time has passed.

When last I put pen to paper, Michael had killed his own cousin, Justin Winterheath, in a pointless duel, whilst doing terrible damage to his own person as well. My husband's knee was shattered, never to heal properly, always to cause him inexorable pain. His drinking, already a problem even before we were married—I had seen that in him and yet refused to accept it as truth—became much worse. He now had the excuse of his injuries.

Phillie, you can imagine the gossip that followed the tragedy at Cheltingham, but I wonder if even you, clever as you are, can anticipate what a web of suffering Michael wove that early morning in the fog.

It was said that Michael was a murderer and should be tried and hanged for his crime. Lady Cheltingham, my mother-in-law, was a fragile wisp of a woman in the first place, and after the tragedy she went into swift decline. Her consumption of laudanum increased by increments, it was said, until she wasn't even bothering to get out of bed. Her husband, the once-blustering Lord Cheltingham, had never been an attentive spouse—I believe some of Michael's more pronounced character flaws came from him—but after Justin was buried, the duke gave up his gaming clubs, his hounds and horses, even his mistress. He shut himself away in his library, not to read, a pursuit which might have done much to mend his spirit, but simply to sit, or so the servants whispered, staring morosely out the windows.

Only Gilbert and I remained strong—Gilbert, because that was his nature, I because Michael needed me. (I was so foolish, Phillie, thinking I could save him, if only I loved him enough!)

Michael became more impossible with every passing day.

He tried over and over again to ride—that had ever been his passion, and love for me had never supplanted it—but his stiff knee made the pursuit wholly impossible. He was thrown on each attempt, and then there was more pain, followed by more drinking, and then more railing and cursing.

In those days when I might still have been a bride, had I wed myself to a more suitable man, I became instead a reminder of all Michael had lost. By that time, he saw himself as the victim of Winterheath's ungovernable temper, and although he must have known what venomous things were being said about him, he never showed a moment's shame or remorse. He hated me, it seemed, as if I'd brought the whole catastrophe down upon us all, and would often mutter the most vile curses at me, or shout. He even accused me of being faithless, Phillie—of betraying him with his own brother.

I don't doubt that you are wondering why I stayed. I am not sure I can answer that question, even now, when I have gained a modicum of perspective. I can only say that I loved Michael completely; my error, no doubt, was in cherishing the man he might have been, instead of the man he was.

At night I slept in a room adjoining Michael's—I did not want him to touch me in a drunken and hateful state. But he came often to my bed and claimed me roughly, and I grew to hate that aspect of marriage that I had so enjoyed at first. I didn't need my magic to disassociate myself from what Michael was doing to me—and I had almost forgotten that I possessed any powers at all.

One spring morning Lady Cheltingham's serving woman woke the household with a shrill scream. The duchess had died in her sleep and lay shrunken and staring in her lacy nightcap and high-necked gown. The ever-present bottle of laudanum stood upon her bedside table within easy reach.

A pall of gloom seemed to settle over the whole of the estate after that, even though the hillsides of Cheltingham were green with sweet grass and the ewes were lambing. Trout stirred in the streams and ponds, and the sky was that fragile eggshell blue that I have only seen in the English countryside. I wanted to be happy, but I could not.

Within a month of Lady Cheltingham's funeral, her husband went into the family chapel in the middle of the afternoon, put the barrel of his favorite hunting rifle into his mouth, and pulled the trigger. The small, ancient *church where countless children had been baptized, where eulogies had been said and vows exchanged, was thus fouled by the literal and figurative carnage of Lord Cheltingham's furious despair.*

Demons seemed to pursue Michael as never before, to stare out of his eyes, to torment him from both sides of his skin. Gilbert tried but could not reason with his brother at all. Michael was beyond both our reaches.

He disappeared for days on end, commandeering one of the carriages and leaving Cheltingham Castle, and me, in temporary peace. During those intervals, Phillie, I prayed that he would never come back. God forgive me, I hoped that he would die. But he always returned, angrier, uglier than before, full of terrible accusations.

By then Gilbert was the Duke of Cheltingham. Though grief-stricken, and bitterly furious with Michael, he was determined to make the estates prosper, to be a good steward. He had long loved one Susan Christopher, a young woman of excellent social standing, and they had planned, since childhood, to marry.

In the wake of the "Cheltingham Scandals," however, Susan's family withdrew their support of the marriage, and Susan herself offered no protest and wed herself to another. She was not steadfast like Gilbert, but I assign her no blame. Although I believe that my own father, as a mortal, was such a man, I have not known another like my brother-in-law.

If you are guessing that I at last knew the worst truth of all, that I had joined myself, under the laws of heaven, to the wrong brother, you are right. I came to love Gilbert, and I believe he bore me some tender sentiment, though of course something within him was broken with the loss of Susan.

Gilbert and I might have taken some comfort from each other, and perhaps not been blamed too much by a merciful heaven, but we did not. Gilbert was far too honorable, though he often looked at me with the same yearning I felt, but it was no such noble notion as honor that stayed me from sin. I might have seduced my husband's brother, so much did I want him, if the act wouldn't have given weight to Michael's constant and otherwise unfounded reproaches.

During this period, Mother, Papa, and Valerian kept their distance. They might have been figures from a mythical tale, for all I knew, and I resented their absence completely, and often summoned them, aloud and in tears. Later, of course, I came to understand that they had stayed away in part because these were battles I had to fight for myself, but there was another reason as well. All of them feared that they would render Michael some unholy punishment, in a moment of uncontrollable fury, and earn my undying hatred in the process.

And so I was alone, except for Gilbert. . . .

The shrill ringing of the telephone jolted both Kristina and Max out of the paper world of the letter; Max leaned his head back on the sofa and closed his eyes, while Kristina went to answer.

"Ms. Holbrook?" an unfamiliar voice asked.

Kristina was watching Max, wondering what he thought of her now, how the information in the letters had affected him. "Yes," she said into the receiver.

The caller gave his name and identified himself as a dispatcher for the alarm company that monitored her shop. "We've had a signal from your place of business, ma'am, and we've sent the police to that address. We're calling to notify you that there may have been a break-in."

Kristina sighed, thanked the man, and hung up. Max was looking at her with raised eyebrows.

"That was somebody from the electronic security firm I

deal with," she said. "They've sent the police to my shop. It's probably just a false alarm, but I've got to go down there anyway."

Max laid the unfinished letter carefully on the coffee table and got to his feet. "Let's go," he said.

Kristina luxuriated in the knowledge that Max wanted to go with her, even though she knew it didn't necessarily mean anything. He was a nice guy, raised to be polite and considerate. Silently she blessed his parents—what fine people they must be.

"You don't seem very worried," he commented when, after helping her into her coat and donning his own, he opened the front door. It was tacitly agreed that they would take his Blazer, which was parked in the driveway beside her Mercedes. "About the shop, I mean."

Something was tugging at the edge of her mind, but she couldn't quite identify it. "Like I said, it's probably just a false alarm. And even if somebody did break in, everything is insured."

Max raised the collar of his coat. An icy breeze was blowing in from Puget Sound, and the promise of a rare Seattle snowfall darkened the eastern sky. "Money doesn't matter much to you, does it?" he asked, opening the Blazer's passenger door for her. There was no surprise in the question, and no criticism. Apparently he was just making conversation.

Kristina waited until he was behind the wheel before answering. "I've always had more than enough," she said.

"And what you wanted, you could conjure," he replied, backing carefully into the street.

"But I didn't," Kristina confessed. "Even in the early days, I wanted so much to be—well—normal."

Max shook his head and smiled. "A lot of us would have taken advantage of that kind of power," he said. "Weren't you ever tempted to strike back at Michael when he treated you so badly?''

Kristina considered for several moments, not weighing the answer because she knew that immediately, but deciding whether or not to make such a confession. ''I imagined a thousand sorts of vengeance,'' she said. ''Frankly, I've never been sure it wasn't my anger that finally finished him.''

Max glanced at her. A few fat flakes of snow wafted down from the burdened sky. ''Are you going to tell me about that?''

She bit her lip. ''You'll come to it in the letters,'' she said.

''Fair enough,'' Max answered.

They reached Western Avenue and the shop within a few minutes. There were two police cars parked out front, and Max tucked the Blazer neatly between them.

Kristina's uneasiness, barely the fragment of a shadow before, rose a notch or two and would not be denied. She got out of the car without waiting for Max to open the door and approached the front door of the shop, which was broken. Huge, jagged shards of glass littered the steps and the sidewalk.

There went the false alarm theory.

''I'm Kristina Holbrook,'' Kristina told the uniformed officer guarding the door. ''This is my store.''

He asked for ID, and she fumbled in her purse, found her driver's license.

The officer nodded, and both Max and Kristina entered the shop. There was almost no glass on the floor, and a quick sweep of the room revealed that very little had been disturbed. The cash register, an antique in its own right, had been slammed through the top of the jewelry counter, probably when the robbers discovered that it was empty.

A plainclothes detective approached, flashing his badge. "Ms. Holbrook? Detective Walters."

Kristina nodded in acknowledgment. Max said nothing, but he stood very close to Kristina, and she was grateful.

"We've got an odd case here, Ms. Holbrook," Detective Graham said. He was a clean-cut sort of guy, nice-looking and neatly dressed. "Looks like it was an inside job. You have any employees? Somebody who might have a key?"

Kristina thought of the glass on the sidewalk. Of course. The door had been broken from the inside. Her uneasiness grew, though she still couldn't pinpoint its cause, and bile burned the back of her throat. "No," she said. "I've always run the shop by myself."

"Any chance somebody could have hidden in here somewhere, when you closed up last night?"

"I wasn't here then," Kristina said, blushing a little. She didn't want to have to explain that she'd been with Max; that was precious and private.

Detective Walters didn't press. After all, one of the advantages of owning a business lies in setting one's own hours. "You having any financial problems, Ms. Holbrook?" he asked instead, in an almost bored tone of voice.

Kristina felt Max stiffen, willed him not to defend her. And at the same time relished the fact that he wanted to protest the implications of the policeman's question.

"No," she said. "I don't need the insurance money."

Walters had the good grace to look mildly embarrassed. "Have to ask, Ms. Holbrook. Fact is, it's an easy thing to check out anyway. Matter of a few strokes to a computer keyboard."

That didn't come as any surprise to Kristina. Her best friend, Valerian's Daisy, was a private detective, and Daisy had long since filled her in on just how easy it was to invade a person's privacy, with or without their knowledge. "I'd like to look around, if you don't mind," she said.

The detective produced a small notebook and a pencil stub from the pocket of his ski jacket. He was wearing jeans, a sweatshirt and sneakers, in lieu of the trench coat Kristina would have expected. "Here," he replied. "Make a list of everything that's missing, if you would."

It finally came to her then, what she had been fretting about ever since the telephone call from the security people had alerted her to the possibility of a robbery.

She headed directly for the back room, where she'd set the doorstop, the ugly brass monkey.

It was gone.

Kristina's knees sagged beneath her; Max caught her elbow in one hand and steered her to the little table nearby, where she took tea breaks in the mornings and afternoons. She sank into one of the cold folding chairs and laid her head on her arms, trembling.

Max touched her shoulder, then crouched beside her chair. "Sweetheart," he said softly. "What is it?"

"The brass monkey," she whispered miserably, turning her head to look into his concerned eyes. "Oh, God, Max—the doorstop is gone!"

"Did this piece have some special sentimental value?" Detective Walters asked, from the doorway. Kristina resented the intrusion, though she did not dislike the man himself.

How could she explain that one night, nearly a year before, a young man had entered the store, bent on rape and robbery, and she'd changed him into a brass doorstop? Obviously she couldn't—not until she and Max were alone, of course.

"Yes," she lied, making herself sit up straight, still dizzy. She knew she was wretchedly pale, and thought she might actually throw up. She hadn't known she was quite human enough to do that. "It wasn't valuable but I—I liked it." She turned imploring eyes to Max, who was still on his haunches beside her chair, watching her closely. "Would you please call my friend and ask her to come down here as soon as she can? Her name is Daisy Chandler." She gave Max the number.

"I'm afraid the perpetrator broke the telephones," Detective Walters said.

Of course. The thief—she'd never troubled herself to learn his name—would have been filled with rage when the spell wore off. It was a wonder he hadn't trashed the whole shop, or even come to Kristina's house to avenge himself. Her home address was printed on the personal cards she kept in her desk, among other places.

"I've got a cell phone in the Blazer," Max answered, and went out to get it.

"What about him?" the detective asked, cocking a thumb in Max's direction. "He have a key to this place?"

"No," Kristina said, unable to keep a note of annoyance out of her voice. "Max is the original solid citizen." She got up, filled a mug with water from the cooler, added a tea bag, and put the whole shebang into the microwave. Nausea roiled in her stomach and seared the back of her throat; maybe chamomile would soothe her nerves.

"Had to ask," Walters said. "Not much more we can do here, today at least. We'll write up a report and ask you to sign it. You probably should get somebody over to either replace that glass or board the place up."

Protecting the rest of her merchandise was the least of Kristina's worries. "Thank you," she said. She didn't exactly mean it, but that was the closest thing to sincerity she could manage at the moment.

Max returned as Walters and the others were leaving. "Daisy's on her way," he said. "While I was on the telephone, I called a friend of mine, a contractor. He'll see what he can do about the door."

Kristina had collected her tea from the microwave. She

made her wobbly way back to the table and sat down. She used both hands to raise the cup to her lips, she was still shaking so badly.

"Do you want to tell me what you meant by that remark about the doorstop?" Max asked when they had both been silent for some time. The police were gone, and a cold draft blew in from outside. Both Max and Kristina were still wearing their coats.

She shook her head. "When Daisy gets here," she promised. "I can't stand to tell it twice."

Max drew back the other chair and sat down across from her. "Daisy would be the woman who gave the Halloween party for the neighborhood kids. The one who keeps a white wolf for a pet and considers herself the wife of a vampire."

It might have been funny, so ludicrous was the situation, if it weren't for the fact that an angry robber and rapist had been turned loose. Kristina couldn't find it within herself to smile. "That's her. She's also a private investigator."

"Figures," Max said wryly. "Never let it be said that your friends and relations lead dull lives."

Kristina managed a ghost of a grin. "Before she came to Seattle, Daisy was a homicide detective in Las Vegas. The word *dull* is not in her vocabulary."

Max pushed his metal folding chair back on two legs, his arms folded, regarding Kristina in thoughtful silence for several seconds. "I'm almost afraid to ask this question," he began. "But what can Ms. Chandler do that the police can't? Isn't she mortal, just like them?"

Kristina let out a long breath. She nodded. "Daisy is quite human. She's also very, very good at what she does."

"And she, like you, has some very powerful allies."

"Yes," Kristina replied. She was counting on Valerian and perhaps Dathan for some aid and advice, but she didn't plan to bother either of her parents with the problem. Calder was doing important work of his own, and Maeve was occupied with the search for Gideon and Dimity.

"How about some more tea?" Max asked, seeing that Kristina's cup was empty.

"Are you always such a nice guy?" Kristina countered, surrendering her mug. "I keep expecting to find out something awful about you."

Max grinned as he dropped a tea bag into water and set the cup back in the microwave. "I leave dirty socks around sometimes," he confessed. "And I'm a sore loser at racquetball."

Kristina spread a hand over her upper chest in mock horror. "Oh, no."

Max leaned down, while the oven whirred behind him, and kissed Kristina lightly on the mouth. "I'm a long way from perfect, okay?"

Suddenly Kristina felt the weight of the ages settle on her slender shoulders. "Maybe," she admitted sorrowfully, "but there's a definition in the dictionary for what you are. I'm something that doesn't even have a name."

The microwave bell chimed; Max took the tea out and set it down in front of Kristina and dropped back into his chair across from her before grasping her hand. "You're a woman," he insisted quietly. "Trust me. I know."

A tear trickled down Kristina's cheek; she dashed it away with the back of her hand. Before she could say anything, however, there was a stir at the front of the shop and the sound of a familiar voice.

"Kris?" Daisy called. "Are you in here?"

"Back here," Kristina replied, rising shakily to her feet.

Max followed her into the shop, where Daisy stood near the broken counter, surveying the damage.

"What happened?" she asked. She was wearing jeans, a turtleneck sweater, hiking boots, and a baseball cap, and her adopted son, Esteban, was perched on her hip. He, too, was bundled against the cold, and his enormous brown eyes were wide as he looked around.

Kristina shoved her hands into the pockets of her coat. Max stood beside her. "You know Max Kilcarragh, don't you?" she asked, stalling.

Daisy nodded. "He came to the Halloween gig," she answered. "Hi, Max. How are the kids?"

"Great," Max replied with another grin. "How's the wolf?"

It was a rhetorical question; no one expected a reply, and Daisy didn't offer one. She was already prowling around the shop, looking at things, assessing the situation. Finally she turned to Kristina again. "Obviously the guy didn't break in, he broke out. What the hell happened here?"

Kristina led the way to the settee and chairs on the other side of the shop, where she and Max had sat talking on another occasion. Daisy took one of the chairs, Esteban settling against her chest and pushing a thumb into his mouth, and Max sat down beside Kristina, on the settee.

Slowly, quietly, Kristina told her friends about the night she'd turned the unwelcome visitor into a doorstop. She admitted that Valerian had warned her that the spell could wear off, and that she had always meant to do something about the thing, but she'd procrastinated.

Now it was only too obvious that the brass monkey had come back to life, torn the shop apart, and left.

"He'd be scared to bother you again, wouldn't he?" Max reasoned. His elbows were braced on his knees; he'd interlaced his fingers and rested his chin on extended thumbs.

Daisy sighed. "As a rule, these guys aren't real smart. That's one of the reasons they commit crimes—because they can't work out the cause-and-effect equation—i.e., 'If I knock off this convenience store, the cops are going to catch me if they can, and then I'll end up in prison.' They don't think beyond what they want at the moment."

Kristina shivered. She hadn't seen the last of her would-be assailant; he'd be back. And now her magic was so weak as to be almost nonexistent. Was she finally going to die, after a hundred and thirty years? And what if Max got in the thief's way, trying to protect her?

She covered her face with both hands and groaned. "Valerian warned me. I should have listened!"

"It's going to be okay," Daisy said. She sounded so certain. Daisy was that kind of person; she never seemed to doubt anything. "First of all, I'm going to bring Barabbas over to keep you company for a while. You could use a pet anyway. And when Valerian—" She glanced briefly at Max, then went on. "When Valerian wakes up, I'll ask him to find this guy."

Max took Kristina's hand and held it tightly between both his own. She felt strength and reassurance surge into her. She saw such love in his eyes that her heart ached with the effort to receive and contain it all.

"My folks could keep Bree and Eliette for a few more days—until this is resolved," he said. "In the meantime, I'll stay at your place. I don't want you alone, even with a wolf to protect you."

Kristina promptly vetoed the idea. "Not a chance, Max," she said. "I won't allow you to endanger yourself that way. Valerian will have some suggestions, and, besides, Barabbas is no ordinary wolf. He'll be a perfectly adequate bodyguard as long as I need one."

Daisy nodded in agreement, but said nothing. There was new respect in her eyes as she looked at Max.

"What are my options here?" Max demanded. "Where this lame-brained plan is concerned, I mean?"

"You don't have any," Kristina said. "If you refuse to let me do this my way, then I'll have no choice but to find this guy and confront him. I have to act, Max. I can't sit around and wait.''

A look of horror dawned in Max's handsome face. *"You expect this bastard to come to your house,"* he rasped.

''It won't go that far,'' Daisy interjected. But she was the only one who felt confident. She stood, easily lifting the now-sleeping child in her arms.

''How do you like motherhood?'' Kristina asked, desperate to change the subject. Max's friend, the contractor, had arrived. Max went to join him at the front of the shop, where the two men conferred about the broken door.

Daisy beamed and kissed the dark, silken hair on top of Esteban's head. ''I like it fine,'' she answered. ''Valerian is having fits, though—it upsets him that the little guy sleeps on the floor and hides food and stuff. You'd think in six hundred years he'd have learned some patience.''

''Not Valerian,'' Kristina said, with a wan smile. She was anxious to see the vampire again, although she knew a heated lecture was inevitable. He had warned her, after all, about casting frivolous spells and failing to follow up on them. ''What about your work as a PI? Are you going to give that up?''

Daisy shook her head. ''I'll be cutting back a little for a while, but I'm a career woman at heart,'' she said. ''We've hired a nanny, through one of those swanky agencies. She came from Brazil, so she speaks perfect Portuguese, as well as English, of course. And Valerian has given up his magic act in Vegas, at least for the time being.'' She paused and grinned mischievously. ''He'll come as quite a shock to the PTA once Esteban starts school, won't he?''

Kristina chuckled, grateful for a few moments of distraction from the new and difficult problem she faced. ''I just hope the nanny can deal with your—er—unconventional lifestyle.'' She thought of the loyal Mrs. Fullywub, who had worked for Kristina's parents for many years, and been fully aware that her employers were vampires.

Daisy shrugged. "Given what we're paying her, I doubt she'll ask all that many questions. Besides, we're not half as weird as some of the people you see on TV talk shows. Listen, I've got to go, but I'll have Barabbas at your place before the sun goes down, I promise. And you can expect a visit from Valerian, too, of course."

Kristina thanked her friend, and Daisy left.

Max introduced Kristina to the contractor, whose name was Jess Baker. Arrangements were made, and Jess prepared to board up the door, until it could be replaced with a new one the following day.

Back at Kristina's house, Max insisted that she sit in the Blazer until he'd gone through the whole place, room by room and closet by closet, to make sure it was safe. Finally he came to the door and signaled that she could come in.

"Are you sure you won't let me move in for a day or two?" he asked, helping her out of her coat.

"Positive," she answered. "Max, we can't keep seeing each other. It's too dangerous—"

He put his arms around her and drew her very close. "Just try to get rid of me," he replied, and kissed her.

Kristina lost herself, lost her troubles, in that sweet, brief contact. "Oh, Max," she said when it was over. "I need you to hold me, to make love to me."

"I think we can arrange that," he answered gruffly.

They went upstairs then, Kristina leading the way, returning to her room. The bed was still rumpled from their last encounter.

Slowly, garment by garment, savoring every moment, every stolen kiss, they undressed each other and lay together on the musk-scented sheets, having flung the covers to the floor. Beyond the windows snow fell, great, fat flakes swaying from side to side, taking their time.

Kristina was filled with a sense of peace, unwarranted as

that was, for while Max was touching her, kissing her, holding her, there was no sorrow in the universe, no pain or treachery or vengeance.

"I love you," she said on a breath as Max moved over her.

His body spoke eloquently, but he did not say the vital words, and even in her need, Kristina took note. And she grieved.

CHAPTER *13*

It was still snowing when nightfall came, and Valerian appeared soon after the earth had reached that crucial degree of turning, the white wolf at his heels. Max felt his hackles rise, but he wasn't sure whether it was the animal that provoked this primitive response in him or the vampire. He suspected there wasn't a whole lot of difference between the two of them—both were ferocious, both were cunning, both were wild, and, as hard as it was to admit, beautiful in a lethal sort of way.

There had been nothing particularly dramatic about their arrival, however—the vampire rang the front doorbell, and the wolf crouched at his heels. The animal's silver-white pelt glistened with flakes of snow; Valerian, too, wore a dusting of the stuff, glimmering in his shaggy chestnut hair and on the shoulders of his expensively cut overcoat. Both the wolf and the vampire studied Max with a hungry glint in their eyes, as though ready to pounce.

He stepped back to admit them. "Kristina is in the living room," he said, gesturing. He was sure Valerian knew the way, and that he had never bothered to ring the doorbell before. Popping in unannounced was more his style, according to Kristina.

The vampire stepped over the threshold and shed his coat in a graceful, shrugging motion, then handed the garment to Max, as though he were a footman or a butler. Amused rather than offended, and understandably fascinated, Max offered no protest.

The wolf, in the meantime, shook himself off in the middle of the entryway's Persian rug, then trotted, puppylike, toward the living room. Valerian gave Max a long, assessing look, then followed the beast.

Max hung up the coat, next to his own ratty ski jacket, and went to join the party.

Valerian stood with his back to the living room fire, which Max had built to a comforting roar, warming his hands. Kristina rested on an elegant Victorian chaise, the pages of an ancient manuscript spread across her lap. The wolf had taken his place on the floor beside her, strange blue eyes watchful, muzzle resting on paws as white as the snow drifting past the windows.

Max bent over Kristina and kissed the top of her head. "You're sure you don't want me to stay," he said. It wasn't a question really, but a statement. He hated the thought of leaving her, but she'd already made her wishes more than clear.

She looked up at him, touched his lips and then his chin with one index finger. Hours had passed since they'd made love, showered together, and gotten dressed again, but he still felt the aftershocks of passion deep in his groin.

"I'm sure," she said.

He met the vampire's gaze, which was level and patently unfriendly, then looked down at Kristina again. "You'll call if you need me?"

"I'll call," she promised, trying to smile. She was looking fragile again; Max wondered if their lovemaking had merely added to the strain of her other concerns, rather than lending comfort.

With a nod to Valerian, Max turned and left the room, collecting his coat and the gym bag containing his dirty clothes on the way out of the house. He sat in the Blazer for a long time before turning the key in the ignition, backing out of the driveway, and heading toward home.

"You've really done it this time," Valerian said when the front door closed behind Max. The vampire's nostrils were slightly flared, and Kristina knew he had had trouble containing his temper until they were alone.

Barabbas whimpered.

Kristina closed her eyes. She'd found the volumes she'd asked to borrow from Maeve's personal library waiting on her desk, when she and Max had come downstairs after making love, and searched the pages for a spell that would get her out of this mess. "How do you mean?" she asked with exaggerated innocence, finally making herself meet Valerian's furious glare. "By letting the doorstop come back to life, or by getting involved with Max Kilcarragh?"

"It's obviously too late to do anything about your infatuation with that mortal, and, as you pointed out the last time we talked, it would be hypocritical of me to condemn you for loving a human being." He paused, pacing along the edge of the hearth, striving hard to retain his composure. "Great Zeus, Kristina—I warned you about that damnable, silly spell, didn't I? Have you tried to find this—this doorstop of yours?"

Kristina bit her lower lip and nodded. "No luck," she said. She tapped the manuscript. "But I did come across an incantation that might turn him back into a brass monkey. At least for a little while, until we, or the police, can find him."

Valerian stopped his pacing and arched one eyebrow in plain contempt. "The *police*? What would you say to them, Kristina? That you changed a man into a doorstop in a moment of pique and now it's all come undone and he's on the streets, looking to commit mayhem and maybe murder?''

She shrank against the back of the chaise, properly chagrined. "Can't you find him?" she asked after a long, difficult silence and at a very heavy cost to her pride. "My powers are dwindling, but yours—"

He shook his head. "I have already tried. Something is veiling him from me—probably a warlock. And he may have powers of his own, this brass monkey of yours."

"He was an ordinary mortal!" Kristina protested. It was too horrible to think of that ghoul using magic.

"I have summoned Dathan," Valerian said, taking an exquisite pocket watch from his vest and flipping open the case. The soft, tinkling notes of a Mozart composition sprinkled the room, light as the evening snowfall. "If there are warlocks involved in this muddle, he'll know about it."

In virtually the next instant Dathan materialized, clad in kidskin breeches, a ruffled shirt, and a waistcoat. The rather dashing outfit was completed by a pair of high, gleaming black boots.

"Did we interrupt a costume party?" Valerian inquired archly.

Dathan was not amused. He dismissed the vampire with a sniff and turned to Kristina. "Have you come to your senses, my beloved?" he asked, taking one of her hands and brushing the knuckles with the lightest pass of his lips. "What a splendid pair we should make."

Valerian made a sound that rather resembled a snort. Another affectation, of course, for his lungs had not drawn breath since the Middle Ages. "How I hate to dash your hopes," he said with a complete lack of conviction, "but you're too late. Alas, our Kristina loves a mortal. I fear it's one of those eternal things, rather like my alliance with Daisy."

Dathan turned at last and leveled a look at his old adversary. Barabbas, who had been watching the warlock intently ever since his appearance, lifted his magnificent head and growled, making it abundantly clear whose side he would take if hostilities escalated.

"I hardly think you invited me here to tell me about Max Kilcarragh," Dathan told Valerian coldly, ignoring the wolf. "I know all about him, as it happens." Here the warlock paused and looked down at Kristina. "He's buried his heart with his dead wife, your Max. He might want very much to love you, but he is incapable of it. Contrary to the stage magician's assessment of the matter, Mr. Kilcarragh's soul mate was—and is—the mother of his children."

Kristina couldn't help remembering that she'd told Max that she loved him that very afternoon, in a most intimate moment, and that he hadn't answered in kind. Max was too honest to offer false vows. "Maybe you're right," she conceded. "In any case, I have other business with you. And it has nothing whatsoever to do with our bargain."

Dathan ran his gaze over her slender form. She was wearing a simple silk caftan of the palest ivory. "Why are you lying there like an invalid? Are you ill?"

Kristina sighed. She'd tried several of the spells she'd found in her mother's books over the course of the afternoon, hoping one of them would work on the escaped doorstop, and the effort had weakened her. The worst part, of course, was not knowing whether or not she'd succeeded.

"No," she said. "I'm just tired, that's all."

A charged silence ensued. Valerian was clearly holding his tongue, though his eyes glittered with malicious amusement, and Dathan actually flushed. No one needed to explain to Kristina that both of them knew what had happened between her and Max.

Kristina gathered the parchment pages of the ancient volume and set them carefully aside. Her relationship with

Max was her own damned business, and she resented both the vampire and the warlock for daring to have any opinion at all on the matter. Quietly, evenly, she explained about the intruder to her shop, telling Dathan how she'd transformed the miscreant into an inanimate object, intending to deal with him later. When the tale ended, Valerian spoke.

"Tell the truth," he said to the warlock, "if that's possible for you. Is any of this your doing?"

Dathan flung out his hands in a gesture of supreme exasperation. Again the wolf growled. "What would I have to gain by such a stunt?"

Valerian had a reply at the ready, as usual. "You could 'save' Kristina, thus painting yourself as a hero, perhaps hoping to win her heart. Brave warlock rescues fair damsel, etcetera, etcetera."

"You forget yourself, vampire," Dathan accused, glowering at Valerian. He was not afraid of Barabbas, probably because he could have broken the beast's neck with a simple motion of his hands. "You are the one who delights in high drama, not I."

"Do not provoke me," Valerian warned in a quiet voice that would have spawned abject fear in almost any other creature. "Kristina is in danger. Were it not for the possibility that you can be of assistance, I would just as soon see you bound in barbed wire and thrown into hell as look at you."

Kristina closed her eyes again. The room fairly crackled with animosity, and the tension was smothering.

"This is not helping," she said.

Valerian turned his back to Dathan and leaned against the fireplace mantel. The mirror above it did not show his reflection. The warlock drew a deep breath and let it out slowly, in an obvious bid for patience.

"I'm sorry, Kristina," Dathan said, putting just the mildest emphasis on her name, so that there would be no mistake, no suggestion that he was apologizing to the vampire. "Naturally, I will do whatever I can to help. And let me assure you—I've had nothing to do with any of this."

Kristina believed him; Dathan, though he could be devious when he chose, was also arrogant. He seldom questioned his own intentions and thus felt no need to disguise them. He was used to power; among warlocks, his word was law. "Can you find him?" she asked.

"I shall certainly try," he promised.

Valerian spoke again, in a more moderate tone than before, but with no greater affection. "Look among your own ranks," he said.

"I would offer you the same advice," Dathan replied. "Beginning with Benecia and Canaan Havermail."

Kristina felt a chill and exchanged glances with Valerian. Dathan had struck upon a possibility she had not considered. Perhaps the doorstop had not come back to life at all. Perhaps, instead, the little fiends had found out about the spell somehow and taken the brass monkey to use against Kristina, or simply to spite her. Benecia, after all, had been furious at Kristina's refusal to consider her as a bride for Dathan.

"I must feed," Valerian said. His magnificent face was utterly impassive; he would not allow the warlock the satisfaction of being right. "Then I shall find the demon babies and make them tell me what they know."

He crossed the room, ignoring Dathan as thoroughly as though the warlock had not been there at all, and bent to kiss Kristina's forehead. "Stay here," he commanded, and then he vanished.

Barabbas merely blinked; he was used to his master's comings and goings. But his fierce eyes followed Dathan closely as the visitor sank into a chair near Kristina's chaise.

"I am calling off our bargain," Dathan announced. "I want only one bride—you, Kristina."

"I don't love you."

The warlock closed his beautiful eyes for a moment, as though she'd struck him a physical blow. "I shall teach you to care for me, and make you queen of all my kind, male and female."

"I do not think witches would take kindly to a queen," Kristina said with a soft smile. "You yourself have told me that they are independent creatures. Besides, I have no wish to reign over anyone."

Dathan leaned forward, sitting now on the edge of his chair, his hands clasped together, his expression so earnest that it caused Kristina pain to look upon his face. "If I swore to keep your Max and his children safe, every moment of every day, until the natural end of their lives, would you agree?"

Kristina started to refuse, but as the implications of Dathan's words sank in, she held her tongue. This was no idle promise; Dathan surely had the power to do exactly that. As matters stood, *she* could offer them nothing but danger.

"It would be a sacrifice," Dathan said very softly. "I know that. But think of it, Kristina. Consider what it means."

She did not need to think, she knew. Just by coming into Max and the girls' lives, she had put them in mortal peril. By leaving them forever, and taking Dathan for a mate, she could undo that.

"I need some time," Kristina said. Her heart was already breaking.

Dathan nodded and rose. "I will make you happy," he vowed.

Kristina didn't respond. Her eyes were brimming with tears, and when she'd blinked them away, telling herself to be strong, Dathan was gone.

*   *   *

Valerian found Benecia and Canaan in a forgotten ceme-
tery, overgrown with weeds, behind the ruins of a church
in a Nevada ghost town. They were conducting one of their
bizarre moonlight tea parties. They had conjured an elegant
table, set with fine china and a gleaming silver service, and
arranged four chairs around it.

Each of them occupied one, of course, their tiny feet
dangling high off the ground in patent leather Mary Janes.
They wore starched dresses, rife with ruffles, and their hair,
as always, was done in gleaming ringlets. Their guests were
a mummified miner and a teenage hitchhiker, freshly
drained of her life's blood and staring mutely into eternity.

The relationship between Benecia and Valerian was not
particularly cordial, although Canaan appeared to bear him
neither rancor nor affection. Canaan was a self-absorbed
creature, concerned, in true vampire fashion, only with her
own pleasures. No doubt the hitchhiker had been her evening's kill. Benecia had probably fed elsewhere, since the
miner was nothing more than a husk, having been dead for
at least seventy years.

Benecia smiled sweetly, all the more horrible for her resemblance to an exquisitely made porcelain doll. "Valerian," she said.

Canaan looked at the newcomer with indifference and
returned to her one-sided conversation with the hitchhiker.

Valerian overturned the table without moving, scattering
the silver coffeepot, the sugar bowl and creamer, the costly
china cups and platters. The miner toppled off his chair,
and what was left of his head crumbled to dust. The hitchhiker teetered, but did not fall.

Canaan vanished in an instant, clearly a vampire who
believed that discretion was the better part of valor, but
Benecia drew back her perfect upper lip and snarled like
the vicious aberration she was. "How dare you?" she spat.

"I would dare considerably more, and you know it," Valerian replied, unruffled. Benecia was nearly as old as he, but he did not fear her. Not for himself, at least. "Do not try my patience, little beast—if there is one penance in all the universe that might keep me from the flames of hell, it is driving a stake through your brittle heart."

The demon-child's cornflower blue eyes glinted with hatred, but she did not advance upon him. "What do you want?"

"An explanation," Valerian replied. "What were you doing in Kristina Holbrook's shop last night?"

She stared at him in silence for a long time, her expression unreadable. Finally she laughed. "There was something I wanted."

"The brass doorstop," Valerian said.

Benecia smiled coyly. "Yes."

"Where is it now?"

"I shall never tell you that," she replied cheerfully, "no matter what you do to me."

Valerian knew she was telling the truth; the fact that she longed for the peace of death was at once her strength and her weakness. Driving a stake through her heart would be a favor at this juncture, and he was in no mood to be merciful.

"What do you want?" he asked, speaking as calmly as he could.

Benecia folded small, alabaster white arms. Her shell-like fingernails were tiny and pink, and she wore a frilly white pinafore over her beruffled dress. Valerian recalled an incident far in the past, when she and Canaan had placed all their dolls in little wooden coffins and buried them in a long-abandoned garden, like corpses.

Inwardly he shuddered, he who hunted human prey with the rise of every moon. The difference was that he rarely killed his quarry, but simply left them in a swoonlike state.

"But you know what I want," she taunted. "So why trouble to ask?"

"Answer me, damn you."

"I want to change the past," she said with a touch of defiance and—Valerian could hardly believe it—sorrow. "I want to grow up as a mortal, become a woman, marry, and have children. Give me that, vampire, and you shall have your ugly brass monkey."

Valerian did not speak. What she asked was impossible; vampires could travel no further back in time than the moment of their transformation from human to nightwalker.

"Those are my terms," Benecia said. And then she dissipated like thin fog, as her sister had done, leaving the ruins of her tea party behind her.

Valerian buried the hitchhiker and the miner and returned to Seattle, where he found Daisy seated in a rocking chair in the nursery, Esteban snuggled in her arms. They were both sleeping, and he did not awaken them.

Instead he stood silently in the shadows, understanding only too well what Kristina must be feeling, now that she had fallen so thoroughly in love with her mortal, Max Kilcarragh. Centuries of wandering, in an incessant cycle of finding his beloved and then losing her again, had marked Valerian's soul with loneliness so deep that the scars would probably never heal. Now he had found her, managed to break the curse that had torn them asunder so many times before, and he was truly happy.

With that joy, however, came a vulnerability unlike any he had ever experienced. Loving took so much courage, so much sacrifice. Always the knowledge was with him that one day, being mortal, Daisy would die. He, on the other hand, would look much as he did at that moment; he had not changed significantly in nearly six hundred years.

She opened her eyes, sensing his presence. Esteban

stirred but did not awaken. "Hello, handsome," she said. "What accounts for the frown?"

"I was thinking that I love you."

"Odd. Thoughts like that make most people smile."

"Most people grow old at the same pace. Daisy, I don't want to lose you—not now and not fifty years from now."

Esteban whimpered in his sleep, and Daisy began to rock the chair gently, one hand patting the boy's thin little back. "You're torturing yourself," she accused softly. "Eventually I'll die. Then I'll be born again as somebody else, and you'll find me, the way you always do. We're meant to be together."

"Suppose I *don't* find you?"

"Vampires are so neurotic," she teased. "Of course you will." Daisy's expression turned serious, and she studied her beloved mate closely. "Did you manage to track down Kristina's brass monkey?"

"Yes and no," Valerian replied, pacing, too restless to sit. He would have to go out again, for he had yet to feed, and his powers were at a low ebb. "Benecia Havermail was behind the robbery, and she's holding the thing hostage."

"Out of spite?"

"She wants to be mortal again."

"That's impossible, isn't it?" Daisy asked, frowning.

Valerian spread his hands. "Aidan Tremayne, Maeve's twin brother, was a vampire for well over two hundred years. Today he is flesh and blood again, with a wife, four children, and no memory whatsoever of his former existence."

Daisy nodded. "I remember now." She had heard the story long before; there were no secrets between the two of them. "If Aidan could be transformed, why not Benecia?"

"Aidan was basically good, and he had been made a

vampire against his will. Benecia, on the other hand, begged for the privilege and has been unabashedly evil ever since she became a blood-drinker.''

''And as a human being, she would still be evil?''

''Unspeakably so,'' Valerian agreed.

Daisy rose, carrying the little boy out into the entryway. At the base of the stairs Valerian took the child gently from her arms, and together they climbed to the second floor. Esteban's nursery was next to their own room; Valerian laid his adopted son gently in his crib. By morning, they both knew, the baby would have climbed over the rail and curled up on the rug in the center of the floor.

Daisy took her mate's hand and led him out of the nursery. The new nanny would arrive the next day; perhaps she could get through to Esteban, explain to him that he was safe now, that he need not fear being abused and neglected anymore.

''Go and feed,'' she said in the hallway.

Valerian nodded, resigned, and kissed her tenderly before taking his leave.

The sun had been up no more than five minutes when Dathan made his way down the circular stone steps to the crypts beneath the desecrated chapel on the Havermail's English estate. The parents of the two beautiful demons were nowhere about—Avery and Roxanne had gone their separate ways long before—but Benecia and Canaan lay side by side upon their beds of stone, immersed in the vampire sleep.

It would be so easy to destroy them, the warlock thought, and he had no compunction about taking their lives. Despite their innocent appearance, these were *not* sweet mortal children, but fiends of the worst order. A stake, an infusion of his own blood, or simply carrying them up the stairs to lie in the sunny courtyard, any one of those methods would suffice.

Only one thing stopped Dathan from killing them both, and that was the brass monkey. As he had suspected, and Valerian had later confirmed, Benecia knew where the thing was hidden, and she had probably confided in her sister.

He drew a steel dagger with a jeweled handle from the scabbard on his belt and for a few moments enjoyed the fantasy of plunging it through those callous little hearts, first one, and then the other. Granted, the doorstop would still be at large, but at the same time, one of Kristina's greatest fears would be allayed: the Kilcarragh mortals would be safe from this pair of monsters.

No chance of Kristina becoming his mate if that happened.

Dathan wasn't prepared to be quite that noble.

He smiled. He could, however, let both Benecia and Canaan know that they were not invulnerable, despite their highly developed vampire powers.

Using the point of the dagger, Dathan pricked his finger and let a drop of blood fall first upon Benecia's barely parted lips, then upon Canaan's. It was not enough to finish them, more's the pity, but when they awakened at nightfall, they would know they had been visited by a powerful enemy. The message could not have been clearer: *Beware, for I, the warlock, have found you.*

Reluctantly Dathan then resheathed his blade and left the tomb.

Within moments of awakening that night, Calder Holbrook went out to feed. He was back in his laboratory, going over the results of Kristina's blood test for perhaps the hundredth time, before an hour had passed.

Hunting, a delightful sport to many vampires, was a troublesome task to him, to be attended to and forgotten as soon as possible. Maeve relished her powers, her adventures, her singular challenges as queen of the nightwalkers. Calder, on the other hand, got all the excitement he needed just loving Maeve and working on his experiments.

That night, however, he was deeply troubled.

Maeve appeared, looking flushed from a recent feeding, just as the small clock on his desk was chiming half past two.

Calder turned from his microscope to kiss her. As always, the old passion surged between them, undiminished by the passage of many, many years. Before the night was over, he knew, they would make love.

"Any luck finding Dimity?"

Maeve shook her head, her blue eyes probing deeply into his, exploring his heart. "What is it, Calder?" she pressed gently. "I know you're upset—I can sense it."

He looked away for a moment. It was difficult, just knowing what he knew. Telling Maeve, and finally Kristina, would be much worse. "Sit down," he said, indicating a nearby stool.

Maeve obeyed, her gaze fixed on his face. "Tell me."

"It's about Kristina," he began, standing before his mate, resting his hands on her shoulders. "I've—well, I took a blood sample from her, because she said she hadn't been feeling well. Maeve, she is undergoing some kind of genetic transformation."

"What does that mean?" Maeve demanded. She was rigid with anguish; like Calder, she cherished their child.

He hesitated a moment, but there was no gentle way to say it. "Kristina is aging. Her blood cells are virtually indistinguishable from those of a mortal."

Tears glimmered along Maeve's dark lashes. Her indigo eyes were wide with horrible understanding. "She's dying?"

Calder struggled against his own emotions. "Yes," he said finally.

During the night the snow melted away, and Sunday dawned gray and murky in Seattle. Barabbas lay curled at the foot of Kristina's bed, apparently taking his guard-dog duties very seriously.

"What do you eat, anyway?" she asked him. "Besides little girls making their way through the woods to Grandmother's house, I mean."

Barabbas made a sorrowful sound.

"You're right," Kristina admitted. "It wasn't a very good joke. Come on—maybe there's a steak in the freezer."

She put on a robe and slippers, because the house was especially cold, and led the way down the rear stairs into the kitchen. After thawing out a top sirloin for the wolf, Kristina poured herself a bowl of cereal and curled up on the family room couch to eat.

She had just finished when Max pulled into the driveway in his Blazer.

"I should have called first," he said when Kristina opened the front door to him, "but I was afraid you would tell me to stay away."

She pulled him inside, closed the door, and then threw her arms around his neck. "Not a chance," she replied.

Barabbas stood in the doorway leading to the dining room, making a low growling sound.

"Hush," Kristina scolded. "It's only Max."

Apparently satisfied, the wolf turned and padded away.

"Did you sleep last night?" Max asked, holding Kristina in a loose but tantalizing embrace.

"Did you?" Kristina countered, smiling a little.

"You know damn well I didn't," he retorted somewhat grumpily. "All I could think about was that creep, the exdoorstop, out there somewhere, dreaming up ways to get to you.'' He kissed her forehead. ''Let's get out of here for a while. Take a drive or something.''

The idea sounded wonderful to Kristina, who was beginning to feel like a prisoner. ''What about Barabbas?''

''He can stay here,'' Max answered, giving Kristina a little nudge toward the stairs. She needed to get dressed, of course, before they could go anywhere.

At the base of the stairway she paused and looked back at Max with a mischievous smile. ''I believe you're jealous of him,'' she teased.

Max shoved a hand through his hair. ''Maybe you're right,'' he answered in all seriousness. ''After all, the wolf got to stay here and watch over you last night. I happen to regard that as my job, not his.''

Kristina shook her head. ''Males,'' she muttered, and hurried up the stairs to get ready for the day.

When she came back down half an hour later, clad in black corduroy jeans, a heavy gray sweater, and lightweight hiking boots, Max was sitting in the living room on a hassock. Barabbas faced him, seated on the hearth rug.

They were staring at each other, man and beast, and Kristina wondered who would have looked away first if she hadn't entered the room when she did.

CHAPTER 14

Bree Kilcarragh took in her surroundings with wonder. Grandmother and Aunt Gweneth said the place was called a flea market, though she had yet to spot even one bug. All she could see was a lot of strange stuff, displayed on shaky tables and in booths.

She tugged at Eliette's hand, while Grandmother and Aunt Gweneth stopped to examine a pair of salt and pepper shakers made to look like little toilets. "Why would anybody want to buy a flea?" she asked in a loud whisper.

Eliette rolled her eyes. She was older and wiser, and she never missed a chance to let Bree know it, either. "That just means there's a lot of junk to buy," she whispered back.

Grandmother turned and smiled at them. It was warm in the large building, so Bree and Eliette didn't have to wear their coats. "Getting tired?" she asked.

Both girls shook their heads vigorously. Although they missed their daddy, they liked staying with their grandparents, and today was extra special because Aunt Gweneth was with them.

"It's almost Christmas," Aunt Gweneth said. "I've got to find something really ugly for Max."

Allison Kilcarragh, also known as Grandmother, smiled. She was so pretty, Bree thought, with her nice clothes and shiny gray hair. "Good heavens, Gwen," she replied, "it isn't even Thanksgiving yet."

Gwen laughed. "I know it seems crazy to you, Mom, but Max and I get a big kick out of our little gift-giving tradition. I think he'd be disappointed if I didn't give him something really awful." She gasped suddenly and strode toward a long wooden table crowded with what looked to Bree like a lot of dirty, twisted metal. "I can't believe it!" Gwen cried, homing in on the weirdest statue Bree had ever seen. "It's an exact duplicate of the doorstop at Kristina's."

Allison made a *tsk-tsk* sound and shook her head. "That is *dreadful*," she said.

Bree agreed, and wondered what Eliette thought.

"It's a valuable piece," said the man behind the table. He had hair sprouting from his ears and his nose, and Bree instinctively took a step backward.

"Strange," Gwen murmured. "The thing feels warm to the touch."

Bree looked at the monkey and wished her aunt wouldn't buy it. Gwen was already rummaging in her purse for her wallet, though.

"How much?" she asked.

"Fifty bucks, plus tax," replied the hairy man. He was dirty, too, and smelled bad. He wasn't like the other people who were selling things behind tables; they all looked pretty ordinary to Bree.

"Thirty-five," Gwen countered.

"Oh, Gweneth," Allison groaned.

But the deal had been made. Aunt Gwen paid the man, and he put the monkey in an old Nordstrom bag and handed it over.

Eliette and Bree looked at each other, imagining the doorstop under their tree on Christmas morning. Bree didn't know why, exactly, but she was scared. She wanted her daddy. And she wanted to leave the ugly monkey right there at the flea market.

Some days, though, you just can't make a wish come true, even if you've been very, very good.

"Don't you tell your father about this," Aunt Gweneth warned her nieces, her eyes dancing with happy mischief as she looked down at them. "I want it to be a surprise."

Bree had no doubt that it would be. This thing was even worse than the moosehead—she just hoped she and Eliette wouldn't have to play this stupid game when *they* grew up.

It was dark when Kristina and Max returned from their ride—they'd gone exploring in the nearby Cascade Mountains, and had made reservations at a secluded lodge for the following weekend. At that high altitude, the snow was deep and white, perfect for shaping into powdery balls and flinging at each other. They'd built a snowman and eaten a hot meal in a roadside restaurant before making the inevitable descent back to the real world.

After a stop at a neighborhood supermarket where Kristina bought a huge bag of dog food for Barabbas, Max drove her home. The wolf met them at the door, making that mournful sound in his throat, wanting to go out. Kristina didn't try to stop him.

Max carried the kibbles into the kitchen, then made the rounds of the house, in case of lurking bogeymen, as he had after the robbery. This time Kristina accompanied him.

"I wish I could stay," he said twenty minutes later, when Barabbas was back inside and munching down on the dog food. Max had built a cozy fire in the family room, and now he stood beside the kitchen door, holding Kristina's chin in his hand.

"Eliette and Bree are probably watching for you," she said.

He nodded. "I've missed them."

Kristina envied him for a moment, this man she so deeply—and so hopelessly—loved. What a glorious blessing it must be, to have children, eagerly awaiting your return, ready to fling themselves into your arms out of sheer joy. She stood on tiptoe and kissed him.

"It was a wonderful day, Max. Thank you."

He touched the tip of her nose. "Keep next weekend open for me," he said. "And if you need anything, if you're scared, either call me or come straight to my place. No matter what time it is. Understood?"

Kristina rested her head against his shoulder for a moment. The cloth was chilly and still smelled pleasantly of mountain air, fir trees, and snow. "Understood," she said softly. But she had no intention of involving Max in her problems if she could avoid it. Only sheer selfishness had kept her from breaking off their relationship already.

Soon she would have to do just that.

Max kissed her again, this time with a thoroughness that left her swaying on her feet, said goodnight, and went out. A moment later she heard his voice from the other side of the door.

"Turn the deadbolt and put the chain on, Kristina."

Dutifully Kristina complied, though she knew it was a case of whistling in the dark. With the possible exception of the brass monkey-man, all her enemies were impervious to locks.

So were her friends and relatives, for when Kristina turned around, Maeve was standing a few feet behind her. The white wolf stood at her side, as though she were his mistress.

Kristina was surprised to see her mother, given the Gideon-Dimity crisis. When her father stepped out of the shadows as well, her incredulity gave way to a stomach-fluttering fear. They had come to tell her something, and it wasn't good news.

"What?" she whispered.

Calder took Kristina's arm and guided her into the living room, where there was no fire burning. He seated her in a chair, while Maeve settled herself in its counterpart.

Calder remained standing, too agitated to sit.

"You have often told us that you wished to be human," he said.

Kristina's heartbeat quickened. She sat up a little straighter in the chair and waited, still fearful, but beginning to hope. "Yes," she answered in a shaken whisper.

Out of the corner of her eye she saw that Maeve was weeping, silently and with dignity, but weeping, just the same.

"I have examined your blood sample over and over again," Calder went on. "I have performed numerous tests, including a DNA analysis." He paused, his dark gaze fixed upon his only surviving daughter, and Kristina remembered that he had lost a child years ago, a little girl born of his first wife. "You are aging, Kristina. For all practical intents and purposes, you are mortal."

At this Maeve covered her face with both hands and sobbed softly. She, too, had lost a loved one—her brother, Aidan, had forsaken the world of vampires to become a man again.

Kristina felt several conflicting emotions—sorrow, joy, fear, exhilaration. To be mortal! "I will die someday," she said.

Calder stood beside Maeve's chair, his hand resting on his mate's trembling shoulder. "Yes," he replied. His voice, though steady, was fractured as well.

"When?"

"I don't know," Calder answered, in his forthright way.

"The process has begun—there's no telling how long it will take."

Kristina was still for a while, absorbing that, considering the ramifications. Her mother's sobs subsided as Maeve gathered her composure.

"That's why my magic has been so unreliable," Kristina mused. It was something of a relief, knowing she had no reason to blame herself. She hadn't neglected her natural gifts after all, but simply lost them.

"You could, of course, be transformed into a vampire," Calder said. "But both your mother and I know that would not be your wish."

"You're right," she answered distractedly. That life, with all its privileges and powers, was not for her.

It was a strange feeling, knowing for certain that she would one day die. She would be subject to all sorts of human ailments—head colds, sore feet, weight gain. "Do you—do you think I can bear children?" She had never menstruated, but perhaps she would start. Perhaps she could be fertile after all.

Maeve and Calder exchanged a tender look, and finally, tentatively, Maeve smiled. "If I did," she reasoned, "I see no reason why you couldn't."

Kristina had been in shock ever since the startling announcement had been made; now she realized what it meant to her parents, and she was filled with love and compassion for them.

"I won't separate myself from you, the way Uncle Aidan did, if that's what you're thinking," she said gently. "I love you too much."

Calder's eyes glistened suspiciously. "We would have watched over you in any case," he said. "Ours is a selfish grief, no lighter for the fact that we share it."

"Because I will die one day," Kristina said. She rose from her chair to embrace her father, then her mother. "Be happy for me," she pleaded softly, looking from one of her parents to the other. "This is what I want, what I've dreamed of as long as I can remember. I have no wish to live forever."

Maeve laid cool hands to either side of her daughter's face. "There is much of Aidan in you," she said. "You are wiser than I, and not so greedy."

"Do you fear death, Mother?" Kristina asked quietly. She had always wondered, but never quite dared to ask.

The queen of vampires considered. "Yes," she said. "I was raised, as a mortal, in an eighteenth-century convent, and the concept of eternal damnation is as real to me as the sky overhead and the earth below."

"And what about you, Papa?" Kristina inquired, turning to Calder.

"I have seen hell," he said. "It is called war, and it exists not in some subterranean realm, but right here on earth."

Kristina went back to her chair and fell into it. She wanted to weep, and at the same time to shout for joy. She might live another fifty years, or awaken with white hair and fragile bones one morning next week.

"What am I going to do?" she whispered.

Maeve stood beside her and laid a gentle hand to her hair. "Live," she said. "Make the most of every moment."

"But I could die tomorrow!"

"Just like any other mortal," Calder put in quietly.

At that, Maeve and Calder joined hands and, without another word, disappeared.

Barabbas laid his large head in Kristina's lap and whined sympathetically. She stroked him, staring into an uncertain future, wondering whether to celebrate her newly discovered status as a woman or to mourn. After an hour or so, still undecided, she went upstairs to get ready for bed.

In the morning she awakened early, with cramps.

At the age of one hundred and thirty, Kristina Holbrook was having her first period. She rolled over onto her side, drew up her knees, and groaned. She'd never expected it to hurt.

After a few minutes wholly dedicated to wretched suffering, she groped for the telephone and punched in Daisy's home number. With any luck at all, her friend would still be there, and not out solving a case.

"Hello," chimed the voice Kristina most wanted to hear.

"Help," Kristina moaned. "I'm human."

"What?" Daisy sounded alarmed, and who could blame her. It had been a strange thing to say.

"I'll explain later," Kristina managed to gasp. "I have the worst cramps—this has never happened to me before—"

"I'll be right over," Daisy said. "Will the housekeeper from hell let me in?"

"She's off this week. Use the spare key," Kristina murmured. "It's under the ceramic frog by the back porch."

"Great security," Daisy scoffed, but with gentleness. She obviously understood what Kristina was feeling and empathized. "Listen—just give me a few minutes to get Esteban settled with the new nanny, then I'll make a quick stop at the drugstore and come right over."

Kristina choked back a whine. If this was what being mortal was all about, maybe it wasn't so terrific and fulfilling after all. "Hurry," she whispered.

"Sometimes a warm bath helps," Daisy offered, and then hung up.

She arrived within half an hour, but to Kristina it felt more like all sixteen years of the FDR Administration, complete with retrospectives. She was still lying in a fetal position in the middle of the bed, clutching her abdomen and gritting her teeth.

"This stuff usually works," Daisy said, ripping the cellophane off a blue and white package. She had a brown paper bag with her, too, but she went into the bathroom, filled a glass with water, and returned. Two pills rested on her outstretched palm. "Swallow these and try to relax. Tension only makes it worse."

Kristina sat up, took the tablets, and swallowed them.

"What's going on here?" Daisy asked, settling into Kristina's reading chair.

She received a baleful look in reply before Kristina said, "Last night my parents broke some startling news to me. I'm completely mortal. And this morning, I woke up with the proof."

Daisy interlaced her fingers and sighed. She wasn't wearing her baseball cap, but otherwise she was dressed in the usual casual-camp way. "Nobody ever said it was easy being human," she pointed out. "Especially being a *female* human." She reached for the brown bag with the pharmacy logo printed on its side and tossed it to Kristina. "Here— you'll have to figure these out for yourself."

Kristina looked inside, saw a box of tampons, and groaned again, flinging herself back onto her pillows. Twenty minutes later the pills had worked, and the tampons were in their place on a bathroom shelf. Daisy returned from downstairs where she'd prepared a pot of herbal tea and toasted a couple of English muffins.

"Feeling better?"

Kristina nodded sheepishly. This was an experience most mortal women endured month in and month out, and she'd carried on as though she were having an appendectomy with no anesthetic. She had a new respect for the female of the human species. "Thanks, Daisy."

Daisy grinned. "After you've knocked back some of the tea and wolfed down a muffin, you should get up and move around as much as you can. Get dressed and take Barabbas out for a walk or something."

"I should go down to the shop."

"Why? Isn't there a construction crew there, fixing the door and replacing the glass in the jewelry counter?"

"Yes," Kristina said. "And I want to make sure things are going okay."

"You've heard, of course, that it was Benecia who took the brass monkey?"

Kristina *hadn't* heard exactly, though Dathan had presented the theory, the night of the robbery, when both he and Valerian were squared off in her living room. They'd all but bared their fangs.

She wondered why the warlock had not come to her with the trophy, the ugly doorstop, as soon as he'd retrieved the thing. It wasn't like Dathan to miss an opportunity to score a point, especially when there was something he wanted in return. "I hadn't heard," she said softly. "Who told you?" The question was a formality, escaping her lips before she'd thought.

"Valerian, of course. Dathan couldn't resist letting him know that a warlock had succeeded where a vampire could not."

Kristina's heart, now all too mortal, was hammering against the base of her throat. "Where is it—he—the monkey, I mean?"

Daisy's gaze was solemn. "Benecia refused to tell. She means to use it against you, if she can."

Kristina set her tea tray on the bedside table and leaned back against her pillows. "How did Dathan respond to that?"

"He was enraged, of course, but he dared not destroy the little demon because the knowledge of the doorstop's whereabouts would go with her. I suspect he found their lairs, Benecia and Canaan's, I mean, and gave them a sample of warlock blood. According to Valerian, everyone in the vampire world heard their wails of fury when they awakened, deathly ill. They had probably been fed just enough to serve as a warning of Dathan's vengeance. Let's hope they are wise enough to heed it.''

Although she still felt a little dizzy, Kristina's pain was mostly gone. She got out of bed, somewhat shakily. She would take a shower, get dressed, and concentrate as hard as she could on summoning the warlock. Max and his children were in more danger than ever before, now that Kristina, too, was mortal and had no magical means to protect them.

Daisy touched her arm. "I'll check on you later. Right now I've got to see how Esteban is making out, then make a run downtown to the agency.''

"Thanks for everything,'' Kristina said, mildly embarrassed that, at her age, she'd had to have the basics of menstruation explained to her.

When she'd showered and dressed, again in jeans, with sneakers and a blue cable-knit sweater to complete the outfit, Kristina hurried downstairs. The bottle of pills Daisy had brought were clasped in her right hand; if the pain came back, she wanted to be ready.

She had barely sat down at the family room table and set herself to concentrating on Dathan's arrival when he appeared. Kristina realized, with a touch of sadness, that it was his magic that had alerted him to her need, and not her own. Hers was gone, and she was going to miss it, even though she'd wished it away for as long as she could remember.

He was dressed like a gentleman who has just attended the opera, most likely one in the eighteenth or nineteenth century. He sported a short cape, a gleaming black top hat, and very elaborate shoes, with ornate buckles and square heels. Like vampires, warlocks were facile at time travel.

Dathan approached Kristina, hardly sparing a glance for Barabbas, who gave a low, throaty growl but did not rise from his resting place on the hearth rug. Taking her hand and sweeping off his top hat in the same grand gesture, Dathan placed a warlock's kiss on her knuckles. She withdrew rather abruptly.

"Why didn't you tell me, instead of Valerian, what you had found out about Benecia Havermail?"

"Because I could not present you with a fait accompli, my dear," Dathan said, looking and sounding surprised that anyone would question his judgment. "A situation is not resolved until it is—well—*resolved.*"

Kristina lowered her head, thinking of Max, of the way he laughed, the way his eyes told her so much of what was in his mind, the way he made love to her. As though she were a goddess, powerful and worthy of worship, and yet fragile, too. She must give him up and make her way alone, as she had always done.

Dathan curved a finger under her chin and raised her face to look deep into her eyes. "You are so troubled, beloved," he said with inexpressible tenderness. "Why? I will protect your Max, as I promised to do, even though it breaks my heart to know how you love him."

She was surprised again; Dathan, for all his intuitive powers, hadn't discerned that she'd changed and become as mortal as her lost Uncle Aidan. When she told him the truth, he would no longer want her for his bride and queen—a fact that came as something of a relief.

"Yes," Kristina said. "I do love Max, very much."

"But someday—"

"No," she interrupted, shaking her head. "Dathan, I have no powers. I am mortal."

"Nonsense."

"It's true. It's part of the reason I've bungled so many spells lately. My magic is gone. I am a woman, and nothing more."

The warlock's face was not crestfallen at this news, as

Kristina had expected, but translucent with some inner joy. "Even better! The mating of a warlock and a mortal—"

"Cannot be that unusual," Kristina said, losing patience. While she didn't relish the prospect of spending the rest of her life, whatever was left of it, alone, she wasn't about to settle for a mate she didn't love, just to have someone to call her own.

Not that any woman could ever call a warlock her own. Like vampires, they were fickle creatures—Valerian and her parents were the only nightwalkers of her acquaintance who remained faithful to their romantic companions. Though when Daisy was between lifetimes, Valerian had certainly been known to engage in a variety of affairs of the heart.

"I think," Dathan said, "that I should take my leave now, and return when you are in a better mood."

"That," Kristina responded, "would be wise. Only don't bother to come back if you're going to hound me about marrying you, because I won't."

Dathan sighed forlornly, spread his elegant cape like black wings, and was gone.

Kristina walked Barabbas around the block—there was a scent of snow in the air again—and then took him back to the house and shut him up inside. A few minutes later she was in her Mercedes, driving downtown to her shop.

The door had been replaced, and Max's friend and two of his helpers were just finishing the repairs to the jewelry counter. The floor had been swept, and as Kristina moved among the familiar antiques, she told herself she could open for business that afternoon, or in the morning at the latest.

She wondered how long it would be, though, before Benecia and her sister returned to wreak more havoc. And where was the brass doorstop? Would he turn up one night, standing over Kristina's bed, a knife in his hand?

She shivered. Barabbas was there to protect her, of

course, but she couldn't depend on a wolf forever. Besides, the animal belonged to Daisy and Valerian; it's rightful home was with them.

Maybe, Kristina thought sorrowfully, it was time to close down her shop and go traveling again. She could simply wander from place to place, the way she'd done after Michael's death. The world had changed a great deal since the days of steamer trunks and great ocean liners; countries had new borders and new names.

There were other differences, too. She was deeply in love, and on this journey she would not have unlimited time. Every moment, every heartbeat and breath, was now infinitely precious.

Max telephoned that night, and he didn't suggest getting together. That was fine with Kristina, because she wasn't ready to tell him about her mortality. He might see the change in Kristina as a reason to rejoice, but she knew it was a very mixed blessing.

"You're okay, right?" he asked. She heard cupboard doors opening and closing, pans clanking. The man was decent to the core, a wonderful lover, and he could cook in the bargain. Amazing. "No creepy stuff has been happening?"

Kristina bit her tongue. It was all in how you defined "creepy stuff," and she didn't want to enlighten him. She needed more of those anti-cramp pills, a warm bath, and a good night's sleep. "Barabbas makes a pretty good bodyguard," she said after a few moments.

"You'll call if you need me?"

"Yes," Kristina promised. She was beginning to wonder, though, if Max had decided she was too much trouble, with all her weird relatives and White Fang for a pet. It would be easier all around if he dumped her, right then, but she found herself braced against his rejection all the same. "I'll call."

He destroyed her theory in the next sentence. "Thursday is Thanksgiving," he said. "My mother is putting on her usual feast, and she's asked me to invite you. Not that I didn't want to, of course." More pan clattering, a brief aside to one of the children, something about fishing somebody named Barbie out of the aquarium. "Will you come with us, Kristina?"

"I'd be happy to," she said, then closed her eyes against a rush of tears. Why, *why* had she agreed, when she knew it was a terrible, even dangerous, mistake to draw the situation out any further? She had already let things go too far.

"It's a long weekend," Max continued, making matters worse. "The kids usually stay with my folks, and you and I do have that reservation at the lodge up in the mountains."

Kristina had completely forgotten that, with all that had happened since. "Maybe you shouldn't be away from Bree and Eliette, over the holidays, at least. I know it sounds silly, but I didn't realize Thanksgiving was coming up so soon."

No pot clanging, no muttered instructions to the kids.

"Don't say no, Kristina," he said. "My daughters aren't being neglected—they *always* spend that weekend with my parents."

Heaven help her, she didn't want to refuse. She yearned to be alone with Max, making love, talking in front of a fire, playing in the snow. The way things stood, that might be the last true joy she ever experienced.

"All right, I'll go," she promised very softly. She would give herself, and Max, that one glorious interlude together, and then she'd do what she should have done long before and put an end to the relationship. She'd tell Max she was selling the store, leaving Seattle and never coming back, and she fully intended to keep her word.

"Pick you up at noon on Thursday?" There was a smile in Max's voice; it warmed Kristina and eased the ache in her heart just a little.

"I'll be ready," she said, silently calling herself every sort of fool.

Then, after taking two more of Daisy's pills, she ate an early dinner, took a brief bath, and crawled into bed with the stack of letters she and Max had been working their way through together. She supposed she should have waited, but that night, it seemed, nothing had the power to distract Kristina from the gloomy future but the past. The days of yesteryear, while grim in their own right, had one advantage on the years to come—they were over.

. . . Michael was inconsolable after his father's death; he blamed himself for both his parents' passing, I think, though he never admitted as much to me. He would have said even less to Gilbert, who represented everything Michael himself was not and could never be—he was good, strong, steady. Even handsome, though in a less fragile way than Michael.

Late that summer Gilbert brought me a strange and magnificent gift, a little baby swaddled in rough blankets. He explained that the poor little mite was a foundling, that his mother had given birth to him beside one of the roads passing through the estate, and had perished there.

I was filled with yearning, for while I had put my own powers firmly out of mind, I was certain that I could not bear an infant of my own. Yes, of course, my mother, a vampire, had brought me forth in quite a normal fashion, but I was an oddity and I knew it. Here was a helpless, needy child that I could love, dote upon, educate.

I felt as though I had been drowning and someone had

flung out a rope, that I might catch hold and be saved.

I recall that Gilbert looked at me, and at the child, with the most moving tenderness glowing in his eyes. "I wish things had been different, Kristina," he said, and that was all.

But I knew what he meant. That we might have been together, as husband and wife, and produced babes of our own. He did not know the truth about me, though Michael did, by then, and had reviled me for it often.

I might have known how my husband would react to the introduction of a foundling into the household, although it was rightfully Gilbert's estate, and not his own. He called the infant a bastard—true no doubt, but surely not the fault of the child and very probably not even the fault of its mother—and ordered me to send him away.

I refused, and Michael tormented me day and night. Then one morning, when Gilbert was away in London, my husband confronted me yet again, in a drunken rage. We were standing at the top of the main stairway leading down into the great hall of Cheltingham Castle—great Zeus, Phillie, why did I challenge him then? And why there?

I had named the baby Joseph and engaged a nurse for him, and I already loved him as much as if I'd given birth to him myself. And so, in a moment of temper, I told my husband I would sooner give him up than the child.

He backhanded me then, did Michael, and I went sailing down the stairs, end over end. Had I not been what I was, I would surely have perished, and even so I suffered incapacitating injury. When I awakened, Joseph had been taken from the house, and my searching, however frantic, was fruitless.

I can write no more just now. I know you understand.

CHAPTER 15

The next of the many letters Kristina had written to Miss Eudocia Phillips, her former governess, was dated nearly six months after the one in which Michael had engineered the disappearance of Kristina's adopted child. Even after all this time, remembering made Kristina's heart ache, for no amount of searching had turned up even a trace of the baby boy, Joseph.

Not then, at least.

. . . Your letters have brought me so much comfort, Phillie. You would tell me, wouldn't you, if you found the story too burdensome, too full of sorrow, and could not bear the telling?

When last I wrote, I told you how Michael had taken my son from me, and struck me when I confronted him for what must have been the thousandth time. The wounds I suffered when I fell down the stairs were insignificant compared to what that final treachery did to my spirit. I was destroyed and could no longer endure living under the same roof with Michael Bradford.

Still, I had cracked several ribs in my fall and could not travel, so I had no choice but to remain at Chel-

tingham, at least until I'd recovered. Michael, in the way I have since learned is typical of such men, was immediately contrite, as solicitous as any husband might have been in the circumstances—rushing down the stairs, shouting that a doctor must be sent for, soothing me and stroking my hand as we waited. I lay there at the base of the stairs, beyond anguish, with servants hovering about, for Michael had decreed that I must not be moved until the village physician had examined me.

How ludicrous it seems that Michael should be my caretaker, my constant companion, when he had been the one to do me hurt in the first place. I despised him and wanted him to go from my sight, not just then but forever, but he would not leave me; even after I was carried to a downstairs bedchamber, where my ribs were bound and I was given laudanum to ease my pain. In some ways, Phillie, that was the greater torture, his continued and doting presence. The drug numbed my flesh but could not reach the anguish in my soul.

Michael held my hand. He stroked my hair. He said he was sorry and swore he had never meant to do me any harm. I believe he meant what he said, as he was saying it, but I hated him as I have never hated anything or anyone before.

"Tell me where Joseph is," I said. I thought one good thing might come out of Michael's remorse, at least— that I might learn the whereabouts of my foster child. When I had sufficiently recovered, I meant to fetch the boy from wherever he was being kept, and then put Cheltingham behind me forever. I would miss no one there, except for Gilbert.

I hoped that my parents and Valerian would come to me at last, once I had truly separated myself from Michael. I felt an almost inexpressible yearning to see them again, but I confess I was embittered, too—quietly furi-

ous that they had refused to step in when I needed them so much. Knowing that they had good reasons, and that the decision was a difficult one for them, was of no consolation then.

Michael hesitated a long time before answering my question about Joseph's whereabouts. Then, the very picture of compassion, he said, "You must cease your fretting over the brat, Kristina darling. We shall make our own babies."

I turned my head upon the pillows; I could not bear to look at him. And I was wiser now; I knew better than to let him see how I despised him. "I want Joseph," I whispered.

Michael brushed my hair back from my forehead. "He is gone," he said. Such a tender motion from the very hand that had bruised me, and sent me reeling and tumbling down a long flight of stairs.

I felt a terrible chill at the words—surely even Michael, with all his sins, would not destroy an innocent child! I was not to know Joseph's fate for a long time, and when I did, it only made me hate Michael more.

It was very late that same night, when my husband had ceased his feverish ministerings at last and left me in peace, and I was half insensible from the drugs the doctor had prescribed, that Valerian appeared at the foot of my bed.

I thought at first that he was an illusion, or part of a dream, so long had it been since I had laid eyes upon this beloved creature who called himself my guardian vampire. He has always had an irreverent sense of humor, but then you knew that.

What I remember most about that visit from Valerian was the sorrow I saw in his face and in his magnificent countenance. "Have you learned your lesson, sweet Kristina?" he asked.

I moved to sit up, but I could not.

I wanted to plead with him to find Joseph, to bring my baby back to me, but something stayed my tongue. "What lesson was that?" I asked, a bit testily, I fear, for he had tarried long in coming to me, and I had suffered so much in the interim.

He feigned one of his melodramatic sighs. "Kristina," he scolded in a quiet voice.

"All right, yes—I chose the wrong man, for the wrong reasons."

"Anyone might have made that error. The worst part, my darling, is that you stayed with that monster. Why didn't you simply leave him?"

"I kept hoping he would change."

Valerian flexed his elegant white fingers. "Do you know what it is costing me, little one, not to rouse the wretch from his drunken stupor and kill him in a manner that would cause Genghis Khan himself to cringe?"

"Yes," I said. "I can imagine."

"I have come to take you away."

I closed my eyes, but tears seeped through my lashes and sneaked down my cheeks. "I hurt so much," I said with a nod.

"I know," Valerian said softly.

"As much as I long to leave Michael, it is difficult for me to go without saying good-bye to Gilbert."

Valerian's lips curved into the thinnest of smiles. "Don't worry, beloved. One day you will undoubtedly see him again, under other circumstances." He rounded the bed, bent over me, and touched my forehead, and instantly I was unconscious.

When I woke, it was morning, and I was back in the house in London where I had been so happy as a child. My parents were asleep in their lair, and Valerian, of course, was in his, wherever it was, but I was surrounded by familiar servants, and they fussed and fetched and tried their utmost to bring me cheer.

My heart was broken, however, and I could not be happy.

That same afternoon there was a tremendous scuffle downstairs, and I was dreadfully afraid that Michael had come for me, perhaps bringing ruffians to assist him. Our servants were all elderly, and the vampires of the household could not help, being in their usual daylight trances, far below ground..

I remember that I grasped the candlestick from the table alongside my bed and summoned up what I could of my neglected magic, prepared to defend myself as best I could. On pain of death I would not return to Cheltingham.

There was more shouting, but then I heard my personal maid, Minerva, who had often attended me at Refuge, our country home near Cheltingham, speak in calming tones to the protesting mob.

Moments later, she entered my room with a little bob and said, "It's all right, miss. You may put aside the candlestick, for it's Lord Gilbert who's come to call, not his brother. Will you see him?"

Before I could reply—my smile would have given away my feelings on the matter already—Gilbert filled the doorway, tall and handsome, his face contorted with a peculiar combination of rage and sympathy. Minerva perched upon one of the cushioned window seats overlooking the back garden; rules of propriety were observed in our household, by the servants if not the primary inhabitants, and I must not be left alone with a man who was not my husband.

Gilbert was dressed for business—he had come to London to attend to matters related to assuming his late father's title and the estates—but he was clearly a coun-

try gentleman in his tweeds and scuffed boots. His brown hair was rumpled where he had repeatedly thrust his fingers through it.

"Oh, God, Kristina," he murmured. "It's true, then. He did injure you."

"I asked again about the baby," I said. "About Joseph."

Gilbert drew a chair close to the bed and took my hand in his. Tears rose in my eyes and in his as well. "I have had the whole of England search for that child," he said raggedly. "You know that."

"He's killed him. Michael has killed my baby."

Minerva, who had been stroking one of the house cats, a tabby called Trinket, and pretending not to listen, gasped at this.

Gilbert and I were silent for a long time, then Gilbert spoke.

"I cannot believe, even after all Michael has done, that he would stoop to murder. Especially a child."

"Then you are a fool," I replied, unkind in my grief.

Gilbert, as usual, was understanding. "You needn't worry about Michael after this," he said. "I'll make a remittance man of him, provided I don't succumb to the urge to do murder myself. In the meantime, Kristina, you must stop tormenting yourself over little Joseph." He paused. "God in heaven, I curse myself every day for ever bringing the infant to you in the first place. I thought—"

I squeezed his hand. "I know what you thought," I said gently. "That you might give me joy."

He nodded, then bent and kissed my forehead. "I will deal with Michael," he said. "And if there is a way to get the truth out of him regarding the babe, I will do it. In the meantime, you must rest and recover."

I knew, somehow, that I would not see Gilbert again,

and clung to him for a long moment when he would have turned to leave the room.

"Good-bye," I whispered.

He kissed my mouth that time. It was light, brief, but in no way brotherly. "Farewell, sweet Kristina," he said. And then he strode out of the room without once looking back.

Minerva, poor dear, was sniffling and dashing away tears with the hem of her apron when I glanced in her direction. "Such a dear man," she said.

"Yes," I replied, staring at the empty chasm of the open doorway, through which Gilbert had just passed.

"I can't see the likes of him raising a hand to a woman," Minerva observed in a righteous tone, rising from the window seat with the cat squirming in her arms.

"No," I agreed, but I feared Gilbert would do violence when he returned to Cheltingham, and I was right. Word came to London, several weeks later, by way of an intricate network of grooms and footmen and others who handled horses and carriages, that Gilbert had gone home to find Michael preparing to come to the city and fetch me.

They had argued heatedly, as the story went, and Michael had taken up a fireplace poker, in a fit of temper, and swung it at Gilbert's head. Gilbert had deflected the blow, fracturing a bone in his forearm in the process, but had managed, all the same, to administer a memorable thrashing. Our stable hands had it on good authority, and passed the word to the household servants, that Michael Bradford had been dumped, bruised, chastened, and humbled onto a ship bound for Australia. As long as he kept himself within those far shores, he would receive an adequate allowance. Should he return to England, for any reason, however, he would be utterly penniless.

I received one letter after that, from Gilbert. He wrote that he was to be wed at last, to one Ethel Grovestead of Devonshire, and that there had still been no word of Joseph. . . .

Kristina laid the letter aside. Joseph.

She seldom allowed herself to think of the little boy, but he was very much on her mind that evening. She had found him, some seven years after his disappearance, with Valerian's reluctant assistance, working with a gang of pickpockets. Once a cherubic baby, the child was now feral and ratlike, hardly even human. Michael had put him into a foundling home after taking him away from Cheltingham in secret, a terrible, cold place where he'd been beaten and half starved. At five he'd fled the institution and taken up with a gang of cutthroats, orphans, and other lost boys like himself, and Kristina had realized at last, looking into his fevered and hateful eyes, that there was no saving him.

Valerian had understood that all along, and perhaps Gilbert had, as well. They had been shielding her, the pair of them, and she did not appreciate their efforts.

She'd given the boy, once called Joseph, all the money in her bag. He'd snatched the coins into his grubby hands, spat at her, and fled. After that, she'd done her best to provide for him, again with Valerian's aid, but after only a few months the child had perished in an alleyway, a small bundle of dirty rags and brittle bones, racked with consumption.

If Kristina had hated Michael before that, it was nothing compared to what she felt afterward. Life might have been so very different for Joseph, for all of them. . . .

She pulled her thoughts forcibly away from that dreadful time. She had dwelt on the past long enough, for one night. Now she must look forward, make plans for a new life.

Kristina switched on the computer at the small desk in

the family room, got out her address book, and began composing letters to other antiques dealers all over the world. Her wares were envied far and wide, and selling them would be an easy matter, once her colleagues knew she was going out of business.

She worked into the small hours of the morning, then went upstairs to shower and crawl into bed. Barabbas slept at her feet, heavy and warm, and hers was a peaceful, dreamless sleep.

The next day she went to the shop and sent off the letters she had written the night before, via her fax machine. By lunchtime she was already receiving offers. Several dealers, in fact, were flying in from other parts of the world, while others asked for a complete inventory list. Kristina kept her stock catalogued on the shop computer and updated the information once a week. It was an easy matter to print out a copy and begin responding to the requests.

All the while she waited for the brass monkey-man to show up, human again and bent on revenge. Benecia Havermail could hold a doorstop hostage as long as she wanted to, but even she wouldn't be able to reverse the spell Kristina had cast. She would, however, have a better chance of defending herself.

At home Kristina let herself in, half expecting her assailant to pounce on her. Instead she was greeted by a whimpering Barabbas, eager for a walk and supper.

Kristina let him out, trusting him to return when he was ready, although she knew he wanted to go home to Valerian, who was his true master. Because the wolf had been commanded to keep watch over Kristina, however, he would do so, no matter how lonely he was.

While Kristina was making supper—a light pasta dish— the telephone rang. She didn't need her lost magic to know the caller was Max.

"Hi," she said.

He let out a long breath, as though he'd feared she wouldn't answer. "How was your day?"

She smiled as she chopped red, yellow, and green peppers to roast and put on top of her pasta, to give it some color and pizazz. "It was pretty good, really. Nothing jumped out at me, or anything like that. How about you?"

Max laughed. "Wish I could say the same," he said. "My players are all keyed up for the four-day weekend, and most of them were on hormone overload in the first place. I spent the day letting the smaller guys out of lockers."

"I don't know how you stand the little devils," Kristina said, cooking as she spoke. A little salad would go nicely with the pasta, she decided.

Max, too, was making dinner; she could hear the homey, accompanying sounds over the wire. "Coming from you, that's an ironic remark," he teased. "Given the sort of company you keep, I mean."

His words reminded Kristina of all she would have to tell him, in the very near future, and dampened her spirits a little. Thinking of Michael, she said, "Considering the cruelty of some human beings I've known, I marvel that Valerian or even Dathan could be called 'monsters.'"

"Did I hurt your feelings?"

That was Max for you. No beating around the proverbial bush; just get right to the point. The concern in his voice made Kristina want to weep.

"Maybe a little, but I know you didn't intend to."

"Sorry," Max said. She hadn't known anyone even remotely like him since Gilbert Bradford, Duke of Cheltingham.

"It's all right," she insisted. Her appetite was gone, though. She turned off the burner under the pasta and took the chopped peppers out of the electric grilling machine she'd ordered off an infomercial one night, a few years before, when she hadn't been able to sleep. "Vampires and warlocks aren't subject to the rules of political correctness."

"Just give them time," Max said ruefully with a grin in his voice.

There was so much she wanted to tell him—that she was human, that she was fertile, that she was closing her shop and leaving Seattle, but none of it could be said over the telephone. She had had to give up Gilbert, and now she would lose Max, but this time she would have some very sweet memories to take away with her, along with a freshly broken heart.

"How are Bree and Eliette?" she asked, holding her breath while she awaited his answer. She was still very afraid of Benecia and Canaan; they could so easily turn their envy on Max's little girls, who had everything they wanted. Innocence. Mortality. Not just one future, but many.

"Only slightly less rowdy than my football players," Max replied. "They're getting excited about Thanksgiving—not that they're all that thankful. It's just that, thanks to TV, they know it's a greased track from Turkey Day to Christmas."

Kristina smiled again, but wistfully. Although she had had plenty of beautiful toys as a child, and a great fuss was made over her birthday, even the boldest vampires did not dare to observe the holy days of any of the great religions. Nemesis and his Superiors were very touchy about such matters, and no sane fiend would invoke their ire.

"That must be fun—filling stockings, keeping secrets . . ."

"To tell you the truth," Max confessed when Kristina's voice fell away, "it's something of a hassle. And it bothers me a lot that the central idea is Getting Stuff. Whatever happened to peace on earth and goodwill toward men?"

"I think both are where they always were—in the hearts of men *and* women. It's just a matter of what you focus on."

"You're right," Max said. "First my mom and dad made Christmas happen, then Sandy took care of it. The last couple of years I've been—well—going through the motions."

Again Kristina's heart was touched with sadness. She wondered if being in love was always like riding a roller coaster, or if her mood swings were connected to her new humanity. "I bet you're not giving yourself enough credit," she said.

"Maybe," he allowed.

It was then that Barabbas scratched at the kitchen door. Kristina stretched but couldn't quite reach the knob. "Hold on a second, will you, Max?" she asked.

His voice was warm and low, sexy as a caress. "Maybe I'd better let you go. The spaghetti is about to boil over. Call you tomorrow?"

"I'll be looking forward to it," Kristina said.

She hung up the telephone and opened the door. Standing behind Barabbas, in the early darkness of late November, were Benecia and Canaan. They were dressed as ludicrous little pilgrims, complete with buckles on their shoes, Puritan bonnets, gowns, and aprons.

"Barabbas," Kristina commanded in an even voice, "bring Valerian."

The wolf darted away into the night, and while Canaan looked unsettled by this development, Benecia smiled. Her uncanny beauty made her all the more hideous, all the more vile.

"Aren't you going to ask us in?" she asked in her small, bell-like voice.

Kristina had no choice, and she knew it as well as they did. She just hoped Valerian wasn't too far away to help.

The fact that Benecia didn't seem particularly worried about the other vampire was not encouraging. Stepping back, Kristina admitted them.

"Where is the doorstop?" she demanded.

"I haven't the faintest idea," Benecia replied. "I gave it to a junk dealer. It'll be interesting to see where the thing turns up, don't you think?"

Kristina might have gone for the little beast's throat if she hadn't known it would mean instant—or worse yet, *not* instant—death. She said nothing. *What* could be keeping Valerian?

"I believe he's busy elsewhere," Benecia said with acid sweetness, as if Kristina had asked the question aloud.

Kristina drew a deep breath and let it out slowly. She must stay calm, at all costs. Vampires of this ilk were like wild, vicious animals, unreasoning, provoked by the scent of fear. "What do you want from me?" she asked in what she hoped was a reasonable and even tone of voice.

"A plan has occurred to us," Benecia said.

Canaan was still keeping an uneasy eye out for Valerian.

"What sort of plan?" Kristina went for a tone of contempt, in what was probably a futile effort to distract Benecia from the terror she felt.

"One that would allow us to be human, to live out normal lives." She paused and smiled, showing her white teeth, as perfect and pearly as a doll's. "We might even be your daughters. Wouldn't that be fun?"

Kristina swayed inwardly as the full weight of Benecia's words struck her. Great Zeus, the little beasts were talking about *possession*, planning to abandon their own vampire bodies and take over those of Eliette and Bree!

"I will do anything to stop you," she whispered. "*Anything.*"

"But can you?" Benecia retorted, almost simpering.

"You have no magic now. You are nothing but a mortal woman."

"Nothing but what you have always wanted to be," Kristina replied.

"Let's go," Canaan said, breaking her silence at last. "I don't like it here."

"A wise child," commented a third voice, but it wasn't Valerian who spoke. Even before Kristina whirled to look, she knew it was Dathan who had materialized in her kitchen, not the fearsome vampire.

Canaan retreated a step, but Benecia advanced, snarling, her china-blue eyes demonicly bright. She held a particular grudge toward Dathan, Kristina recalled; something on the order of a woman scorned.

"You," the vampire accused. "It was *you*, warlock, who gave us your vile blood while we slept!"

Dathan was, once again, dressed for either the theater or the opera. Kristina deduced, stupidly, that he must be quite an aficionado of the arts. He dusted the impeccable sleeves of his greatcoat with white-gloved hands before replying. "Hold your tongue, you demon's whelp, or I'll give you a dose that will make arsenic seem like ambrosia."

Benecia made a primal sound, like the hiss of a jungle cat about to spring, and Dathan raised one hand and snapped his fingers.

A circle of flame danced around Benecia's feet.

Canaan shrieked and fled immediately; sensible vampires fear fire as they do sunlight and the point of a wooden stake. Benecia, though visibly frightened, glared at the warlock as the blaze grew.

Kristina clasped both hands over her mouth, horrified. "Stop," she whispered. "Please, Dathan—stop."

He sighed, and the flames died down to a black circle on Kristina's floor.

"Get out," he said.

Benecia scowled at him a moment longer, then vanished.

Kristina turned and flung herself against Dathan's chest, utterly terrified. "You must help me—they're planning to take over Max's children—can they do that?"

Dathan gave her a gentle shake, then held her close again. "We shall not allow it, you and I," he said tenderly, kissing the top of Kristina's head. "Leave the 'littlest vampire' and her more judicious sister to me."

"What will you do?"

He touched a finger to her lips. "Shhh," he said. "Do not worry yourself with such matters, Kristina. After all, you will soon be my queen. Think on that instead. Imagine what it will mean."

She could not bear to consider the full scope of her vow, not then. She had told Benecia and Canaan she would do anything to save Eliette and Bree from them, and she'd meant it. The price was high indeed, but Kristina would not stint.

"You must give me just a few more days to end things with Max."

"I cannot pretend I am not jealous," Dathan said. "But I will grant you that request or virtually any other. But you must give me your word, Kristina. You will become my bride."

She swallowed hard, blinked back tears, and then nodded. "I promise," she whispered.

With that, Dathan bent his head and kissed her gently on the mouth. She was not unmoved—he was a creature capable of great passion—but there was no spiritual connection as there was with Max. No sense of rightness, of something ordained in a time when stars, now long dead, were tumultuous and new, bursting with fire.

Then suddenly he vanished.

Valerian arrived an instant afterward, popping in in his usual spectacular fashion, bringing Barabbas with him. Or did Barabbas possess that talent in his own right? It didn't matter, for Kristina had just sold her soul, and she was as good as damned.

"Where have you been?" she demanded, and then gave a deep, wrenching sob.

Valerian put his arms around Kristina, in the way her father might have done, ignoring her outburst. He was not at her beck and call, and he had the good grace not to point that out—though he could be depended upon to raise the subject later. "I have been doing what I could to assist your mother," he said simply.

Kristina looked up into his face, full of sorrow, glad that she was human, that she would die. "I will be wed to Dathan within a fortnight," she said.

Valerian looked truly startled, an emotion she had not seen in him in all the length of her memory. "*What?*" he demanded.

She explained Benecia's threat, brokenly, trembling all the while, and the somber expression on the vampire's face told her that such a thing was indeed possible.

"They have made some unholy bargain," Valerian reflected. "They must be destroyed before they can carry out their plans, or other vampires will do the same. I do not believe I need to tell you how Nemesis would react to that."

"What can I do?" Kristina asked, desperate.

Valerian cupped her chin in his hand, wiped away some of her tears with a thumb as smooth and cool as marble. "Only wait," the vampire said. "You were very foolish to promise yourself to Dathan, however. He will not release you from the pact."

"It is worth it to me," she replied.

The vampire kissed her forehead. "I hope so," he answered. And then he, too, was gone.

Kristina took Barabbas, drove to Max's, and knocked on

the front door. Maybe she couldn't protect Bree and Eliette, with her lapsed magic, but there was a chance that the wolf could. And besides, she wanted to be able to summon Dathan if Benecia and Canaan decided to put in an appearance.

Max didn't ask questions, bless him. He just led Kristina to the guest room, kissed her lightly, and left her alone.

Sometime in the middle of the night, Bree and Eliette joined Kristina in the double bed, cuddling up close, but she knew it wasn't because they were afraid. They had sensed her sorrow, somehow, and wanted to console her.

Kristina was sipping coffee the next morning in the kitchen when Max found a moment to talk to her alone. The girls were on their way to their separate schools, via the neighborhood carpool.

"Okay," he said. "What's the deal? How come you showed up in the middle of the night?"

"I got lonesome," Kristina hedged. "Besides, you invited me, didn't you? You said I could come over any time I wanted."

"And I meant it." He glanced at the clock over the kitchen sink, and his jaw tightened. "I have to get to work. We'll talk about this later."

Kristina nodded, though she had no intention of explaining, *ever*, that two vampires wanted to possess his daughters. She had all day to think up some story that would bear a resemblance to the truth.

"I'll stop by the shop after practice. Around five o'clock?"

He would find out that she was liquidating her stock and getting ready to close down the business, but that was the least of her problems. In fact, she needed to hurry home to shower and put on makeup and a power suit, because two of her European colleagues were arriving that day to take their choice of her merchandise.

"Make it six, and I'll take you out to dinner. Bring the girls."

If Bree and Eliette were along, they could avoid a lot of subjects Kristina didn't want to talk about just yet. Like why she'd showed up at their house after midnight with a wolf in tow.

Max didn't fall for it. "I think I can get Cindy from down the street to babysit," he said. "I'll see you at six."

Forget the battle, the whole war was already a lost cause. Kristina was putting herself through hell just so she could have that one special weekend in the mountains with Max before she told him it was over, and it was selfish and unfair of her to do it.

But then, she had never claimed to be perfect.

CHAPTER 16

Two of Kristina's European colleagues were still at the shop when Max arrived that evening, at five after six. Between them, Adrian and Enrique had purchased nearly everything in the place, and the few items they hadn't claimed had been sold via telephone and fax to still other dealers. Both men had hired shipping companies, and Kristina's treasures were being bound up in bubble wrap, taped into boxes, and put into huge wooden crates with shredded paper for padding.

Adrian and Enrique oversaw the whole process, each one jealously guarding his spoil, and many things had already been taken away in trucks. Adrian's purchases would go to a small shop in Avignon, and Enrique owned an exclusive place in Toronto.

Max, who had had no idea what to expect, in that charming way of mortals, was flabbergasted to find the shop in the process of being emptied.

Adrian and Enrique paused in their noisy supervisory duties just long enough to assess the newcomer, then ignored him. He was definitely not their type.

Max was still standing just inside the door, looking stunned, when Kristina went to him, took his hand, and gently pulled him into the back room, where they could have a modicum—though not much more—of privacy.

"What in hell is going on here?" Max demanded in a loud whisper. Kristina knew he was worried, not angry.

"There are some things I need to tell you," she said. "We established that this morning. Now, are you ready to go out for pizza and some intense conversation, or shall we stay here and make sure Adrian and Enrique don't kill each other?"

Max's large, football player's shoulders rolled under his sports jacket; he might have flung out his arms if the back room hadn't been so small and so jammed with Kristina's personal belongings—the microwave, the stash of herbal teas, the mugs, the table and chairs. There was also a small desk, which held a laptop computer, a miniature printer, and her fax machine.

"There are *definitely* some things you need to tell me. How about starting right now?"

She moved close to him, slipped her arms around his waist, laid her cheek against his chest. He smelled of a recent shower and crisp, fresh air, and she wished she could hold Max like that forever.

It was then, of all times, that she realized who he was— or more properly, who he had been, once upon a time. The knowledge nearly buckled her knees, but she wouldn't let herself fold up now. There were too many things to be done.

"I don't want to talk here," she said, blinking back tears, her forehead pressed against Max's breastbone. "Please— there's a quiet place down the street, with candlelight and soft music and tables tucked away in the shadows. Let's go there."

Max held her tightly for a moment, then took her shoulders in his hands and looked down into her eyes. "Fine,"

he said. "But what about those hairdresser types out there?
Do you trust them?"

Kristina couldn't help smiling at Max's description of
her colleagues. "They're art and antiques dealers, Max, not
cat burglars. Besides, I've already put through their Gold
Card numbers. Thanks to the wonders of electronics, the
money for what they've bought is being transferred into my
business account even as we speak."

He smiled at that, and kissed her forehead, but she knew
he was still troubled. "Let's get out of here," he said. "Unlike most people, I get hungry when I'm stressed."

In the main part of the shop the circus of labeling, packing, and arguing in four languages continued. Kristina explained that she and Max were leaving, and would be back
later to lock up. She didn't bother with introductions.

It was a short walk to Luigi's Ristorante, only a block
or so, and the night was cold. The stars were out, but
seemed somehow more distant than before, as though they
had taken a step back from a doubtful Earth. Max held
Kristina's hand, but neither of them spoke until they had
checked Kristina's coat and taken a seat at one of the most
private tables.

They chose a red wine and ordered the house specialty:
a wonderful, thick-crusted pizza with an astronomical cal-
orie count, preceded by *insalata mista*—a simple mixed
salad.

Max held his peace until the greens arrived. Then he
stabbed a forkful of lettuce leaves and said, "All right,
Kristina. What's the deal?"

"Are you asking why I showed up at your house in the
middle of the night or why I'm shutting down my business?"

Max laid his fork down again, the food untouched.
"Both," he said. He looked like a man who didn't want to
hear the answer he himself had demanded.

"Unfortunately it wouldn't be quite accurate to start with either of those events," Kristina said, resigned. Amazingly, she found she had an appetite and began to nibble at her salad. She hoped she wasn't going to turn out to be one of those mortals who ate when they were stressed, like Max— with her circle of friends and relations, she'd double her weight in a month. "I've discovered something very inter- esting about myself, Max. I'm human. I mean, fully, com- pletely, flesh-and-blood *human*."

She had expected him to be pleased, but as Kristina watched Max's reaction, she saw something peculiar in his face. Not fear, exactly. She couldn't be sure what it was she'd glimpsed, and it wasn't the right time to ask. He began to eat.

"Maybe you were always mortal and just didn't know it."

Kristina shook her head. "I had magical powers, and they're gone now. My father has performed tests—he was—*is*—a doctor, you know. There's no doubt that I've changed."

Max let out a long sigh, polished off his salad, and started on the breadsticks. "Why didn't you tell me last night?"

"It was late, and I felt bad enough about disrupting your household that way as it was. Besides, the timing wasn't right."

"Okay. Let's move on to that. What brought you to my door in the wee small hours, with Barabbas at your heels, looking as though you'd just barely outrun the devil?"

"Maybe I had," Kristina said, reaching for her wine, a rich Chianti, and taking a thoughtful sip. She set the glass aside. "I wanted to protect you and the children, and I knew I couldn't manage without my magic. So I brought Barabbas to serve as a sort of watchdog."

Max leaned forward, his second breadstick forgotten in

his hand. "Protect us from what?" he pressed quietly.

Kristina was still a little wounded that he wasn't happier about her being mortal, which didn't make sense, of course, because she was going to have to tell him, very soon, that they couldn't see each other anymore. What she would *never* tell him was that Benecia and Canaan had plans to possess his children; he could do nothing to save them and would only be tormented by the knowledge that they were in danger.

And he'd hate her for bringing that peril into their lives.

"Just—things in general," she answered after a long, painful silence, during which she indulged in several more sips of wine. "I've already explained about my unfortunate connections with the supernatural underworld, Max. Please don't force me to say more, because it would serve absolutely no purpose."

Max was quiet, indulging in his own wine, though in gulps rather than sips. Finally, pale under his year-around suntan, he said, "Let's get back to the subject of your mortality for a moment. I don't give a damn about your lost magic, and it isn't your job to protect me or my family anyway, though I appreciate the effort. Does this mean that you can die, like everybody else?"

The food arrived, with exquisitely bad timing. They both sat in silence while the waiter gave them plates and forks and red-and-white-checked napkins, then cut the succulent pizza into wide sections dripping cheese.

Kristina watched Max the whole time, feeling as though she'd been struck. Maybe Max had never truly cared for her at all. Maybe he'd only wanted her because he thought she couldn't get sick or be killed in an accident. The way Sandy had been.

"Yes," she said when the solicitous waiter had finally left them alone. "I'm as vulnerable as anyone else." She tried to smile but didn't quite achieve it. "Guess I take after my father's side of the family—he was still a mere man when I was conceived.''

Max waited until Kristina had taken a serving of the steaming, fragrant pizza for herself, then slid a double helping onto his own plate. He ate with his fingers, while Kristina used a fork.

"Why are you closing the shop?" he asked, after refilling both their wineglasses. She knew, though, that he was still mulling over what she'd just told him, that she wasn't going to live forever.

Kristina bit her lower lip. Lying had never come easily to her, and it was almost impossible with Max. She was already straining the limits of her abilities. "I guess I'm tired of working for a living," she said. "I don't have to, you know—I have more than enough money."

"I'd guessed that," Max replied. "That you weren't poor, I mean. But you've got to admit the decision might seem sudden to the casual onlooker."

"I'm impulsive," Kristina said with a little shrug. She hadn't meant to sound flippant, but there was so much she couldn't say. Not yet.

"Am I about to be dumped?" Another Max-ism. If you want to know something, ask. A simple concept, in theory at least, but damn hard to emulate in practice. Or so it seemed to Kristina, who felt mired in lies and omissions.

She didn't want to give up Thanksgiving dinner with a real family, or the long, delicious weekend in the snowy mountains. It was pure selfishness, and she knew it, but there it was. The rest of her life looked too long and too lonely to survive, without the comfort of these last few precious memories.

"I was wondering the same thing," Kristina said. "Whether or not you'd decided to break things off."

"I don't know," he finally replied, meeting her gaze straight on. She loved him for that, for so many things. "I love you, Kristina—I'd like nothing better than to marry you and make babies—but it scares the hell out of me, and I'm not talking about warlocks and vampires here. It's the idea that you could—that what happened with Sandy could happen all over again—''

Kristina reached out and touched his hand. "It's okay, Max," she said softly. "I understand."

He interlaced his fingers with hers and squeezed. "I'm not going to ask you what your plans are," he said hoarsely, "because I don't think I could deal with the answer right now. So let's just take things one day, one *moment* at a time, at least until after this weekend. Agreed?"

Kristina swallowed a throatful of tears. "Agreed," she said.

They ate a good deal of the pizza, and then Max walked Kristina back to the shop, where Enrique and Adrian were still packing and giving orders and arguing. Kristina gave Adrian a spare key—she had several, because of the new door—and asked him to lock up when they were finished.

Adrian kissed her on both cheeks, which made Enrique feel compelled to do the same, though he seemed a bit put out that his competitor had been the one chosen to close the shop. Max waited patiently by the door, then drove Kristina to her car, which was parked in a lot several blocks away.

"Feel like spending the night?" he asked, getting out of the Blazer to open her door for her and see her inside and properly seatbelted.

Kristina considered, then shook her head. She'd imposed enough as it was by showing up unannounced the night before. Another appearance would probably worry Bree and Eliette, or at least confuse them. "I could send Barabbas over, though."

Max rolled his eyes. "Thanks," he said, "but no, thanks." He bent and kissed her through the open window of the driver's door. "Try not to worry so much," he said, when it was over. He'd left her dizzy, but he didn't seem to have a clue how his kisses made her feel. "There are fiends and ghouls in the world, mortal and otherwise. I wouldn't have believed the 'otherwise', if it hadn't been for you, but you reminded me of something else, Kristina. Something I'd almost completely forgotten, because I was so furious that a woman as sweet and smart and innocent as Sandy could die like that."

There were tears on Kristina's face, and she didn't try to hide them. Nor did she speak.

Max dried her cheeks, first one and then the other, with the edge of his thumb. "You made me remember how much good there is in the world. For every demon, there's an angel."

An old memory brushed Kristina's heart, like the soft, feathered wing of a passing cherubim. Once, when she was very young, Benecia Havermail had told Kristina that she was doomed, being the child of two vampires, and would surely burn in hell forever. Kristina had been terrified and had run to her governess, the unflappable Phillie, with the news that she was damned.

"Heaven bears you no ill will, child," Phillie had said, smoothing Kristina's hair with a tender motion of her hand. "While the bodies of innocents sometimes suffer, their spirits are inviolate. Do you understand what that means?"

Kristina, being seven or eight at the time, and uncommonly bright, had gotten the gist. Flesh was temporary, spirit was eternal.

She brought herself back to the here and now, heartened, but still wishing for Phillie. How reassuring it would have been to tell her troubles to her old friend, the way she had as a little girl, as a young bride, as a lonely wanderer.

"You'll be okay?" Max asked, caressing her cheek.

Kristina nodded, and as she pulled away she said a little

prayer that Eliette and Bree would be guarded, with special care.

There was no word from Dathan, or from Valerian, her parents, or any of the other vampires of her acquaintance, that night. Only Barabbas greeted her, trotting over and plopping down beside the chair in her bedroom, when she sat down to read another of the ancient volumes she had borrowed from her mother.

She couldn't have said why she bothered, for even if she found a spell to protect Bree and Eliette and Max, it would be of no real use, now that her magic was gone.

She learned nothing at all in fact, and her sleep that night was crowded with dreams, all of which stayed just out of conscious reach when she awakened in the morning.

After showering, dressing, and feeding Barabbas, Kristina drove back down to the shop. Adrian had locked the place, as promised, and he and Enrique and all their little hired elves were gone.

The place was practically empty, except for those things that had still to be boxed for shipment to other dealers. Kristina could have hired the work done, of course, but she wanted to be busy, to keep her mind off Benecia Havermail's aspirations to be human and well away from the absolute necessity of breaking things off with Max. She most certainly didn't want to consider the implications of her inevitable union with the warlock, so she kept her brain as blank as she could and worked furiously until the sun had gone down and she was exhausted.

Again there were no visitations from supernatural creatures, and Kristina was boundlessly grateful. She made a simple supper, attended to Barabbas's canine needs—i.e., a walk and a bowl of kibbles—and finally settled herself in front of the family room TV. Unable to face the old letters to Phillie that still remained to be read, or the volumes that were yielding no solutions to her problems, she tuned in to the shopping channel and sat sipping herbal tea. By the end of the evening, she owned two gold bracelets and a combination grill and waffle maker.

She would figure out what to do with this largess some other time.

Morning brought some good news, however minor. Her period was over.

Kristina went through the showering, dressing, and eating ritual and, clad in jeans and a sweatshirt, returned to the shop to finish packing the last of her stock. Only a few items had not been sold; she would take those home and, like the loot from the shopping channel, dispense with them later.

By noon a delivery van had arrived, and the driver was wheeling boxes out to his truck in relays. Kristina signed the necessary papers, supplied her account number, and then stood in the near-empty shop, wanting to cry but not quite able to manage it. She'd loved building the business, but she knew it was the process of doing that that she'd truly cared about, not the establishment itself.

She wondered, with wry depression, what her duties would be as queen of the warlocks. How could there even *be* a queen of the warlocks, for pity's sake, if witches, the female of the species, were an entirely separate group? Come to that, how could there be warlocks *or* witches if the two genders hated each other too much to mate?

Kristina had decided to donate the microwave, table and chair, fax machine, etc., to a charitable group. They arrived with a truck of their own and took away the contents of the back room, the place that had been her refuge during hectic work days. She threw in the unsold antiques for good measure so she wouldn't have to carry them to her car, and then went home.

She'd been in the house approximately five minutes

when Daisy called. From the electronic choppiness of the transmission, Kristina guessed that her friend was using the cell phone she carried in her fanny pack.

"You might tell a person you're closing up shop," snapped Valerian's bride, "instead of just folding your tent like some sheik and stealing silently off into the night."

Kristina smiled, even though she felt more like crying. Daisy usually had a cheering effect on her, and she hoped her upcoming, lifetime alliance with Dathan wouldn't interfere with their friendship. "Sorry," she said. "It was a sudden decision."

"Like agreeing to become Dathan's bride?" Daisy demanded between crackles. "Damn, I always forget to charge this thing. Stay where you are—I'm coming right over."

Kristina sighed, put on water for tea, and waited.

Daisy arrived within twenty minutes. Barabbas greeted her with pitiful delight, squirming at her feet like a puppy.

"You've got to take him back to your place," Kristina said. "I can't bear the guilt—I feel like the villainess in a *Lassie* movie."

Daisy shrugged out of her jacket. "Okay," she said, opening the kitchen door and cocking one thumb. "Barabbas, go home."

The wolf shot through the slim gap as though he had springs in his haunches.

Daisy closed the door. "Valerian is pretty crazy over this marriage of yours," she said. There was no judgment in the remark; it was just an observation.

"It's none of his business," Kristina replied in the same tone. The tea was ready, and she carried the pot to the family room table on a tray, along with sugar cubes, a small pitcher of milk, and two cups and saucers. The irony of the phrase "family room" struck her, and she laughed, though the sound came out sounding more like a sob.

'You're right,'' Daisy agreed, letting the sob pass with-commenting or commiserating. "But since when has tnat stopped Valerian from meddling?'' She sat down across from Kristina. "I guess you gave up the shop because you'll be leaving here.''

Kristina nodded, stirring sugar into her tea. "There is that. And I've been in the business of collecting and selling antiques for about seventy-five years.''

"Because you loved it,'' Daisy pointed out. She could be implacably blunt, like Max. It was one of her most endearing, and most annoying, qualities.

"It's gone,'' Kristina said. "That's the bottom line.''

"You own the building, don't you? Maybe you could start up again sometime. If you get bored with being queen of the warlocks.'' There was a twinkle in Daisy's eyes, along with a great deal of empathy. "What exactly will you do, anyway?''

Kristina shook her head. "I don't have a clue—beyond the obvious, of course.''

Daisy, who had been a homicide cop in Las Vegas and consorted with all sorts of sleazeballs in her more recent career as a private investigator, actually blushed and averted her eyes. Although neither of them took the subject any further, Kristina was pretty sure they were both wondering what it would be like to have sex with a warlock.

She felt a new yearning for Max, deeper and more desperate than ever.

"Where will you live?'' Daisy asked.

Kristina didn't know that, either. And since she no longer possessed magical powers, she wouldn't be able to transport herself from one place to another at will as she had done in the past. "Probably in Transylvania,'' she said, trying to make the best of a bad situation by turning it into a joke. It didn't work.

"Don't,'' Daisy said.

At last Kristina broke down and cried. "I'm going to have one weekend with Max," she sobbed, "just one weekend. And the memories of that will have to last for the rest of my life."

Daisy lowered her head for a moment, obviously feeling Kristina's pain, bowed by it, probably imagining what it would be like to be separated from Valerian, once and for all. She tried to offer consolation. "You're mortal now. Maybe in another lifetime . . ."

Kristina's sobs had subsided to inelegant sniffles, but her sorrow was as great as ever. "No," she said. "I knew Max once before—he was someone else then, of course—and it just wasn't meant to be."

"Don't tell me he was that Michael character who threw you down the stairs and left your foster son in a workhouse!"

Kristina didn't need to ask how Daisy had known those things, details she had confided to no one else besides Phillie and her "guardian vampire." Valerian had told her, of course. "No," she said. "Max wasn't Michael." But she didn't offer any more information than that.

"Have some more tea," Daisy said. "Have you got any brandy? If you ask me, you could use a shot of firewater."

"No, thanks," Kristina replied. She would have liked to escape the pain, but she didn't care for the idea of dulling her senses, especially now that Barabbas was no longer there to guard her. "How's the new nanny working out? Not to mention motherhood in general?"

Changing the subject proved a good tactic. Daisy's face brightened, and the uncomfortable subjects of Dathan and Max were forgotten, at least temporarily. "She's a wonder worker—now that she's told Esteban he's safe with us, that we're not going to starve or beat him, he's doing better. He still sleeps on the floor once in a while, but he's not hiding food, and he's trying to learn English. He adores Valerian.''

Kristina remembered how tenderly the legendary vampire had held the little ragged boy that night in Rio, and was touched. Ah, but it was not a simple thing, this matter of good and evil. Was Valerian, who preyed upon mortals and sustained himself on their very life's blood, a monster? What of Esteban's birth mother, who would sell her own child into an unthinkable fate? Was *she* not the true fiend, though a human heart beat within her breast and her soul might still be salvaged through grace, should she repent, however unlikely that seemed?

''To know Valerian,'' Kristina answered at last with a slight smile, ''is to love him.''

Daisy laughed. ''I certainly do,'' she said, ''but you've got to admit—it's a matter of perspective.''

It was a comfort just having Daisy's company for a little while, and by the time her friend left, Kristina felt better, if a bit lonely. She built a fire, took a nap on the family room sofa, and lapsed into a dream. She couldn't remember it after she woke up, and that troubled her, for she'd been left with a sense of urgency, part terror, and part hope.

The next day was Thanksgiving.

Kristina packed a small bag for the weekend in the mountains with Max and dressed carefully in a tan cashmere skirt, high brown leather boots, and a long, ivory-colored silk sweater. When Max and the girls arrived to pick her up, she saw by the warmth in Max's eyes that she'd chosen well, and that was something of a relief, for with all her sophistication, Kristina did not know exactly what one wore to a family feast. She'd never attended one before.

Max took her bag and put it in the back of the Blazer while Bree bounced around him, babbling questions. Was

Kristina taking a trip? Where was she going? Was he going along, too? Could she and Eliette go?

Eliette walked more sedately, keeping close to Kristina's side. She was usually reserved, but she'd been the one to cuddle closest the other night, when Kristina had slept over in Max's guest room and his children had joined her in bed. "Bree is just a kid," she confided to Kristina. "She doesn't know about these things."

Kristina tried not to smile. She also felt bruised inside, for she guessed that Eliette had begun to let down her guard a little, to see her as a friend. Which meant the child would be hurt again, to some degree, when Kristina and Max went their distinctly separate ways.

"What things?" she asked, casually offering her hand.

Eliette took it, after a brief hesitation. "Oh, kissing and stuff. Like you do with Daddy."

"Oh." Not a very original or profound reply, but Kristina was stumped.

Mercifully they had reached the Blazer, and Eliette pulled free and scrambled into the back beside Bree, who was already buckled in. Max helped Kristina into the passenger seat and then went around to get behind the wheel.

He was whistling softly under his breath.

"Aunt Elaine moved to Arizona," Bree chimed from her booster seat. "She breaked her heart. I think she fell down."

"She didn't fall down, ninny," Eliette said. "She wanted to marry Daddy, and he said no."

Out of the corner of her eye, Kristina saw Max tense slightly, but she had to hand it to him. When he spoke, his voice was matter-of-fact. "Aunt Elaine missed your grandparents," he said. "Besides, they're getting older and they need her."

Max hadn't exactly lied; he hadn't denied that Sandy's sister, Elaine, was in love him. It was probably true that she missed her parents, and they might even need her help, if their health was poor or something like that. But he had certainly steered the conversation away from the subject of his sister-in-law.

Kristina gave him a teasing, sidelong look, to let him know she wasn't fooled.

He chuckled and shook his head.

The day was wonderful, straight out of the fantasies Kristina had cherished all her life.

Max's parents lived in a large colonial-style house, built of brick, in one of Seattle's better, though certainly not exclusive, neighborhoods. There was a small duck pond out back, and the spacious property was fringed with fir and maple trees. A few gloriously yellow, brown, and crimson leaves still clung to the wintry branches of the maples.

The people in the living room, some gathered around a piano singing, and others in front of the fire arguing politics, looked like figures from some painting celebrating Americana. The air was filled with lovely aromas—roasting turkey, spices, scented candles, and a variety of perfumes.

Mrs. Kilcarragh came immediately to greet Max with a kiss—the girls had already shed their coats and gone running to sit on either side of the piano player, whom Kristina deduced, by the resemblance, to be Max's father.

"Kristina," Mrs. Kilcarragh said warmly, taking both Kristina's hands in hers. "It is a joy to meet you at long last. I'm Allison, and that handsome devil at the piano is the girls' grandfather. Do come in and meet our other guests."

There were an overwhelming number of people in the Kilcarragh house, but that only made it better. Kristina loved the laughter, the music, the talk, and the food, and she could not remember a happier day in all of her life.

After the meal, which was unbelievable, the men retired to watch the football game, Max included, and the women cleaned up. Kristina was thrilled to help—she had not known this particular kind of female camaraderie ever, and being part of it was an experience so sweet that it swelled her heart. Oh, to be a part of this family, to share in other celebrations, to belong.

But it wasn't to be, and all the pretending in the world wouldn't change that. Nor would she squander such a precious gift by looking ahead to a bleak future, however. Kristina kept herself firmly in the present, listening to the women's chatter.

Gweneth, Max's sister, whom she remembered from her one visit to the shop when she'd wanted to buy the brass monkey, was in charge of drying water glasses as they were washed and rinsed. Since Kristina was doing sink duty, they were in close proximity.

"I've found the world's ugliest gift for Max," Gweneth announced to the room at large, with glee and an obvious sense of accomplishment. "He'll never be able to top this."

"What?" asked one of the aunts, grinning.

"Yes, what?" echoed somebody's cousin's sister-in-law.

Gweneth's eyes twinkled as she shook her head. "I want it to be a complete surprise. Trust me, though—he will *hate* this. And the best part is, I've hidden it right under his nose."

Allison shook her head, looking less than amused. "You and Max are getting too old to play such silly games," she said. She looked around the room in general, as if seeking confirmation for her statement. "Why can't they give each other regular presents like everybody else?"

"That wouldn't be any fun," Gweneth answered.

Soon the china and silver were clean and put away, and the football game was over, and practically everybody over the age of thirty was stretched out somewhere in the big, cozy house, taking a nap.

Max found Kristina standing at a window in the dining

room, watching the light change on the waters of the pond behind the house. He slipped his arms around her waist, kissed her nape, and drew her back against him gently.

"Ready to go?" he asked.

Kristina turned in his arms, looked up into his face, and smiled, even though her heart was breaking.

"Ready," she said.

CHAPTER 17

"You have a wonderful family," Kristina said softly as she and Max drove out of the city and onto the freeway leading to Snoqualmie Pass. She had watched him say good-bye to Eliette and Bree, and had thought that Eliette clung a little at the parting, as though unwilling, even afraid, to let him go. Perhaps the child had been remembering another day, when she'd lost her mother, and very nearly her father as well.

"Thank you," Max replied, flinging her a sidelong grin. "Since I've never met your parents, I can't return the compliment, but if they made you, they have to be special."

" 'Special,' " she said, with a smile and a nod. "You missed your calling, Max Kilcarragh—you should have been a diplomat."

He laughed at that. "I wonder if my players would agree," he replied. "You might not believe it to look at me, but I'm one of those guys who paces the sidelines and shouts when things aren't going well in a game."

Kristina studied him soberly. "Do you care that much about winning?"

"I don't give a damn about it," he answered, eyes mirthful. "I just think a little yelling and an occasional dose of pressure make the kids better prepared to live in the real world. And, no, I don't use the same techniques with Bree and Eliette, if that's what you're wondering.''

''I was,'' Kristina confessed. ''It's a bit hypocritical of you, though, wouldn't you say, to shout at other people's children?''

Max smiled, flipped on his signal light, glanced into both the side and rearview mirrors, and changed lanes. ''No,'' he replied with certainty. ''The guys on my team are all at least sixteen years old. There's a big difference.''

By tacit agreement, they avoided the subject of Kristina's closed shop and all it might mean. It was as if nothing existed beyond the darkest edges of the upcoming Sunday night; everything difficult, if it had a bearing on the present, would be discussed then.

''I guess you're right,'' Kristina conceded. ''So someday when your daughters are that age, and they complain that a teacher is pressuring them—''

''I'll try to stay out of it, unless I think there's a deeper problem.'' The freeway was crowded with holiday travelers, and dusk had descended before they left Max's parents' house. He concentrated on his driving and did not look away from the road when he spoke again. ''What about the letters? What happened after both your in-laws died so quickly?''

Leaning back against the seat and closing her eyes, Kristina sighed. Although she had been rereading the letters, she didn't need to do that to remember. It was just that the process made her feel close to Phillie, who had been her dearest and truest mortal friend except, perhaps, for Gilbert Bradford.

In a quiet voice she brought Max up-to-date from the place where he'd left off—explaining, though it was difficult, about Joseph, and the injuries she'd suffered at Michael's hand when she finally confronted him one too many times. She made very little mention of Gilbert, however, except to say that he'd sent Michael away to Australia, never to return.

"And did he?"

Kristina shook her head. "No," she said. But there was much more to the tale, and, as they drove, she began to tell it, unconsciously lapsing into the accent of her English upbringing and the formal phraseology of the time. . . .

"After Michael had gone away, I believed I should have peace at last, but I did not. I was frantic over Joseph's passing—ironic, isn't it, that one's life can be even more horrible than so wretched a death as he suffered? But such children were common in nineteenth-century London.

"For five years I worked among the poor—I could not remarry since I was still legally Michael's wife—but in the end the hopelessness of it was simply more than I could bear. I needed a respite, but did not know what to do.

"Finally, I decided to go traveling, simply to get away. I rode elephants in Burma and climbed mountains in Peru and Africa. I was in China, perhaps eight years after I had left England, when I began having the dreams.

"They were extraordinarily vivid and always terrifying. In them I was visiting Australia—a place I would never go, as large and fascinating as it was, because I feared encountering Michael. I could not be sure I wouldn't kill him with my bare hands if I saw him again. I blamed him completely for what had happened to Joseph.

"In the nightmares I saw a debauched Michael, aged by drink and whoring and the use of opium. He was in a small courtyard, beating a woman, slapping her again and again, first with the front of his hand, then with the back. She flinched, of course, for she was smaller, but she did not cry out, nor did she attempt to defend herself. She simply glared at him with such hatred that her dark eyes glinted in the moonlight.

"At last he hurled her down into the dirt of a flower bed. She put out her hand, only to balance herself, but her fingers closed round the handle of a small gardening trowel. In that moment I became her, entered her body, took over her thoughts.

"Now I was the one clasping the trowel. And I had no compunction about striking back. I raised my hand and, with a strength born of years of hatred, drove the point of the tool straight into Michael's throat, and deep. He had not expected the attack—indeed, it had all happened very fast, in that way of dreams.

"Blood spurted from his open jugular vein, staining his shirt, his coat, the very stones of the courtyard. He put his hands to his throat, eyes bulging with horrified rage, as if to stem the flow. Of course, he could not.

"With a gurgling sound I shall remember as long as I have the capacity to recall anything at all, he slumped to the ground and perished there at my feet, and even then I felt no remorse. My hands and dress—indeed, *her* hands and dress, whoever that ill-fated woman had been—were sticky with the crimson evidence of my guilt, but I would have celebrated, rather than mourned.

"It was always the same dream, and it went on for months on end, in exactly the same manner. Each time it ended as other people rushed into the courtyard, grasping at the woman, crouching over Michael, squashing the delicate flowers under the soles of their shoes.

"About eight months had passed, I suppose, and I was in Paris, because my mother had bid me to come to that city on other business, when I happened to pick up an English newspaper left behind at a table in front of a sidewalk café. In it was a discreet report of Michael Bradford's murder, somewhere in New South Wales. He'd been stabbed with a garden trowel, by an unnamed woman who had subsequently been taken into custody. Before the alleged killer could be tried, however, she hanged herself in her cell.

"I was so stricken that I took to my flat for three days and would not come out for any reason. It wasn't that I spared any grief for Michael, but every time I thought of that poor woman, I was bludgeoned with guilt. Had she been blamed for a crime I had actually committed, while thinking I was merely dreaming? How else could I have known so much about Michael's death if I hadn't been there?

"Eventually I had to stop asking myself those questions, for it was pure torture, and there was no way to learn the answers. But sometimes it haunts me still, even now, when so much time has passed.

"I could not seem to stop moving about the world after that. I was always on board a steamer bound for somewhere, or a train, or rattling along in a coach. I still insisted on doing things the human way, you see, but if I'd really *been* human, I'm sure the pace I kept would have done me in. Even my parents, who can go anywhere they wish, provided the sun is not shining in that place, of course, simply by thinking of their destination, were hard put to keep up with me.

"I began to collect things on my journeys—a jade figure here, a painting or a sculpture there, but the idea of going into business did not occur to me until 1925, when I finally opened a shop in San Francisco. I had garnered some friends in that city, and the need to wander lessened, though it certainly hadn't abated.

"By the time air travel was prevalent, I was off again, though I kept the San Francisco shop for many years.

"My friends grew old and died, and that was nearly unbearable for me, being left behind over and over again. I became almost reclusive and then left California, because there were too many memories.

"Finally I settled in Seattle—I'm not sure why, beyond

the fact that it's beautiful, with the water and the trees and the mountains all round. I know I had a sense of belonging that I had never really known before, in any other place on Earth, as if I had come home at last.

"I was dreadfully lonely, but careful not to make many friends. I confined my social life, such as it was, to the company of my parents, Valerian, and a few other diverting vampires.

"For want of something to do, I opened my store on Western Avenue under the name of Kristina Tremayne. When some years had passed, I went away for a while and came back as my "daughter," Kristina Bennington. Then, when enough time had gone by, I reinvented myself again, this time as Kristina Holbrook. As my uncle Aidan had done before me, I willed my assets to myself, as though I were my own descendent. Otherwise, obviously, a lot of difficult questions might have been asked.

"I grew set in my ways, over the years, as mortals and monsters alike will do. I ran my shop, made occasional buying trips, attended estate sales, and the like. I read extensively and I was excruciatingly bored. Sometimes, when the dreams of Michael's murder in the Australian courtyard threatened, I didn't sleep for weeks at a time.

"Finally I met you, and everything changed. . . ."

She had almost said "I met you *again*," but caught herself just in time. Max had enough to deal with without adding an account of one of his past lives to the tale. There were reasons, after all, why most people did not recall earlier incarnations—good ones. The past, for mortals at least, was gone, and looking back, except to learn, was a waste of the precious present.

"It sounds like a lonely life," Max said gently. They had reached the mountain lodge where they had booked reservations the week before, and there were snowflakes dancing in front of the headlights.

"It was," Kristina replied.

"Wait here," Max said, reaching out to touch her arm. "I'll register us and get the key to our cabin."

She nodded. After so many years of doing everything by herself, for herself, it was lovely to be so thoughtfully attended. She looked forward to being alone with Max, to the privacy of the cabin, and the freedom to make love as much and as long as they wanted.

True to his word, Max returned within five minutes, climbing into the warm Blazer, tossing the huge old-fashioned key into Kristina's lap with a grin, shifting the engine into reverse. A fire had been laid in their one-room cottage, but not lit, and the air was so cold that they could see their breath.

Max crouched beside the hearth, struck a match, and got a good blaze going. Then, with a light in his eyes, he turned to Kristina, who was shivering inside her cloth coat.

"I think you need a little warming up," he said, rising.

Kristina felt a thrill go through her as he came toward her, drew her into his arms, and kissed her. It was tentative at first, that kiss, but as Max put his hands inside Kristina's coat and boldly cupped her breasts, it grew deeper and more demanding.

She had made love with this man before, of course, and known true rapture, but that first contact was a portent of something still more powerful, something rooted in eternity itself.

He stripped her of the coat, then her boots. He took off her sweater and her bra, and then, after kissing each of her taut nipples, he began unhooking her skirt. She was covered in goose bumps and at the same time approaching melt-down, so great was the heat within her.

Finally Max removed her skirt and slip and pantyhose,

and she stood before him utterly naked, trembling with anticipation. The fire on the hearth was just beginning to warm the room, but a thin film of perspiration glistened on Kristina's bare flesh.

"I've been wanting to do this ever since I first laid eyes on you," he said. He was still fully dressed, except for his jacket, which he had tossed aside at some point, and now he knelt in front of Kristina like a worshiper before a goddess.

"W-What?" she whispered. Though she knew, somehow.

The cabin was dark, except for the flickering light of the fireplace, but Kristina was in a fever. She didn't know whether she had turned out the single lamp or if Max had.

"To taste you," Max answered. He caressed her belly with his fingertips, then held her hips for a moment, as though aligning her for possession. Then he began to massage her most private place, making it ready, causing it to harden in the same sweetly painful way her nipples had done earlier, at the touch of his tongue.

Kristina had nothing to hold on to, but it didn't matter, because Max was supporting her. He widened her stance a little, moved his hands to clasp her buttocks, and delved through musky silk to take her full in his mouth.

She cried out throatily, letting her head fall back, not at all certain that she could bear such pleasure.

But bear it she must, for Max would show her no quarter.

He teased her mercilessly, now suckling hard, now nibbling, now laving her with his tongue. She groaned aloud, grinding her hips without shame, desperate to be vulnerable and more vulnerable still.

Finally Max eased her back into a chair, draped her trembling legs over its arms, and consumed her in earnest. Kristina bucked under his lips and tongue, hairline and body drenched in sweat, begging him in senseless, disjointed phrases for release.

In his own sweet time he granted her appeal, but it was a brief victory. As soon as her body had ceased its violent spasms of pleasure, he proceeded to make her want him all over again. By the time Max carried Kristina to the bed, which was covered with a bright, heavy quilt, she was all but delirious and could not honestly have said whether the room was cold or warm.

She herself was burning, but the fever was an ancient one.

Max undressed at his own maddening pace, the way he did everything, but when he lay beside Kristina on the bed, and she reached out to touch him, to clasp his staff in her hand, she knew how much he wanted her. He had paid a great price to make certain that Kristina's needs were accommodated.

"I love you," she said, rolling on top of him.

"I—love—you—" The words came hoarse and splintered from his throat, for she was still holding him, her knees astraddle of his hips.

"By all rights," Kristina teased, leaning forward to nibble at his lower lip, "I ought to put you through the same exhaustive paces you put me through, but I won't. Not yet, anyway."

Max groaned. He was at her mercy now, and she was enjoying the power this benign dominance gave her. To his credit, so was he.

"There are all sorts of things I could do to you, you know," Kristina said, passing a thumb back and forth over the moist tip of his erection, guiding it slowly toward its natural sheath inside her own body. She proceeded to name a few.

Max was half out of his head with need by then. Exactly what he deserved. "Kristina—"

She took him into her, but lingered infinitely at every fraction of an inch, feeling herself tighten instinctively around him, feeling him swell and grow harder still in response. Finally, with a warrior's cry, Max grasped her hips and thrust his own upward, possessing her completely.

There was a power shift in that instant, but not to one or the other. They were true equals, Max and Kristina, as they rode the tempest into a storm of spinning lights and shattering ecstasy.

Finally Max arched high off the bed, his powerful body flexing as he emptied himself into Kristina, once, twice, three times. For her, the climax lasted even longer—she was still descending, and occasionally catching on still another orgasm, each one sweet but less intense than the last, when Max kissed her temple.

"Ummm—I think we forgot something," he said.

Kristina closed her eyes, crooned low in her throat, and then snuggled against him again. "What?" she asked.

"A condom."

"I haven't slept with anyone in a hundred years, Max," Kristina reminded him. "You?"

"Just Sandy, though it hasn't been quite that long, so you're safe with me. But what if you got pregnant?"

Kristina's eyes flew open. On the one hand, the prospect of bearing Max's child delighted her. On the other, it was terrible, because she could never marry him. She had promised herself to Dathan, and it was a vow she must keep, no matter what her own feelings in the matter might be.

"You don't suppose—?"

"Could happen," Max said. "After all, this is the standard method."

Kristina held on to him very tightly and buried her face in his chest. "Would you be angry?" she asked in a small voice.

"Angry?" The word ruffled the soft hair at her temple,

which was still moist from their earlier passion. "God, no. I love kids, Kristina. And I love you."

Kristina fought hard not to cry. She was afraid Max was going to ask her to marry him, and equally afraid that he wasn't. She made a circle on his bare back with the palm of her right hand, greedy for the feel of his flesh. "I thought it made a difference—my turning out to be mortal, I mean."

"What kind of difference?"

"In how you felt about me. You admitted that part of my charm might have been the fact that I couldn't die."

"Yeah," Max said with a long, deep sigh, his arms tight around her. "I've thought a lot about that. What it all comes down to, though, is that love is a risk, plain and simple. And everybody has to die someday. I mean, everybody's human."

"Even vampires can die," Kristina said, thinking of a story her mother had once told her, about the original vampires. They'd called themselves the Brotherhood and had become blood-drinkers on the island continent of Atlantis, while participating in a scientific experiment. They had grown weary, after many thousands of years, and willed their own deaths.

Max raised himself on one elbow and looked down at her. "Really? How? Do they have to be shot with a silver bullet?"

Kristina didn't laugh, though the thought was ludicrous enough to provoke a certain grim amusement. "That's werewolves, and I don't even know if it's true, because I've never encountered one. Vampires must have blood, of course, and they can be killed by fire, by sunlight, and by having a stake driven through their hearts, just like in the movies. They have one other known vulnerability as well— the blood of warlocks is poisonous to them. Given a sufficient dose, they will slip into something resembling a coma and gradually die of starvation.'' She stroked his cheek, where a five o'clock shadow had sprouted. ''Can't we talk about something else?''

''I'm sorry,'' Max said. ''I should have left the subject alone.'' He touched the tip of her nose. ''Are you hungry? Believe it or not, they have room service in this place. No doubt everything comes by dogsled.''

Kristina laughed. ''Hungry? After that dinner your mother served today? I may never need to eat again!''

''Well,'' Max said, resting on his elbows, ''I'm starved.''

Kristina fell back with a groan and pulled the covers over her head, and Max reached for the phone on the bedside table and called the restaurant in the lodge. She was hiding in the bathroom—up to her chin in bubbles in an old claw-foot tub actually—when his late-night snack was delivered.

He joined her, after dispensing with the food, a devilish glint shimmering in his eyes. With a growl, he flung off his robe, which came with the room, and stepped into the bath, nearly causing the water to overflow.

They made love again, there in the tub, and got the floor so wet in the process that Kristina figured the bathroom would be a skating rink by morning, if they let the fire go out.

Eliette liked staying at her grandparents' house. She enjoyed sleeping in the room that had been her daddy's once, and still had some of his things in it. She liked floating boats on the duck pond, though she and Bree weren't allowed to go near it unless an adult was with them. She especially liked all the sounds—people talking quietly in a nearby room, soft music playing somewhere, the creaks and squeaks as the old house settled itself for a winter's night. In the morning there would still be a crowd, but just like always, Grandmother and Gramps would belong only to her and Bree, for that special Friday.

They would start by going out to breakfast, just the four of them. Even Daddy wasn't invited on those outings, or Aunt Gweneth. Bree and Eliette could order anything they wanted to eat—even a chocolate sundae or a corn dog, if they chose—but they always picked scrambled eggs and orange juice and waffles.

Then, once they were all full, they would get back into Grandmother's Volvo—Gramps didn't drive anymore because he had a disease in his eyes, and every year it was harder for him to see—and drive to a big mall called South Center. There they went into practically every store, choosing presents for their daddy, for Aunt Gweneth and Aunt Elaine and their Arizona grandparents, Molly and Jim. They even bought stuff for each other, one going off to shop with Grandmother while the other went with Gramps.

They'd have lunch then—they usually went to a Mexican place close to the mall—and in the afternoon they saw a movie.

By the time they got back to the big brick house, they always had lots of packages, and Gramps always took a long nap before dinner. Grandmother ordered out, then sat down in her favorite chair and put her feet up, sipping tea and dozing a little. Bree and Eliette were usually pretty tired, too, but they were too excited to sleep. After supper, though, and their baths, they would barely get into their pajamas before they crashed.

Eliette smiled, just to think about it. It was so much fun.

She closed her eyes, willing herself to drift off. In the twin bed across from hers, Bree was sound asleep. But she was smiling, too.

Eliette snuggled down deeper in the covers. It was a cold night, and the weather man had said it might snow. That was relatively rare in Seattle, and Eliette hoped there would be such a deluge that they wouldn't have school again until after Christmas.

Fat chance.

Thinking about Christmas made her think about the awful brass monkey Aunt Gweneth had bought for Daddy at the flea market. It was already wrapped, first in bright red paper and then in that heavy brown stuff, and tucked away on a shelf in one of the cabinets in their garage. On Christmas Eve, Aunt Gweneth said, Santa Claus would bring it inside and put it under the tree.

Eliette made a face. She didn't like the monkey any more than Bree did; it was ugly, and besides, it gave her a creepy feeling. She didn't regard herself as a sneaky sort of kid, but if that doorstop thingy had been handy just then, she might have carried it out and dumped it in the duck pond.

"Kristina can't do magic anymore," Bree said from the other bed, startling Eliette. She'd been convinced her sister was asleep.

"That's okay," Eliette answered, feeling the need to put in a good word for the ordinary. "Most people can't anyway."

"Do you lIke her?"

Eliette considered. "Yeah. Do you?"

Bree nodded; it was a good thing Eliette was looking. Half the time the kid just assumed you could hear her shaking her head. "She's going to go away, though, so I guess I'd better not like her too much."

Eliette felt alarmed. Ever since her mom had died, she'd been trying to make herself stop needing people, but it hadn't worked very well. "What makes you say a silly thing like that?"

"An angel told me."

Eliette made a contemptuous sound. "Angels don't go around delivering messages, like Federal Express or somebody."

"Yes, they do," Bree insisted. "Grandmother told me

that's what the word *angel* means—a messenger. And I saw one.''

"Okay," Eliette scoffed. "When did you see this angel? And what did it look like?"

"Not *it*—she. She was pretty, like one of those dolls nobody wants you to touch. She had yellow hair and blue eyes and a ruffly dress with lots of lace trimming. I saw her the night Kristina came to stay in our guest room, when I got up to go to the bathroom.''

Eliette felt a chill. Angels were scary, as far as she was concerned. "You ate too much pumpkin pie," she said. "Either that, or you've been dreaming. Or both."

"No," Bree insisted. "She was real. She told me she had a sister, too."

Eliette sighed, but she pulled the covers up to her chin at the same time. "This angel really had a lot to say, it seems to me. On top of all this, she told you Kristina was going away?"

"To marry a king," Bree said with awe and not a little sorrow.

Eliette felt sad, too. She hadn't wanted Kristina around at first, but lately she'd been counting on her staying and marrying Daddy and being their stepmother. "I don't want her to go," she said.

"Me, neither," Bree answered. "But grown-ups do what they want to."

Eliette nodded. That was certainly true enough. Some adults didn't even seem to *see* little kids; it was as though they were invisible or something. But Kristina wasn't like that—she noticed people, whether they were big or small— and if she went away, Eliette would miss her more than she cared to admit.

She was getting really tired, because it had been a long day. Thanksgiving always was, she thought. When a person got to be seven, they started to see a pattern in things like that.

"Go to sleep," she said to Bree. "We've got to get up early."

Bree yawned loudly. "I'm going to buy Kristina something really beautiful. Then, even if she marries that king, she'll remember us."

Eliette's throat felt tight. She gulped and let her eyes drift half closed. After a few moments she thought she saw a blond angel through her thick lashes, standing at the foot of the bed and smiling. She was just as Bree had described her, but in a blink she was gone.

Eliette told herself she was dreaming and soon enough, she truly was.

In the morning Max and Kristina ate a room-service breakfast in bed, made love, then got dressed and went outside into a fresh fall of snow. They made snow angels and flung balls of the stuff at each other and laughed like kids. They didn't go inside until they were breathless and so cold that their feet and hands were numb.

They made love again and then slept, warm and sated.

That evening, after having dinner in the lodge restaurant, they joined half a dozen other guests for a sleigh ride over perfect, moon-washed snow. It was a magical experience, and Kristina thought she would remember the singular music of the horses' harness bells for the rest of her life.

It was an idyllic weekend, but it went by very fast, as such interludes always do. On Sunday night they sat together on the rug in front of the fireplace in their cabin, the room still resonating faintly with the power of their lovemaking, like a concert hall after a great symphony has been played.

Max took Kristina's hand, and she knew the moment had arrived, that the enchantment was over, the spell broken.

He said her name, running his thumb lightly over her knuckles. Then he whispered, "Marry me."

She looked away in a useless attempt to hide the tears that burned in her eyes. She wanted nothing more than to marry Max Kilcarragh, but she dare not accept his proposal. She had already pledged her life, perhaps her very soul, to another.

Max caught her chin in his hand and made her look at him, though gently. With the pad of his thumb, he smoothed away the tears, then touched her lower lip, leaving behind the taste of salt. "Was that a 'no'?"

"I can't," Kristina whispered. It was agony to say the words, to turn down her greatest desire, her shining dream.

He let his forehead rest against hers for a moment, and his broad shoulders moved in a great sigh that broke Kristina's already fractured heart.

"Because?" Max prompted.

"Because I'm going to be Dathan's mate."

He stared at her. "The *warlock?*"

Kristina only nodded. There was no point in explaining.

Max pushed to his feet, abandoning her, ripping himself away. "You came here and slept with me, knowing that? That you were going straight from my bed to his?"

Kristina could not speak. She merely nodded again.

Max began gathering their things, his motions wild, furious, full of hurt, and Kristina offered no protest, no words of consolation. There was nothing to be said.

CHAPTER 18

Kristina and Max had left their cozy cabin at the mountain lodge far behind before either of them spoke. The atmosphere in the Blazer was thick with tension, and a fresh snowfall enclosed them in white gloom.

"Why didn't you just leave me alone in the first place?" Max ground out. He didn't look at her; understandably, he was keeping his eyes on the slippery, treacherous road.

Kristina bit her lower lip for a moment before answering. She wanted to cry—no, to sob and wail—but somehow she held onto her composure. "You make it sound as though I sought you out and deliberately led you on. I was in love with you, Max—and I always will be."

The sound he made was low and contemptuous. "And all along you intended to mate with that—*thing*."

A shiver moved down Kristina's spine, and it had nothing to do with the cold that had somehow settled in the marrow of her bones, despite the Blazer's more than adequate heating system. It was dangerous to speak of creatures like Dathan in such a desultory way, especially for Max. The warlock was already jealous of him.

"It wasn't like that at all," she said evenly. There was no way to assuage Max's pain, or her own, but she owed him some kind of explanation. Even though anything she might say would probably only serve to deepen his sense of betrayal.

The snow was blinding now, and traffic slowed to a crawl, then a full stop before Max replied. "What *was* it like, then?"

A state trooper approached the driver's side, and Max rolled down the window. Kristina held her tongue.

"Sorry, folks," the policeman told them, shivering but genial. "The pass is closed. You'll have to turn back and find a place to wait out the storm." Through the weather-fogged windshield, Kristina saw other cars making U-turns and heading in the opposite direction. Soon enough, Max and Kristina were going that way, too.

"Great," Max murmured. "Couldn't you just zap us back to Seattle or something?"

Kristina folded her arms and blinked back tears. "You know I can't," she said, shrinking into the seat.

Max reached for his cell phone and punched a single button. A moment later he was talking. "Hi, Mom—it's Max. Listen, the pass is closed, so we aren't going to make it back tonight. Will you explain to the girls? And be sure they understand that everything is okay?" There was a brief pause, then Max smiled, and the expression bruised Kristina's heart somehow because it wasn't, might never be, directed at her. "Thanks, Mom. See you."

The cordiality was gone from Max's voice and manner when he glanced at Kristina, after replacing the cell phone in its little plastic bracket on the dashboard. "I guess we're stuck with each other, for tonight at least."

Kristina pretended to be looking out the passenger window and quickly dashed at her tears with the back of one hand. "We'll be lucky if we don't have to spend the night in the Blazer, with so many people turning back," she said, hoping he wouldn't hear the slight sniffle she hadn't been able to disguise.

They were lucky, as it turned out. Their room at the mountain lodge had not yet been rented, though the whole place was full.

Kristina sensed the fine hand of Valerian, or perhaps her mother, at work, but mental efforts to summon either of them met with resounding failure. With their help she and Max could have been, as he'd put it, "zapped" back to Seattle.

Max carried the bags back in and rebuilt the fire. The bed had not been made up, since they'd left the lodge well past check-out time.

"I meant it when I said I loved you," Kristina said, huddling inside her coat and staying very near the door, as if to bolt. It was a silly urge, she soon realized—after all, where could she go? Besides, this wasn't Michael she was dealing with, it was Max, her beloved, sensible, mentally healthy Max. No matter how angry he might be, or how hurt, she had nothing to fear from him.

He turned from the hearth and rose, shedding his ski jacket and tossing it aside. "Call it off, Kristina," he said, his dark gaze holding hers. "If you mean what you say, then tell the warlock there won't be a wedding."

Kristina flushed. "I can't," she said, wishing with everything inside her, everything she was and would ever be, that she could. "I promised."

"*Break* your promise."

She shook her head. She could not tell him, even now, why she had made her heinous bargain with Dathan—to save Eliette and Bree from possession. That was worth whatever she might have to suffer in consequence of the pact and, as much as she longed to be free to marry Max instead, she hoped with all her soul that the warlock would succeed.

"At least tell me why," Max said. He went to the service bar and rummaged for a beer and a diet cola.

At last Kristina removed her coat and crossed the room to accept the can of soda, which Max knew she preferred over every beverage except water and herbal tea.

"You were right," Kristina conceded miserably, "when you said I should never have let things get started between us in the first place. I can't begin to explain the kind of danger I've put you in, not to mention your children. I'm doing this to protect you, Max, all of you—and that's all I can or will say about it."

He sighed and shoved his free hand through his hair. "Doesn't it matter that we love each other?"

She sat down in one of the chairs near the hearth, still feeling chilled, and Max perched on the arm. "Of course it matters. It's the whole reason we have to say good-bye." Kristina raised her eyes to his face. There was one thing she had to tell him, even though he probably wouldn't believe her. "We were in love once before," she said very softly. "A long time ago. It was a star-crossed match, just like now."

Max's brow furrowed into a frown. The hurt was still plainly visible in his eyes, but he was calmer than before. "I think I'd remember that," he said, sounding bewildered.

Kristina smiled, though her heart was breaking, falling apart bit by fragile, splintered bit. "Not necessarily. Your name wasn't Max Kilcarragh then—it was Gilbert Bradford. You were the Duke of Cheltingham, Michael's elder brother."

Max's eyes narrowed. "Reincarnation?"

"Sort of. It's really more complicated than that. Time is not linear, so human beings actually exist in all their various incarnations at once. They're usually not aware of it, of course."

Max set the beer aside. "I was—am—Gilbert? The good guy?"

Kristina laughed. "Yes. And probably a lot of other people, too."

He frowned. "Is this what Albert Einstein was talking about with his theory of relativity?"

"In a way," she agreed.

Max was silent, absorbing it all.

Kristina took a sip of her diet cola, wishing it were something stronger, a potion capable of quelling the terrible heartbreak she felt. "It would seem," she said carefully, "that we simply aren't destined to be together." The next part was one of the most difficult things she had ever had to say. "Very likely, Sandy is your true mate, for all of time."

Max rose suddenly from his seat on the arm of the chair and went to stand on the hearth, his broad back to Kristina, his hands braced, wide apart, against the mantelpiece. "I loved her very much," he said at great length, in a voice so low and hoarse that Kristina could barely hear him. Then he turned and looked deep into her eyes. "But I love you, too. And even though I don't remember being Gilbert Bradford, I know from the letters you showed me that he felt something similar to what I'm feeling now." He paused to draw a long, ragged breath and once again pushed his fingers through his hair. "I don't understand about eternity— I'm an ordinary man, Kristina. All I know is what I want this moment, in *this* lifetime. And that's to marry you."

Kristina looked down at her hands, which were knotted painfully in her lap. She tried to relax her clenched fingers. "That's what I want, too," she admitted. "But we can't be together, Max. It's impossible, and the sooner we accept that, the better off we'll be."

Even as she spoke the words, she knew she would never be able to accept losing Max, never get over this particular farewell. She dared not think beyond the moment when they would part, once and for all.

He came to her then, drew her up out of the chair and into his embrace. He held her close, and they wept together in silence, while outside the little cabin the snow continued to fall.

In a cabinet inside Max's garage, the package stirred. Brown paper fell away, followed by the festive Christmas wrap beneath. The thing quivered, grew hot enough to singe the paper, and toppled out onto the concrete floor with a metallic crash.

It rolled a little way, and then, in a mere flicker of time, Kristina's spell was broken. Billy Lasser, boy criminal, came back to life.

He was only eighteen years old, but in the course of his brief existence, he'd pulled off more than his share of convenience-store heists, muggings, and rapes. Once he'd even done murder, if that was what you wanted to call it, killing a whore down on the Sea-Tac strip and dumping her off out by the Green River.

Billy smiled, remembering his cleverness. No doubt about it, the cops would have chalked that one up to a certain serial killer they'd been tracking for as long as he could remember.

But his pleasure quickly faded, replaced by rage. He had another score to settle, with that weird chick who'd turned him into a goddamn monkey. Billy wasn't overly bright, and it didn't occur to him that messing with somebody who could do stuff like that might not be a good idea. He knew two things: that he was hungry and that he was pissed off.

He looked around, his eyes adjusting to the darkness, and realized more from the smells than anything that he was in somebody's garage. Maybe if he broke into the house he'd find that bitch who'd locked him up inside a hunk of metal and make her wish she'd never been born.

After he'd had a sandwich and maybe some beer, if there was any.

Billy tried the inside door and found it locked, but that hardly slowed him down. The light switch was right there handy, and he turned it on. There was a toolbox on a work-bench nearby; he took a screwdriver, and in no time he was inside.

He paused, waiting, listening. The place was empty; he'd have bet on that. There was no dog and probably no alarm system.

Billy flicked on the kitchen lights and went straight to the refrigerator. There was plenty to eat—he stuffed two packages of lunch meat down his throat without bothering to find the bread, then guzzled two beers in a row before taking a third one to sip as he went through the house.

He figured out right away that the bitch didn't live here, but he found some cash in a cookie jar on top of the fridge and stuffed that into the pocket of his jeans.

Billy checked out the upstairs, reckless with relief that he was finally free, and high on the beers he'd downed so fast. Two little girls shared one room, and one was obvi-ously reserved for company. The third belonged to a man, judging by the clothes in the closets and bureaus. No mommy in this family.

What a pity, Billy thought.

He went downstairs, feeling a little less reckless now that the food was getting into his system, and tried to figure out what to do next. It was cold outside, and all he had was his fake leather jacket, bought at a swap meet a couple of years before.

He helped himself to a beat-up down-filled coat he found in a closet by the front door and pulled it on. It didn't fit, hung clear to his knees in fact, but Billy didn't care. It would keep the chill off.

It was snowing, and Billy walked a long way before he finally managed to catch a bus headed downtown. The weather in Seattle was usually mild, and when they got a little white stuff, the whole place freaked out.

The bus driver gave him a look, and Billy barely suppressed an urge to strangle the bastard then and there. Instead, he brought out some of the money he'd lifted from the big man's cookie jar and paid the fare.

The shop on Western Avenue was closed, of course, since it was late. Billy let himself in through the back door, a little disappointed to find that it wasn't even locked. A few seconds later he knew why—the place was empty to the walls—and now he was even more pissed than before.

He paced the darkened shop restlessly, barely able to contain his agitation. Nobody—*nobody*—was going to get away with treating him the way that woman had. What was her name?

He'd been able to hear things, once in a while, since he'd sat, helpless, for weeks, maybe even months, in this prissy-assed store, though most of that time he'd just sort of drifted, as if he'd been high on top-grade stuff.

He thought hard.

Kristina, he recalled at long last. Kristina Holbrook.

Billy went out the same way he'd come in, hurried through the bone-chilling cold to the nearest phone booth, and shut himself in. Sure as hell, the stupid slut was right there in the book, big as life, along with her fancy address.

It was almost too fucking easy, Billy thought, but he was grinning as he left the booth. Feeling triumphant, he hailed a cab.

The driver bitched about the snow all the way, and that was good, as far as Billy was concerned. Kept the guy from wondering what business a hood like him would have in such a ritzy area of the city. Not that it mattered, Billy reflected smugly, what some dumb-ass cabbie thought about anything.

Her house was big and expensive-looking.

It was also dark.

Billy blessed his continued good luck as he paid the cabbie with cookie-jar money, crossed the sidewalk, opened the front gate, and walked up to the door. He was running on attitude now, and adrenaline.

The cab pulled away, it's taillights glowing red through the heavy white flakes.

Billy sprinted around the side of the house to the back, where he broke in through a basement window. The lots were big in this part of town, and the neighbors wouldn't have heard the glass breaking anyway, he figured, because the snow was still coming down thick and fast. Billy was no weatherman, but he knew from TV that snow muffled sound.

He crawled through the space and found himself in a pretty standard basement.

It was dark as hell, but he couldn't risk turning on any lights, not yet, so he just stood there, waiting and breathing hard, until his vision had adjusted again.

Then he made his way to the cellar stairs.

No big surprise: They opened onto a kitchen.

Billy found a flashlight in one of the drawers—he'd burgled a lot of houses in his time, and they'd all had a little cubbyhole where things like that were stashed, along with a lot of assorted junk.

After pausing once more to listen, Billy switched on the flashlight and, keeping the beam pointed low so there was less chance of it showing at one of the windows, he began to explore the home of the woman he meant to punish.

He went upstairs first, found her bedroom, touched the perfume bottles on her vanity table, and fingered the jew-

elry lying in a pricey, Chinese-looking box on one of the
dressers. These rich bitches, they didn't even care enough
about nice things to take care of them right. Just left them
laying around, waiting to be stolen.

Billy dangled a strand of pink pearls from one index
finger. They were real all right, and old. They glowed, even
in the darkness, as though there was moonlight inside them.
His ma would have given anything, including him, probably, to own a necklace like that.

Not that his old man woulda let her keep it very long.
Thing like that you could pawn for serious change.

Billy dropped the pearls into his pocket. He'd check out
the other jewelry later, after he'd made himself at home for
a while, after he'd had revenge on *Ms.* Holbrook. When
she got home from wherever she was, she'd find a big surprise waiting for her.

He grinned at the thought and opened drawers until he
found her nightgowns and underwear. Silk, all of it. A single pair of her panties probably cost more than everything
he had on, even when it was new.

His grin faded, though his fingers worked the smooth silk
back and forth. It wasn't fair that some people had so much,
while guys like him got squat.

He'd make her pay, he thought, and felt better. Lots better.

Billy put the panties back and scooped an armload of
nightgowns out of the drawer. Then, carefully, still with
only the fading beam of the flashlight to guide him, he
began laying the costly garments out on the bed, one by
one, tracing the lace edgings with his fingertips, running
his hands over the cloth. It felt as fine as a butterfly's wing.

God, he thought, he was getting to be a regular poet.

It took a long time to pick out which gown he wanted
the bitch to wear when he took her, but he finally chose a
little thigh-length number the same pink color as cotton

candy, with ivory trim. He draped it over the back of a chair for later.

Then, very neatly, taking his time, he refolded all the other garments and put them back in place. After that, he went back downstairs, found a roll of duct tape, scissors, and fresh batteries for the flashlight, all in the same junk drawer he'd raided before.

Finally Billy Lasser stretched out on Kristina Bitch Holbrook's satin bedspread, hands cupped behind his head, booted feet crossed at the ankles, and waited for her to come home. He drifted off to sleep with a smile on his face, dreaming of sweet, sweet revenge.

Max and Kristina spent the whole night making love. Their couplings were poignant, frantic, even greedy, for both of them believed that this would, indeed, be their last night together.

In the morning they awakened to find that the snow had stopped. According to the weatherman on TV, the pass was clear again, and traffic was moving at a steady rate in both directions.

Resigned, Kristina and Max showered, had breakfast in the lodge's restaurant, and set out for Seattle. Max was already running late, and although he'd called the school office from the cell phone that morning to explain his absence, he was anxious to get to work.

Or did he just want to get away from Kristina?

They stopped at her house first, of course, and Max walked her to the door, waiting while she let herself in. The pain in his eyes was so intense, such a clear reflection of what she herself felt, that Kristina could barely look at him.

"Do you want me to come inside and have a look around?" he asked.

Kristina's heart might have been in agony, but her brain

was numb. She shook her head. "It's okay," she murmured.

Max touched her cheek with the backs of curled fingers. "Shall I call later?"

"It would be better if you didn't," she answered.

He nodded, leaned forward to kiss her forehead briefly, then turned and walked away. Kristina watched him until he'd gotten into the Blazer and driven off, longing to run after him, convince him that somehow everything could be all right. But that was a lie, and they both knew it.

Thoroughly weary, Kristina went into the kitchen and put on a pot of coffee. It was a paradoxical thing to do, considering how badly she needed sleep, but nothing about Kristina's life made much sense at that moment. She was too soul-weary to sort things out in any reasonable fashion.

If she slept, she would dream. If she stayed awake, she would think of nothing but Max, and how she'd lost him forever.

She couldn't win.

She dialed Daisy's number at home and got the new Brazilian nanny. Ms. Chandler, the woman told her pleasantly, was on a case at the moment, but Kristina's message would be relayed.

Kristina sighed and hung up, feeling utterly alone.

It was only when she'd poured her coffee and climbed the stairs that she realized she was not alone. There was a faint, strange scent in the air, something dangerous. And things seemed disturbed, out of place, though this last was strictly a subjective matter, a fact discerned in her gut rather than her head.

She paused, almost on the threshold of her room, the hairs on her nape standing upright. Some of the coffee splashed over her hand, burning her, but she barely noticed the resultant sting.

Her visitor could not be Benecia or Canaan—they were

vampires and thus asleep in their lairs. Dathan, though fully capable of being abroad in the daylight, liked to make flamboyant entrances, à la Valerian.

Who, then . . . ?

Kristina closed her eyes for a moment and swallowed hard.

Of course. It was only her housekeeper, Mrs. Prine, back at last from her vacation.

Kristina stepped into her room and stood frozen in place, staring into the grinning face of the young man she had turned into a doorstop months before. He was lying on her bed, cleaning his fingernails with the point of her antique letter opener.

He gestured toward the chair, and she saw one of her silk nightgowns there, laid out for her. A shiver went down her spine.

"Put that on, baby," he said. "Billy-boy wants to see you in it."

Kristina's response was two words long and most unladylike.

"That's kinda what I had in mind," Billy answered, sitting up. She'd have to burn her white satin bedspread after he'd lain on it, with his filthy clothes and greasy hair. "Only it ain't gonna be good for you, honey. Just me."

"No," Kristina said flatly. If her life was to end in this room, at the hands of this awful man, that was that. But she wasn't about to cooperate in any way, and she would die fighting.

"Come here," he said.

She did, but only to fling the scalding hot coffee into his face.

Billy was screaming in fury and pain when she turned, an instant after the deed, and bolted for the rear stairway.

She was halfway across the family room, headed for the side door that led out onto the deck, when he caught up to her, grasping a handful of her hair and wrenching her back against him. Bile rushed into her mouth, and the pain in her scalp was blinding.

Billy intensified it by giving her a little shake. She caught her breath; nearly fainted.

"Let me go," Kristina said, forcing herself to speak calmly, "or I'll turn you into a toad."

Billy laughed. "I figure you would have done something like that already, if you could. What's the matter, little witchy-bitch? Have you lost your magic somewhere?"

Tears of fury and frustration filled Kristina's eyes. She didn't want to become the warlock's bride, but neither did she want to die.

Dathan, she thought desperately. *Help me.*

Billy tightened his hold on her hair, nearly pulling it out by the roots. "Answer me," he said.

Kristina spat another ungracious invective and tried to stomp on his instep.

He hurled her back toward the stairway, and she landed on the steps, bumping one shoulder hard. "I've got plans for you," Billy said with a leer that made her stomach roll again. She hated being so defenseless, and yet she was glad she'd turned down Max's offer to check the house for her before he left. Max was much bigger and stronger than Billy, not to mention brighter, but the little creep might have gotten the jump on him somehow. There was no question in Kristina's mind that Billy was armed.

She gave him a look of contempt and got to her feet slowly, using the wall for support. She was breathless with fear, on the verge of vomiting, but she wasn't going to let this little weasel know it.

"I'm afraid you're just going to have to cancel your plans," she said.

He produced a .38-caliber pistol from the waistband at the back of his jeans. Kristina recognized the weapon from the night he'd tried to rob her shop and wished she'd made him eat it. The idea had occurred to her at the time, but she'd dismissed it as gauche.

"No, ma'am," Billy answered, brandishing the .38. "We've got business to attend to. It's going to hurt, it's going to take a long time, and face it, baby doll, it's going to happen." He was standing by then, with his back to the window over the kitchen sink, leaning indolently against the counter. "First, you're going to take off all your clothes, then I'm going to look at you for a while. Have a little fun, maybe. Then you're going to put on that silky thing—"

Kristina's gaze was caught by something at the window—a flash of white—and then suddenly the glass splintered in a thousand directions, and Barabbas came through the chasm, all sleek, glorious, snarling wolf. Billy shrieked as the animal landed on him from behind, catching him by the nape and shaking him as though he were no heavier than a rat.

Wide-eyed, both paralyzed and speechless with shock, Kristina simply stood there, unable to believe what she was seeing.

There was blood and glass everywhere, and, after an indeterminate length of time, Billy stopped screaming. Barabbas flung him aside and trotted over to Kristina, as docile as a lapdog, nuzzling her thigh with a bloody muzzle.

Sobbing, she dropped to her knees and flung both arms around Barabbas, burying her face in his lush fur. Billy lay still a little distance away, and Kristina knew without touching him that he was dead. She clung to the wolf, who sat patiently, and waited.

Kristina knew she should call the police, but she couldn't move, and her mind was doing peculiar things. One moment she would be cognizant, then she'd drift off into a dream. The hands of the clock over the stove had advanced significantly every time she looked at them, and finally the quality of the light began to change and soften. Gold became lavender, and then charcoal, then black. A cold wind blew in through the broken window over the sink, bringing flakes of snow with it.

That was how Valerian found them when he arrived only moments after sunset, woman, wolf, and dead man.

Muttering an expletive, Valerian rushed to Kristina and drew her into his arms. "What happened?" he demanded, and Kristina felt him trembling.

"The—the brass monkey—" she managed to grind out. "He was here—Barabbas broke the window—I think he's dead."

Valerian carried Kristina into the family room as tenderly as if she were a fragile child and laid her on the sofa. After covering her with his cloak, he rummaged through the liquor cabinet until he found a bottle of Grand Marnier. After pouring her a double dose and ordering her to drink it immediately, the vampire returned to the kitchen.

She heard him speak softly to the wolf, but Valerian spared no word for the man whose blood covered the floor and cabinets.

"He's dead all right," he said flatly upon returning to the family room.

Barabbas followed, and Kristina noticed that the blood that had stained his coat and muzzle was gone. No doubt the kitchen had been Valerianized as well; the body had probably vanished already, along with all traces of the killing. This was not a matter any of them would want to explain to the police.

"Please don't say 'I told you so,' " Kristina whispered, recalling how many times Valerian had warned her to use her magic with caution.

He smiled and drew up a chair. "I won't. Not until you're over the worst of it, anyway."

"Did you—is he—?"

"Yes, darling," Valerian said gently. "He's gone. And this time it will be forever."

Kristina was almost sick with relief. She held out a hand to Barabbas, and he came to her, licking her fingers affectionately. "Thank you, my friend," she told the animal. "I don't know how you knew I needed you, but your timing couldn't have been better."

Barabbas made a whimpering sound and sank to his haunches.

"And thank you," she added, turning her gaze to Valerian.

He blew her a kiss. "Don't mention it. By the way, the Dimity-Gideon crisis has been resolved somewhat."

Sipping her Grand Marnier, Kristina was beginning to feel calmer. "Really? How?"

"I'll leave that tale for your mother to tell, since it was mostly her doing. She'll be along shortly, I should guess. By now she's probably sensed that you've had a near miss and are something the worse for wear." He glanced at his watch, another affectation, or perhaps just a habit since, like all vampires, he always knew the time. "I must feed," he said. "Unless you need me to hold your hand until Maeve arrives, I'll send Barabbas home and take my leave."

"I'll be all right," Kristina said, and she knew it was true, despite all her problems.

Valerian vanished, after planting a light kiss on the top of her head, without reclaiming his cloak. He hadn't been gone more than a moment when the telephone rang.

Kristina reached for the receiver of the cordless phone, which was lying on the lamp table at the end of the couch. "Hello?"

"Kristina?" The voice on the other end of the line was Max's, and even though he'd only spoken a single word, her name, she knew he was in a terrible state. "Oh, God, Kristina—I need your help. Bree and Eliette are missing!"

CHAPTER 19

Max's children were gone.

Kristina's personal ordeal was forgotten in the face of all that might mean. "What happened?" she whispered into the receiver, one hand raised to her throat. She held her breath, waiting for the answer, and could see Max shove a hand through his hair as clearly as if she'd been standing in the same room with him.

"I picked them up from my parents' house after work," he said evenly. Kristina knew what a supreme effort it was for him to remain calm. "They were playing in their room. I phoned for a pizza, and when it was delivered, I called to the kids to come down to supper. They didn't, so I went up to look for them. They were gone—nowhere in the house."

Kristina closed her eyes, agonized. "Have you called the police?"

"Of course," Max answered. He couldn't be faulted for snapping a bit; he must have been frantic with fear. Kristina certainly was, and Bree and Eliette weren't even her children. "They're sending somebody over," he finished, less abruptly.

"What did they say on the phone—the police, I mean?"

Max let out a long sigh, and in it Kristina heard frustration as well as terror. "That the girls are probably at a neighbor's house or hiding somewhere. They asked if I was divorced—I guess the non-custodial parent is usually the culprit."

Kristina bit her lower lip. She felt a fluttering motion at her side and was relieved to see Dathan standing there, his brow furrowed as he eavesdropped.

"I'll do whatever I can to help, Max. This is my fault."

"We can argue about whose fault it is later," he replied. "Just get over here, *please*—if I don't find my kids, I don't know what I'll do."

"I'm going to find Bree and Eliette," Kristina answered, meeting the warlock's steady gaze.

"But your magic—"

"I have somebody to help me," she said gently. "We'll resolve this as soon as we can, Max—I promise. Just try not to panic."

Without speaking a word, Dathan took Kristina's free hand while she hung up the receiver with the other.

"Benecia and Canaan, I think," Kristina said, answering Dathan's unasked question. "God, I hope it's not already too late!"

Dathan tightened his hold on Kristina, and together they vanished.

Kristina was breathless when, only moments later, they reassembled.

She had expected a cavern far beneath the earth, like the one in the stories Valerian and Maeve had told her about the Brotherhood, the lost forefathers of all vampires. Or the inside of some elaborate tomb. Instead they were in a sunlit garden next to a cottage with a thatched roof and painted wooden shutters.

Kristina glanced nervously at her future mate, confused. "Benecia and Canaan are here? But the light—"

"An illusion, all of it," the warlock said. "And quite probably a trap."

Benecia appeared in the open doorway of the charming cottage, a beatific smile on her face. "So," she chimed, "you've come at last." She was looking at Dathan, not Kristina, who might have been invisible for all the notice the vampire gave her.

"Yes," he replied, his tone absolutely expressionless. "Where are the Kilcarragh children?"

Benecia gestured. "They're inside. We're having a tea party. Do come in and join us."

Kristina started toward the door, desperate to reach Bree and Eliette, gather them in her arms, protect and reassure them. Dathan stopped her by extending an arm, and though he said nothing, the sidelong glance he gave her was a stern one.

He bowed at the waist—this grand gesture was, of course, directed at Benecia—and then walked toward the fairy-tale house and his hideous little hostess.

"You've certainly taken your time to come courting," Benecia said, pouting prettily. "Canaan said nothing would entice you, but I knew she was wrong."

"You must allow me to serve the tea in order to make up for being remiss," Dathan said smoothly. His smile and manner were charming now; he would have made a fine actor.

Benecia's cornflower gaze found and acknowledged Kristina at last and lingered maliciously. "Why is *she* here?"

"She wants the Kilcarragh children," Dathan answered, standing close to the small vampire now, casting back a warning glance at Kristina. "That is the bargain, isn't it, my sweet? I take you to wife, and you give us the little girls, unharmed."

"How do I know you'll keep your word?"

"You don't. That is one of the perils of entering into an affair of the heart." He took her doll-like hand, bent, and kissed the knuckles. "No more arguments, my darling. We shall drink a toast to our future together." With an elegant motion of one wrist, he conjured a golden goblet, probably medieval, studded with emeralds and rubies, diamonds and amethysts. It glittered in the false sunlight.

Kristina did not want to obey Dathan's unspoken edict that she stay where she was; every instinct compelled her to storm the bastions, to collect Bree and Eliette, to see for herself that they were all right.

Max's children, the children of her own heart. But she dared not move or speak.

Benecia stepped daintily into the cottage, and Dathan followed.

Kristina waited in anguish for something, anything, to happen.

All that came from inside the cottage was an eerie silence.

Then Bree and Eliette stepped out, holding hands and seemingly unharmed, although they appeared to be sleepwalking. They looked blindly in Kristina's direction, plainly not seeing her.

All the same Kristina held her arms out, and they came to her, slowly, and with bewilderment, still entranced. She sank to her knees in the sweet, imaginary grass and gathered them close, terrified that it was too late, that Benecia and Canaan had already done irreparable damage, had begun the process of possession.

Kristina clutched the speechless children more tightly, weeping now. She would never, never forgive herself if they did not recover. If their souls had been stolen, the blame was hers to bear, for all of time and eternity.

The scene around them was chillingly idyllic, almost cartoonlike, with twittering birds, a fresh breeze, apple trees blossoming pink and white in a nearby orchard. A butterfly with kaleidoscope wings fluttered past, and the sky was china blue and cloudless.

A perfect spring day in a place that did not exist.

"Bree? Eliette?" Kristina spoke softly to the little girls, holding one in the curve of each arm. They were wearing jeans, T-shirts, and sneakers—their after-school clothes, no doubt. Their eyes were absolutely blank, and although they did not resist Kristina's embrace, they didn't cling to her, either.

Suddenly a terrible shriek pierced the air, coming from inside the cottage. It was immediately followed by another. Then, silence again, more frightening in some peculiar way than the screams had been.

Kristina stiffened, but if either Bree or Eliette had heard, they gave no sign of it, but simply stood unmoving against her sides, staring at nothing.

Dathan came outside again, pausing to close the door tidily behind him. His smile bordered on cocky as he met Kristina's gaze; he dusted his hands together, in the time-honored gesture of a job not only completed, but well done. And despite the profound relief she felt, there was also remorse.

He had destroyed Benecia and Canaan, as promised, and that had been a service to mortals and monsters alike. All the same, they had once been *children*, those horrid little beasts; it was a matter for sorrow, their perishing, though in all truth they'd died long ago.

The warlock came to stand over Kristina, gesturing with one graceful hand toward the cottage. There was no sign of the jeweled chalice he had produced at the doorstep, before stepping inside to work his cruel mercies.

"Go and see for yourself, Kristina. The vow I made to you is now kept."

Kristina did not want to see, did not want to leave Bree

and Eliette for even a moment, but she knew she must go and look upon her dead enemies with her own eyes. If she did not, she would wonder, through all that might remain of her life, if they were truly gone.

Kristina nodded and got to her feet.

"Bree and Eliette—?"

Dathan looked fondly upon Max's children. "They believe they are dreaming."

"They won't remember?"

He sighed. "Subconsciously they will know that something weird happened to them. With proper love and care, however, they'll overcome any remaining trauma. The loss of their mother was far worse."

Kristina's eyes filled as she looked down at these two precious, innocent children. They'd been through so much in their short lives, and she was sick with the knowledge that they would never have encountered Benecia and Canaan, if not for her.

Once again, Dathan read Kristina's thoughts. "You saved them," he said gently. His hand rested lightly on the small of her back, urging her toward the cottage, which was even then shifting, blurring at the edges. "Bree and Eliette will be safe with me. Go inside, Kristina. Let it be over at long last."

She walked reluctantly forward, through the swinging gate, up the walk, onto the step. After drawing a deep breath and releasing it very slowly, Kristina pushed open the door and stepped inside.

The cottage was furnished like a playhouse, with everything to scale. A table had been set with miniature china dishes and a silver tea service. Benecia and Canaan, ludicrous shapes of pulp and powdery ash, slumped in two of the four tiny chairs.

Dathan's chalice stood between them, with one drop of shimmering warlock's blood still glistening on the brim. It seemed unlikely, given their great age, that they had been tricked into drinking what was, for a vampire, the most potent hemlock. No, Kristina thought sadly, they'd known what they were doing.

Benecia had wanted, even yearned for, oblivion and peace.

Canaan had no doubt followed her sister into the darkness voluntarily, preferring death to eternal solitude.

Kristina turned and left the cottage.

Dathan, Bree, and Eliette waited in the dooryard. The great warlock held one child in each arm, their heads resting upon his shoulders, sound asleep. For a moment Kristina was reminded of Valerian and the vast tenderness he showed for his adopted son, Esteban.

"Stand very close," Dathan said, his eyes soft and somehow sad as he surveyed Kristina.

She nodded and stood with her chest pressed to his, her arms around his neck.

In an instant they were all in Max's house, in the room Bree and Eliette shared.

Dathan stood behind Kristina, holding her in a loose embrace, and she knew he had somehow rendered them both invisible.

Bree and Eliette, meanwhile, were suddenly animated again, sitting on the floor between their two beds, as if nothing had happened, putting two Barbie dolls through a spirited argument.

"Hey!" Max yelled from downstairs. "The pizza's here. And don't forget to wash your hands!"

With shrieks of pure joy, Bree and Eliette abandoned the dolls and bounded out of the room. A tear slipped down Kristina's cheek as she listened to their footsteps on the rear stairway.

"You turned the clock back an hour or so," Kristina said, turning to look up into the splendid face of the warlock. How she wished she could love him, but it was Max she cared for, and Max alone.

Dathan shrugged. "I thought it would be better this way."

She nodded. "Thank you, Dathan," she whispered.

He laid his hands to her shoulders and kissed her, ever so lightly, on the lips. Then, in the next breath, she found herself standing in the middle of her own family room in Seattle. There was no sign of the warlock.

The telephone rang again, suddenly, shrilly, startling Kristina out of her daze. Her hand trembled as she reached for the receiver.

"Hi," Max said.

Kristina held her breath, and her heart swelled like an overfilled balloon, ready to burst. "Hi," she replied.

"Look, I know you and I didn't exactly part on the best of terms this morning—"

Kristina closed her eyes, even more grateful than before for Dathan's magic. The kidnapping hadn't happened, as far as Max and the girls were concerned, and he need never know about her encounter with Billy Lasser. "It's okay," she said. They'd made love over and over the night before, at the mountain cabin, and that would sustain her. "Saying good-bye is never easy."

"No." His voice was gruff. Kristina loved him so much that she very nearly couldn't bear it. "We've got a lot of pizza over here," he said. "How about joining us for supper?"

Kristina was an emotional wreck, after all she'd been through, and as much as she loved Max and the children, she needed to eat something, take a hot bath, crawl into bed, and sleep. She simply could not spend an evening with the three people she considered to be her family, knowing she was fated to spend the rest of her life as Dathan's mate.

"I can't, Max," she said softly. "Please understand."

"I do," he replied, just as softly. There was no sarcasm in his voice.

She sighed and pushed a hand through her hair, the way she'd seen Max do a hundred times. "There are a couple of things I need to say," she told him. "I love you. And you don't have to worry anymore, because you and the girls are safe."

"Kristina—"

"That's the end of it, Max," she broke in, her eyes burning again. "Good-bye." With that, she hung up.

The phone rang again immediately, but she ignored the sound until it stopped.

It was the middle of the night when Kristina awakened, sensing that someone was standing at the foot of her bed. She opened her eyes, mildly alarmed, to find her mother there, looking like a vision in her flowing gown and cascading ebony hair.

Maeve smiled. "Hello, darling," she said.

Kristina sat up. "Is everything all right?"

"I came to ask you the same question. Valerian told me about the incident with that brass monkey of yours."

Kristina shivered at the memory. "Fortunately that's over. Thanks to Barabbas." She remembered something else Valerian had said. "I hear Dimity and Gideon have been found."

Maeve took a seat on the edge of Kristina's bed, smoothed her hair back from her forehead with a gentle motion of one cool hand, the way she'd done when Kristina was small. "After a fashion, yes," she said. "Dimity found her way into a parallel dimension, where she can live as a woman instead of a vampire."

Kristina thought, with some unhappiness, of Benecia, who had wanted to do that, too. "And Gideon?"

"An angel is, and must always be, an angel. He tried to

follow her, but he could not, and he is inconsolable.''

"He loved Dimity very much," said Kristina, who had heard the stories as a child. Too, she knew what it was to care so deeply for someone forbidden.

"It is denied to angels, that sort of love," Maeve said firmly. "Don't worry. Gideon will be fine in time, and Dimity is happy where she is."

"And Nemesis? What is his state of mind?"

Maeve looked grim for a moment. "He is furious, but since all the blame cannot be laid at Dimity's feet, and thus put upon all vampires, he has withdrawn his armies."

"He had *assembled armies*?" Kristina whispered. "Are you saying that we—that all of us—were on the brink of Armageddon?"

"Yes," Maeve answered without hesitation. "But that danger—though it will inevitably come again—is past. You will become Dathan's mate, now that he has lived up to his part of the agreement?"

Kristina nodded. "I have no choice. And I *am* grateful for what he did."

"Gratitude is a poor basis for such a union," Maeve said.

"Yes," Kristina agreed. "But I don't have any alternatives."

Maeve took Kristina's hand. "No," she answered. "Neither do I, under the circumstances. Still, I have learned some things that I feel you need to know—from Nemesis, as a matter of fact. It was he who told me I would bear a mortal child, before I knew you were growing in my womb."

"What did he say?" Kristina asked, hardly able to breathe.

"You are carrying Max's babe," Maeve said.

Kristina fell back against the pillows, stunned. Full of sorrow and of exultation, in equal measure. She could not speak, though tears slipped down her cheeks.

"There is more," Maeve went on very gently, her hand tightening on Kristina's. "On some level, you were waiting for Max to come back into your life. You've probably already guessed that he was Gilbert Bradford. In any case, that is the reason you didn't begin aging until recently. You wanted to be in step, so to speak, with Mr. Kilcarragh."

Kristina let out a long, broken sigh. She'd come so close to complete happiness, so close to living all her dreams. "Perhaps Dathan will change his mind, once he knows I'll bear another man's child."

Maeve's expression was gently skeptical. "I know this warlock. While he has certain redeeming qualities, he is not above claiming Max's babe as his own. Dathan wants you very badly, Kristina."

"Can't you help me?"

The queen's beautiful, ink-colored eyes glittered with vampire tears. "A pact was made and kept. I cannot interfere."

Kristina nodded and leaned forward to kiss her mother's cheek. "You won't abandon me, will you? Like when I married Michael?"

"I have often regretted that," Maeve confessed. "No, darling. I shall be available to help you in any way I can. Mayhap you will come to love the warlock one day—it could be, you know, that he is your destiny, after all, rather than Max."

Although Kristina did not want that to be so, she had already considered the possibility. No doubt Max would find Sandy again, in another lifetime, and anyone he married now could only be an interim love. "Yes," she said. "It could be that Dathan and I were meant to be together, at least for a while. But I shall never love him."

Maeve embraced her tenderly. "No," she said, understanding. "But there are other joys. And you will surely cherish the child."

"Do you know about this babe—whether it's a boy or a girl? Mortal or immortal?"

Maeve smoothed Kristina's tears away with palms as smooth as polished marble. "Nemesis offered no other information than the fact that you and Max had conceived. And I did not ask him to tell me more." The great queen kissed her daughter's forehead. "And now I must hunt. Dream sweet dreams, my darling."

As surely as if Maeve had cast a spell, Kristina fell immediately back into a deep sleep. When she awakened the next morning to another light snowfall, she wondered if she truly *had* been dreaming.

Until she descended into the kitchen and found Dathan standing there, dressed for a wedding, that is. Kristina felt nothing but despair, but some quirk caused her to look down at her long flannel nightie and then at her future groom, her expression rueful.

"I'm afraid my wedding gown leaves something to be desired," she said.

Dathan raised his right hand high, palm up, and as he lowered it, a wondrous dress formed itself to Kristina's body. It was made of the finest ivory silk, the skirts embroidered with hundreds of appliquéd doves, outlined in tiny pearls. The bodice was lacy and sprinkled liberally with diamonds.

"There has never been a more beautiful bride in all of time," Dathan said.

Kristina swallowed hard. Dathan conjured a small hand mirror, and she saw that her veil, a trail of gossamer white netting, tumbled from a circlet of small white orchids on the crown of her head.

"Okay," she said, resigned. "So where's the preacher?"

Dathan arched an eyebrow. "It isn't done in exactly that way," he said.

"Then how *is* it done?"

"We will simply clasp hands and make a promise to each other."

"Here?" Kristina asked. "In the kitchen?"

Dathan sighed. "Wherever you wish, my darling. Just name the place, and we'll be there in a moment."

"Beside the point," observed a third voice.

Both Dathan and Kristina turned in surprise to see Valerian standing just a few feet away. Given the fact that it was broad daylight, that was amazing.

"How—?" Kristina croaked.

"Call it astral projection," Valerian said with an impatient wave of one hand. "I'm a magician, remember?" His gaze was fixed on Dathan, and the vampire looked as solid as he ever had. "There is a point in human wedding ceremonies that I rather like," he told the warlock. "The clergy member always says, 'Is there anyone here who can give just cause why these two should not be joined in holy matrimony?' "

Dathan flushed. "I am not human," he pointed out in a dangerously even voice.

"But Kristina is," Valerian offered reasonably. "Furthermore, I can show just cause. She loves one Max Kilcarragh—has waited a hundred years to be his wife. Even now, his child is curled beneath her heart—a heart in which Max, not you, will always live."

Dathan looked down at Kristina. "Is this true? The part about the child, I mean?"

Kristina nodded. She guessed she hadn't dreamed her mother's late-night visit after all.

"Can you never learn to love me?" the warlock asked.

A great sadness welled up within Kristina. "No," she said.

"If you care for Kristina," Valerian put in, very gently and very carefully, "you will set her free."

"We had a bargain!"

"And only you have the power to break it," Valerian reasoned quietly.

"Damn you," Dathan spat, glaring at the vampire. "How dare you speak of bargains? You once promised me a bride, and instead you set Roxanne Havermail on me like a mad dog!"

Valerian tried his very best to look contrite, but there was, Kristina thought, a certain merry twinkle in his eyes. "A nasty trick, I confess. Allow me to rectify the matter."

Dathan narrowed his gaze upon the fiend, while Kristina just stood there, resplendent in her conjured wedding dress, apparently forgotten. She did not want to remind the warlock of her presence before Valerian had made his point.

"Why should I trust you?" Dathan demanded.

"Kristina's happiness is at stake," Valerian replied. "She is like my own child, and only Daisy and Esteban matter more. I would not play you false in such a case as this."

Dathan turned and looked down into Kristina's upraised face. "So beautiful," he whispered, almost regretfully.

"But so mortal," Valerian said. "There is a female vampire—I have trained her myself—by the name of Shaleen. Meet me this night on the north entrance to All Soul's Cathedral in London, and I will prove myself truthful."

"If you lie—" Dathan murmured.

Kristina held her breath. She wasn't even sure her heart was beating.

"If I lie, you have only to come and take Kristina back."

Dathan considered, while Kristina flashed her "guardian vampire" a scathing look. She hadn't wanted that last option to be part of the deal.

"Well?" Valerian finally prompted.

Dathan gave a great sigh. "All right," he said. He kissed Kristina, first on the forehead, then on each eyelid. When she looked again, he was gone, and so was Valerian. The magical wedding dress had turned back into a chenille bath-robe.

"Cinderella, eat your heart out," Kristina muttered.

She waited three full days before she called Max, just in case Dathan's blind date with the vampire, Shaleen, had gone wrong. During that time, Kristina busied herself by sorting through old papers and other things she no longer needed or wanted. She read the last of her letters to Phillie and burned all of them.

The past was truly gone.

"Hello?" Max answered when Kristina finally called him. It was 6:05 and she could tell by the background sounds that he was cooking dinner.

"Hi," Kristina said with a smile in her voice. "This is a mysterious woman from your recent past."

He laughed. "The meter maid who gave me a parking ticket this morning?"

"No," Kristina replied in a naughty undertone. "The one you spent the weekend in bed with."

"Oh, that one." There was hope in Max's voice now, as well as humor.

"I was wondering if you could come over. There are some things we need to talk about."

"Just give me half an hour to round up a babysitter," he replied.

He arrived in twenty minutes flat.

Kristina pulled him inside, wrapped both arms around his neck, and kissed him soundly. It was a greeting, that kiss, but it was an invitation, too. If she had her way, they would be upstairs, in her bed, very soon.

"Did you mean it when you said you wanted to marry me?" she asked when it was over, and Max was standing there, still in his coat, with snow in his hair. His mien was one of pure, dazed confusion.

"I did indeed," he said. "But you had other plans, if I remember correctly."

"They've changed."

"You're not going to marry the warlock?"

"I'm going to marry you, if you'll have me. But there's something you have to know first—something that might make you feel trapped. And I only want a willing husband, Max Kilcarragh."

"What?" he asked in a voice so tender that it brought a lump to Kristina's throat and tears to her eyes.

"I'm pregnant. With your baby."

For a moment Max looked as though she'd struck him with a blunt object. She was just beginning to worry when a grin flicked up one corner of his mouth and then slowly spread until it seemed to cover his whole face.

"That's the second best news I've heard all day," he said, and despite his smile, there were tears shining in his eyes.

"What's the first best?" Kristina asked, unzipping his jacket, slipping her arms inside to embrace and warm him.

"That you're going to marry me. Oh, God, Kristina—I love you."

She took his hand. "Upstairs," she said, pulling him in that direction. "If we don't start now, we may end up making love right here in the entry hall, or on the stairs—"

They made it as far as Kristina's bed, but just barely.

In the attempt to undress each other, they became entangled in each other's clothes and finally landed on the mattress in a laughing, twisted knot of flesh and fabric.

Soon enough they'd sorted that out, and Kristina lay on her back with Max poised over her, gazing down into her eyes.

"Hurry, Max," she whispered.

He smiled. "No way," he answered, and bent his head

to her breast, teasing the nipple unmercifully with the tip of his tongue.

Kristina began to writhe and moan. "Max," she said with a gasp, "we don't *need* foreplay—I've been thinking of nothing but this for three days!"

He moved to the other breast, subjected a second nipple to slow, sweet torment. "Good," he said. "That ought to make it all the better."

With that, he suckled in earnest. There were long interludes where he teased her with his fingers and with his tongue. He whispered shameless, wicked things in her ear and nibbled at her lobes.

Kristina was out of her mind with need, her body drenched in perspiration, when Max finally parted her legs and gave her just the tip of his shaft. When she begged— and he made her do it prettily—he finally entered her in a slow, deep thrust.

She pleaded some more, and the thrust quickened, deepened, but only slightly.

Finally she shouted out what she wanted, not caring who might hear, and with a sound that was part chuckle and part animal need, Max took her in earnest. Placing his strong hands under her buttocks, he raised her high to receive him, and she undulated against him, her hands moving restlessly, feverishly, up and down his muscle-knotted back.

They reached a simultaneous climax, their bodies arched high off the bed and slick with sweat, and hung there, suspended, flexing spasmodically, for what seemed like forever. Finally, replete, exhausted, they tumbled to the mattress and lay entwined in each other's arms and legs, struggling to breathe, transported.

"Tell me what changed your mind," Max said sometime later, when shadows filled the room. "About marrying me, I mean."

She explained about Valerian's intercession, but left out

the near-miss with Benecia and Canaan. There was no need for Max to suffer over that—the incident of Bree and Eliette's disappearance had been erased from his mind, and that was for the best.

"Did you know I've been waiting for you? That that's why I finally became completely mortal?"

He kissed the tip of her nose. "Was I worth it?"

She smiled. "So far, so good," she replied, and pulled his head down so that his mouth found hers.

EPILOGUE

The question of whether or not Jaime Maxwell Kilcarragh had been blessed—or cursed—with magical powers was as yet unresolved. He was a healthy, strapping boy, however, greatly loved by his parents, two elder sisters, and a weird but devoted extended family.

Downstairs in the large family room of the house Max and Kristina had bought together shortly before their marriage, Valerian heard happy laughter. Daisy, Esteban, Maeve, and Calder were all there, along with Max and Kristina, of course, and their daughters, Eliette and Bree.

The great vampire closed his eyes for a moment, listening, nearly rapt, for the sound was like music. It courted the ear, then went deeper to swamp the soul, causing a sweet ache there.

As he watched, the babe awakened. The room was dark, except for a small night-light near the crib itself, and the flow of autumn moonlight through the window. Valerian knew this child was safe, and yet he felt compelled to look out for him, just as he had for Kristina and, once, a long time ago, for Aidan Tremayne.

He closed his eyes briefly, for the thought of Aidan was still poignant, if not actually hurtful.

When Valerian looked again, he was no longer alone in the room. Esteban stood beside him, a sturdy, solemn-eyed lad, ready for school.

"Papa?" he asked softly, taking Valerian's hand. He'd come so far, this beautiful little one, in a short time. He spoke clearly, worked his lessons, no longer slept on the floor or hid stashes of food all around the house.

Valerian lifted Esteban into his arms, sensing his uncertainty. "Shhh," he said against the boy's small temple, where dark, gossamer hair grew, fine as fairy-floss, and a warm heartbeat pulsed. "We mustn't wake the baby."

"We are going to have cake," Esteban confided in an accommodating whisper, his brown eyes very wide. Daisy seldom allowed such treats; she was into health food.

There were times when Valerian was more than grateful that he wasn't required to eat the way mortals did.

"Don't you want some?" the child prodded, glancing back once, at the babe.

"What's the real question?" Valerian prompted. They understood each other more than passing well, this father and son.

Esteban sighed. "Do you like him better than me?"

Valerian shook his head. "No."

Reassured, Esteban began to squirm. He was probably thinking of the cake, perhaps fearing that the others would consume it all before he had his share.

With a chuckle, Valerian set the boy on his feet, and Esteban ran off again.

Valerian went to the crib side and looked down at the handsome babe, who returned his gaze directly. Then, with the slightest smile, Jaime Kilcarragh shifted his gaze to the teddy bear at the foot of his small bed, and raised one tiny hand, wriggling his fingers. The toy had been summoned, and it came obediently to lie beside Jaime, who snuggled close and went back to sleep.

Smiling slightly, Valerian turned and walked out of the nursery.

The adventure wasn't over, he thought.

No, indeed—it had only begun.